DEADLY

HARVEST

DEADLY
HARVEST

LEONARD GOLDBERG

A DUTTON BOOK

DUTTON
Published by the Penguin Group
Penguin Books USA Inc., 375 Hudson Street, New York, New York 10014, U.S.A.
Penguin Books Ltd, 27 Wrights Lane, London W8 5TZ, England
Penguin Books Australia Ltd, Ringwood, Victoria, Australia
Penguin Books Canada Ltd, 10 Alcorn Avenue, Toronto, Ontario, Canada M4V 3B2
Penguin Books (N.Z.) Ltd, 182–190 Wairau Road, Auckland 10, New Zealand

Penguin Books Ltd, Registered Offices:
Harmondsworth, Middlesex, England

First published by Dutton, an imprint of Dutton Signet,
a division of Penguin Books USA Inc.
Distributed in Canada by McClelland & Stewart Inc.

First Printing, May, 1997

10 9 8 7 6 5 4 3 2 1

REGISTERED TRADEMARK—MARCA REGISTRADA

CIP data is available upon request.

Printed in the United States of America
Set in New Baskerville
Designed by Leonard Telesca

*In memory of my father
and Donna Sue*

Diseases desperate grown
By desperate appliance are relieved
Or not at all.

—Shakespeare, Hamlet

PROLOGUE

August 2, 1986
Los Angeles

Karen Kessler walked out of the Women's Reproductive Clinic and looked into the barrel of a high-powered rifle. In the distance she saw something glittering in the dense shrubbery, but it lasted for only a moment and then it was gone. There were rolling hills surrounding the clinic, and Karen knew that they sometimes caused the sun's rays to reflect peculiarly. That was probably it. Or maybe her eyes were playing tricks. She shrugged her shoulders, unconcerned, and went to a nearby park bench.

A middle-aged man dressed in camouflage clothing lay prone in the thick brush and followed the woman with the telescopic sight mounted on his weapon. Now she was sitting on the bench, crossing her legs and lighting a cigarette. He zeroed in on her sharp features and large, doelike eyes. She was in her mid-thirties, he estimated, forty at the most. Slowly he lowered the telescopic sight until the crosshairs were on the front of the woman's scrub suit. There was a large spot of perspiration between her breasts, circular, with a pale area in its center. A perfect target. His finger was on the trigger and he applied gentle pressure, imagining what would happen if he squeezed it at that moment. Her chest would explode, heart and aorta shredded, death almost instant.

But she was not the person he wanted to kill. She was probably just a nurse, following orders. No, she wasn't to blame. The blame rested squarely on the shoulders of a doctor. A murdering son of a bitch. The assassin's jaw tightened as he thought about the doctor who had killed his sister. The doctor would never be convicted in a court of law. Hell, no! After all, the doctor hadn't done anything illegal, hadn't broken any laws. All he had done was cause the death of a beautiful young woman.

The assassin cradled the stock of the rifle against his shoulder and waited patiently, not moving although sweat was now dripping off his forehead and onto his weapon. The day was very warm with a bright sun, and the assassin was uncomfortable because of the combat fatigues he was wearing. He ignored his discomfort and thought about the head shot he would use to kill the doctor. Then a carefully planned route of escape. Up the hill, through dense brush to a walking path where his motorcycle was hidden, then to the San Diego Freeway, less than a mile away. But if he didn't escape and was caught, that was okay too. The assassin was prepared to die if need be.

The door to the clinic opened and the doctor walked out into sunlight. He was a tall, slender man, middle-aged, and wearing a long white laboratory coat. The assassin quickly lined up his sight, the doctor's head now in the crosshairs. He started to squeeze the trigger—but suddenly the doctor bent down to pick up something he'd dropped. The assassin refocused as another doctor stepped out of the clinic. He was shorter, older, and also had on a white coat. Now the two doctors were standing together talking and the assassin couldn't get off a clear shot. *Goddamn it! Move!*

But the second doctor didn't move, and now the men were joined by the nurse in the scrub suit. All the assassin could see was the very top of the target's head. A shot might kill him, but then again it might not. Too risky. Better to wait for them to turn to go back inside.

A large hawk circling overhead screeched loudly and the trio looked up at the sound, the nurse pointing to the bird. Her hand blocked out the doctor's face. In a moment she would lower it and a fifty-caliber slug would find its way into the doctor's brain. No more murders for that son of a bitch. Just the gates of hell, where he'd burn forever.

The nurse's hand came down, and for a fraction of a second the assassin saw the doctor's head. But then a long, black limousine pulled up in front of the clinic, blocking the trio on the steps. The driver and another large man jumped out of the limousine and surveyed the area, ignoring the medical personnel. The door to the limo opened and a woman stepped out, followed by a man. The assassin focused in on the couple with his telescopic sight. The woman was young and beautiful with flowing brown hair and a striking figure. The assassin zeroed in on the woman's breasts. The scope was so good he thought he could see the outline of a nipple. The assassin moved the scope over to the man. He was well into his middle years with heavily grizzled hair and a paunch that was obvious despite the expensively tailored suit he was wearing.

Then the assassin saw the man's face. William Arthur Warren! The assassin stared through the scope, not believing his eyes. Impossible! It couldn't be William Arthur Warren, but it was. Warren was a multimillionaire, a staunch conservative and a major supporter of the Pro Life movement in America. The assassin had seen the old man on television a dozen times, condemning liberal causes and pledging his wealth to crush them. And now the old bastard was walking into a women's clinic with a honey who was young enough to be his daughter. It didn't take a genius to figure out why. The assassin watched Warren through the telescopic sight, the crosshairs now on the old man's face. Warren was smiling, now laughing, and his whore was laughing with him.

The assassin wished he had a video camera with a long-range viewfinder. Some tabloid or television show would pay a fortune for a videotape like that. He wondered how much it would bring. $100,000? $250,000? Maybe even more. Jesus! His heart pounded at the thought of so much money. Then the assassin remembered his dead sister and in an instant he pushed his greed aside. The only picture he wanted to see was that of a doctor with his head blown off.

The assassin heard something rustling in the brush behind him. Quickly he looked over his shoulder and searched the thick shrubs and bushes. Nothing stirred. He concentrated his hearing, listening and waiting, but the sound did not recur. It was probably a squirrel or a coyote, he thought, but he waited another ten seconds before turning back and again peering through the telescopic sight.

Now the group was on the patio, walking toward the clinic entrance. The assassin moved down the line of people. First the nurse, then Warren and his whore, then the doctor he wanted to kill. The assassin focused in on the doctor's head, positioning it squarely in the center of the crosshairs.

Close by a twig snapped loudly. The assassin twisted his body around, but it was too late. A huge gloved hand came down karate style and caught him high on the neck. Stunned, he tried to roll away, but a tree trunk stopped him. The assassin felt himself being lifted up by his hair, then came a terrible pain. Then nothing.

January 8, 1996

There was a drenching downpour in the mountains separating
West Los Angeles from the San Fernando Valley. Rain pounded on
the canvas canopy that had been constructed to protect the grave
site. Detective Lieutenant Jake Sinclair huddled beneath the covering as the wind swirled and water streamed in from the sides.
The freshly turned earth was rapidly becoming a muddy pool.

"You'd better hurry it up," Jake shouted above the noise, "or
that skeleton is going to wash away."

He was standing in a shallow ravine with two medical examiners. On the ridge above were attendants from the coroner's office
and a Highway Patrolman, and beyond them a dozen police officers were combing the hills, looking for clues. A sudden gust of
wind pulled at the canvas canopy, and Jake had to grab a sup-
porting pole to keep it from toppling over. The rain came down
harder and he had to turn away as the droplets stung his face.

"We need another ten minutes, Lieutenant," Girish Gupta said
in a clipped British-Indian accent. He was a middle-aged, pudgy
medical examiner, born in New Delhi and trained in London. "Fifteen minutes would be perfect."

"You'll be lucky to get five," Jake said, feeling his shoes sink
deeper into the mud.

"Is there not some way to stop the water from coming in?"

"Use a board," Lori McKay suggested.

Jake squinted his eyes. "A what?"

"A board or a piece of wood," Lori said, on her hands and knees, now examining a small metallic object with her magnifying glass. "You know, use it like a dam."

"It won't work," Jake told her. "You put a board into the ground and it'll cause the mud to slide and then you'll have no crime scene left."

"Don't drive the board into the ground. Just use it to divert the water." Lori examined the metallic disk once more, then placed it in a plastic envelope.

"Won't work."

"Just do it, Lieutenant. And maybe we'll buy ourselves enough time to finish our work."

Gupta glanced over uneasily at the junior medical examiner, trying to get her attention. *Don't be so demanding,* he wanted to tell her. A little deference would get her a lot more cooperation. Particularly when dealing with a tough, no-nonsense homicide detective like Jake Sinclair.

Gupta reached out to touch Lori's arm, to signal her to tone it down. But she was moving away on all fours, crawling toward a small, rotten log.

"This will do fine," Lori said, pulling on the log, which was stuck in the mud. It didn't budge. She looked up at Jake. "Want to lend a hand here?"

Jake leaned over and with effort pried the log free. He helped Lori drag it over to the shallow grave and watched her stuff towels between the log and the ground. She was young, he thought, too young, and without experience. And this was going to be a bitch of a case. The toughest kind. A man had been killed so many years ago that all that was left was bones and shreds of clothing. And a rifle. The victim had been a man—they could tell by the shape of the pelvis—but there was no way to identify him, no way to determine the date of his death. All one could say was that the victim died a long time ago. And there sure as hell weren't going to be many clues left in the surrounding area, not after all these years.

"See," Lori said, stuffing in another towel. "The water is not pouring in anymore."

"Great," Jake said absently, now studying Lori's face. She was pretty, with long, auburn hair, green eyes and flawless skin except for a few scattered freckles across her nose and cheeks. She was probably smart, Jake thought, at least book-wise. But whether she was any good in the field was another question. She hadn't shown him anything yet and her manner was beginning to bother him. She talked too much and her tongue was too sharp too often. He wondered if that was just a reflection of her insecurity or whether she was one of those irritating feminists.

"There is no evidence of trauma to the skull," Gupta reported. "Nothing to indicate violence."

"Maybe he didn't die as a result of a criminal act," Lori said thoughtfully.

"Oh, yeah," Jake said in a flat voice. "Maybe the guy died of a heart attack, then buried himself."

Lori glared up at Jake, her eyes steely. She didn't like being talked down to by some damn cop. "There are possibilities other than murder, you know."

"I'm listening."

"Let's say he was a hunter. He tripped on the ridge above and fell into this ravine, hitting his head. Trauma can cause a massive hemorrhage into the brain without actually fracturing the skull. It happens to boxers all the time."

Jake nodded. "Fine. How did he bury himself?"

Lori thought for a moment. "He was in a ravine. Maybe the rains came and washed mud down from above."

"Three feet of mud?"

"It's possible."

"There's a dozen holes in your theory," Jake said matter-of-factly. "And the biggest flaw is that this guy wasn't a hunter."

"He had a rifle," Lori said quickly.

"That has a telescopic sight and a silencer attached to it. That's not the kind of equipment a hunter uses."

Lori stared down at the rifle, its silencer half buried in the mud, and cursed at herself for not seeing it. A damn silencer right in front of her and she'd missed it. So stupid! Her eyes suddenly narrowed as she looked up at Jake. "Do you think he was a soldier of fortune type? Or maybe one of those loony militiamen?"

Jake shrugged and said nothing. There were a lot of possibilities, but only one really made sense. The guy had to have been a professional. The telescopic sight, the silencer. And the type of rifle. A Ruger Mini-14, the weapon preferred by professional snipers. But what the hell had he been doing out in the mountainous terrain of West Los Angeles?

Jake looked around at the rolling hills with their thick, scrublike vegetation. It was a remote, deserted area. Nobody lived there or even nearby. In his mind's eye Jake tried to envision the surrounding communities. He knew that the San Diego Freeway was at least a mile to the east and beyond that the million-dollar homes of Bel Air. Far to the south was Brentwood and farther yet to the west was Pacific Palisades. But what was to the north? Nothing, unless it had been constructed recently.

Jake waved up to the Highway Patrol officer on the ridge. "Are there any houses in the area north of us?"

"Not until you reach Encino," the officer yelled back.

"Any buildings at all?"

"There's a big medical clinic a mile or so up."

"Can you get there from here?"

"No way! The only road is off Mulholland Drive."

"Nothing else around here, huh?"

"Nothing but coyotes and brush."

"Double-check it for me, will you?"

"Will do," the CHP officer shouted above the rain. He had been the first peace officer to arrive at the scene. Two UCLA students hiking through the mountains had come upon the skeleton, which had been partially uncovered by the steady rain of the past week. They called the Highway Patrol and directed them to the site. The CHP officer kept the students at the grave scene until they could be questioned by the homicide detectives. The students clearly knew nothing.

"The mud is sliding!" Lori screamed out.

The mud slide pushed at the retaining log and caused it to roll toward the edge of the grave. Large chunks of earth broke free and fell atop the skeleton.

Quickly Lori reached for the log and tried to hold it in place. Gupta and Jake were at her side, straining against the tide of oozing earth. Jake grabbed a shovel and jammed it against the log, propping it up. The flow was stemmed, but it didn't stop altogether.

"We'd better move fast or we'll end up with a buried skeleton," Jake said.

"Bring the gurney down," Lori shouted up to the attendants.

An attendant called back, "We'll bring a canvas stretcher. It'll be easier."

"I don't give a damn about easy," Lori snapped. "You bring the gurney down here pronto!"

"Quite right," Gupta said, knowing that the bed of the gurney was very firm and that the skeleton could be placed on it and kept in the same position that the bones had in the grave. A canvas stretcher, on the other hand, would allow things to move about and become scrambled.

Lori turned to Jake. "My log didn't cause the mud slide, you know. The mud came from above the log."

"Your log caused the slide," Jake said evenly. "The log allowed water to pool above it and saturate the earth. That's why the mud formed an ooze and moved."

"Well, I don't—"

"And next time," Jake cut her off, "listen when you're given good advice."

Lori glared at Jake, eyes blazing. They had rubbed each other the wrong way right from the start. When she arrived on the crime scene, he had treated her like some type of underling or trainee, not as a medical examiner, and she wasn't about to put up with that.

Lori took a deep breath, trying to calm herself. Jake Sinclair's reaction to her had been typical of every man she'd ever worked with or for. She was young and pretty and female, and that meant she couldn't be bright. All of her life people had initially underestimated her. Even her parents. Before she was two, she could speak in complete sentences. Her parents thought it was cute. But when she taught herself to read at the age of four and could memorize the dialogue in the Sunday comics with a single reading, they realized she was extraordinary.

Lori was placed in a school for gifted children and did well, excelling in the sciences. She graduated from high school at fourteen, college at seventeen, and medical school at twenty-one. But her youthful appearance continued to plague her. When she was an intern, her patients thought she was a nursing student or a hospital volunteer. Gaining their trust and confidence was a real problem. Lori decided to go into pathology, where she didn't have to concern herself with interpersonal relationships. But pathology was too static and straightforward, so she specialized in forensics, excelling again.

She was hired by the Los Angeles County Coroner's Office, and this was her first day on the job. Her first case. On the drive over she could barely control her excitement. Her first case! And now Jake Sinclair was ruining it for her.

A loud clap of thunder shook the ground, bringing Lori's mind back to the present. "Hurry up with that gurney!" Lori barked out as the attendants carefully made their way down the side of the ravine.

She pushed more towels under the log, hoping to stem the flow of mud. Now Jake was helping her, repositioning the log at a slight angle so that the mud streamed to the base of the grave, where there were no skeletal remains.

Lori watched the detective stand and brush the dirt from his hands. He was a big man in his mid-forties with powerful shoulders, high cheekbones and pale blue eyes. His hair was thick and brown and swept back, just covering the tops of his ears. On his chin was a jagged, well-healed scar, just a white line now. Lori stared at it, wondering how he'd gotten it.

"Okay, Doc, how do you want to do it?" asked a coroner's attendant as he pulled the gurney next to the canopy.

"Very carefully." Lori went down to her knees and cleared the mud away from the skeleton. There was no soft tissue remaining, nothing to hold the pieces of bone together. The wind gusted again and blew a sheet of rain into Lori's face, stinging her eyes and blinding her for a moment. With the back of her hand she wiped at her eyelids.

"Maybe we can get a piece of canvas under it," the attendant suggested.

"No," Lori said at once. "You'll just jumble everything."

Another blast of rain came under the canopy and Lori turned away. When she looked back, the water had washed the skull free of debris and dirt, and beneath it Lori saw wood. She quickly brushed away the mud surrounding the bones. "There's a piece of plywood under the skeleton!"

Gupta bent down for a closer look. "You're right, quite right."

"Why would someone bother to make a plywood floor for the grave?" Lori asked.

Gupta shrugged and glanced over at Jake. "Any ideas, Lieutenant?"

Jake nodded. "Now we know that there were at least two killers involved."

Lori looked at Jake strangely. "What are you talking about?"

"That plywood wasn't used as a floor," Jake explained. "It was used as a stretcher to carry the corpse here to bury it. That's my guess."

Lori wrinkled her brow in thought. "Maybe the corpse was placed on the board and dragged along by one very strong man."

"That's not very likely. Not over this rugged terrain." Jake looked out at the surrounding hills with their steep slopes and ravines. "And if they used that plywood as a stretcher, that tells us our victim wasn't killed nearby. They needed a stretcher because they had to carry that body some distance to bury it here."

"Jesus," Lori said softly, marveling at Sinclair's ability to make so much from so little. But she still didn't like him. She poked a finger into the soft plywood. "It's rotten. If we lift it the wood will crumble."

"I think we need to put supports under it," Gupta advised.

"We had a case like this in Culver City a few years ago," the second attendant, a young African-American man, said.

"How'd you work it?" Jake asked.

"We all reached under the wood and lifted it real quick and all together."

"How'd you do?"

"It came out okay."

Jake, the two medical examiners, and the two attendants dropped to their knees and dug their fingers beneath the wood.

"On three," Jake said. "One! Two! Three!"

They lifted in unison and the wood cracked loudly and split, but not before the skeleton was atop the gurney. Gupta picked up the rusted rifle with a gloved hand and placed it in a large plastic envelope.

"Which coroner is going to work this case?" Jake asked Gupta.

"I am," Lori said promptly.

Jake looked at her at length. "This is going to be a real tough one."

"I've done tough cases before," Lori said.

"You've worked on just skeletons before?"

"Yes."

"How many times?"

"Once," Lori had to admit.

Jake turned to Gupta. "You'll have to bring in some experts."

"Most definitely," Gupta said agreeably. He and Jake had worked together countless times over the years.

"Wait a minute. Wait one minute!" Lori said in a high-pitched voice. "This is my—I mean—this is our case. We don't need any outside help."

"Sure you do," Jake said flatly. "We're going to need all the help we can get."

Lori was fuming. "I think I should remind you that this is a coroner's case and that decision can only be made—"

"By me," Gupta interjected. "I'm the senior examiner and I'll make the call."

"It's not fair, damn it!"

Jake touched Lori's arm. "This isn't personal."

"The hell it isn't!" Lori snapped, pulling her arm away. "You're cutting me out."

"The simple fact, Dr. McKay, is that we have no choice but to bring in experts," Gupta said in a consoling tone. "And I shall tell you why. First, the forensics laboratory we have is five years behind the times. It's outmoded with no hope of obtaining new equipment. Second, we have no experts in bones and skeletons. And third, we are so backed up with corpses that we'll never complete all the autopsies we have to do. Never. Now, if we take this skeleton to the County Morgue it'll be placed on a shelf and never worked on. These are the facts and you have to accept them."

Gupta turned to Jake. "I suggest we bring in Dr. Blalock."

Jake stared at Gupta for a moment, a faraway look in his eyes. "Fine. If she'll do it."

"Oh, she'll do it," Gupta said confidently. "She's now a paid consultant for the County Coroner's Office."

"Doesn't she still work at Memorial?"

"Yes, yes," Gupta said quickly. "But only part-time. She has an outside consulting service, and from what I hear she's doing very well."

"I see," Jake said slowly. He hadn't seen or talked with Joanna since they had split up six months before. Their relationship had been off and on for the previous five years. Sometimes wonderful and passionate, other times cold and distant, with no in between. They had decided to break up once and for all, having caused each other enough pain.

"Who is Dr. Blalock?" Lori asked, resisting the urge to tell both men to go straight to hell, then pack her things and return to Baltimore, where she had a position waiting.

"A very fine forensic pathologist," Gupta told her. "She's director of forensics at Memorial Hospital and has the best laboratory in the entire state."

"So I won't be involved at all, huh?" Lori asked, tight-lipped.

"Oh, I didn't say that," Gupta said cheerfully. "I plan for you to work with Dr. Blalock and help her solve this riddle."

"But how will I find the time to get over to Memorial?"

Gupta smiled pleasantly. "You're a very bright woman. I feel confident you'll find a way."

Jake studied the skeleton for a moment, then looked over at Gupta. "When you talk with Joanna, ask her if there's any way to approximate how long the body has been buried."

"I will do that, first thing."

Jake studied the bones again, now seeing a wedding band on the skeleton's fourth finger. A simple gold ring. Jake wondered if the man had children. "Tell her I'm interested in approximate times—like five-year increments. Was the body buried five, ten or twenty years ago?"

Gupta squinted an eye. "I'm not sure she'll be able to give you that answer."

"The body has not been in the ground for more than ten years," Lori said evenly.

Jake smiled thinly. "You're sure of that, huh?"

"Positive."

"You reached that conclusion on gross inspection?"

"Right."

Jake waved away Lori's approximation. She was just guessing. "We'll see what Joanna says."

"Twenty bucks says I'm right," Lori challenged him.

"You're on," Jake said promptly.

"I'll take the payment in cash," Lori said, grinning. She reached into her pocket and took out a small plastic envelope. "I found this in the ground next to the corpse."

Jake leaned over, trying to see through the plastic. "What is it?"

"It's a dime with the date 1986 on it. It was buried with the corpse. Thus, the body has been in the ground ten years or less."

Jake watched as Lori climbed out of the ravine. He reminded himself not to underestimate her again.

2

Joanna Blalock paced back and forth across the freight platform at the rear of Memorial Hospital. The loading dock was deserted. No workers, no trucks, all equipment neatly stacked against the walls. Joanna glanced out at the security guards roping off the surrounding area. No one except for essential personnel was allowed within a hundred feet of the platform.

Joanna heard a siren approaching and quickly went to the end of the dock and strained her neck to catch sight of the ambulance. She saw nothing but the misty afternoon air.

The siren whined down, then stopped altogether. It was probably parked in front of the hospital, Joanna thought, at the emergency room entrance. That meant the ambulance wasn't carrying Joanna's sister, who was being flown up from Guatemala with some terrible febrile illness that was killing people by the dozens. It was most likely caused by a virus, but no one knew for sure. All they knew was that the infecting agent was highly contagious and lethal. Very, very lethal. Joanna started pacing the platform again.

The door behind her opened and Dr. J. Mack Brown, director of infectious diseases at Memorial, walked out. He was dressed in surgical garb, capped and gowned, mask around his neck.

"Put these on," he said, handing Joanna a pair of latex gloves and a small packet of talc. "And tuck the ends of your sleeves under the gloves."

Joanna dusted her hands with talc and snapped the gloves on. She too was dressed in a surgical outfit, capped and gowned. "Has the plane landed?"

"About twenty minutes ago. The patients will be here shortly."

"Has there been any change in their condition?" Joanna asked softly.

"Not that I know of." Mack Brown was a tall, lanky Texan in his late forties, with rugged good looks and a squared-off jaw. He was named after a famous cowboy film star, Johnnie Mack Brown. "They're all very sick."

"I know."

Mack Brown scratched at his ear absently, regretting that he'd given Joanna permission to be on the platform. She'd only be in the way and could be exposing herself to real danger. But she had persisted and pleaded, and she was pretty as hell with a great body and Johnnie Mack Brown was always a pushover for great-looking women, so he'd reluctantly said yes. And besides, he owed her a favor. "Now remember, Joanna, don't touch or kiss your sister. And if by chance one of the patients vomits on you or you get splattered with any of their bodily fluids, you run like hell for the decontamination area."

Joanna nodded and looked down at the long, well-lighted corridor. At the end was an elevator, doors opened, ready to take them down two floors to the basement, to the Virology Research Center.

"Do you have any questions about the decontamination procedure?"

"I know what to do," Joanna said. A research nurse had walked her through the decon procedure, step by step, a dozen times. "Have they identified the virus?"

"Not yet. The scientists in Guatemala made some electron microscopic slides and thought they saw some unusual viral particles. But the sections were distorted and they couldn't be sure. They've sent the specimens to the good old U.S.A. for definitive identification."

"Who's doing the studies?"

"The boys at the CDC and USAMRID," Mack Brown said. The Center for Disease Control was in Atlanta and the United States

Army Medical Research Institute of Infectious Diseases was in Fort Detrick, Maryland. Mack Brown didn't mention that specimens, frozen in ice, had been flown from Guatemala to Los Angeles as well and were now being studied feverishly in the Virology Research Center at Memorial. He decided it was best for people not to know that a deadly, highly contagious microorganism was being studied in the basement of a major Los Angeles hospital.

Deep down Mack believed that the infecting agent was a new virus—a new strain—and his laboratory was every bit as well equipped as the CDC or USAMRID to identify it. Of course, the new virus would be named after the locale or area in which it had been found, but everyone would know who identified it. It was an opportunity that most virologists lived for but never saw. "Within a week we'll know what type of virus we're dealing with."

"What sort of viruses are commonly found in Guatemala?"

"The usual run. Yellow fever, dengue, HIV, influenza. But your sister's group was digging around in a primitive rain forest, untouched for hundreds and hundreds of years. Who knows what could be in there?"

Joanna wiped at her brow, thinking about her sister Kate, a young archaeologist digging in central Guatemala when the epidemic broke out. In quick succession, patients developed fever, chills, and hemorrhagic rashes, followed by jaundice and delirium. Of the sixteen Americans in the expedition, twelve were dead, and four were terribly ill. "Do they know how the virus was transmitted?"

"Probably via bodily fluids. The best evidence for this is the twenty Guatemalan natives who died of the illness and were buried by their families. The only family members who came down with the disease were those who repeatedly hugged and kissed the corpses. None of the hospital workers got the disease as long as they used adequate protective measures. You know, gloves, masks, the usual isolation procedures."

"So why not just put my sister in a regular hospital room with strict isolation rather than in the Virology Research Center?"

"Because I don't know what the virus is, and until I do I'm not taking any chances." Mack paused to scratch at the back of his neck. "This bug is a real nasty bastard. It kills almost all the people it infects."

"But some recover from it?"

"Some," Mack said somberly.

They heard sirens in the distance and turned their attention to the rear of the huge lot behind the hospital. The afternoon air was thick and misty, but Joanna could still clearly see the wire mesh gate at the far end of the lot. The sirens grew louder and Joanna could make out a string of flashing lights. Slowly the gate opened and two ambulances entered, escorted by a squad car in front, motorcycle policemen on the sides.

"Mask up!" Mack told Joanna, then reached into a paper bag and took out two sets of goggles, handing one to Joanna. "Put these on."

Joanna pulled up her mask and put on the goggles, which immediately fogged up. She wiped at them with her sleeve. Joanna felt her body temperature begin to rise, just as Mack had said she would. Most of her skin was covered by cloth, plastic or rubber, and there was very little ventilation to keep her body comfortable.

The ambulances pulled up to the loading ramp and their rear doors opened. Nurses—also wearing full protective gear—jumped out, pulling gurneys after them.

Joanna saw only two gurneys and turned quickly to Mack Brown. "I thought there were four patients."

"There are. Two were sent to another facility."

"Is—is my sister . . ."

"She's here. I made certain of that."

The first gurney up the ramp came by Joanna. It held a young man, mouth open and eyes rolled back. His skin had a peculiar greenish yellow tint in the bright daylight.

Joanna held her breath, hoping against hope as the next gurney approached. She looked down at Kate and her heart sank. Her sister looked awful, more dead than alive. Kate's eyes were closed, her skin so deeply yellowed it appeared to be painted. There was caked blood around her nostrils and mouth. Joanna wanted to call to her sister but the gurney went by in an instant.

Moments later they were in a freight elevator descending to the Virology Research Center. The elevator car was just big enough to accommodate the group. The nurses had to squeeze between the two gurneys. Joanna and Mack were pressed tightly against a side wall. Everyone was close and touching involuntarily. The air was still, filling up with the odor of stale bodies. Like most freight elevators, this one moved very slowly, creeping downward.

The young man on the gurney began to speak in a mumble, then babbled incoherently, his words a mixture of English and Italian.

"They've both been in and out of delirium," a nurse said.

"Are their vital signs stable?" Mack asked.

"Pretty much," the nurse said. "The girl has a bradycardia with a pulse of fifty-four, but her blood pressure is okay."

"That's common in viral infections," Mack said, now thinking about the virus multiplying in the young man's brain and causing encephalitis. That alone could kill.

Joanna looked down at her desperately ill sister and resisted the urge to touch her, to tell her she was home and that everything was going to be all right. *Oh, Lord! Help her! She's so young. Please don't let her die.*

The elevator jerked to a stop and the door opened. The medical team hurried down a long corridor pulling the gurneys along. At the far end of the hall was the Virology Research Center, a facility built over ten years before and continually updated ever since. Its purpose was to serve as a backup for USAMRID, the government's major viral research center. Like USAMRID, the facility at Memorial studied some of the most virulent viruses known to man. Memorial had been chosen as the site for the facility because Johnnie Mack Brown had worked at both the CDC and USAMRID and was considered one of the country's leading virologists. He was the world's expert in the virus that caused Lassa fever. The Virology Research Center was restricted to employees and patients only. No one was allowed in the research section of the facility unless he or she had been vaccinated against yellow fever, Rift Valley fever, Q fever, and a complex of horse brain virus.

Suddenly the young man on the gurney struggled against his restraining straps and tried to sit up. He was babbling nonsensically again.

"Just lie back, Tommy," a nurse said softly. "We'll have you in bed in no time."

"*Mal di testa!*" Tommy cried out.

"What's he trying to say?"

Tommy brought his head up and dry heaved. Then he heaved again and black vomitus flew through the air. All the medical personnel ducked, hands going up to protect their faces. Tommy retched again, but this time it was mainly spittle that stuck to his lips.

"Shit!" the taller of the two nurses hissed. The front of her gown was soaked.

"There's some splatter on your mask," Mack said quickly. "At three o'clock."

The nurse reached up and moved the mask away from her mouth. She prayed that none of the vomit had soaked through.

"It's on me too," Joanna said, her voice barely audible. She held up a gloved hand dotted with black liquid.

Mack moved in for a closer look at Joanna. "You've also got some on the rim of your goggles."

Fear flooded through Joanna. She thought she felt something wet on her eyebrow. Automatically she reached up.

"Don't touch it!" the tall nurse barked and grabbed Joanna's arm.

The nurse pulled Joanna through the door and down a short corridor that led to the decontamination area. They went through a metal door with a thick glass window and entered a small room bathed in deep-blue ultraviolet light. The light gave off no heat but it destroyed viruses, smashing their genetic material and making them unable to replicate. Joanna tried to stay calm, but she kept wondering if the vomitus on her goggles had penetrated through to her eyes, where the conjunctiva would readily allow the virus to pass into her body.

"Let's go," the nurse said and pushed Joanna into a small adjacent room, all metal with no windows. Silver nozzles protruded from the walls. The nurse quickly pulled her mask down to see if any of the black vomitus had penetrated through. It hadn't. She thanked God. She brought the mask back up as the intense shower-spray began.

The initial spray was water to wash away blood or vomit or any other contaminated materials. Then came a powerful blast of Eviro Chem, a disinfectant that kills viruses on contact. Joanna remembered what the nurse had told her when they had rehearsed going through the decontamination procedure. "And after the Eviro Chem shower you hope to God that some virus wasn't hiding in some crack or crevice of your body, away from the Eviro Chem and the ultraviolet light." It hadn't bothered Joanna when the nurse had told her this the day before. But it was scaring the hell out of her now.

They went into an adjoining room, again all metal with no windows, and stripped out of their garb, leaving everything on the floor.

"Check your goggles for leaks," the nurse said.

"How do I do that?" Joanna asked.

"Put them under a strong stream of water," the nurse told her. "The guy's puke landed on the upper, outer part of the rim on your left."

Joanna went over to the basin and tested the goggles under a forceful stream. She breathed a deep sigh of relief. "No leaks."

"Good."

They dressed in fresh scrub suits and returned to the corridor, now deserted. The air had a peculiar aroma, like a stale deodorizer. To the right was a metal door, tightly sealed. A sign on the door read:

CAUTION

EXTREME BIOHAZARD

DO NOT ENTER

DANGER

HIGHLY CONTAGIOUS AGENTS

To the left was another door with a thick glass window. It was marked with another sign.

CAUTION

PATIENT ISOLATION AREA

AUTHORIZED PERSONNEL ONLY

BEYOND THIS POINT

The nurse pressed on a pedal on the floor and the door to the patient isolation area opened. They entered a small area with a large window that looked into the isolation ward. There were only two beds in the unit, each surrounded by sophisticated monitoring equipment. A nurse was starting an IV on one of the patients, but Joanna couldn't tell if the patient was Kate. All she saw was two feet sticking out from under the sheets.

"It looks like a totally self-contained unit," Joanna said.

"It is," the nurse told her. "Not even air can get out. There's negative pressure in the room, so if there's a breech anywhere air is sucked in and nothing gets out."

"You've had patients in here before, I take it."

The nurse hesitated, then nodded. "Some sloppy people in the lab got themselves infected."

"With what?"

The nurse hesitated again. "You don't want to know."

The door to the patients' ward opened and Joanna could feel the negative pressure suck air in. Mack Brown walked out, pulling down his mask.

"Did any of the boy's puke penetrate?" Mack asked.

"No," the nurse said. "We're fine."

"Good. That boy is loaded with tons of virus."

Joanna asked, "Why do you say that?"

"Because he's so sick," Mack Brown explained. "That virus is multiplying at an incredible rate in every cell in his body." And the virus could continue to multiply, Mack thought, until it destroyed every cell and killed the patient. Then the virus, which cannot multiply outside the host, would sit around for weeks or months or years or even centuries until a new host came along and offered it a nice place to stay. Then it would start multiplying again.

"Is there anything you can do for the patients?" Joanna asked softly.

Mack shook his head. "Nothing."

"Not even something experimental?"

"Well," Mack said carefully, "once we identify the virus we could get plasma from those Guatemalan natives who survived the infection and see if they have antibodies against the virus. And if they do, we could give the plasma to our patients."

Joanna brightened, now seeing a ray of hope. "Do you think it'll work?"

Mack Brown gestured noncommittally, thinking that in all like-lihood the patients would be dead before the virus was identified. "I wouldn't bet on it."

The phone on the wall sounded. It didn't ring. It buzzed and a red light above it flashed.

The nurse picked it up and spoke briefly. She looked over at Brown. "It's for you. It's Wally."

Mack took the phone and held it to his ear. "Yeah, Wally?" He listened intently, then furrowed his brow. "Are you sure?" A pause. "Make double damn sure."

Mack put the phone down and stared through the window at the patients. "That was Wally Orenstein, my head technician. Wally says he's growing a virus out of the patient's blood that we received from Guatemala. It's early, but it's there." Mack Brown took a deep breath and exhaled loudly. "And it has a threadlike appearance. It looks like a filovirus."

"Oh, shit!" the nurse said, real fear in her voice.

Joanna's jaw dropped open. She tried to swallow but couldn't. "It's—it's not ebola, is it?"

"We'd better hope to God it's not," Mack said and went back to the phone. He dialed the number for the CDC in Atlanta.

3

Bright flowers were everywhere in the library, giving the room a cheerfulness that Pamela Warren did not feel. She sipped brandy from a snifter and watched her husband, William Arthur Warren, as he paced behind a large mahogany desk. He was talking to his lawyer on a cellular phone.

"Don't give me any of that legalese crap! I want a yes or a no. Is my prenuptial agreement absolutely, positively airtight? Good. Good. Make sure it stays that way. Start the divorce proceedings tomorrow."

Warren put the phone down and turned to his wife. "The prenuptial agreement is solid as a rock. You signed it and now you'll have to live by it."

"My lawyer says I can get more," Pamela said flatly.

"Try it and you'll end up with nothing." Warren was a slender man with thin gray hair and a heavily lined face. "You just try it."

"My lawyer says you have to continue to support me in the manner I was accustomed—"

"Not with a prenup," Warren cut her off. "And if we go to court, keep in mind you'll have to pay your own legal fees. And I'll see to it you stay in court for a long time before you lose."

"Bastard," she growled, hating him and the power he held over her. "Ten years of marriage and all I'm getting is two hundred thousand dollars."

"That's what you agreed to. Twenty thousand a year for each year of marriage. It seemed reasonable at the time, didn't it?"

"Yes."

"But now you want more?"

Pamela nodded slowly, thinking how naive she had been when she'd agreed to marry William Arthur Warren. He was fifty-two then, nearly double her age, with a slowly progressive form of hepatitis. They had met at Memorial Hospital, where she had been one of the private nurses hired to look after him. He was a dynamic, strong-willed man who had been one of the first to cash in on the information highway. His holdings in the communication and computer industries were vast and estimated to be worth well over a hundred million. He pursued Pamela the way he went after anything he wanted. Intensely. He showered her with expensive gifts and took her on fantastic trips aboard his private jet.

At first she thought he was just an ailing old man who wanted a nurse close at hand. But his health began to improve when he was treated with immunosuppressive drugs and his liver function stabilized. And the stronger he became the more he pursued her, finally convincing her to marry him. But only after the tests.

The goddamned tests. He had insisted she undergo a battery of tests, including a total body MRI, scans, blood analyses, even DNA and chromosome studies to make certain she wasn't a carrier for some god-awful inherited disease. William Arthur Warren wanted children. And he wanted them to be perfect.

Pamela took a deep breath and sighed audibly as she looked around the library. The room was spacious, with a polished hard-wood floor, brick fireplace, and furniture upholstered in dark-brown leather. Despite the richness of the decor, it had no warmth, no feeling. The room pretty much summed up William Arthur Warren, Pamela thought. At length she asked, "Is there another woman?"

"Not yet."

"But you've been thinking about it."

"Of course."

"Well, you'd better look far and wide, because I think you'll have a problem finding a woman who'll go through all the tests you demand."

Warren smiled thinly. "People will do anything for money."

Pamela swirled the brandy in her snifter, studying it. Behind her a grandfather clock ticked quietly. "Are you divorcing me because I couldn't conceive a child?"

"You just couldn't get the job done," Warren said.

"So it's my fault, huh?" She spat out the words, glaring at him. "Maybe if you could have performed a little better—"

"I've got sperm," he snapped loudly.

"Which my uterus saw once every two weeks if I was lucky."

"Why is it that when a woman wants to hurt a man she impugns his cockmanship? Why is that?"

"In your case, because it's true."

"Let's talk about your uterus." Warren picked up a Davidoff cigar and examined it for a moment, then placed it back on the desk. "It was your uterus that couldn't hold a perfectly fertilized egg."

"That procedure only works a third of the time," Pamela said defensively.

"Well, you had your three tries."

Pamela felt a hollowness deep within. The failure to conceive had been the biggest disappointment of her life. She had gone to a world-renowned infertility clinic in West Los Angeles and had undergone the ordeal of in vitro fertilizations. First she'd had to take injections, which caused her to superovulate. They also caused her to be miserably nauseated and bloated. Then she'd had to undergo laparoscopic surgery to obtain the eggs. Finally the eggs were fertilized with her husband's sperm and implanted in her uterus. She had gone through the entire procedure three times, all for naught. "All for nothing," she said softly.

"What?"

"Nothing." Pamela finished the last of her brandy and raised her glass. "I'd like another drink."

Warren went over to the button on the wall that rang for the butler.

"This is Tuesday. Charles's night off," she reminded him.

"Then you'll have to pour your own drink."

"Jesus Christ!" Pamela said irritably. "Touching a bottle of brandy isn't going to harm your new liver."

Warren patted the right side of his abdomen. "I've got a nice, new transplanted liver and it works damn good. I'm not touching any possible hepatic toxins. As a matter of fact, I think I'll throw all of the alcohol out of my house."

"Alcohol has to be ingested before it can damage the liver."

"I'm not taking any chances," Warren said, "I've had this liver a year and it's a perfect match. The donor and I had almost identical tissue types. Do you know how lucky I was to get a damn near perfect match?"

"Who did you have to buy off to get it?" Pamela asked derisively.

"You can't buy those transplant people off. It's a carefully regulated—"

"Bullshit!" she said sourly. "You buy and sell people all the time. Now you've bought yourself some additional years of life. What's next? A youth transplant? Maybe somebody will turn you into a virile twenty-year-old."

Warren glared at his beautiful young wife, despising her for making him feel so old. "I want you out of this house first thing in the morning. Take only the clothes you can carry. Nothing else."

Pamela fingered the diamond necklace she was wearing, wondering if the bastard was going to snatch it off her neck. "I can take my car," she said defiantly.

"You can take a taxi," Warren snapped back. "The car is in my name, not yours."

"You really are a heartless son of a bitch, aren't you?"

"Not really." Warren grinned malevolently. "I gave you everything for ten years."

Outside there was a loud noise of a metal object hitting cement and rattling around. A dog barked in the distance, but only for a moment.

Warren jerked his head toward the window. "What the hell was that?"

"A dog knocking over a trash can in the street," Pamela said, unconcerned.

"It sounded closer than that," Warren said. "I think someone is in the garage area."

"If that was the case, the alarm system would have picked it up."

Warren walked quickly over to the bay window and looked out at the darkened lawn. Everything was quiet with no sign of an in-truder. Warren stretched his neck to the side, his head touching the pane, as he studied the lighted area in front of the garage. The door was down, the garbage cans upright. A neighbor's dog barked.

Pamela came up to his side. "Do you see anything?"

"Nothing unusual." Warren looked out once more at the front lawn of his two-story colonial-style house. He studied the house across the street with its lights on. Then he scanned the deserted sidewalk. There was an eerie silence in the affluent Brentwood neighborhood. Then the dog barked again, louder this time. "I'd better check the alarm system."

Warren hurried out of the library and down a hallway lined with lithographs and watercolors. He came to the large kitchen, tiled in white with built-in refrigerators and freezers, then went into an adjacent laundry room. On the wall was a panel of blinking green lights, indicating that the alarm system was working.

Warren decided to check the garage, where his restored 1939 Packard convertible was parked. He walked to the side door and began to unlock it, then realized that the door was already unlocked. He was reaching for the wall phone when he felt cold metal at the back of his neck.

"Don't move and don't make a sound or I'll blow your god-damn head off," a rough voice said behind him.

Panic flooded through Warren, and all he could think about was that he was going to die and his transplanted liver would die with him. The new lease on life he'd been given was about to be taken away. "Take whatever you want and please leave," Warren managed to say.

"I want your money. You must have a shitload of it here."

"Ten thousand dollars," Warren said, his voice shaking. "That's all I've got here."

"Where is it?"

"In a wall safe."

"Lead me to it." The burglar pushed the gun deeper into Warren's neck. "If you set off any silent alarms or I hear any sirens coming I'll kill you. Do you understand?"

"I understand."

"Then move your ass," the burglar said, prodding Warren with the gun.

They walked slowly through the kitchen and down the hallway, the gun always up against Warren's skin. Warren's heart was pounding in his chest as he tried to gather his wits. He remembered that there was a gun in the wall safe. A .38-caliber Smith & Wesson. But he hadn't fired it for years and he wasn't even sure it was loaded. "My—my wife is in the library where the safe is."

"You tell her to keep cool unless she wants a husband without a head."

They entered the library and Warren said in a voice louder than he had intended, "Pamela, this man has a gun in my neck. Please do exactly as you're told."

Pamela stared up at the masked man, wide-eyed. The snifter fell from her hand and dropped to the hardwood floor, shattering into pieces.

The burglar shoved Warren forward. "Now open the goddamn safe!"

Warren moved to an oil painting that hung on the wall behind the desk. He pushed it aside and began turning the dial of the wall safe. On the first try it didn't open.

"I'm nervous. I'm sorry," he said, voice quaking.

"Get the damn thing open!" the burglar growled.

Warren turned the dial again, very slowly this time. In his peripheral vision he could see the burglar. A tall man, well built, wearing a Lone Ranger–type mask. His hair was long and black and swept back into a short ponytail.

Perspiration dripped from Warren's face as the final tumbler clicked into place. He opened the safe and saw the stacks of hundred-dollar bills and the handgun next to them. For a moment he was tempted to go for the gun. He pushed the urge aside.

"Put the money on the desk!" the burglar ordered.

Warren placed the stacks of bills on the desk and stepped back. "There's your money. Now please leave us alone."

The masked man reached for a stereo set that was located on a shelf. He pushed a button and classical music came on. Tchaikovsky's 1812 Overture. He turned up the volume. Cannons were booming in the music.

Warren stared incredulously at the burglar, not comprehending. "What the—"

The burglar fired two shots in quick succession. The bullets ripped into Warren's thorax and shredded his aorta. Warren grabbed at his chest, blood gushing out of the wounds and onto his fingers. He stumbled forward and, unable to keep his balance, reached out for the wall. His bloodied hand made streak marks on the white wall as he slowly sank to the floor.

Pamela pushed herself up from the chair and hurried over. She knelt and felt for Warren's carotid pulse.

"Is he dead?" the burglar asked.

"Yes." Pamela walked over to the man and kissed his lips lightly. "Now I'm going to have you and all of his money. Millions and millions and millions."

"Jesus," he said softly. "It's going to be paradise."

"You know it." Pamela pecked his cheek and reached over, turning off the stereo set, then moved quickly to the bay window. Outside all was quiet. No neighbors shouting, no dogs barking. She closed the drapes and turned back to Tony Boyette. He was trying to flip through a stack of hundred-dollar bills but was having difficulty because of the latex gloves he was wearing.

Tony was a good-looking part-time actor in his late thirties, with a great smile and sharp, chiseled features. Pamela had met him at an acting class and had been having an affair with him for the past three months. When she overheard a phone conversation and learned of Warren's intention to divorce her, she persuaded Tony to help her kill her husband, promising him a lifetime of love and never-ending wealth. "Put those bills in your pocket and take off your mask."

Tony stuffed the stacks of hundreds into the front and back pockets of his jeans. "Easy money," he hummed and removed his mask. He saw a cigar on the desk and picked it up, biting off the tip. He spat out the piece of tobacco and reached for a match.

"We don't have time for that," Pamela said sternly.

"Right," Tony said and dropped the cigar on the desk.

"Now take the gun from the safe and make certain it has ammunition in it."

Tony quickly checked the weapon's chambers. "It's loaded."

"Good. Now drop the gun by his right hand."

"In the blood?"

"It doesn't matter," she said irritably. "Just do it."

Tony put the gun in a small pool of blood, then removed Warren's Rolex watch and his wallet. He looked in the billfold and saw two five-dollar bills. *Shit,* he grumbled to himself, *the old fart was a multimillionaire and carried around only ten bucks.* Tony pocketed the money.

"Remember, don't hock or sell anything," Pamela said firmly. "Take everything—wallet, watch and your gun—and put it in a plastic bag, then dump it in the ocean."

"Way out in the ocean?"

"Way out," she repeated. "Then we'll have a very happy ending."

"You and me, babe," Tony said and kissed her hard.

"You and me," Pamela said and slipped out of his embrace. She stepped back and took a deep breath, readying herself. "Let's get the last thing done."

"Jesus," Tony said, hesitating. "I don't know if—"

"Just do it!" she snapped.

Tony made a tight fist and punched her on the side of her face. She went down to her knees, cheek bruised, lip bleeding. With effort she pulled herself up.

Tony reached out to her. "Does it hurt bad?"

She shrugged off his hand. "Finish it."

"Are you sure?"

"Finish it, goddamn it!"

Tony slammed the barrel of his gun down on Pamela's head.

She dropped to the floor like a dead weight.

4

"How the hell did he get in?" Jake Sinclair asked.

Sergeant Lou Farelli shrugged. "Don't know. The windows and doors were locked. There was no evidence of forced entry."

"Maybe he had a key."

"Or maybe he just picked a lock. The back doors would have been easy for a pro."

"Were there any scratch marks on the door locks?"

"Naw. But the keyholes were big enough to shove a pencil through. A pro would have stuck a pick in on the first try."

They were standing in the kitchen of the Warren home. Bright sunlight flooded into the room, causing the white tiles to glisten. Outside Jake could see policemen combing the manicured lawn, looking for clues. Across the street curious neighbors lined the sidewalk.

Jake glanced over at the alarm panel on the wall, green lights blinking. "Did you check with the security company to see if an alarm went off last night?"

"It was quiet all night, they said."

"So our pro knew how to get around the alarm system too."

Farelli grunted sullenly. "Oh, yeah. This guy is good. He even knew the butler would be away."

Jake looked over at the butler, Charles Horton. He was sitting at the breakfast table, nervously puffing on a cigarette. "How many people knew you took Tuesday night off?"

"A great many, I'm afraid," Horton said with a British accent. He was tall and thin and carefully groomed. "There was Mr. and Mrs. Warren, of course, and some of their friends. And most of the house workers—maids, cooks, yardmen. And you know how they talk and gossip with friends who work in nearby houses."

"Yeah," Jake said sourly, thinking that the pro didn't even have to case the house to find out when the butler would be away. All he had to do was talk with one of the maids or yardmen. "Tell me, who knew the code to shut off the alarm?"

"Only Mr. and Mrs. Warren, a few of Mr. Warren's closest aides, and myself," Horton said at once. "But that may not be of much help to you because the alarm system was always malfunctioning."

"Always?"

"At least twice that I can recall." Ashes dropped from Horton's cigarette onto the table and he quickly brushed them into an ashtray. "Last year a burglar tried to break into Mr. Warren's garage, presumably to steal his restored Packard. We were alerted by the noise he made. The alarm never went off."

"Did you call the security company?"

"Of course," Horton said. "They claimed we hadn't set the alarm correctly, which was nonsense."

"So you think the alarm may not have worked last night?"

"It's entirely possible."

Or maybe the pro just disarmed the system, Jake thought. Some pros were magicians when it came to alarm systems, and most home security systems were simple and easy to disrupt. "Have there been any attempted break-ins since last year?"

"No, sir."

"Could there have been any attempted robberies that Mr. Warren didn't mention to you?"

"Oh, no. Never," Horton said with certainty. "Mr. Warren confided absolutely in me in such matters. You see, I've worked for him for nearly twenty years."

"He didn't seem edgy or nervous to you?"

"Quite to the contrary. He seemed more robust and self-assured than ever."

"When did you see him last?"

"Just before six yesterday evening," Horton said. "I was on my way to the opera in San Diego and he wished me a good journey."

"And you were the one who found him this morning, right?"

"Yes," Horton said, his voice now sad. "I came back just after seven this morning and found them in the library."

"Thanks for your time." Jake turned away, then turned back. "One more question. Did Mr. Warren get along well with the other people who work in the house?"

"Oh, yes," Horton said promptly. "They're good and loyal and he treated them well."

"Don't leave the grounds. We may have more questions later."

"Very good, sir."

Jake and Farelli walked out of the kitchen and down a carpeted hallway. A detective from the Crime Scene Unit was on his knees carefully examining a dirty footprint in the thick carpet. It had ridges and grooves like those found in athletic shoes.

"What type is it?" Jake asked.

"It's probably an Adidas," the detective said. "I'll give you the size and model later."

Jake and Farelli walked on, passing a row of paintings on the wall. One looked like a Picasso, but Jake couldn't tell if it was an original or a very fine print.

"Get a list of all the household workers and check their bank accounts," Jake told Farelli. "And check over the next few weeks to see if any of them make big purchases. You know—cars, expensive stereos, things like that."

Farelli smiled thinly. "But Horton said they were good and loyal servants. Don't you have any faith in them?"

"None at all," Jake said without expression. "And check out Horton too."

They went into the library. The drapes were still closed, lights on, the air stale and smelling of old blood. Jake and Farelli stepped aside as the Crime Scene Unit filed out carrying their special equipment.

Over by the desk Farelli saw a young woman on her knees studying the bloody handprint on the wall. He squinted his eyes and moved in for a closer look. "Who the hell is that?"

"That's Lori McKay, the new medical examiner," Jake said.

"Jesus," Farelli winced. "She looks young enough to be my daughter."

"That's because she is."

Farelli lowered his voice. "Is she any good?"

"Yeah," Jake said, "but not as good as she thinks she is."

They strolled over to the desk, both looking at the opened wall safe behind it. On the carpet was the body of William Arthur Warren, his eyes open, mouth agape. A dried stream of blood ran from his chest to the carpet. A Smith & Wesson revolver was near his hand.

"What have you got, Doc?" Jake asked the medical examiner as she stood up.

"I prefer you not call me Doc," Lori said evenly. "McKay is fine or Dr. McKay, but not Doc."

"Fine," Jake said, holding his temper and wondering if young people were always such pains in the ass. "What have you got, McKay?"

"What I've got is what you see," Lori said and pulled off her latex gloves. "Our killer comes in some time after eight—"

"How do you know the time?" Farelli asked.

Lori studied his face for a moment. "Who are you?"

"Farelli, Sergeant Farelli."

"I'm Dr. McKay," she said formally, then pointed to a partial muddy footprint on a small Persian carpet. "Somebody tracked mud in here last night and it had to be after eight because that's when the lawn sprinklers went on. There's no mud on the corpse's shoes, so I think it was brought in by the killer."

Jake asked, "How do you know the carpet was clean before the killer came?"

"Because I asked the butler. When he left at six p.m. the carpet was spotless."

"Good," Jake said and meant it. She might be a pain in the ass but she was a smart pain in the ass.

Lori went on. "The killer comes in and surprises the Warrens. Mrs. Warren is sitting in the chair by the sofa drinking a brandy. She's badly frightened and the snifter drops from her hand and shatters on the hardwood floor. The killer orders Mr. Warren to open the safe and the old man does it. Then, for God knows what reason, Mr. Warren grabs the gun from the safe and turns to the killer. William Arthur Warren is shot and dies because of his stupid move. His wife runs over to help and gets conked on the head. She's got a lump the size of an orange on her temple. The killer grabs the money and runs."

Something didn't fit, Jake thought. If old man Warren really cared about his wife, he wouldn't have pulled a revolver on a burglar who was holding a gun on them. Such a stupid move for a man who was supposedly so smart. It didn't make sense.

Jake saw a small piece of brown paper on the floor. He picked it up and carefully sniffed it. "It smells like tobacco."

Lori pointed a gloved finger at the desk. "There's an unlit cigar with its end bitten off next to the ashtray. There's also a pack of Davidoffs in Mr. Warren's coat. So I suspect the bitten-off cigar belonged to the victim."

"Maybe," Jake said and turned to Farelli. "Make sure the Crime Scene boys match the piece on the floor to the cigar on the desk. And check out the cigar for fingerprints."

Farelli took out a small pad and quickly scribbled a note.

A young, lanky cop hurried into the library and came over to Jake. "Lieutenant, Mrs. Warren's doctor would like to talk with you."

"Bring him in."

The cop turned to the door and signaled to Dr. Steven Kaye. The doctor was tall and middle-aged with prematurely gray hair and inquisitive brown eyes. He had been the Warrens' family physician for the past ten years.

"Sorry to bother you, Lieutenant," Kaye said with a Boston accent.

"No problem," Jake said. "What's up?"

"Mrs. Warren will need to be hospitalized," Kaye said, fingering the stethoscope around his neck. "She's suffered a severe concussion. There may be a skull fracture as well."

"Any chance of us talking with her?"

Kaye shook his head. "She's in and out of consciousness. I don't think you could rely on her answers."

"If there's any change, let us know."

Kaye looked down at the corpse of William Arthur Warren and

sighed sadly. "So tragic after all he's been through. And the transplant was working so well."

Jake's eyes narrowed. "What transplant?"

"A liver transplant," Kaye told him. "Mr. Warren suffered from a slowly progressive form of hepatitis and went into liver failure last year. He had only weeks to live when they found him a replacement liver. An almost perfectly matched liver from a teenager who had died in a traffic accident."

Kaye took the stethoscope from his neck and placed it in his coat pocket. "It might be a good idea for us to contact the people at Memorial who performed the transplant. They may want blood and tissue samples to see how well the transplanted liver had worked."

Lori McKay stepped forward, her expression firm. "This is a coroner's case. Nobody touches the body."

Kaye studied the name tag on Lori McKay's coat. "Of course all such decisions should be made by you as medical examiner. But the studies I mentioned could give valuable information and be very important to those who receive transplants in the future."

"When I do the autopsy we can invite one of their people over to observe," Lori said, not budging.

"That might be helpful," Kaye said doubtfully. "But as you know better than I, sometimes corpses lie around morgues for days before the autopsy is done. And the organs may not be placed in the correct preservative for the studies the transplant people require."

Lori gestured with her hands, palms out. "I can't promise you when the autopsy will be done."

"Exactly," Kaye said, nodding to her. "Perhaps we could solve the problem by having a pathologist from Memorial come over and take needle biopsies of various organs."

Lori didn't answer right away. She squinted her eyes, considering the proposal.

Jake couldn't help but be impressed with Dr. Kaye. The doctor was soft-spoken with a nonconfrontational manner. He knew how to defuse situations and he knew how to handle Lori McKay.

"I don't want people sticking a hundred needles into this body," Lori said finally.

"Of course not," Kaye assured her. "It would have to be done under your supervision."

"Okay," Lori said reluctantly. "Just make certain they send someone over who knows a little about forensics. That way he won't screw things up too much."

"Yes, someone in forensics," Kaye said agreeably.

Joanna Blalock edged her way through the crowd of reporters and television cameramen outside the Warren home. She ducked under the crime scene tape and walked up the lawn past a hedge of roses. The policeman at the door recognized Joanna and gave her a half salute.

"They're in the library, to the left, Doc," he said.

Joanna entered a gleaming white marble foyer. In front of her was a huge living room with cream-colored carpet and furniture upholstered in a deep-blue silk fabric. On the far wall were two exquisite paintings by Joan Miró. The room was beautiful, but it struck Joanna as being unused and lacking in warmth.

She went to her left down a carpeted hallway and came to the library. On the floor was a partial footprint circled with white chalk. She stepped around it and into the library. It was a large, dark room with everything done in deep brown. The bright floral arrangements seemed out of place to Joanna. She saw Jake standing over a body and talking with a young, pretty woman.

He really hadn't changed, she thought. Maybe a little heavier but still good-looking and still able to attract just about any woman he wanted. He had a lot of good features—and some bad ones too, she quickly reminded herself. Like his insensitivity. God! How unthoughtful he could be, not willing to bother with other people's needs. When she'd needed him, really needed him, he disappeared. Well, now she was over that. She'd learned—the hard way. Never depend on Jake Sinclair.

"Hello, Jake," she said neutrally as she walked over.

"Hey, Joanna." Jake grinned, exposing even, white teeth. "How have you been?"

"Just fine. What about yourself?"

"Still trying to catch bad guys," Jake said and turned to Lori.

"Let me introduce you to one of our new medical examiners. Dr. Lori McKay, this is Dr. Joanna Blalock."

The women nodded formally and said, almost in unison, "Nice to meet you."

Joanna studied Lori briefly. The new medical examiner seemed so young. Or maybe it was just her getting older. "How long have you been with the coroner's office?"

"This is my first week," Lori said.

"I'll bet you feel like it's been a lot longer," Joanna said. "I know the workload there is incredible."

Lori shrugged, not interested in small talk. She was already way behind in her schedule. There was another murder in the mid-Wilshire area she had to investigate and two autopsies were awaiting her at the County Morgue.

"Where did you train?" Joanna asked.

"Does that make any difference?" Lori asked, losing patience.

"It might," Joanna said, stung by the young woman's brusqueness. "If you trained in a place that has expertise in a particular area, it might be very important. If not here, then perhaps in the future."

Lori took a deep breath and exhaled loudly. "Johns Hopkins."

"Did you have a chance to work with Kidderman?"

Lori shook her head. "He died before I started."

"He was a wonderful man," Joanna said softly, remembering the professor who had taught her so much. "His death was a real loss."

"Well, things change and time moves on."

This woman has the warmth of a table, Joanna thought and decided to end the pleasantries. She looked down at the corpse of William Arthur Warren. "Do you want to fill me in?"

Lori's eyes narrowed noticeably. "Fill you in? Just get your liver biopsies so we can finish up here."

Joanna raised her eyebrows. "What the hell are you talking about? I'm director of forensic pathology at Memorial and I don't do liver biopsies for you or anybody else."

Lori glared at Joanna, then turned to Jake, eyes blazing. "You set this up, didn't you?"

Jake shrugged his shoulders innocently. "All I did was call Memorial and ask for someone with a background in forensics."

"And that someone just happened to be the *director* of forensics?" Lori's voice was high-pitched, almost a shriek. A detective by the door turned and looked over.

"That's right."

Lori was fuming, her face reddened. "This is my case, a coroner's case. Nobody touches this body and nobody examines it without my permission. You got that?"

"I've got neither the time nor the patience to put up with this nonsense," Joanna said to Jake and turned to leave. "Good luck on this case."

"Wait a minute! Wait a minute!" Jake said hurriedly. "Just take a quick look at the corpse while I talk with Dr. McKay."

"I'm not very good at quick looks," Joanna said.

"Sure you are," Jake said and took Lori's arm, guiding her across the library and out the door into the hallway. A cop was nearby, and Jake gave him a thumb signal to move away.

"I'm not going to let you bully me, Lieutenant," Lori said and pulled her arm away from him. "I know the duties of a medical examiner, and I'm going to follow them to the letter."

"Great," Jake said.

"And I also know the powers that the law gives me, powers that you can't do a damn thing about." Lori spoke in a calm, even voice but she was still furious at him for bringing in Joanna Blalock. "It is I and I alone who determines what happens to this body. So, as far as I'm concerned, you can go piss off."

Jake took a deep breath and tried to control his temper. "Now you listen and listen real good. I'm giving you a chance to cover your ass without losing any face and you're too stupid to see it."

"What are you talking about?"

Jake looked around to make certain no one was near. He pointed into the library. "This is not some old skeleton that nobody gives a damn about. That body belongs to a multimillionaire with more power and pull than you could ever dream about. He's what's called a high-profile case, and the news media will be all over this like flies on dogshit."

"So?"

"If we don't crack this case soon—and chances are we won't— the news media is going to ask why we haven't. And then they're going to learn that you are the medical examiner on the case. And when they find out you look about sixteen and that you've only been out of training a week, they're going to crucify you. They'll eat you alive. Maybe they'll call you Shirley Temple McKay. And if by chance a more senior examiner picks up something you missed—well, you're as good as gone. You'll never get another decent job anywhere. You'll spend the rest of your career in the back of the L.A. morgue doing routine autopsies on month-old corpses."

"I—I may not have missed anything," Lori stammered, caught off guard.

"But then again you might have," Jake said, keeping his voice low as a policeman walked by. "And I might have too. That's why I'm never bothered by a good second opinion."

Lori looked away and carefully considered what Jake had said. Again, she thought miserably, her youthful appearance was working against her. But as much as she hated to admit it, she knew the detective was right. Having Joanna Blalock as a consultant in the case would cover Lori's ass in the event something was overlooked. "It'll still be my case. I'll be the head investigator."

"Absolutely."

"Regardless of what's found?"

"Regardless," Jake lied.

Lori turned toward the library. "You know, Lieutenant, I don't like you very much."

"I can live with that."

They walked into the library, now filled with light since the drapes had been opened. Joanna was on her knees, carefully studying William Arthur Warren's hand and the gun beside it. She glanced up briefly at the approaching footsteps, then went back to examining the gun with a magnifying glass.

Jake watched her, thinking that she was still beautiful, maybe even more beautiful than when he'd first met her six years before. She had fine, patrician features with deep-brown eyes and sandy-blond hair that was pulled back and held in place by a simple barrette. Her skin was flawless except for some early crow's-feet that were noticeable only when she smiled broadly. The smile that took his breath away. It always seemed as if it was meant just for him. She had the kind of beauty that would last a lifetime, Jake decided.

"We'd value your opinion," Lori said, as if nothing had happened. "If you'd like, I can fill you in."

"Fine," Joanna said, getting to her feet and wondering how Jake had managed to change the examiner's mind so quickly.

She listened as Lori carefully reconstructed the sequence of events that led to the death of William Arthur Warren. The young medical examiner dramatized how the mortally wounded Warren dropped his gun and staggered to the wall, leaving a bloody handprint before falling to the floor.

"There are only two small puddles of blood on the floor," Lori pointed out. "So I suspect he bled out internally."

"There are no streams of blood between the puddle and the chest wounds," Joanna observed.

Lori shrugged, unconcerned. "There was plenty of blood on the front of his shirt. Some of it could have dripped to the floor before Warren fell. I figure the gun slipped from his hand and he bled some. Then he staggered to the wall. That's why the gun is lying in a pool of blood."

Joanna nodded slowly. "So you believe that Warren was shot, dropped his gun and bled on it before he hit the floor."

"That's what the evidence indicates," Lori said.

"Then why is there no blood on the side of the gun facing up?"

Lori quickly looked down at the weapon, its metal gleaming without a trace of blood. She lifted the gun with a pencil. Beneath it was coagulated blood. "Maybe he was on his knees for a little while bleeding, then dropped the gun into the blood."

"Then he stands back up and puts a bloody handprint on the wall?" Joanna shook her head. "That won't work."

"Are you saying that someone else dropped the gun in that blood?"

"That's one possibility." Joanna paused in thought, wondering if Warren had attempted to fire the gun and the killer grabbed it away, then shot him. The killer could have thrown the gun down at any time. Joanna looked down at the fully loaded weapon again. Warren probably never had a chance to fire it. "Maybe the killer picked it up. Make sure the weapon is checked carefully for prints."

Jake was thinking about other possibilities to explain the position of the gun. Maybe the killer kicked it accidentally on his way out or maybe the butler picked it up and dropped it without thinking when he discovered the murder. There were a dozen possible answers, none of them very good. But one thing was damn sure. There should have been blood all over that gun if Warren had dropped it. And there wasn't.

Joanna moved to the desk and studied the unlit cigar with its end bitten off.

"We found the bitten-off piece on the floor," Lori volunteered. "Warren may have been about to light up when the killer came in."

Joanna used a magnifying glass to examine the cigar, focusing in on the bitten-off end. "How do you know it was Warren who bit off the end of the cigar?"

"Because he had a pack of Davidoffs in his pocket," Lori said at once.

"That means nothing. The killer may have taken one from Warren's body. Maybe he was celebrating."

Jake said, "We're going to check it for prints."

Joanna nodded. "Also have someone in forensic dentistry examine the cigar and see if there are any unusual features to the bite mark."

Lori's face colored. Damn it! She hadn't thought of that. She'd had all the time in the world and had overlooked it like some damn amateur.

Outside there was the sound of an approaching siren. Jake looked out the bay window and watched an ambulance pull into the driveway. The news reporters tried to follow it in, but two big cops kept them behind the yellow tape. "Where will the autopsy be done?"

"At the County Morgue," Lori said promptly. "And that's final. No ifs, ands or buts."

"I wish you'd reconsider," Joanna said diplomatically. "The transplant people learn so much from these postmortem studies."

"Well, they're welcome to come to the morgue when I do the autopsy."

"That's not the same and you know it," Joanna said, her temper flaring briefly. She sighed wearily and wondered how to deal with the immature medical examiner. "Would you consider doing the autopsy at Memorial?"

"I don't have privileges there."

"I could arrange that with no problem," Joanna said.

"And I would do the autopsy? No interference?" Lori said slowly, thinking that privileges at Memorial meant a clinical appointment to the staff, probably at the level of assistant professor. It would look good on her curriculum vitae.

"Correct."

"And all tissues go to the coroner's lab for further study?"

"Except those specimens taken by the transplant people."

Lori nodded cautiously. "That might work."

Joanna nodded back. "That way everybody will be happy."

Lori's eyes narrowed suspiciously. "And that way you'll be able to keep a close watch on me, won't you?"

Joanna smiled sweetly. "That too."

Dr. Steven Kaye stepped into the library and called out to Jake. "Lieutenant, we're taking Mrs. Warren to the hospital now."

"Doc, can we ask Mrs. Warren a couple of questions?" Jake asked. "It's really important."

Kaye hesitated, a man unhappy with the decision he was about to make. "You've got thirty seconds."

Jake hurried out of the library, Joanna and Lori a few steps behind. Pamela Warren was strapped onto a gurney, a sheet up to her shoulders. She was a very pretty woman despite the large, abraded lump on her temple. Her hair was disheveled, her eyes puffy and almost closed. She was wearing a diamond-and-pearl necklace.

Jake leaned over Pamela Warren. "Mrs. Warren, can you describe the man who shot your husband?"

Pamela Warren shook her head ever so slightly and spoke in a whisper. "He had a mask on."

Shit! Jake cursed silently. "Did your husband pull a gun on the man?"

"I—I'm not sure," she said, her voice faint. "It happened so quickly." Her eyelids dropped shut.

"All right," Kaye said to the ambulance attendant. "Let's go."

Jake watched the gurney move down the hall and into the marble foyer. "Sloppy burglar, huh?"

"Or just stupid," Joanna said.

Lori's eyes darted back and forth between Jake and Joanna. She wondered what she had missed. "What are you talking about?"

"The diamond-and-pearl necklace," Joanna said.

"What about it?" Lori asked, her brow now furrowed in thought.

"The burglar didn't take it," Jake said. "The guy empties the safe, takes the old man's watch and wallet, but leaves behind a necklace worth at least ten grand. It doesn't make sense, does it?"

"Maybe he got all flustered after he shot the victim," Lori suggested. "Then he just grabbed what he could and ran."

"Maybe," Jake said thoughtfully, not believing it. The rest of the process was too deliberate, too good. He left damn few clues behind. Some muddy footprints. Maybe a bitten-off cigar.

Abruptly, Jake started down the hallway. "Let's go talk to the butler."

In the kitchen, Horton, the butler, was still sitting at the breakfast table, now starting his second pack of cigarettes of the day. Farelli was sitting beside him, writing up a report.

"Horton, did Mr. Warren smoke cigars in the library?" Jake asked.

"Oh yes, sir," Horton said promptly. "That's where he usually smoked."

"Did he bite the ends off his cigars?"

"Never. He used a clip."

"So, he wouldn't have spat a piece of tobacco onto the floor, huh?"

Horton made a face of disgust. "Of course not. Mr. Warren was a very meticulous man."

"Well, now," Jake said, pleased with himself, "it seems our guy wasn't all that flustered. Hell, he even took time to chew a cigar. He had plenty of time to see the necklace."

"Mrs. Warren's hair is long," Joanna said, thinking out loud. "If she fell to the floor face down, the burglar might not have seen the necklace."

Jake turned to Farelli. "Did they find Mrs. Warren face up or face down?"

"Face up," Farelli said.

Joanna nodded. "He saw the necklace."

"Then why didn't he take it?" Jake asked.

Joanna shrugged and shook her head.

"It just doesn't make sense, does it?" Jake said again and left the kitchen.

5

"Your sister is terribly ill," Mack Brown said gravely. "Her liver enzymes are sky-high and still going up."

"Isn't there anything we can do?" Joanna asked, her voice barely above a whisper.

"Nothing that I know of. We just have to watch and wait and hope she turns the corner," Mack said, wondering when would be the best time to tell Joanna Blalock that her sister wasn't going to make it. The girl was as good as dead, all of her organs infected with some dreadful virus. But the liver was worst of all. It couldn't hold up much longer. Soon the girl would go into hepatic failure and die.

Joanna's eyes began to tear up as she looked through a thick glass window into the isolation ward. Her sister just lay there motionless while a nurse started an IV. The nurse was capped, gowned and masked and was wearing goggles. Joanna had to fight to keep her voice from breaking. "What about giving her plasma from the Guatemalan natives who were infected but survived the illness?"

"The plasma is supposedly on its way to us now, but I won't be able to give it to her," Mack said. "At least not yet."

"Why not?" Joanna snapped, her emotions raw. "My sister is in there dying and you're telling me—"

"Listen to me, Joanna," Mack said, putting his hands on her

shoulders and squeezing gently. "We still don't know why those natives survived. We don't know if they had antibodies in their plasma or whether they had some other form of natural immunity. And most importantly, we don't know whether they're still carrying around a ton of virus in their blood despite the fact that they're feeling well. The last thing we want to do is give your sister even more of the virus than she's already got."

"Can't you test the natives' plasma for the virus?"

"We haven't identified it yet," Mack said wearily. "It's a real son of a bitch that grows for a while, takes on peculiar shapes, then dies away."

Joanna nodded, now understanding the problem. Until the virus was isolated and identified, there was no way to determine whether someone's blood or plasma had antibodies against it. And unless one had the virus isolated, it would not be possible to design methods to determine who had the virus in their blood. It was like the AIDS story. Until they isolated the HIV virus, nobody knew how or why the disease was transmitted and spread. But it could take weeks, maybe even months, to identify the virus infecting Kate. Too long, much too long. "If my sister continues to go downhill, I think we should give her the plasma, regardless of whether the virus has been identified."

"That could be very risky," Mack warned her.

"I'm not just going to stand here and watch her die," Joanna said, setting her jaw.

That's exactly what they were going to do, Mack thought, unless a miracle happened. "Let's wait a little longer. Maybe things will improve."

"Are you saying there's still a chance she'll make it?"

"A chance," Mack said, hating himself for giving Joanna false hope.

"May I see her now?"

"Of course."

Mack stepped on a floor pedal and a thick metal door hissed open. They walked into the ward and felt the pull of negative pressure before the door closed behind them. The room was windowless, the air filled with a sweet-smelling disinfectant. Above Kate

Blalock's bed a series of monitors visually displayed her pulse and blood pressure.

"Remember," Mack said quietly, "you can touch her, but don't kiss."

Joanna looked down at Kate, resisting the urge to kiss her and hold her and tell her that everything was going to be all right. Joanna felt so helpless. She was supposed to protect and care for her younger sister, now that both of their parents had passed away, but all she could do was stand by and watch and do nothing.

Joanna's goggles misted up, and she wiped them clear with the sleeve of her gown. Carefully she leaned over Kate. "How are you feeling?" she asked softly.

Kate's eyes fluttered and slowly opened. Her skin was deeply jaundiced, her lips parched and flecked with dried blood.

"Are you having any pain?" Joanna asked.

Kate focused her eyes on the person above her, but all she saw was someone wearing cap, mask and goggles. "What?"

"It's me. Joanna."

"Hi," Kate said, her voice low and hoarse. She tried to smile but it caused her lips to stretch and the cracks in them to hurt. "I feel awful."

"You've got a bad virus."

Kate nodded very slowly. "Everybody who went into the cave got it."

"What cave?" Mack asked, coming up beside Joanna.

"An old cave in the jungle," Kate said weakly, her voice barely audible. "It was full of spiderwebs and bugs and bats."

Mack leaned in closer. "Did anyone get bitten?"

"Not that I know of."

Mack remembered a similar event that had occurred in a rain forest in Central Africa. A group of natives had gone into a cave, exploring, and within days had come down with a fulminating type of hemorrhagic fever. All of them had died. It was thought to be an outbreak of ebola, but that was never proven. "How long after the visit to the cave did people become sick?"

"The next week it started," Kate said as her eyelids dropped.

Mack needed her to be more precise. "How many days?"

"Four or five days."

That would fit, Mack thought and took a step back. Some of the filoviruses, like ebola, had a short incubation period.

Kate groaned.

"Hang in there," Joanna said, squeezing her sister's hand. "You're going to be fine."

Kate took a deep breath and, closing her eyes, drifted off.

Joanna looked down at her sister, now frightened by what she saw. Kate was emaciated, her color awful, and now there was a trickle of blood coming from her nostrils. "Why is she bleeding?"

"Her platelet count is down," Mack said.

"Why?"

"She's having intermittent disseminated intravascular coagulation."

"Oh, Lord!" Joanna turned away and shook her head sadly. When a provoking agent, like a virus, activated the patient's coagulation system, blood clots began to form within the blood vessels. As clots formed, the body's platelets and coagulation factors were used up and the patient would start to bleed. Thus, one had the paradox of a patient forming clots and bleeding at the same time. It was an ominous sign. "How severe is it?"

"It's only moderate. She's had no major hemorrhages." Mack studied the overhead monitors briefly, watching the pulse change from 96 to 88 per minute. "I don't think it necessarily worsens her prognosis."

"It sure as hell doesn't help it either," Joanna said dejectedly, hating to feel so helpless.

She gently patted Kate on the shoulder and stepped back. Her gaze went to the bed next to Kate. It was now empty, the mattress stripped bare and rolled up. "Where's the other patient?"

"He died early this morning."

Joanna stared at Mack at length, then poked a finger at his chest. "I want my sister to receive that plasma as soon as it arrives from Guatemala. Thaw it and give it to her."

"It might be wise to wait," Mack cautioned.

"Wait for what? For my sister to die so we can roll up another mattress?"

Mack was about to say something but knew it was useless to

argue further. "We'll have to check the plasma for HIV, the hepatitis virus and syphilis."

"That shouldn't take more than a few hours."

"Please keep in mind that plasma may have no effect whatsoever on your sister's illness."

"Call me the moment the plasma arrives. Day or night."

Joanna turned and exited the isolation ward, then went through an ultraviolet decontamination room before stripping off her garb and goggles and changing into a fresh scrub suit. She put on a long white laboratory coat and left the Virology Research Center.

The freight elevator door was open, the car empty. Joanna stepped in and pressed the B-level button. As the elevator slowly began to ascend, Joanna leaned back against the wall and told herself she was making the right decision. The virus was so lethal it had already killed thirteen of the sixteen Caucasians it had infected. A kill rate of over 80 percent. It was every bit as deadly as ebola. And deep down she knew Kate would die without the plasma. She just knew it.

Joanna took a deep breath and forced herself to face the very real possibility that Kate was going to die even with plasma therapy. She could only hope that Kate didn't have the Blalock family curse of premature death. Everybody passed away so young, it seemed. An only uncle had died at thirty-two of a massive myocardial infarction, and their father had been killed at forty-four in a plane crash. Their mother came down with a strange neurologic disorder and died in her mid-fifties. Kate was the only family Joanna had remaining, and the thought of losing her and being left all alone in the world both frightened and saddened Joanna. *Lord! She's so young! Please help her!*

The elevator jerked to a stop and Joanna stepped out. She walked down a long corridor, past the autopsy room, and entered her office. Her secretary, Virginia Hand, was on the phone, busily scribbling down a message.

Joanna reached into a desk drawer and took out a candy bar. She quickly unwrapped it and wolfed it down, licking her fingers at the same time. Her gaze drifted up to the wall clock. It was almost three o'clock and there were still two autopsies to be done. She'd be lucky to finish up by eight.

Virginia put the phone down and looked up. "How's your sister?"

"The same."

"I went to mass and said a prayer for her this morning."

"Thanks," Joanna said warmly. Her secretary was middle-aged with frizzy hair and always had time and concern for others despite a miserable home life that included an alcoholic husband and a teenage son heavily into drugs. "Is the Warren autopsy all set?"

"All set and ready to go." Virginia picked up a message slip. "The transplant surgeon is running a little late but he'll be down shortly. Dr. McKay—she's a real cutey, huh?—is here, and Harry Crowe is mad as hell and bitching to anyone who'll listen."

Joanna flicked her wrist disdainfully. Harry Crowe was the diener of the morgue and had worked at Memorial for over thirty years. He was obnoxious and a bully. "What's bothering him now?"

"Oh, a long list of things," Virginia said, holding up a hand and counting on her fingers. "First, you're starting the autopsy too late in the afternoon. Second, you're bringing in an outsider to do the autopsy, someone who's not on staff at Memorial. Third, he doesn't trust anybody from the coroner's office because they're all foreigners who don't treat him with respect and he's not going to put up with it."

"Well, that's too bad," Joanna said, unconcerned, and licked the last remaining dab of chocolate from her fingers. "Give the transplant service a call and tell them we're starting the autopsy. If their guy can't get here, ask if there's a special way they want us to handle the liver."

"Right," Virginia said and reached for the phone.

Joanna crossed the corridor and went through two sets of swinging doors before entering the autopsy room. She unbuttoned her laboratory coat and reached for a black plastic apron, then changed her mind. Let Lori McKay do the autopsy unassisted, Joanna thought. That way they'd find out if she was any good, and if she wasn't, they'd repeat the postmortem examination later.

Joanna strolled by rows of stainless steel dissecting tables, all empty except for the one that held the body of William Arthur

Warren. Next to the corpse was Harry Crowe. He was leaning against the tiled wall, his eyes boring into Joanna.

Harry pushed himself away from the wall and walked over. He was carrying an electric saw in one hand, a chisel in the other. "Why the hell are we starting so late?" Harry bitched. "Why not wait until tomorrow?"

"It's an important case," Joanna said, disliking the man even more than usual.

"Important? Why?" Harry demanded. "Because he's got money?"

"Because he was murdered."

"Oh, I see," Harry said, nodding to himself. "That's why they're letting that schoolgirl do the autopsy. She looks fifteen years old, for chrissakes!"

"She's a qualified medical examiner," Joanna said sternly. "And you'll treat her the same as you would a visiting professor from Harvard."

"I checked upstairs. She's not even listed on the clinical staff."

"She has temporary visiting privileges and that's good enough."

"We never let someone from the coroner's office do an autopsy here. Never." Harry Crowe was a short, stocky man in his early sixties, balding, with a round face and BBs for eyes. "And we shouldn't start now."

"I decide who does the forensic cases here," Joanna snapped. "Not you. *Me*. Understood?"

Harry narrowed his eyes, despising Joanna Blalock, hating her and the power she held over him. He yearned for the old days when .the pathology department had been run by distinguished men and not by a bossy woman.

The swinging doors opened and Lori McKay entered the autopsy room. The scrub suit she was wearing seemed to swallow her petite frame. The top hung more like a dress than a shirt, almost touching her knees. The pants were rolled up to keep them from dragging on the floor. She took a black apron from a wall hook and slipped it on. The bottom of the apron almost touched her shoes. The overall effect, Joanna thought, was that of a child wearing her father's clothes.

"Oh, Sweet Mary, save us!" Harry groaned under his breath. He bit down on his lip and tried not to laugh as she approached.

"I should have brought my own scrub suit and apron," Lori said sheepishly. "I feel like I'm swimming in this outfit."

"The problem is ours," Joanna said apologetically. "We should have a wider range of sizes."

"Yeah," Harry scoffed. "That's what we need. More sizes."

Lori gave Harry a hard look. "Have you opened up the head?"

"Yes, I have, Doctor," Harry said, emphasizing the word *doctor* in a derisive tone.

"Then we won't be needing you anymore."

"What?" Harry's jaw dropped open. He blinked rapidly, taken aback by her brusqueness.

Joanna smiled to herself, enjoying the stunned look on Harry's face. "Yes, you can go, Harry. If we need you, we'll call."

Lori watched Harry angrily coil the wire around his electric saw and stomp toward the door. "He doesn't like me very much, does he?"

"He doesn't like women in positions of power."

"Why?"

"Because he thinks we belong in either the kitchen or the bedroom."

Lori looked at Joanna oddly. "Maybe someday he'll wake up and find out he's in the twentieth century."

"Don't bet on it."

As Harry reached for the swinging doors, they suddenly burst open and a short, well-built man wearing surgical garb walked in. He was in his early forties, dark-complected and good-looking with tousled, gray-black hair. The front of his scrub suit was covered with perspiration. He brushed by Harry Crowe, who quickly stepped back.

The surgeon hurried over to the autopsy table. "Who's Blalock?"

"I am," Joanna said, briefly glancing at the surgeon's unlined face and prematurely gray hair.

"I'm David Dellacorte," he said formally. "Sorry I'm late but a patient on the ward suddenly went sour."

"No problem," Joanna said and gestured to Lori. "This is Lori McKay from the coroner's office."

Dellacorte studied Lori for a moment, then smiled.

"Is something wrong?" Lori demanded.

"Yeah. You've got a piece of lint on the end of your nose." Dellacorte reached out and picked it off, then showed it to her. "Have you got any use for this?"

"No." Lori grinned.

Dellacorte flicked it away and looked down at the corpse of William Arthur Warren. He sighed wearily. "What a waste. We found him a perfect liver—an almost perfect match—and some damn thug kills him."

"Did you do the surgery?" Joanna asked.

Dellacorte nodded. "He received his transplant a year ago last week. Mr. Warren sent me a box of Davidoffs to celebrate the anniversary."

"And his liver was functioning well?"

"It couldn't have been better." Dellacorte scratched at the back of his neck. "At least he got a year of good life from it. He wouldn't have lasted another month with his old liver. It had been virtually destroyed by some damn virus."

Joanna glanced away, reminded of her sister and the awful virus that was also destroying her liver. Maybe the plasma from Guatemala would arrive late that night, Joanna hoped, maybe even sooner. She'd check on Kate again as soon as the autopsy was completed.

"Let's start the postmortem, shall we?" Lori broke into Joanna's thoughts.

"Fine," Joanna said absently, still thinking about Kate and hoping for a miracle. With effort she forced herself to concentrate on the corpse of William Arthur Warren. "I like to start with a careful examination of the external features."

"Be my guest," Lori said, uninterested. The pathology here was inside the body, not outside.

Joanna meticulously examined the corpse, beginning at the feet and working her way up. She paid particular attention to the hands, gunshot wounds, face and back. Then she repeated the examination once more. She looked over at the X rays mounted on a wall viewbox and studied them. "Do you know his past history well?" Joanna asked Dellacorte.

"Very well," he answered.

"I take it he was a good amateur boxer."

Dellacorte smiled. "How do you know that?"

Joanna pointed to the knuckles on Warren's hands. "There's a marked hypertrophy of the metacarpal heads and the X rays show a lot of soft tissue calcification. You see those changes in boxers."

"How did you know he was an amateur and good?"

"Because he didn't have a lot of scars or scar tissue on his face, like the professional fighters do. And his skill shows in that he had a boxer's hands and an unmarked face. That means he hit the other guys a great deal more than they hit him."

Dellacorte nodded admiringly. He had heard that Joanna Blalock was good. But not this good.

Lori moved in closer, now very interested. She hadn't seen the boxer's hands, damn it. Missed it altogether. She wondered what else she might have missed. "You spent a lot of time on the gun-shot wounds. Was there something unusual?"

"Yes," Joanna said and turned the corpse on its side. "There are two entrance wounds and only one exit wound."

Lori shrugged. "Well, then, one of the slugs is still in the body."

Joanna pointed over to the X-ray viewbox on the wall. "Not by the X ray, it isn't."

Lori studied the X ray, feeling stupid. Another oversight. God-damn it! What was wrong with her today? "Then there's one other explanation."

"Which is?"

"Both bullets exited at the same place."

"Good," Joanna said approvingly. "Do you know how often that happens?"

"It's pretty rare, I'd guess."

"One in eight hundred," Joanna said, "according to a very fine Italian forensics expert who did his studies on animal carcasses."

Lori studied the purplish discoloration on the corpse's back. She pressed it to see if it would blanch. It didn't. "At least we know he died where we found him."

"Probably," Joanna agreed.

Dellacorte asked, "How can you determine that?"

"Because blood settles to the most dependent part of the body when a person dies," Lori explained. "the livido discoloration is on the corpse's back and that's how we found him—on his back."

"Is that important?"

"Sure," Lori said, looking into Dellacorte's pale-blue eyes and thinking they were almost turquoise. He stared back at her and she felt herself blush. She quickly turned her attention to the corpse. "Let's say, for example, we found the body on its back but the livido discoloration in its lower extremities. That would mean he died sitting and that the body had been moved and placed on its back."

"Like a concocted crime scene, huh?" Dellacorte asked.

"Exactly."

Dellacorte moved in and studied the livido color, thinking he would have made nothing of it. But then again, this was not his area of expertise. He knew nothing of forensics. But he knew a hell of a lot about taking out a diseased liver and putting in a new one.

He watched the two women carefully examining the corpse once more. One would make a comment or finding and the other would expand on it, quoting the research literature or referring to some case they'd previously worked on. Both women were so sharp, Dellacorte thought, trained to see things others would miss. Blalock was obviously the more experienced of the two, but Lori McKay was holding her own. Dellacorte wondered if Lori was innately bright or if she, like himself, had to work like hell in order to excel.

His gaze went to Lori, with her long auburn hair pulled back with a ribbon to keep it out of her way. There were a few loose strands that came across her forehead, giving her pretty face a sexy, slightly disheveled look. Dellacorte glanced down at Lori's hand and studied her ring finger. She was wearing latex gloves and he couldn't tell if she had on a wedding band.

"Let's move on," Lori said, picking up a scalpel and quickly making a deep incision, sternum to pubis. She used a metal cutter to split the sternum and open the rib cage. It was filled with unclotted blood. Lori placed a thick tube in the thoracic cavity and turned on a suction machine. With a slurping sound the machine sucked the blood out, clearing the cavity.

"Jesus," Lori said, finding the ends of the shredded and transected aorta. "He must have bled out in under a minute."

"He was for all intents and purposes dead before he hit the floor," Joanna said, remembering back to the unusual finding at the crime scene. The gun sitting in blood with no blood on its face-up side. Warren hadn't had time to bleed a puddle and then drop his gun on it. "He would have dropped his gun and bled atop it," she said, thinking aloud.

"What?" Lori asked.

"Nothing," Joanna said absently, her mind going to the bloody handprint on the wall. There was something amiss there too, but she couldn't put her finger on it. Maybe it would come later. She shook her head, clearing it. "I know Dr. Dellacorte has a very busy schedule, so why don't we go right to the liver?"

"Okay with me," Lori said and went to the abdominal cavity. She carefully dissected out the liver en bloc and held it up to the light, blood vessels and bile duct dangling in the air.

"It looks rather small," Joanna commented.

Dellacorte said, "That's because it came from a fourteen-year-old boy."

"It appears healthy," Lori said, feeling its texture. She placed the liver on a scale. "Eight hundred grams. It *is* small."

"But it got the job done," Dellacorte said somewhat defensively. "Mr. Warren's hepatic function tests were excellent."

Lori held up the liver again, studying its under surface where the common duct came out. "Everything seems to—"

"Hold it right there," Joanna said and quickly snapped on a pair of latex gloves. She gently palpated an area adjacent to the hepatic vein. "This looks like a cluster of nodules. Were they there at the time of transplantation?"

"Absolutely not." Dellacorte moved in for a closer look. "I would have seen them, particularly in the area of the hepatic vein, where I spent a lot of time doing an anastomosis."

Joanna picked up a scalpel and cut into a nodule. Blood oozed out. She punctured another, and even more blood came out. "They're hemorrhagic cysts and there's plenty of them."

Dellacorte's face suddenly lost color. "Oh, shit!"

"What's wrong?"

Dellacorte took a deep breath and slowly exhaled. "We have another transplant patient upstairs with the same thing. His liver is filled with hemorrhagic cysts and his hepatic function is deteriorating because of it."

Joanna asked, "Has this ever been reported in liver transplants before?"

"Never."

"Do you have any idea what's causing it?"

"None," Dellacorte said gravely. "Not even a clue."

6

"You stupid ass!" Pamela Warren hissed quietly. "What are you doing here?"

"I wanted to make sure you were all right." Tony Boyette was standing at the door to the hospital room, a bouquet of flowers in his hands. "The television news said you were really hurt."

"Well, come in," Pamela said irritably as she slowly propped herself up on a pillow. Her head was still throbbing and any movement made it worse.

Tony closed the door and came over to the bed. "Where do you want these flowers?"

"Just put them on the table."

Tony placed the bouquet down and leaned over Pamela, carefully studying the large bruise on her temple. "Jesus! I didn't mean to hit you that hard."

"Shhh!" Pamela held a finger to her lips, quieting him. The door had cracked open and she pointed to it.

Tony hurried over and closed it, then came back to the bed. "Does it hurt a lot?"

"Like someone has got a jackhammer inside my head."

"I shouldn't have hit you so hard."

"I'll survive."

"I was so damn worried when I heard the TV report," Tony said and meant it. The television reporter had made it sound like

Pamela was almost dead. If Pamela died, Tony's one and only chance at real wealth would die with her. The thought of losing all that money terrified him. "I'm really glad you're better."

"Thanks," Pamela said flatly. "Now tell me, did you follow my instructions completely?"

"Sure did."

"Did you dump everything—gloves, gun, watch, wallet—into the ocean?"

"Everything," Tony assured her. Everything except for the watch. A Rolex President model that cost at least $14,000. Tony couldn't throw away that kind of money. He just couldn't. He had hocked the watch for $2,000. "Do you think I should dump my sneakers?"

"Why?"

"Just in case I left some footprints outside the house."

"Good idea," Pamela said, now thinking that Tony might be smarter than she'd given him credit for. But he still wasn't very bright, and he talked too much. Once everything was finished he'd have to be dealt with. "And remember, don't make any big purchases with the cash. And don't flash a big roll of bills in front of your friends."

"What do you think I am? Stupid?"

"Of course not." Pamela reached up and gently touched Tony's face. "I don't get myself involved with stupid people."

"Me neither." Tony leaned over and kissed her cheek. He again glanced at the nasty lump on Pamela's forehead. The skin above it was broken and encrusted with blood. "How long will you be in the hospital?"

"Another day or two. But no more than that. I want to attend my husband's funeral."

"Yeah, it's the right thing to do," Tony said solemnly. "You've got to be there. You know, the grieving widow."

"Dressed in black." Pamela grinned. With no veil, she decided, so everyone could see her head injury. She'd rub some salt water into her eyes just before the service to make certain they were red and full of tears. It was a trick she'd learned in acting class.

"When can we start seeing each other again?"

In about fifty years, Pamela wanted to say. "Soon."

"How soon?" Tony asked abruptly.

"We'll have to wait at least a few months."

"Why so long?"

"Because I don't want people to talk or for anyone to get any ideas."

Tony looked at her strangely. "But everybody thinks your husband was killed in a robbery."

"And I want everybody to continue to think that."

Tony rubbed his chin pensively. He wanted to keep seeing her, to keep screwing her on a regular basis. Otherwise she might drift away. With all that money. "Maybe we can do like before. You know, meet secretly at the motel."

"We'll see," Pamela said evasively.

"Are you saying we shouldn't see each other at all?"

"It's the smart move." Pamela reached over and squeezed his hand, but she could see the worry in his face. He was worried about losing her, she thought, cursing herself for giving him an inkling of what the future held. She kissed his fingertips. "But somehow I've got to see you. I just can't go too long without being close—real close."

Tony's face brightened. "Yeah. We'll find a way to meet. You can come to acting class and tell people you're only trying to keep your mind occupied. You know, some kind of bullshit excuse like that."

Pamela kissed his hand once more and held it to her breast for a moment. "Perfect! I'll let a month or so pass, then go back to class."

"That way we can see each other once a week."

"Maybe more," Pamela said, wondering how she was going to deal with Tony. She couldn't just buy him off. He'd keep coming back again and again. There'd be no end to it.

"We could always fly down to Mexico. I know a place that nobody—"

There was a discreet knock on the door.

Tony quickly moved away from the bedside. He ran his hands through his hair and smoothed it in place.

"Yes?" Pamela called out.

The door opened and Jake Sinclair walked in. Lou Farelli was a step behind.

Jake came to the bedside. "Mrs. Warren, do you remember me?"

"I don't think so," Pamela said and tried to place the vaguely familiar face.

"I'm Lieutenant Sinclair from Homicide. This is my partner, Sergeant Farelli. We're investigating your husband's murder. I hope you feel well enough to talk with us."

"I'll try," Pamela said, keeping her voice weak. With effort she nodded toward Tony. "This is Tony Boyette, a friend of mine from acting school. My classmates were kind enough to send some flowers with Tony."

Jake measured the visitor carefully. The man had swarthy good looks and was neatly groomed, yet there was something sleazy about him. He had tried to dress expensively but the clothes didn't fit that well and looked like they had been bought at a discount store. "Did you know Mr. Warren?"

"No. I just know Pam from class," Tony said evenly, but sweat was pouring down his back. He shook his head sadly. "It's a terrible thing when a man isn't safe even in his own home."

"Yeah, it sure is," Jake said, looking over at Pamela Warren and thinking she was incredibly beautiful, even with the lump on her head. She had black hair and deep blue eyes and flawless skin and perfectly contoured lips. Her resemblance to Ava Gardner was striking.

Jake had to pry his eyes off her. "Tell me, Mr. Boyette, how many students are in this acting class?"

Tony thought for a moment, then shrugged. "Like ten or twenty. It depends on who's working at the time."

Pamela tried to get Tony's attention with her eyes. She wanted him to leave before he said something really stupid, something that might tip off the police.

"So some of the class are professional actors?" Jake asked.

"Most are," Tony said and scratched at his piles without thinking. "We come to the class to refine our craft."

"How's business been?"

"Slow, real slow," Tony admitted. "But I got a good chance for a part in a daytime soap. They're supposed to call me back next week."

The eternal optimism of the would-be Hollywood star, Jake thought. They usually end up working in gas stations or convenience stores. And sometimes they robbed them. "What's the name of this acting school?"

Tony hesitated, wondering if he'd said something he shouldn't have. "I—I don't want to cause them any trouble."

"There won't be any trouble," Jake said. "We just have to be absolutely thorough in a murder investigation. Now, what's the name of this acting school?"

"First Act." Tony glanced over at Pamela and saw the hard look on her face. What the hell was she so upset about?

"Where's it located?"

"On Vine in West Hollywood."

Jake took out a notepad and jotted down the information. He looked over at Tony and studied him briefly. The guy was getting antsy. "How can we reach you if we need to talk with you?"

Tony's eyes widened. "Talk with me about what?"

Jake shrugged harmlessly. "You never know."

"I'm in the phone book."

Pamela groaned weakly and rubbed at the bridge of her nose. She closed her eyes, grimacing. "My headache is worse."

"Should I call the nurse?" Tony asked, concerned.

"No," Pamela said, her voice barely audible. "It'll pass."

"Maybe I should go," Tony said, happy to have a reason to leave and get the hell away from the nosy cop.

Pamela nodded, eyes still closed. "And thank everyone for their concern."

Jake watched Tony Boyette leave the room, then turned to Pamela Warren. "Will you be able to answer some questions for us?"

"Yes," Pamela said very quietly. "I'll try. But please keep it as brief as possible."

Jake studied her for a moment. Her color was pale, her jaw

clenched against the pain. This was no act. She was hurting. "We can come back later if you'd like."

Pamela sighed, opening her eyes. "Let's get as much done now as we can."

"All right," Jake said and moved closer to the bed. "When we questioned you at your home, you said the killer was wearing a mask. Was it a ski mask?"

"No," Pamela whispered. "It was the Lone Ranger type. Just over his eyes."

Jake had to strain to hear her. "Did he have a mustache or goatee or any facial scars?"

"No."

Farelli asked, "Did your husband pull a gun on the burglar?"

Pamela hesitated for a moment. "I'm not sure. Everything happened so fast."

"Start at the beginning," Jake said. "Start at the moment you first knew something was wrong."

Pamela looked at the window and blinked at the sunlight flooding into the hospital room. Her headache was mild now but she grimaced, wanting to give the impression that she was in a lot of pain. It gave her an excuse to be very slow and deliberate and to take a lot of time between the detective's questions and her answers. "We heard a noise outside, like a trash can being knocked over. Then a dog barked. My husband went to check the alarm system, and when he returned a masked man had a gun pointed at my husband's head."

"Is that when you dropped your glass of brandy?" Farelli asked.

Pamela closed her eyes, wondering what the hell difference that would make. She decided to play it safe. "I don't remember."

"Did the burglar walk up to you?" Farelli asked.

Pamela nodded. "He came within a few feet and told me not to move."

Jake smiled to himself, now seeing what Farelli was driving at. If the burglar had been that close he got a real good look at Pamela Warren's necklace. Before the shooting started. "Did your husband put up any resistance?"

"None that I saw. The masked man forced my husband to open

the wall safe and when my husband turned around—" Pamela's voice broke and she swallowed, like someone holding back tears. She sniffed gently and continued. "When my husband turned, the man shot him."

Farelli jotted down a note. "Did your husband pull his gun from the safe?"

"I can't be sure," Pamela said ambiguously, her forehead now furrowed in concentration. "I think I saw something in his hand, but it all happened so quickly. There was a loud gunshot and I saw my husband fall. I jumped up and ran over to him and—and that's all I can recall."

"When you jumped up, you probably spilled your brandy, huh?" Farelli asked.

"I guess," she said, deciding to end the interview in another minute or so. Her headache was almost gone and her stomach was growling with hunger. She wondered if she could order out from the hospital.

Jake asked, "Do you know what was in the safe?"

"Some cash, usually around ten thousand dollars. Some important papers and a gun." She paused and feigned deep thought. "That's about it."

"Did you know the combination?"

"No."

Jake looked down at his notepad and flipped a page. "When your husband was found, he had no watch or wallet. Did he usually have them on his person?"

"Yes," Pamela said promptly. "He rarely carried cash, but his wallet was full of credit cards. And of course he had a watch. An eighteen-karat Rolex."

"Do you have the serial number of the Rolex?"

"I didn't know they had serial numbers."

Jake closed his notepad. "Thanks for your time, Mrs. Warren. We'll do everything possible to catch the person responsible."

Pamela nodded gratefully and closed her eyes.

Jake and Farelli walked out into the hall, shutting the door behind them. They stepped back as a gurney passed by. Both men glanced down, briefly studying the patient. An old man with his eyes closed and mouth agape. He looked more dead than alive. An IV was running into his arm, a tangle of plastic tubes hanging from the sheet that covered him.

Jake looked around to make certain no one was near and lowered his voice. "That actor guy bothers me."

"Yeah," Farelli agreed. "A real piece of sleaze. He ain't the type to bring flowers for just a friend."

"Check him out," Jake said and waited for a nurse to pass and move out of hearing distance. "Check out the whole acting class. See if anybody has got a record. And find out if somebody suddenly got rich."

"Right," Farelli said and tucked his notepad into his pocket.

"And that missing Rolex sounds like it's the Presidential model. It'll have a serial number. Maybe the butler can give it to you or at least know where you can get it."

Farelli nodded. "I'll check out all the pawnshops on the west side."

Jake looked up at the ceiling and shook his head. "That damn diamond necklace she was wearing."

"Yeah," Farelli said. "The perp goes for the Rolex but leaves the diamond behind. It doesn't make sense."

Jake's eyes narrowed. "Unless he was a real pro."

"How do you mean?"

Jake quickly turned back to the door of Pamela Warren's room. He knocked and waited.

"Yes?"

Jake opened the door and looked in. "I have one more question, Mrs. Warren."

"Of course," she said, instantly on guard.

"Was the necklace you were wearing the night of the crime made of real diamonds?"

"I assume so. It was a gift from my husband. Why?"

"Because the burglar didn't bother to take it."

Pamela blinked rapidly and tried to come up with a reason why the necklace wasn't taken. *Stupid! Stupid!* It would have been so easy for Tony to grab that too. *Think of a reason, damn it!* But her mind went blank and her face started to pale. "Maybe he was in a hurry."

"Yeah, maybe," Jake said, now seeing the sickly look on Pamela Warren's face. "Are you all right, Mrs. Warren?"

"Yes, I'm fine," she said, but she wasn't. Her headache had returned with a vengeance.

7

Joanna ran into the Virology Research Center. She saw Mack Brown standing by the thick glass window and went to join him. He stared into the isolation ward for a moment longer, then pushed himself away from the window. His face was tense.

"Your sister was having seizures," Mack said softly. "Grand mal seizures."

Joanna gasped. "Oh, no!"

"I've had a neurology consultant see her. He thinks she has encephalitis." Mack slowly shook his head. "That damn virus is everywhere."

Joanna glanced through the window at Kate. Her sister was lying still, absolutely motionless. A nurse at the bedside was adjusting an IV. "Is there anything that can be done?"

"We're controlling her seizures with Valium and Dilantin, but that, of course, has no effect on the virus."

Joanna's heart sank. She knew her sister was dying, all hope fading. "The plasma from Guatemala didn't arrive, huh?"

"It's a nightmare," Mack said sourly. "The village where the survivors live is a day-and-a-half drive from Guatemala City. The medical people got there, obtained the blood and started back. Then the rains came and washed out the roads. There was no refrigeration, only ice that melted, so the blood spoiled."

"What do we do now?"

"I've got some pull down there. The people at the medical school owe me big time." Mack stroked his chin absently. "They're going to send a Land Rover in and bring some survivors back to Guatemala City, where their blood will be drawn."

"How long will it take to get the plasma here?"

"Three days or so."

Joanna sighed sadly, feeling so helpless, doubting that her sister could hold out that long. Inside the isolation ward Joanna saw Kate's arm begin to twitch. A nurse hurried over and readjusted the IV drip. A moment later the twitching stopped. "What about her liver?"

"No worse." And no better either, Mack thought. The blood level of hepatic enzymes was still sky-high, the liver still badly inflamed. It was only a matter of time before the liver failed altogether. "By the way, it's not ebola."

"It's nasty enough to be."

"And then some," Mack said, nodding. He reached into his pocket for a snapshot. It showed viral particles detected by an electron microscope. "Here's the bugger. It's an RNA-type virus that has some similarities to the dengue fever virus. That may explain why some of the Guatemalan natives who were infected survived."

"I'm not sure I follow you."

"Dengue fever is fairly common down there, and it's almost never a fatal disease," Mack explained. "Now, our virus seems similar to the one that causes dengue fever. If these natives had dengue fever in the past, then they may have some natural immunity against the new virus."

"And that would explain why the disease was less severe in most of the Guatemalans."

"Exactly. But," Mack said and held up a finger of caution, "there's no guarantee. It's all hypothetical at this point."

"Is there any way we can get the plasma up here quicker than three days?"

Mack shook his head and forced a laugh. "By Guatemalan standards they're already moving at the speed of light."

"Please make another call," Joanna pleaded.

"It won't help."

"Please." Joanna's lower lip began to quiver, and she bit down on it. "Maybe they can use a helicopter."

"You're going to owe me a ton, Joanna."

"I already do."

Joanna entered the forensics laboratory just as her chief technician was leaving for lunch. A row of ultracentrifuges against the wall were spinning at high speed, filling the air with a loud humming sound.

"What's wrong with your eyes?" the technician yelled above the noise. "They're all puffy."

"It's my allergies," Joanna lied easily.

"Yeah, I get them too." The technician pointed with her thumb to the centrifuges. "The automatic timers are starting to screw up again. The centrifuges are set to shut off in thirty minutes, but I can't stick around to watch and see if they do. I've got a dental appointment for a cracked filling. Could you check and see if the machines turn off like they're supposed to?"

"Sure," Joanna said and wrote a note to herself in pencil on the sleeve of her white coat.

"And you've got company in the back."

"Who?"

"A cop and a coroner."

Joanna walked over to a small office and took a hand mirror from the desk drawer. Her face was a mess, eyes red and puffy, lipstick almost gone. She made quick repairs, but despite the new makeup her eyes were still red with dark circles beneath them.

She straightened her white coat and went through a door into the rear of the forensics laboratory. The back room seemed more spacious than the front because it contained no heavy equipment or workbenches. All of the cabinets and counters were built into the walls, leaving plenty of floor space. There were a few small tables with magnifying devices and microscopes atop them. She saw Jake sitting on a countertop and walked over. He was intently watching Lori McKay as she studied skeletal remains laid out on a gurney.

Jake looked up at Joanna. "You got anything to tell us about the skeleton that the rains uncovered?"

Joanna shook her head. "We've only done some preliminary studies."

Lori's head came up abruptly. "But you've had the skeleton for almost a week."

"Bones take time," Joanna said, glancing up at the wall clock. The day was half gone and she was already way behind. A lecture to give, slides to review, an autopsy waiting. "But if you think you can do it more quickly, be my guest."

Lori's face colored and she went back to studying the skeleton, concentrating on the wedding band on the ring finger. With the magnifying glass she saw scratches and embedded dirt but nothing else.

"Tell us about the ring," Joanna said.

"It's a wedding band, so obviously he was married," Lori said carefully. "There are a lot of scratches on its surface, indicating it had been worn for a while, so he was not newly married at the time of his death."

"Good," Joanna said approvingly. "Can you give us any idea what his name was?"

"Not from the ring. There's no way you can—" Lori stopped in mid-sentence, suddenly aware of her oversight. She quickly removed the ring and studied the inner surface with a magnifying glass. She squinted, barely able to make out the engraving. *J.R.* "His initials were J.R."

Jake took out his notepad and flipped to an empty page. "Probably his first two initials, huh?"

"Right," Joanna agreed. "His friends may have even called him J.R."

"Wait a minute," Lori said, breaking in. "J.R. could be the initials for his entire name."

"Possible, but unlikely," Joanna told her. "The band was probably given to him by his wife. She wouldn't have used the initial for his last name. That has no warmth, no love to it."

"That still doesn't exclude it," Lori said stubbornly.

"We're going to have to deal with probabilities here," Joanna said firmly. "Otherwise we'll never learn his identity."

Lori said, "I still think you should run it both ways through Missing Persons."

Jake groaned impatiently, wishing the young coroner would shut up and listen. Missing Persons, hell! This guy was a professional. The chances of him turning up in a Missing Persons search were nil. But Jake wrote himself a note to do it anyway.

"And you can narrow your Missing Persons search down to the last ten years," Lori added. "He was buried no more than ten years ago."

Joanna's eyes narrowed. "How do you know that?"

Lori smiled thinly and decided to let Joanna Blalock wait. "Something I found at the crime scene."

"Obviously," Joanna said, annoyed. "What was it?"

"A dime, dated 1986."

"That's good," Joanna said, nodding. "Was the coin in his hand or in a pocket?"

"No, but it's still damn good evidence," Lori said defensively.

"Oh, I think your time frame is right," Joanna said. "And I have physical evidence to back it up. Evidence that's better than your dime that could have conceivably been washed by the rain from another site to the grave."

"What evidence?"

Joanna reached over to the counter and held up a slender cylinder with a tooth atop it. "This is one of the dental implants I removed from the skeleton. It's a cylinder screw-in type. I had the people in the School of Dentistry check it out for me. It was made by a corporation that was started ten years ago. This was their first product."

"You got the dental X rays?" Jake said at once.

"Sure do," Joanna said.

Jake got to his feet and started pacing. "How many dentists do these implants?"

"A lot," Joanna told him. "Hundreds, maybe thousands."

"Can we send copies of the dental X rays to all the dentists in Southern California?"

"Yeah, we can," Joanna said, offering no encouragement. "But don't get your hopes up. It's a long, long shot."

"And this guy is probably from out of town," Jake said sourly.

"Which makes it an even longer shot."

Lori watched the interchange between the detective and Joanna

Blalock, admiring their ability to interact and make quick, logical progress. It was almost as if they had rehearsed, as if one knew what the other was thinking. But in the process they were talking around her, making her feel left out. *The hell with it,* she thought, *this is my case and they're not going to take it away from me.*

Lori's gaze went to the legs of the skeleton and she saw a metal plate attached to one of the femurs. It was grimy and caked with mud, but she could still see a few areas of exposed silver metal. "Did you know he broke his leg?"

Jake leaned over and studied the metal. "What is this?"

"A supracondylar femoral plate," Lori said, her tone now clinical. "It's used to hold fractured ends of the bone together so it heals properly." She looked over at Joanna. "Any idea how he fractured his femur?"

Joanna pointed to the X rays on the viewbox. "You tell me."

Lori went over to the viewbox on the wall and studied the X rays carefully. The femur had healed nicely with good alignment. The femoral plate was screwed in place. Around the plate and in the bone itself were scattered flecks of metal. "Something exploded in his leg."

"Like what?"

Lori shrugged. "Any one of a dozen things could have done it."

Joanna pointed to the irregularly shaped flecks of metal. "What about these?"

"They're small bits of metal from whatever exploded."

"Try a bullet."

Lori studied the X rays again and slowly nodded. "I guess that's possible."

"More than possible," Joanna said, wondering whether Lori's head was really that hard or whether she was just being argumentative. "These are classic findings for injury caused by a high-velocity missile. Those metal fragments are called shrapnel."

"You can't prove that," Lori challenged.

"Sure I can," Joanna said promptly. "I'll obtain a sample of that shrapnel and send it for metal analysis. That'll tell me whether it came from a bullet."

Lori was about to say something but held her tongue. She was out of her depth and knew it. Gunshot wounds weren't her strong point. Stab wounds were.

Jake was wondering how the victim got himself shot. Maybe the guy was a thug or maybe it was an accident or maybe he got it in a war. "Do we know how old this guy is?"

"In his late forties, according to bone density studies," Joanna said.

Jake did some quick arithmetic in his mind. "So he could have fought in Vietnam."

"That would fit," Joanna agreed and studied the metal plate screwed into the victim's femur. She scratched away some of the dirt and grime, exposing more of the metal. "I'll have an orthopedic specialist look at the plate. Maybe he'll be able to date it, like the dentist did with the implant."

"So," Jake said, pacing again, "we've got a forty-something-year-old married man whose initials are J.R. He may have fought in Vietnam and he sure as hell wasn't poor."

Lori squinted an eye. "How do you know he wasn't poor?"

"Because dental implants are expensive and often not covered by insurance," Joanna said without thinking. "We can also approximate his height to be five feet ten inches, and he probably weighed between one-sixty and one-seventy."

Lori knew that the length of the skeleton allowed one to estimate the victim's height. But how did Joanna Blalock know the weight? How? The bones wouldn't tell you that. Or would they? "How can you be so sure about the weight?"

Joanna pointed to a small plastic label attached to a shred of the camouflage uniform near the victim's cervical spine. Jake and Lori leaned over for a closer look. On the label was the letter *M*, indicating size medium.

Jake started pacing again. "So we've got a forty-something-year-old married man with the initials J.R. He's five-ten and weighed about a hundred and sixty-five. And he may have fought in Vietnam." Jake abruptly stopped pacing and glanced over at Joanna. "With that plate in his leg, do you think he had a limp?"

"I don't think so," Joanna said carefully. "The fracture was well healed and there was no shortening of the femur. But I'll ask our orthopedic consultant about it."

Lori stared at Jake and Joanna, mouth agape, dazzled by the amount of information they had garnered from an old skeleton. Unbelievable! And Joanna Blalock had only done preliminary studies thus far. Lori couldn't even imagine what they'd come up with once Joanna got down to the serious stuff. Lori was still unhappy about the case's being taken away from her, but at least now she understood why. "I'd like to be here when the orthopedic specialist examines the skeleton."

"It's usually catch-as-catch-can with surgeons, but I'll see if I can set it up for late tomorrow afternoon. Say about five?"

"That'll be fine," Lori said and stripped off her latex gloves. "Would it be possible for us to review the slides from the Warren autopsy tomorrow as well?"

"They should be ready by then," Joanna said. "We're waiting on some special stains to be done on Mr. Warren's liver. Maybe they'll tell us why his liver was full of hemorrhagic cysts."

Jake turned to Joanna quickly. "What kind of cysts?"

"Cysts that were filled with blood," Joanna told him. "They were studded throughout his entire liver."

"Did it have anything to do with his death?" Jake asked.

"No," Joanna said. "But they were certainly destroying his transplanted liver."

"Do you know what caused them?"

Joanna shook her head, now thinking about the second liver transplant patient who was similarly affected. "We don't even have a clue."

"Well," Lori said, reaching for her knapsack and putting it on one shoulder, "I've got to run."

"See you tomorrow," Joanna said.

Lori nodded and looked down at the skeleton once more. There was so much information in those bones, she thought, so much. If one only knew how to go about getting it. "There's a lot to be learned down here, isn't there?"

Joanna detected a softening in Lori's attitude and nodded back. "Yes, there is."

Joanna watched Lori hurry out of the laboratory, knapsack bouncing up and down. The medical examiner looked so young, more like a student than a specialist. But she had a good brain,

Joanna decided, a very good brain. Only judgment and experience were lacking, and that would come with time.

Joanna's stomach suddenly growled loudly. "I think I'm running on empty."

"Do you have time for lunch?" Jake asked.

"No. I don't have time for lunch or dinner," Joanna said tersely. "Not today or tomorrow or the day after."

Jake took a deep breath and sighed wearily. "Look, what we had was a failure to communicate."

"There was no failure of communication," Joanna snapped. "You knew exactly what was going on. And when the times got rough, you disappeared, just like you always do."

"Christ almighty!" Jake blurted out, losing his temper. "Are you talking about your illness again?"

"My illness! You make it sound like it was the damn flu or something."

"Look, we'd already split apart when the thing—"

"The thing! What the hell is wrong with you?" Joanna fumed, her face coloring with rage. "Can't you call it by its name? It was a lump, a nodule in my breast."

"Well, the lump turned out not to be cancer, didn't it?"

"You just don't understand, Jake. You really don't."

Joanna breathed deeply and tried to calm herself. She still remembered the first time she'd felt the lump in her breast. It was small, no more than a centimeter in diameter, but it was there and it scared the wits out of her. She'd never known terror like that. The mammogram confirmed the presence of a mass and she was scheduled for a needle biopsy. That's when she'd called Jake.

"God! I needed you then, Jake. I was so frightened. I had no one to talk to, no one to hold on to except you. And then I found out I didn't even have you."

"It was a lump," Jake tried to explain. "But that didn't mean it was cancer."

"It was the thought of it," Joanna said, her voice now quiet. "You have no idea what a woman feels like when that occurs. The fear is beyond description. You feel for the damn lump a dozen times a day, hoping it will disappear, but it doesn't. You dwell on losing a breast, on the disfigurement. And that's almost as awful as the thought of death itself."

"I know," Jake said, staring into space.

"No, you don't," Joanna insisted, a sharp edge returning to her voice. "If you did, you wouldn't have left me all alone. You would have been there for me."

"I've got to tell you a story about—"

"I'm not interested in your stories anymore," Joanna said, cutting him off. "I'm not interested in anything about you. Our relationship is now strictly professional."

"Look, just listen—"

"Strictly professional. Get used to it."

A bell sounded loudly in the front laboratory. Joanna glanced at the wall clock. It was 12:55 P.M. There wasn't even enough time for a quick lunch before the next autopsy.

She went into the front room and heard the giant centrifuges whining down. The machines had stopped ten minutes later than they were supposed to. The automatic timers were still malfunctioning. She looked down at the note she'd scribbled on her sleeve, promising to check the timers and make certain they were working properly. She hadn't, and now the experiment was ruined. Shit!

Nothing was working right in her life, Joanna thought miserably, and stomped out of the laboratory.

8

"Now we have two patients whose transplanted livers have developed hemorrhagic cysts." Simon Murdock, the dean at Memorial Hospital, paced back and forth behind the desk in his office. He had a rolled-up newspaper in his hands and he kept twisting it tighter and tighter. "First there was Rudolph Ettinger, then William Arthur Warren. And Mr. Ettinger has decided to sue the hell out of us."

"Bringing a lawsuit doesn't necessarily mean he's going to win," Joanna said calmly.

"Oh, he'll win it—big time," Murdock said bitterly. "Even our lawyers suggested we try to settle out of court. But this patient isn't interested in money. He's got tons of it already. What he wants is for us to fix his transplanted liver."

"Which, of course, we can't do."

"Goddamn it!" Murdock slammed the newspaper against an open palm. "How does a perfectly good transplanted liver become filled with nodules and cysts? *How*?"

Joanna shrugged, still wondering why Murdock had called her in. She certainly wasn't an expert in liver disease or transplantation, and there was no evidence that any criminal act had been committed.

"Have you got any ideas?" Murdock asked.

"There are only a few possibilities," Joanna said, now concentrating. "One is that the liver had the nodules and cysts prior to the transplantation."

"It didn't," Murdock said promptly. "According to the surgeon who transplanted the liver and the people at Donors International, the liver was healthy prior to transplant."

"What is Donors International?"

"It's a for-profit corporation that scans the world for organ donors. They charge the recipients a fortune, but they almost always come up with an excellent match."

"Do we know where this patient's liver came from?"

"A young boy in Hungary who was hit by a car." Murdock picked up an index card from his desk and studied it briefly. "A fourteen-year-old boy. His liver was normal, according to the Hungarian surgeon and the specialist from Donors International. And the boy's blood showed no abnormalities in liver function."

Murdock placed the index card down. "So that means our patient received a normal liver and that the hemorrhagic cysts developed after transplantation. Now, what can cause hepatic cysts and adenomas to form?"

"Drugs—like androgens and contraceptive pills."

"Which he wasn't taking."

"Maybe certain toxins."

"Which weren't present in his blood or in his liver biopsy."

Joanna tried to think of other causes but couldn't. "I think you're going to have to call in the liver specialists on this one."

"I already have and they gave me the same answers you just did."

Murdock went over to the window and stood by it. The day was overcast, the rain starting to fall. In the distance he saw the Cancer Research Center and the Neuro-Psychiatric Institute, both built during his tenure at Memorial. Murdock had spent the past twenty years transforming Los Angeles Memorial into a world-renowned medical center. Endowments had tripled. Honors had been bestowed. It was rated the number-one hospital in the West, number two in the country.

But Memorial had had its share of problems too. There had been murders, sex scandals, drug dealing. Yet Murdock had always managed to smooth things over. This problem was different, though. The patient involved was Rudolph Ettinger, a billionaire who controlled newspapers and television stations all over the world. He could permanently damage Memorial's name with one phone call. "We've got to come up with an answer here."

"I wish I could help," Joanna said.

"I think you can," Murdock said, now seeing an opening. "I want you to lead an investigation to determine why these transplanted livers are developing cysts and adenomas."

Joanna was caught off guard. "This is not my area of expertise, Simon. I'm a forensics specialist, not a hepatologist."

"I looked up forensic medicine in the dictionary. By definition, it's the application of medical knowledge to questions of civil or criminal law, especially in court proceedings. I think that fits our situation here rather well."

Joanna thought quickly, looking for an excuse out. "I just don't have the time it would require. I'm only here part-time, as you well know."

Murdock's face hardened. He'd known it was a mistake to allow Blalock to work part-time and still maintain her professorship at Memorial. It gave her all the freedoms and none of the responsibilities of academic medicine. "Well, you give me no choice but to start looking for someone to be a full-time forensic pathologist at Memorial."

"You do what you have to do," Joanna said, calling his bluff.

Murdock felt like throwing Joanna Blalock off the staff, and he could do it, too. She was a part-time employee, no longer tenured, and that made dismissal much easier. But he needed her now, just as he had needed her back when he agreed to let her work part-time. Goddamn it! "Let's see if we can reach a middle ground," he said smoothly. "Let's see if I can offer something that will persuade you to lead the investigation."

"What do you have in mind?"

"Suppose I decide to bring in another forensic pathologist but with the following condition. It would be a junior position and you would choose the person to fill it." With another forensic pathologist, Murdock thought, Memorial wouldn't be so dependent on Joanna. And if the new pathologist turned out to be good, then Memorial wouldn't need Joanna at all.

Murdock narrowed his eyes, thinking back. "What was the name of your chief resident a few years ago? You know, the attractive woman?"

"Emily Ryan."

"Yes, Emily Ryan. Perhaps she might be interested in the position."

Joanna thought about the proposition for a moment and slowly nodded. It could work out fine. A good assistant would free up more of her time. "I'd like it in writing."

"I'm afraid that's not possible."

"Then no deal," Joanna said, not trusting Murdock even a little.

"What if I write a letter to Emily Ryan and tell her that we're planning to expand our forensic staff and ask her if she's interested in the position?"

"Only one letter will go out?"

"Unless you give me more than one name."

"All right," Joanna said cautiously, knowing that Murdock was a master when it came to breaking his word and screwing people over. "But I have two conditions. First, the transplant investigation will go on for only one month and no more. If more time is needed, someone else will take over for me. Second, I'll need an open-ended budget to bring in whatever consultants and do whatever tests I want."

"Agreed."

"And I'll have to talk with the other patient who has adenomas in his transplanted liver."

"Good luck," Murdock said sourly. "Mr. Rudolph Ettinger is not a very nice person to begin with, so you can only begin to imagine what he's like now. When he found out there was yet another transplant patient with hepatic adenomas and cysts, he nearly went through the roof."

"How did he learn about William Arthur Warren?"

"That idiot surgeon Dellacorte told him." Murdock sat down heavily in an oversized swivel chair and reached into his desk drawer. He took out a filtered cigarette and studied it. It had been over eight years since he last smoked. "What a damn idiot!"

"It doesn't really matter," Joanna said, not surprised at Murdock's badmouthing another doctor on staff. "Chances are he would have eventually found out about William Arthur Warren and then he would have accused us of hiding important medical information. And he would have been right."

"But Dellacorte didn't have to tell him right now," Murdock said tersely. "He could have waited a week or so until we had a chance to look into the matter."

Joanna nodded slowly. "It might have been better to wait."

"I thought people of his background knew the value of silence."

"What background is that?"

"Sicilian," Murdock said, as if that explained everything.

Joanna looked at Murdock oddly. "So?"

"When I was a boy growing up in New York, his grandfather controlled one of the most powerful families in the city," Murdock explained. "David's father was also thought to be in the business but died prematurely when he fell from a fifth-story window. An accident, of course."

"But David is not part of that, is he?"

Murdock gestured with his hands. "Let's say he was exposed to it."

"The sins of the father are visited on the son," Joanna said quietly.

Murdock barely heard her. His mind drifted back fifteen years to the time Dellacorte was thrown out of his junior residency position at Memorial for smoking pot while on call. Intense political pressure was put on Murdock to let the young doctor back on staff after he did a year of immunology research as penance. Murdock had reluctantly agreed, and Dellacorte had turned out to be an outstanding transplant surgeon. But Murdock always wondered who was behind Dellacorte's political clout. "What?" Murdock asked absently.

"Just thinking about ethnic stereotypes."

"Whatever," Murdock said, waving away the remark. "Just get to the bottom of this mess and do it quickly."

Joanna arrived on the transplant ward just in time to hear David Dellacorte chew out a surgical intern. The house officer was young with curly hair and wire-rimmed glasses.

Dellacorte glared at the intern. "The patient's hematocrit

dropped from thirty-four to twenty-six percent and you think it's due to hemodilution?"

The intern wrinkled his brow, concentrating. "We had to give him four units of fresh plasma because he was bleeding and—"

"*Bleeding,*" Dellacorte cut him off. "That's the key word here. He's losing blood, damn it!"

"But the bleeding stopped after we gave him the fresh plasma."

"Well, it's started again."

"But from where?"

"You find out," Dellacorte said curtly. "You're supposed to be his doctor."

"Maybe we should get an angiogram."

"Maybe you should examine the patient first."

The intern stared at Dellacorte for a moment and started to speak, but decided against it. He hurried away from the nurses' station, mumbling to himself.

Dellacorte turned to Joanna. "The New Age house officer," he said wearily. "They know all about MRIs and CAT scans and angiograms. And they expect those machines to think for them. It just doesn't work that way, does it?"

"It never has."

They stepped aside as a huge X-ray machine pushed by a male nurse rumbled by, then they walked down a long corridor. The air was filled with the aroma of sickly sweet disinfectant. They went by the visitors' lounge and Joanna heard people crying but couldn't see them.

"So you're leading the investigation, huh?" Dellacorte asked.

Joanna nodded. "Simon Murdock was very persuasive."

"Yeah, the old man is good at that," Dellacorte said. "But you've got to give him his due. He usually picks the right person for the job."

"I'm not certain there is a right person for this job."

Joanna reached into the pocket of her long white coat and took out a stack of index cards. "Are we certain this patient wasn't taking any hormones or drugs?"

"He denies it. The only drugs he takes are the antirejection medications."

"Did you screen his blood and urine?"

Dellacorte smiled to himself. Joanna Blalock might not be an expert in liver disease, but she was a superb investigator. She wasn't going to overlook anything. "All negative. We even did an open liver biopsy and checked the tissue for toxins. *Nada.* Nothing."

Joanna went to the next index card. "Has anyone ever reported the presence of hepatic cysts and adenomas in patients taking immunosuppressive or antirejection drugs?"

"Never," Dellacorte said promptly. "We've thoroughly checked the literature and even called the drug manufacturers. They've never seen it. We also reviewed the microscopic slides from other patients with liver transplants who died. We saw some scarring and fibrosis, but no cysts or adenomas."

Everything negative, Joanna was thinking, no easy or straight-forward answers. Still, there were only two ways to explain the hepatic adenomas in the transplant patients. Either the livers they received were abnormal or the livers became abnormal after transplanta-tion. "Both livers came from Donors International, correct?"

"Right."

"I understand they have a fine reputation."

"The best," Dellacorte said without hesitation. "We've gotten livers, kidneys and hearts from them. All were excellent matches, some so good we had to debate whether or not to use antirejection drugs."

"Do you know anything about the people who run it?"

"Oh, sure." Dellacorte stopped in front of a patient's room, its door closed. "The man in charge is a very well-known transplant researcher. His name is Jason Adler."

Joanna's eyes narrowed. "So Donors International does research as well as provide organs for transplantation?"

"I think so," Dellacorte said, uncertain. "You can check that out with Ben Wintrobe down in Immunology. Wintrobe is some sort of consultant to D.I."

"Donors International is located here in Los Angeles?"

"Yeah. They've got a big medical complex out in the Santa Monica Mountains."

Dellacorte straightened his white coat and took a deep breath.

"The patient you're about to meet is not very pleasant. You'd better brace yourself."

"He can't be that bad."

"You'll see."

Dellacorte knocked and pushed the door open. He held it for Joanna to walk in. "Mr. Ettinger," Dellacorte said formally, "this is Dr. Joanna Blalock from our forensics department."

Rudolph Ettinger stared at Joanna, measuring her as she approached. "What the hell do *you* want?"

"They've asked me to look into why your liver developed cysts," Joanna said evenly.

"Oh, great," Ettinger said disgustedly. "My liver has gone to hell and now everyone is suddenly interested in why. I guess my fifty-million-dollar lawsuit lit a little fire under your asses, didn't it?"

"This is not about money, Mr. Ettinger," Joanna said, trying not to lose her temper.

"Everything is about money," Ettinger snapped.

"There's much more at stake here," Joanna went on. "What we find may be crucial to every person who has received a liver transplant and to every person who will receive one in the future."

"You'll pardon me if I'm not too interested in what happens to others."

Ettinger was an emaciated man, balding, with a hawklike face. He strained for a moment and burped loudly, not bothering to cover his mouth. "You pay a goddamn fortune for a liver and they give you one that isn't worth a damn."

"I'd like to ask you a few questions," Joanna said, wanting to get finished and get out. "Have you taken any drugs at all other than the antirejection pills?"

"I've already given those answers to Dr. Pelligrini here," Ettinger said, grinning slightly and enjoying the insult.

Dellacorte's eyes narrowed and his face colored, but he said nothing.

"You're going to have to help us, Mr. Ettinger, if you expect us to come up with answers," Joanna said firmly.

"Are those answers going to save my liver?"

"I can't guarantee that," Joanna said carefully. Then she added, "Probably not."

"Then I don't give a damn about your answers," Ettinger said disdainfully. "All I care about is the liver slowly dying inside me. You got that?"

"We're only trying to help—"

"You're only trying to save your own asses!" Ettinger spat out. He turned to Dellacorte. "I hope you've got a lot of malpractice insurance, boy, because you're going to need it. And don't think when I die, everything will just fade away. That won't happen. I've already instructed all of my newspapers and television stations to give the story their closest attention. That means you're going to be famous, Pelligrini, but famous for the wrong reason."

"I think that would be a mistake," Joanna said, her chin jutting. "Dr. Dellacorte is a fine doctor and is highly qualified to look after you. If you want him to continue to be your physician—"

"Oh, but I don't," Ettinger bellowed out. "I've asked the chief of surgery to take over my case and he's agreed to do so. Now you get the hell out of my room and take Pelligrini with you."

Joanna led the way out into the corridor. She took several deep breaths, calming herself, then turned to Dellacorte. "I think he's just upset over the failure of his transplant. I wouldn't take anything he said personally."

"Yeah," Dellacorte said. But his eyes were cold as ice and just as unforgiving.

9

Joanna pressed up against the glass window and looked into the isolation ward. Kate just lay there, motionless, with no signs of life. "Is she conscious?" Joanna asked Mack.

"She occasionally responds to her name, but nothing more."

A nurse was turning Kate on her side, placing a pillow beneath her to keep her in that position. Joanna knew that the turning procedure was used to prevent pressure sores in comatose patients. Everything had to be done for Kate, everything. Fluids and calories had to be given intravenously, her bladder and rectum emptied with catheters and tubes. She was so ill, so terribly ill. "Maybe if I flew down to Guatemala, I could hurry things up," Joanna suggested.

"That's not a good idea," Mack said, feeling for her and knowing what it was like to watch someone close to you die. "You'd only get in the way."

"I feel so helpless," Joanna said. "Isn't there something I can do?"

Mack shook his head as he briefly studied Joanna. Her face was tired and drawn, the worry eating away at her. "Why don't you go home and get some sleep? I'll call you if there's any change."

"I'd rather be here."

"Go home and go to bed and get some sleep," Mack said firmly.

"I've tried it, but I can't sleep. I just lie there and think about Kate."

"All night?"

"All night."

Mack thought for a moment, strumming his fingers against the glass. "Get your coat and meet me at the front entrance to the hospital."

"Why?"

"For some medicine."

"I don't need—"

"Just be there."

The bar was well hidden on a side street two blocks from Memorial. From the outside the Alamo looked like a real dive. Its front window was filled with neon lights advertising Bud Light, Coors, and Miller Genuine Draft.

"I really don't feel like drinking," Joanna said wearily.

"Good! You can watch me." Mack took her arm and guided her in.

The bar was larger than it seemed from the outside. All of the booths against the wall were empty, as were the half dozen small tables in the middle of the room. At the rear was a narrow stage where a pretty woman with blond hair and a cowgirl hat was tuning her guitar. There was a microphone in front of her.

As they walked to a table the men sitting at the bar turned and gave them a quick look, then went back to their drinks.

They took off their coats and draped them over the backs of wooden chairs, then sat. A waitress appeared instantly. She was young and tall with close-cropped, brown hair.

"How you doing, Doc?"

"I'm doing good, Chrissy," Mack said, his Texas drawl now obvious. "How's little Sam?"

"He's trying."

"He'll get there," Mack assured her. "You'll see."

"Lordy! I hope," Chrissy said, casting her eyes heavenward. "You want the usual?"

"Two of 'em."

Joanna watched the waitress walk away, then asked, "Who's little Sam?"

"Her two-year-old son," Mack said, tilting back on his chair and stretching out his legs. "He had meningitis and lost some of his hearing. And it's affected his speech learning. But he's getting better."

Joanna shook her head sadly. "It seems that just about everybody has got heartaches, doesn't it?"

"Without exception."

Joanna glanced over at the bar, where men were drinking and smoking and laughing. She didn't feel like being happy and having a good time. She wanted to be back at the hospital, near Kate. That's where she should be. Joanna was about to push her chair back when the waitress reappeared.

"Announcing the arrival of Mr. Jose Cuervo," Chrissy said playfully and placed two shot glasses of tequila along with salt and slices of lime on the table. Then she put down two Bud Lights, cold and dripping. "Just holler when you're ready for another round." She stepped over Mack's outstretched legs and noticed his boots. "I like your new boots."

"They're lizard."

"What'd they set you back?"

"Two hundred."

Chrissy whistled softly under her breath and walked away.

Mack turned to Joanna. "You ever drink tequila?"

"No," Joanna said a bit sharply. "And I'm not starting tonight. I'll just sip my beer."

"You're missing out on one of life's great pleasures."

"I have no need to numb my brain."

"Tequila doesn't numb your brain. It sort of cleanses it."

"Of what?"

"Excess baggage."

Joanna looked at Mack stonily. "You think worrying about my sister is excess baggage?"

"No. I think worrying about something full-time that you have no control over is excess baggage."

"Are you telling me that no one has control over what happens to my sister?"

"Only God," Mack said matter-of-factly. "Now, let me show you how to drink tequila. If you don't do it right, it'll poison the way you think about it forever."

Joanna continued to stare at Mack. "You don't think doctors play a role in whether or not a patient lives."

"I believe in the words of a famous battlefield surgeon who said, 'I treat, God cures.' " Mack placed a pinch of salt in the crook of his thumb and picked up the shot of tequila with the other hand. "Now watch carefully." He licked the salt and in an instant swallowed the tequila. Mack ignored the lime slice and took a swig of Bud Light. "Wonderful stuff!" he pronounced.

Joanna picked up her tequila and sniffed it. It had a strong, stinging aroma. She pinched off her nostrils and raised the shot glass.

"Jesus, Joanna! You're supposed to drink it, not dive into it."

Joanna smiled, then laughed, then laughed harder.

"That's better." Mack grinned. "Now go for it."

Joanna licked the salt, swallowed the tequila in a flash and chased it with beer. She braced herself for the burning sensation but it never came. "Not bad," she said. "Not bad at all."

Mack signaled the waitress for another round. "You need two tequilas to get the cleansing process going real good. Three will make everything sparkle like new."

Joanna smiled again, enjoying Mack's Texas drawl and humor. She realized she'd been all work and no play since splitting up with Jake six months before. Mack was so different outside the hospital, so loose and easy, so much like the cowboy he was named after. And he was good-looking enough to be a Marlboro man. "Are you married, Mack?"

"Sort of."

"What does that mean?"

"That means my wife thinks I'm a shitty husband," Mack said and took a long swallow of beer. "You know, I'm not thoughtful and caring and I spend too much time at the hospital and not enough with her and my boys. She thinks we're better off apart."

"So you're separated?"

"For now."

"Think you'll ever get back together?"

"We're supposed to be talking about you, not me."

"Do you think you'll ever get back together?" Joanna persisted.

"Who the hell knows?"

The waitress came over with another round of tequila and beer. Mack and Joanna quickly downed the tequila and chased it with beer. Joanna's head began to swim a little. A nice high. It felt good. The microphone on the stage gave out a burst of static as the songstress introduced herself. Her name was Patsy Willis.

"Is she any good?" Joanna asked.

"Depends on the song," Mack replied.

Patsy Willis had a nice, sweet voice that went well with a guitar. Her song was sad, lamenting over and over, "You were my strongest weakness."

Joanna leaned back and thought about Jake. No matter what she did, she could never really get him out of her mind. He was like an addiction, a habit she couldn't break. "Do you think everybody has a person who's their strongest weakness?"

"Sure."

Joanna sipped her beer, thinking. "How do we let ourselves get involved with people like that?"

"Oh, that's easy," Mack explained. "First, you're both on your best behavior so you become very attached to a person. Then, since you're perfect, you expect the other person to be perfect too. Then the other person turns out to be flawed and you find yourself attached to a flawed person. You know that you ought to get rid of them, but you can't. So there they are, flaws and all, sitting right there in your heart and mind." Mack smiled briefly, enjoying a private thought. "It's a common affliction."

Joanna smiled back. "It reminds me of a line from an old movie called *Scarlet Street* with Joan Bennett and Dan Duryea. She says, 'If I had any sense I'd walk out on you.' And he tells her, 'You don't have any sense.' "

Mack chuckled. "You like old movies, huh?"

"Anything black and white before 1960."

"Me too," Mack said. "I watch them all the time."

"Got any favorite lines?"

Mack leaned his chair back, thinking. "Well, I don't know if it's my favorite, but once you hear it you can't forget it. The line is cold and hard, but it paints a hell of a picture."

"How does it go?"

"It's a tough-guy line from *The Big Combo*. Cornell Wilde says, 'I treated her like a pair of gloves. When I was cold, I called her up.' "

Joanna shivered to herself. "And of course she was always there, waiting for him."

"Of course," Mack agreed. "Because, like the rest of us, she didn't have any sense."

"Maybe she needed him."

"That too. Hell, everybody needs somebody."

Joanna studied Mack briefly. "You don't seem to be the kind who needs people."

"You'd be surprised." Mack finished the last of his beer. "Want another round?"

"No, thanks," Joanna said, pushing her chair back. "My alcohol level is right where I want it to be."

They put on their coats and left the bar. Outside the air was cool and misty, the moon barely visible through the clouds. A taxi was parked across the street, inside lights on, the driver reading a newspaper.

"Thanks for the drinks and conversation," Joanna said, turning to Mack. "It was just what I needed."

"My pleasure."

"Too bad the effect of the tequila isn't permanent."

"It's not meant to be," Mack told her. "The booze just gives you a temporary break. Now you can go home and get some sleep, and tomorrow you can go back to worrying full-time."

Joanna nodded, knowing that tonight she'd sleep soundly, very soundly. "I'm going to catch that cab home."

"Don't be silly. I can give you a lift."

"I don't trust cowboys." Joanna giggled, now feeling the full effect of the tequila. She started across the street, then came back to Mack. "There's something I forgot to tell you."

"What?"

"I think your wife is crazy." Joanna put her arms around Mack's neck and kissed his cheek. Then she ran for the cab.

10

Raindrops splattered against the windshield of Joanna's car. She was driving carefully down a steep road through the Santa Monica Mountains. On one side the road was bounded by the face of a cliff, on the other by boulders and scrub brush. A coyote darted in front of her car, and Joanna quickly braked to avoid hitting it. Her car swerved and skidded on the wet asphalt and she had to fight to control it. She slowed down, cursing under her breath, and again wondered how anyone could build a medical facility in such a mountainous patch of wilderness. Then again, she remembered, Los Angelenos built on top of anything and everything, defying nature.

As she rounded a curve Joanna caught a glimpse of buildings with red rooftops in the valley below. Then they were gone from view. The road curved again, then suddenly widened as the land flattened out. Ahead Joanna saw a tall metal gate with a kiosk adjacent to it. She slowed and lowered the car window.

"I'm Dr. Blalock, here to see Dr. Adler," she told the uniformed guard.

"I'll need a photo ID," the guard said.

Joanna handed him her driver's license and noticed that he was armed. Inside the guard's kiosk was a panel of electronic instruments, including two small television screens.

The guard gave her license back and checked a clipboard for

Joanna's name. He pushed a button and the metal gate slowly opened. "Just follow the signs to the parking area."

Joanna drove into the compound and turned off her windshield wipers. The rain had stopped but the sky was still dark and filled with gray clouds. The air smelled fresh and clean with no trace of smog. Around her the landscape had changed from scrub brush and boulders to trees and manicured lawns. A sign with an arrow directed Joanna to the visitors' parking area. From ground level Joanna couldn't see any buildings.

She parked her car and walked down a winding road, following the arrows. There was no sidewalk. Joanna had to step around large puddles of water that remained from the heavy morning rain.

Off to the left she saw a path on higher ground and decided to take it, hoping it was a drier shortcut. The path was pebbled and mercifully dry and lined with thick shrubbery. Overhead the tops of trees blocked out the daylight, giving Joanna the feeling she was in a tunnel. She walked out into an open area and came to a beautiful Japanese-style garden. There were small waterfalls and ponds and streams with bridges over them and more pebbled paths. From somewhere nearby she heard a soft whining sound and looked up to see a surveillance camera mounted on a light pole.

She walked on, now seeing a high chain-link fence with children behind it. The children were small and moved about noiselessly. A bell rang and the children ran to a two-story wooden structure. It was shaped like a rectangle with plenty of windows and appeared to be a dormitory or school.

"Can I help you?" a voice said from behind her.

Joanna turned to face another security guard. He was a very large man, uniformed and armed.

"I'm afraid I'm lost," she said. "I'm Dr. Blalock, here to see Dr. Adler."

The guard pointed to the pebbled path. "Go back to the main road and follow it around to the complex."

"Thanks."

Joanna walked away, still feeling the guard's eyes on her. She heard the static of a walkie-talkie and the guard muttering something into it.

Joanna went back to the road and again followed the signs with the arrows. She moved over to the side as a motorized cart approached and passed by. In it were two men who appeared to be gardeners, but they too had walkie-talkies. She wondered why so much security was needed at a medical facility. All Donors International supposedly did was track down organ donors and match them up with potential recipients. That shouldn't require the presence of armed guards and surveillance cameras.

She came to the front of the medical complex, water now soaking through her shoes. There were wooden steps leading up, and beyond them Joanna could see a large building made of redwood. In the distance she saw a stream of gray smoke but couldn't determine where it was coming from. She started up the steps and saw a tall, distinguished-looking man waiting for her. He was wearing a dark, pinstriped suit with a vest.

"Hi, Dr. Blalock," he said warmly. "I'm Jason Adler."

Joanna shook his extended hand. "Sorry I'm late," she said. "It seems I got myself lost."

"That happens to our visitors all the time," Adler said easily. "We need to put up better signs."

Joanna looked around, scanning the complex of redwood buildings. There were three large, single-story structures, all unconnected and separated by small courtyards. "I had no idea Donors International was so big."

"Donors International is only a part of what we do here," Adler said, taking her arm and guiding her toward the largest of the three buildings. "This, for example, is the Women's Reproductive Clinic. It was specifically designed to treat infertile couples."

Joanna nodded, remembering an article about the clinic in the *Los Angeles Times*. "I've heard it has one of the best success rates in the country."

"It has *the* best success rate in the country," Adler corrected her proudly. "Fifty-five percent of the infertile women referred to us eventually become pregnant and deliver healthy babies."

"Amazing," Joanna said and meant it.

"But it's becoming a bureaucratic, red-tape nightmare," Adler went on. "Ever since that scandal at the University of California–

Irvine, the paperwork has tripled and the state and federal govern-
ments are demanding more and more safeguards and double-
checks."

Joanna, like every other physician in Southern California, was
aware of the horrible scandal at U.C. Irvine. Eggs had been taken
from one woman and fertilized, then implanted in another woman
who thought the eggs were really hers. In at least a dozen cases
women had given birth to children who weren't theirs biologically.
Multimillion-dollar lawsuits had been filed. The doctors involved
had fled the country.

"Do you plan on keeping the clinic open?" she asked.

"Oh, yes," Adler said with certainty. "We feel we're doing a real
service. And to be frank, it's very lucrative. We support a lot of
research with the money we make from the clinic."

Joanna tried to place Adler's accent. It sounded almost English
with a hint of Boston. She glanced over at him and briefly studied
his face. She had expected him to be older, at least in his fifties.
But he seemed ten years younger than that. His features were
sharp and chiseled, the skin smooth and unlined. The only sign of
aging was a few flecks of gray in his short brown hair.

Joanna's gaze went back to the Women's Reproductive Clinic.
To the rear was a smaller building that was attached to the main
structure. "All of this is the fertility clinic?"

Adler nodded. "The front section serves as the hospital clinic.
The annex at the back is where ova and sperm are stored. It's
where the in vitro fertilization is done."

"Can I take a look?"

Adler hesitated for a moment, then shrugged. "I'm not certain
any work is going on now. We can check and see."

They entered the annex and walked down a long corridor tiled
with polished granite. There were no windows and the air was stale
and stuffy. They went by a walk-in freezer, its door securely locked.
Above the door a thermometer shaped like a clock registered the
temperature inside: 20 degrees Fahrenheit.

"The ova and sperm are stored in here," Adler said.

"I thought they required deep freezing," Joanna said, looking
up at the thermometer.

"They do," Adler told her. "We keep them in canisters of liquid nitrogen."

They came to a door at the end of the corridor. On it a sign read:

FERTILIZATION LABORATORY
DO NOT ENTER

Adler led the way into a darkened room. Light flooded in from the corridor and Joanna could see a man hunched over a microscope. Beside him was a woman, tall and thin, but she was in the shadows and Joanna couldn't make out her face.

"Can't you knock, for chrissakes?" the man at the microscope snapped.

"We have a visitor, Matthew," Adler said evenly and switched on the light. "I hope we're not disturbing anything."

"Another thirty seconds and you would have been," the man said, clearly displeased by the interruption. He spun around in his swivel chair and studied Joanna at length. "Who is this?"

"Dr. Joanna Blalock," Adler said. "She's a visitor from Memorial Hospital. Dr. Blalock, meet Dr. Matthew Dunn."

Dunn continued to stare at Joanna, his eyes narrowing. He was a slender, very tall man, middle-aged, with graying hair and thin lips. "Don't tell me you're from their fertility clinic."

"She's a forensic pathologist," Adler told him.

Dunn raised an eyebrow. "Who happens to be interested in in vitro fertilization?"

"Curious is a better word," Joanna said. "If you don't mind, I'd like to see how it's done."

Dunn hesitated, still not trusting her.

Adler rubbed at his eyes. "I'm afraid Dr. Dunn is a little paranoid. He thinks everyone is after his method."

"They are," Dunn said, tight-lipped. "They'd give anything to have my success rate."

Adler sighed wearily. "Just give her the outline, Matthew. You can keep the specifics to yourself."

Dunn reached for a stick of chewing gum and slowly unwrapped it. He placed it in his mouth and began chewing. "What do you know about in vitro fertilization?"

"Very little," Joanna replied.

"You think we just mix an egg with some sperm and hope for the best?" Dunn smiled thinly, then looked over at his assistant. She was young, no more than twenty, with a pretty face and long, fine blond hair.

"I would guess there's more to it than that," Joanna said, now irritated by Dunn's condescending manner.

"There sure is." Dunn put on a pair of latex gloves and picked up an ultrafine pipette. "We use this to actually inject a sperm into the egg. No ifs, ands or buts. The sperm gets in."

"One sperm?"

"That's all it takes."

Dunn signaled to his assistant and the room went dark. He turned on the microscope light and an image appeared on a small screen above the scope. Carefully he focused on it until a human ovum came clearly into view. Then he used the pipette to draw up human sperm. With slow, delicate movements he punctured the outer surface of the egg and injected a sperm into its cytoplasm. "The moment of conception," Dunn said tonelessly.

Joanna watched, awestruck. She had heard of intracytoplasmic sperm injection and had always thought of it as being nothing more than a novel scientific technique. But it was another matter to actually see the sperm disappear into the ovum, to imagine the chromosomes now mixing and lining up to begin the first cell division, the earliest definable moment of life. It took her breath away.

"Unbelievable," she managed to say as the light came back on.

"Kind of grabs you, doesn't it?" Dunn removed the petri dish from beneath the microscope and gently swirled it before handing it to his assistant. "And in a little while we'll implant this egg in a waiting mother-to-be."

"Will you implant it in the Fallopian tube?" Joanna asked.

Dunn's head jerked up. "What do you know about Fallopian implants?"

"Just what I've read," Joanna said, smiling to herself and enjoying Dunn's discomfort.

"What else did you read?" Dunn asked suspiciously.

"That when you freeze eggs and later thaw them, about half of the eggs disintegrate."

"If you don't know what you're doing."

"Unless," Joanna went on, "you freeze them in DMSO and when you thaw them you put them in a culture of Fallopian tube cells."

Dunn jumped to his feet. "How the hell do you know that?"

"I read it in *Newsweek*," Joanna said innocently.

Bullshit, Dunn was thinking. *They'd never give those kinds of details in a news magazine, never.* He wondered what Joanna was doing in his laboratory and how much she really knew.

In her peripheral vision Joanna saw Adler give Dunn some sort of signal. She thought it was a hurry-up sign but she couldn't be sure. "So you do use Fallopian tube cell cultures when you thaw the ova?"

"Something like that," Dunn said evasively, annoyed with himself for being so loose-tongued.

"And do you—"

"We've got to move on to the next stage," Dunn said abruptly and turned his back to Joanna. The conversation was over.

"Thanks for the demonstration," Joanna said.

Dunn nodded as the technician handed the petri dish back to him. He made a mental note to call a colleague at Memorial and find out who Joanna Blalock was and how she'd come to know so much about in vitro fertilization.

Joanna followed Adler out of the laboratory. Scientists were all alike, she thought. They were so frightened someone might steal or copy their work, that someone else might get the credit and praise for their discovery. But, she conceded, their paranoia was well founded. The scientific community was like the rest of society. It certainly had its share of thieves.

Outside the sky was growing darker. The air was heavy with humidity. Joanna could feel the rain coming. She looked up at the surrounding mountainsides, soaked with water from the repeated rains of the past month. "Have you had any mud slides here?"

"Not yet," Adler said. "But we certainly worry about them. We've planted the hillsides with evergreen shrubbery to stabilize the soil and installed retaining walls and large drainage pipes. But whether they'll do any good is another question. From what I've been told, there's nothing that can stop a moving wall of mud."

"Living in paradise has its price, doesn't it?"

"I'll say."

They came to a fork in the path and went to the right, heading for a large single-story building. Gardeners were tending to the plants and flowers that seemed to be everywhere. An armed guard was leaning up against a tree, smoking a cigarette. When he saw Adler approaching, he quickly crushed out his cigarette and disappeared into the dense shrubbery.

"You seem to have a lot of security here," Joanna commented.

Adler nodded. "Not so much for the medical complex as the day-care center."

"Oh, yes, I saw it on the way in," Joanna said, thinking back and frowning. "Those children seemed a bit old for day care."

"They are," Adler said, taking Joanna's arm as they walked up the wet steps to the entrance of Donors International. "They have learning disabilities and their mental age is about half their physical age. We've set up a model day-care facility to see if it's workable and profitable."

"But why the guards? Do the children try to escape?"

"No, no," Adler assured her. "The children are happy where they are and never try to leave. The problem is that the children come from very wealthy families and we're always worried about the possibility of someone kidnapping a child for ransom. It's not a very pleasant world we live in."

"Do the children spend the night here as well?"

"On occasion. If the parents are out of town or traveling, we have facilities to care for the children," Adler said. "And frankly, some of the children prefer to be here rather than at home."

Joanna looked back at the sprawling medical complex. "So this entire facility is owned by one group?"

"Yes."

"Is it a publicly owned corporation?"

"It's privately held," Adler said, his face now closed. He reached for the door and opened it. "Ah, here we are."

They walked through a small reception area and entered a square room that contained a dozen or more cubicles. Workers were speaking into headphones and typing information into computer keyboards on their desks. The air was filled with the hum of conversations. Mostly English, some Spanish, a little French.

"Information on possible donors comes in here from all over the world," Adler explained. "It's processed and fed into a computer, which tells us whether we have a recipient for the donor's organ."

Joanna looked at Adler quizzically. The people working the phones seemed like ordinary office workers. "These—ah—secretaries make that decision?"

"Oh, no," Adler said, leading her through the maze of cubicles. "They simply gather the information. If the computer tells us we've got a match, then all the data is double-checked by the transplant coordinator before a decision is reached."

"So the transplant coordinator makes the final decision?"

"No. I do."

They came to another door. Adler punched a five-number code into a panel on the wall, then waited a moment before using an oddly shaped key to open the door.

They entered a surprisingly large room. To Joanna, it looked like the control room at NASA. On the walls were giant video screens, all with blue backgrounds, all blank except for a blinking white dot in the center. Off to the side of the room there were large mainframe computers making whirring noises. The light was dim but Joanna could see a woman sitting at a console, punching numbers into a keyboard.

Suddenly one of the video screens lit up and clinical data on a patient began to appear.

NAME: PIERRE DUPRES

SEX: MALE

AGE: 11 YEARS

NATIONALITY: FRENCH CANADIAN

RACE: CAUCASIAN

CLINICAL HISTORY: MASSIVE HEAD INJURY—AUTOMOBILE ACCIDENT. CLINICALLY DEAD. 2 EEGs AT TORONTO GENERAL HOSPITAL SHOW NO ACTIVITY.

PAST MEDICAL HISTORY: EXCELLENT HEALTH USUAL
                        CHILDHOOD DISEASES
MEDICATIONS: NONE
ALLERGIES: NONE
FAMILY HISTORY: PARENTS HEALTHY; PATERNAL GRANDFATHER
    HAS ADULT ONSET DIABETES MELLITUS.

Joanna watched as another screen lit up, showing the young boy's blood and tissue types. His blood type was A+. His tissue type was a very long set of numbers, some interspersed with letters.

"The boy is brain dead," Adler said quietly. "He's been on life-support systems for the past twenty-four hours."

The woman at the console punched more numbers into the keyboard, then turned in her swivel chair and looked up at a blank screen. The screen suddenly lit up and the word *processing* appeared.

Joanna asked, "How long will it take for the computers to determine if there's a suitable recipient for the boy's organs?"

"The shorter it takes, the better," Adler said.

The screen went blank again. Then numbers began flashing so rapidly the eye couldn't keep up.

Joanna felt a chill as she watched the screen, thinking that the numbers really represented human beings. All dying, all waiting and hoping for a transplant that would prolong their lives with quality years. Joanna remembered seeing an advertisement that encouraged people to donate their organs. The slogan was "Give the Gift of Life." But there was something almost macabre about it. One person had to die to give another person life. And although Donors International provided a worthwhile service, giving its clientele excellently matched organs, it was also a for-profit organization. It was like an expensive store that was selling organs to the highest bidder.

And everything was done legally. Patients from Donors International were placed on a waiting list at the medical centers where the transplants would be performed. They moved up the list as others received their organs or died while waiting for one. When the time came for their transplant surgery, there was little or no waiting. Perfectly matched livers or kidneys were rapidly located and transported to the medical centers where the transplants were done. The donors almost always came from foreign countries, particularly those in middle Europe. It was rumored that Donors International paid the donor's family handsomely for the organ.

The screen went blank for a long moment, then flashed a message:

NO GOOD MATCH
SORRY

"Too bad," the woman at the console said and sighed heavily. "The kid would have made a good donor."

"Well, we can't win them all," Adler said. He sat on the edge of the desk and introduced the women. "Dr. Blalock, this is our transplant coordinator, Karen Kessler."

The women nodded formally.

"Dr. Blalock is investigating the abnormal transplanted livers I told you about," Adler said.

Karen lit a cigarette and blew smoke up at the ceiling. For a moment she thought about William Arthur Warren and his absolute joy when told they'd found a liver for him. "What in the world is happening to those livers?"

"That's what we're trying to find out," Joanna said.

"Well, they were in great shape when we got them," Karen said. "That's for sure."

"How can you be so certain?"

Karen punched numbers into the keyboard and clinical data began appearing on the video screen. "These are the patients who donated the livers to Mr. Warren and Mr. Ettinger. The donors couldn't have been any healthier before their accidents." Karen pointed to the screen directly in front of her. "This is Mr. Warren's donor."

DONOR B.S. #88

NAME: BOROS SARKOZY
SEX: MALE
AGE: 14 YEARS

NATIONALITY: HUNGARIAN

RACE: CAUCASIAN

CLINICAL HISTORY: MASSIVE HEAD INJURY—MOTORCYCLE ACCI-
DENT. CLINICALLY DEAD. 2 EEGs AT BUDAPEST INTERNATIONAL
HOSPITAL SHOW ISOELECTRIC ACTIVITY.

PAST MEDICAL HISTORY: EXCELLENT HEALTH

MEDICATIONS: NONE

ALLERGIES: PENICILLIN

FAMILY HISTORY: PARENTS HEALTHY
   GRANDFATHER—EMPHYSEMA (SMOKER)
   GRANDMOTHER—PSEUDOGOUT

LABORATORY EVALUATION:
   LIVER FUNCTION STUDIES (BLOOD):

FILIRUBIN	.8
SGOT	24
SGPT	40
GGTP	52
ALBUMIN	3.8
ALKALINE PHOSPHATASE	112

   LIVER-SPLEEN SCAN—NO ABNORMALITIES
   LIVER—INSPECTED AT SURGERY—NO
      ABNORMALITIES

"So," Karen said, crushing out her cigarette, "Mr. Warren received a perfectly normal liver. There wasn't even a hint of abnormality."

Joanna watched as Karen Kessler punched in another set of numbers. The transplant coordinator was a very attractive woman with high cheekbones and lovely eyes. Her hair was brown and long and hung down past her shoulders. Joanna guessed that the coordinator was in her early forties.

The screen flashed up information on the boy who had provided the liver for Rudolph Ettinger.

DONOR P.P. #102

NAME: PETROS STAMATIPOULOS

SEX: MALE

AGE: 12 YEARS

NATIONALITY: GREEK

RACE: CAUCASIAN

CLINICAL HISTORY: ACCIDENTAL GUNSHOT WOUND TO HEAD. CLINI-
CALLY DEAD. 2 EEGs AT ATHENS GENERAL HOSPITAL SHOWED
NO ACTIVITY.

MEDICATIONS: NONE

ALLERGIES: NONE

FAMILY HISTORY: PARENTS HEALTHY
   GRANDFATHER—CANCER OF THE LUNG (SMOKER)
   GRANDMOTHER: OSTEOARTHRITIS

LABORATORY EVALUATION:

BILIRUBIN	1.1
SGOT	28
SGPT	21
GGTP	70
ALBUMIN	4.2
ALKALINE PHOSPHATASE	118

LIVER-SPLEEN SCAN—NO ABNORMALITIES

LIVER—INSPECTED AT SURGERY—NO ABNORMALITIES

"You can't get any more normal than that," Karen said. "There's nothing to even suggest a cyst or adenoma in these livers."

"I'd like copies of all the information on these two donors," Joanna said.

The transplant coordinator hesitated, then looked over at Adler.

Adler nodded. "Okay," he said slowly, "but there are conditions. You can't use the donors' names in any publication of any type or form. The information is privileged and confidential."

"Of course," Joanna said and waited for the coordinator to print the patient data. "I'll also need the names of the surgeons who removed the livers and the names and phone numbers of the families of the donors."

"Whoa!" Adler said, holding up his hands, palms out. "We'll give you the names of the surgeons, but we can't release any information on the families."

"Why not?" Joanna demanded.

"Because they want it that way," Adler said at once, an edge to his voice. "They don't want to be bothered anymore. I talked with them by phone and they gave me permission to release the data to you, but nothing else. And they specifically asked not to be contacted again. I have to abide by their wishes, and so do you."

Joanna felt the tension rise in the room. It was as if she had touched a raw spot, a sensitive nerve. But why? She couldn't believe it was the donors' families. If anything, they'd want to know if there was some abnormality in the boys' livers or if other children in the family could be similarly afflicted. No. There was something else. "I really need to talk with the families."

"Forget it!" Adler said sharply.

Joanna decided to back off. She would talk with the surgeons who removed the boys' livers. Maybe they could help her get to the boys' families. "How many livers have you provided for transplantation?"

"Close to a hundred and fifty."

"Could I have all the names and clinical data—"

"No way," Adler said, cutting her off. "I can't give you any of that information because it's all confidential. Our lawyers have advised us to seal those files until this business is cleared up."

"It'll never get cleared up if you continue to put obstacles in my way," Joanna said, briefly losing her temper.

"Well, you just do the best you can," Adler said.

"You don't seem to understand that Mr. Ettinger is going to sue the hell out of you."

"Maybe, maybe not," Adler said, unconsciously straightening his tie. "His attorneys seem to think that the real fault lies with Memorial, not us."

Joanna seethed inwardly. So, they had bought their way out. A private little transaction out of court. She wondered what it had cost them. It wasn't just money. Ettinger had plenty of that already. "Are you going to help Ettinger point the finger at Memorial?"

Adler shrugged. "If that's where the blame belongs."

"I'll give you some free advice," Joanna said angrily. "Whatever deal you're making with Ettinger, you'd better have all the i's dotted and all the t's crossed. Rudolph Ettinger is notorious for double-dealing and breaking his word whenever it suits his purpose."

"Thanks for the advice," Adler said, unconcerned. "Our lawyers will make sure we're protected."

Joanna forced a laugh. "By what? Some legal contract that can be broken the day after it's signed? You may not wish to believe it, but if we don't come up with an answer as to why those livers went bad, you'll end up in the same boat as Memorial."

"We'll see," Adler said.

"Yes, we will," Joanna said, watching Adler's face for signs of worry. He didn't show any. "Well, I've taken up enough of your time."

Adler handed the computer printouts to Joanna. "Let me show you out."

They left through a rear door and walked out into a small courtyard. There were wooden benches and tables and off to one side vending machines under a shed roof. A technician and a nurse were on a break, drinking coffee from Styrofoam cups. They jumped up when they saw Adler approaching. He waved them back down.

Adler took out a pipe and lit it carefully, sending up a plume of smoke. "Sorry about my abruptness in there. These abnormal livers have got us all on edge. I feel like I'm walking on legal eggshells."

"That's because you are," Joanna said evenly.

"Those livers were fine when we delivered them. Something happened at Memorial to damage them. I'm certain of that."

"Do you have proof?"

Adler shook his head slowly. "Not really."

"Then you're in the same boat as Memorial Hospital." Joanna buttoned up her tweed blazer as the wind picked up, now chilly and very damp. The sky overhead was growing darker and more threatening. So much for the myth that it never rained in Southern California. "And if that boat sinks you're going down with us."

Adler sighed wearily. "I doubt if we'll ever get to the bottom of this."

"We'll never know unless we try."

Adler looked away, thinking, trying to come up with a compromise. He didn't want to go against the advice of his lawyers. Things were bad enough as they were.

"I need the medical records of everyone who donated a liver,"

Joanna said, wondering if there was some legal way to obtain them. "And I need to know all about their families."

Adler's pipe went out and he slowly relit it. "The best I can do is to arrange for you to talk with the family doctors of the boys who donated the two bad livers. You can do it by phone. I'll check and see if you need a translator. How does that sound?"

"It's a start," Joanna said and again thought that if necessary she could use the family doctors to persuade the families to talk with her. "What about the other liver donors and their families?"

"Their records remain sealed," Adler said firmly. "There is no way we're going to break the confidentiality we agreed to."

"Can I have the names of all the patients who received livers from Donors International?"

"Out of the question."

"Why not?"

"Again, confidentiality."

"Do these people know their livers may be rotting away inside them?" Joanna snapped.

"Look," Adler said sharply. "Just because two livers develop cysts and adenomas doesn't mean the others will."

"I think the patients will want to know."

"Bullshit!" Adler blurted out, momentarily losing his composure. He took a deep breath and calmed himself. "Look, these transplant recipients have normally functioning livers. Do you expect me to scare the hell out of them by telling them their livers may go bad? Do you want these patients to feel like they're walking around with ticking time bombs?"

Joanna could see Adler's point. It was a good one, one she hadn't thought of. "Can I at least get copies of their most recent laboratory studies? No names?"

Adler thought for a moment. "We'd have to get the data from their physicians, but I don't think it would be a problem."

"What about obtaining ultrasound studies of their livers?"

"No," Adler said promptly. "The patients will immediately know something is amiss."

"Not necessarily," Joanna said, thinking quickly. "Tell them it's part of an ongoing study to make certain their livers are every bit as good as they seem to be. We'll pay for the tests, of course."

Adler hesitated and carefully considered the proposal. "I'll have to check with our attorneys."

"It would really be important. And it just might help us solve this riddle."

"I'll do the best I can," Adler said noncommittally.

Joanna tried to read his face but couldn't. Somehow she had the feeling he wasn't going to try very hard.

They left the courtyard and walked down wooden steps, heading for the sidewalk. Beyond a grove of trees to the rear was another building, larger than the others. It had a tall brick chimney with gray smoke coming out of it.

Joanna pointed to the building. "Is that also part of Donors International?"

"In a roundabout way," Adler told her. "It's where we do our research."

"What sort of research?"

"Research that's going to revolutionize the science of transplantation," Adler said, his mood suddenly lighter.

"How so?"

"We're going to create universal donors."

Joanna's eyes widened. "A source of organs that can be given to anyone?"

"Exactly."

"This I've got to see."

Adler nodded and guided her along a narrow path to the building beyond the trees. The wind was beginning to swirl, and it blew the smoke from the chimney toward them. It smelled sweet, almost appetizing.

"What's the chimney for?" Joanna asked.

"It leads to an incinerator where we dispose of animal carcasses."

They entered the building through a side entrance and walked down a long, well-lighted corridor. The doors were all closed, but Joanna could hear animals making noises behind them. She also recognized the stale stench associated with a vivarium.

"What kinds of animals do you use in your experiments?" Joanna asked.

"Goats, sheep, dogs," Adler said as they turned down another corridor. "And baboons."

Joanna's eyes widened. "You keep baboons here?"

"No. We buy them only as we need them, and their stays are very short. Baboons are very expensive to keep, but you've got to have them. Baboon tissue types are quite similar to those of humans."

"So I've been told," Joanna said, wondering if Adler was going to try to transplant baboon organs into humans. Again. Joanna had learned from colleagues at Memorial that Adler's earlier scientific career had been devoted entirely to trans-species organ transplantation. Depending on whom one talked to, Adler had once been considered the most thought-provoking transplant scientist of his time—or the most reckless.

Early on, his star had shone brilliantly. As a graduate student at Harvard he had discovered a method to genetically alter mice so they would accept transplants of human skin. Research money poured in, and Adler went on to devise a procedure by which pigskin could be grafted onto human burn victims. Adler claimed the results were spectacular, but they couldn't be reproduced by others and Adler's work became controversial. Then he became involved in the first baboon-to-human heart transplant, which failed miserably. He fought publicly with university officials about the need to continue cross-species transplants. And lost. Adler's research grants were not renewed and he left Harvard, disappearing for several years before showing up at Donors International.

They came to a set of swinging doors with a sign that read AUTHORIZED PERSONNEL ONLY. Adler pushed the doors open and they entered a large room that was cluttered with sophisticated equipment. Off to one side were Echocardiogram and EKG machines attached to oscilloscopes and monitors. Next to them Joanna saw a technician at a blood gas machine, determining the O_2 content of a blood sample. In the center of the room was a treadmill, its motor whirring noisily as the belt moved at full speed. A sheep was tethered to the treadmill, its feet moving faster and faster to keep up. EKG electrodes were taped to the sheep's chest. The animal's face was impassive. It didn't seem to be straining at all.

Adler guided Joanna over to the far side of the treadmill where an intense-looking scientist was seated on a metal stool.

"Dr. Blalock, meet Dr. Kurt Rhinemann, who is head of our research division," Adler said formally.

Joanna nodded, but Rhinemann didn't even bother to look up. His eyes were fixed on the sheep running in place on the treadmill.

"How's the experiment going?" Adler asked.

"Fantastic," Rhinemann said, his accent strongly Germanic. He pointed to a nearby monitor. "He goes up to one hundred sixty beats per minute easily and his EKG remains normal. The goat's heart is working wonderfully."

Joanna studied the animal again. "You mean the sheep's heart."

Rhinemann smiled. "No. It's a goat heart inside of a sheep."

"How long has it been in place?"

"Two weeks," Rhinemann said, jotting down numbers in his data book. "Are you in transplant research?"

"No. I'm a forensic pathologist."

Rhinemann flicked his wrist at Joanna, as if she were an annoying insect. He was a short, slender man, totally bald, with an oversized head and wire-rimmed glasses. His face was smooth, his lips thin and pressed together.

"What's the longest period of time that a cross-species heart transplant has lasted before rejection?" Joanna asked.

Rhinemann shrugged. "It depends. There are a lot of variables," he said evasively.

"Like what?" Joanna persisted, awed by what she was seeing.

"Like whether we use minimal or maximal doses of immuno-suppressive drugs to prevent rejection," Adler said, now studying the EKG monitor. "This animal is receiving only small amounts of antirejection drugs and is doing beautifully at two weeks. That's unheard of."

"How do you get by with such small doses?" Joanna asked.

Adler smiled thinly. "By stripping the antigens off the surface of the transplanted organ. That way the sheep's immune system doesn't recognize the goat heart as being foreign tissue."

Joanna leaned forward, now even more interested. If one could remove *all* surface antigens, any organ could be successfully transplanted into any recipient. "How do you remove the antigens?"

Rhinemann's head suddenly came up. "By a new method I've devised. And that's all we should say about it."

"Oh, come on," Adler urged Rhinemann, "you can tell her a little about how you treat the organ's surface with—"

"Enough!" Rhinemann shouted, his face coloring. "Once we've perfected the method and published it, you can talk about it all you want."

Adler stared at Rhinemann for a moment, then nodded reluctantly. "Perhaps you're right. We probably should wait until the work is published."

Rhinemann gave Adler a long hard look. He started to say something, but changed his mind and abruptly turned away.

"Well," Adler said, breaking the uneasy silence. "Dr. Blalock has a very busy schedule and needs to be on her way."

"Thanks for your time," Joanna said to Rhinemann. "Your work is absolutely fascinating."

Rhinemann shrugged at the compliment and turned back to the sheep running on the treadmill.

Adler and Joanna took a rear door out and walked to the front of the medical complex. The sky was now very dark, rain clouds almost touching the tops of the mountains.

"Thanks for the tour," Joanna said.

"It was my pleasure."

"And please talk to your lawyers about letting me examine the data on the transplant donors and recipients. It could be of crucial importance."

"I'll do what I can," Adler said.

Joanna walked away, still not convinced that Jason Adler was going to try very hard. But at least she had persuaded him to set up phone conversations with the family doctors of the liver donors in Greece and Hungary. That was a start.

Joanna was at the wooden steps when she stopped in her tracks and thought about the livers that had come from Greece and Hungary. Both countries were at least fifteen hours away from Los Angeles by jet. Wasn't that too long to keep organs for transplantation on ice? Maybe the length of time between the removal of the livers from the donors and their placement in the recipients was what had damaged the organs. Maybe. She'd have to find out what the longest permissible period of time was for an organ to be on ice before transplantation. She'd ask David Dellacorte about that.

Raindrops started to fall, a few drops at first, and then the sky opened up. Joanna ran for her car.

Joanna donned a surgical gown, mask and gloves and hurried into the isolation unit at the Virology Research Center. Other than the beeping monitor, there were no sounds in the room. Mack Brown was at the bedside, adjusting the IV drip going into Kate Blalock's arm.

"When did the plasma arrive?" Joanna asked.

"About two hours ago," Mack told her. "We called your office but you were out."

"How many units did you get?"

"Three. But one tested positive for syphilis so we discarded it."

"Shit!"

"Yeah."

Joanna moved in closer to the bed. Her heart sank as she studied her sister. Kate looked awful. Her skin was still deeply jaundiced, and there was bloody mucus caked around her nostrils. Her chest barely moved when she breathed. Joanna glanced up at the monitors. The vital signs were good. Pulse sixty per minute, respirations twelve per minute, blood pressure 100/72. "Has her mental status improved any?"

Mack shook his head. "She responds to pain, but nothing else."

"There's not much hope, is there?"

"We might get lucky," Mack said, not believing it for a moment.

"But even if she does survive, there's bound to be some residual damage," Joanna said quietly.

"I know of no way to predict that." But as a rule of thumb, Mack knew that the more intense the encephalitis, the greater the chance for residual sequelae. The young woman was almost surely going to end up brain damaged—if she lived.

"How will you administer the plasma?"

"We'll give one unit now, then wait twelve hours and give the second."

"And if we need more?"

"If two units have no effect, it's unlikely more will."

An alarm went off. A loud beeping noise from machines above Kate's bed.

Joanna froze for a moment and felt a terrible hollowness deep in her gut. Quickly her gaze went to the monitors. Kate's electrocardiogram showed an undecipherable squiggle. But her pulse and blood pressure were normal.

Mack reached up and shut off the alarm. Then he leaned over Kate and reattached an electrode that had slipped from her arm. The EKG pattern returned to normal.

False alarm, Joanna told herself, but her heart was still in her throat.

Mack turned to a nurse at a nearby desk. "Keep a close eye on the patient. Check her from stem to stern every five minutes for urticarial lesions."

"And if I see urticaria, what should I give her?" the nurse asked.

"Fifty milligrams of Benadryl IV. And if that doesn't work, call me." Mack turned back to Joanna. "Come on. I'll buy you a cup of coffee."

Joanna reached down and gently squeezed Kate's hand. She had the horrible feeling that she was seeing Kate alive for the last time.

They left the unit and after removing their surgical garb went into Mack's cluttered office. There were files and bookshelves pushed up against the wall, and above them were framed diplomas and certificates and photographs of Mack with colleagues in various parts of the world. He poured coffee from a pot on his credenza into Styrofoam cups and handed one to Joanna. With a sigh he folded his lanky body into the swivel chair behind his desk.

Joanna leaned back in her seat and closed her eyes, thinking about all the problems she faced. The investigation of the abnormal liver transplants, the search for the identity of the skeleton uncovered by the rains, her affair with Jake that was over and done with forever. But everything put together paled when compared to Kate's terrible illness. Joanna had never felt so desperate. All she could do was watch and wait.

"It's really difficult when you're very close to the person who's sick, isn't it?" Mack asked, breaking the silence.

"You'll never know how difficult until it happens to you."

"It has happened to me," Mack said, his thoughts going back twenty-two years to a pretty technician at the NIH whom he'd married. She'd become infected while working with meningococcus in the laboratory and had died of meningitis. "My first wife."

"I'm sorry," Joanna said. "I didn't know."

Mack flicked his wrist, waving off the apology. "It was a long time ago."

Joanna nodded, but she could tell from the tone of Mack's voice that his dead wife was still in his mind and heart. Joanna sipped her coffee and brought her thoughts back to Kate and the deadly virus that had infected her. "Do we know any more about this damn Guatemalan virus?"

"No more than I've already told you. Except that it's now come and gone. There hasn't been a new case in weeks."

Joanna looked at Mack oddly. "Are you telling me it's just disappeared?"

"That's how these viruses behave." Mack glanced up at the wall and briefly studied a photograph of himself and a group of other specialists in Nigeria during the last reported epidemic of Lassa fever. A nasty son-of-a-bitching virus that had killed hundreds. "They come, they kill, they mutate and they disappear."

"Forever?"

"Oh, no. They just sit around, waiting for the right host to come along. A man, a bat, a spider. It doesn't matter much to the virus. It only wants a nice place to grow and replicate."

Joanna nervously drummed her fingers on the arm of her chair.

"What about using some of the antiviral drugs, like Symmetrel? Could they help Kate?"

Mack shook his head. "Symmetrel works only on type A influenza, and you have to give the drug early in the infection or it doesn't work at all."

"Is it worth trying?"

Mack shook his head again. "That drug can have some peculiar effects on the brain. That's the last thing Kate needs."

Joanna gestured helplessly. "I'm just searching for something, anything that might help."

"I know," Mack said. "But let's don't give up. Maybe Kate will get lucky."

"Good luck doesn't run in my family," Joanna said sadly and stared down at the floor.

Mack sipped his coffee, watching Joanna over the top of the Styrofoam cup. She resembled his first wife in some ways. Both had well-defined cheekbones and sandy-blond hair and brown eyes that were impossible to read. And both were wonderfully bright. His mind drifted back to his first wife and, as always, he envisioned her lying in bed on her side, her hair flowing over the pillow. But now the face he saw wasn't Laura's. It was Joanna's. "*Casablanca* was on TV last night," he said as he pushed the image out of his mind. "It's my favorite."

Joanna looked up and nodded. "It has some great lines."

"None better than Claude Rains telling Humphrey Bogart, 'How extravagant you are, throwing away women like that. Someday they may be scarce!' "

Joanna smiled, her mood suddenly lighter. She liked the way Mack could distract her and take her mind off awful things. She also liked his smooth, easy manner and rugged good looks. Too bad he was married, she thought. Separated, but still married. "I really enjoyed my drinks at the Alamo," she said. "I slept like a log."

"That happens when you clean your brain out." Mack grinned. "I drop in there a couple of times a week. Let me know when you're ready to go again."

"I will," Joanna said, her eyes meeting his and locking in for a moment. She felt her face starting to blush and glanced away.

There was a discreet knock on the door.

"Yes?" Mack called out.

The door opened and a nurse wearing a scrub suit looked in. "I just got a call from Sara Conn."

"And?"

"She's got a temperature of a hundred and three with chills and headache."

Mack abruptly stiffened in his chair. "Is she home?"

"Yes."

"Tell her to stay put. I'm on my way over."

Mack stood up and quickly wriggled out of his white coat. "We may have trouble here. Big trouble."

"What's wrong?" Joanna asked.

"Remember the sick boy who came in with your sister from Guatemala? The boy who vomited on the nurse in the hallway?"

Joanna nodded slowly, thinking back. "Yes, I remember."

"Sara Conn is the nurse he vomited on."

"Oh God, you think he might have spread the virus to her?"

"It's possible," Mack said carefully. "She was the one who caught most of the vomitus."

"But—but some of it also splattered on me."

"I know."

Joanna's throat went dry.

12

The tension was high in the law offices of Cole, Cox and Harrington. On one side of the conference table were Pamela Warren and her attorney, on the other side William Arthur Warren's sons, Richard and T.J. Their faces were all grim and strained. There was no small talk, only icy stares.

Pamela glared back at her stepsons, hating them for the meanness and pettiness they'd shown her during her marriage. They had gone out of their way to make her feel unwelcome. When they interacted at social gatherings the sons refused to acknowledge her as part of the family, never speaking to her or introducing her to others. The most they ever gave her was a nod.

Pamela leaned over to her attorney, Allen Diamond, and whispered to him behind a cupped hand. "What's going on?"

Diamond whispered back, "I don't know. But say nothing until you check with me."

Pamela wondered if there was going to be a reading of the will, like in old movies she'd seen on television. She could envision her dead husband planning a public reading just to embarrass her once more in front of his sons. Or maybe he'd found a way to get around the prenuptial agreement. Maybe there was something in the will that would supersede the agreement or make it difficult if not impossible for her to get the money due her. The thought of losing millions of dollars made her almost physically ill.

The door to the conference room opened. Alexander Cox walked in. He was tall and thin with short white hair and hard features that looked as if they had been chiseled from granite. He wore a dark suit and tie and didn't project even a hint of warmth.

"I see we're all here," Cox said brusquely and seated himself at the head of the conference table. He studied the man next to Pamela Warren for a moment. "Do you represent Mrs. Warren?"

"Yes. My name is Allen Diamond."

"Very well." Cox nodded and began flipping through a folder on the table. "I'm Alexander Cox and I, of course, represent the Warren family."

Pamela's cheeks flushed at the insult. Even the goddamn lawyer refused to include her as part of the Warren family. She looked across at her stepsons. They were smiling at her.

"I'm afraid we have a problem with William Arthur Warren's estate," Cox said impassively.

The smile left Richard Warren's face. "What kind of problem?"

"We cannot find your father's will," Cox said.

There was a stunned silence in the room.

"What!" Richard blurted out, jumping to his feet. He leaned forward, knuckles resting on the table, and stared at Cox. "What the hell do you mean, the will can't be found?"

"The will is lost," Cox said evenly. "Against my advice, your father took all of the originals. He said he would keep them in a safe place. Since his death we've checked high and low. They cannot be located."

"You goddamn well better find that will," Richard growled, his face reddening.

Cox gestured with his hands. "We will do everything in our power to come up with the will. But again, I remind you that it was your father's decision to keep all copies."

Richard glared down at Pamela. "You stole the will, didn't you?"

"You're out of your mind," Pamela snapped.

"Like hell I am!" Richard was the older and the meaner of the brothers, a mirror image of his father. "You took the will from the safe the night of the robbery."

"Oh, sure," Pamela said sarcastically. "I waited for the burglar to crack my skull and while I was unconscious I got up and stole the will."

The veins in Richard's neck bulged. "Everybody here knows you—"

"My client has no knowledge of the whereabouts of the will," Diamond cut him off sharply. "And I will not allow you to insult or threaten her."

"And how do you plan on stopping me?" Richard scoffed.

Diamond smiled thinly. "By walking out of this room with my client."

There was another silence, long and awkward.

Pamela studied her recently manicured nails and chuckled to herself, wondering where the will was. It had to have been in the wall safe, she thought. That was where he kept his important papers. Maybe Tony Boyette had inadvertently taken the will when he cleaned out the safe. Yes, that was probably it. And that meant the will, along with the gun and watch and wallet, was now sitting at the bottom of Santa Monica Bay. She wondered if losing the will would benefit her in any way. "Was the prenuptial agreement I had with my husband found?"

Cox shook his head. "That too is missing."

"I have a copy," Pamela said innocently.

Richard Warren's face lit up, a big smile spreading across it. He couldn't believe what he'd just heard.

Pamela felt her lawyer kick her under the table, but she ignored it, knowing that she'd outsmarted even him.

Alexander Cox leaned toward Pamela. "An original or a Xerox copy?" he asked softly.

"A Xerox copy. But it's not signed."

Cox flicked his fingers disdainfully. "It's of no value."

Richard's jaw dropped. "But—but it's still a legal document."

Cox shook his head again. "You must have a signed document for it to be binding."

"Well, I just might have to get another legal opinion," Richard said angrily.

"As you wish," Cox said amicably, but his face began to color.

"Richard didn't mean that." T.J. Warren spoke for the first time. He was slight and blond and fine-featured. "My brother and I have every confidence in you. It's just that we don't want this woman to receive anything more than our father allowed. Not a cent more. And if there's any way to contest the amount the will called for, we'd—"

"You can't make something null and void," Diamond interrupted smoothly, "if it doesn't exist. And until you prove its existence, Mrs. Warren will continue to live in the Warren home with its full staff. She will also receive a monthly allowance so that she can continue to live in the style to which she's become accustomed. That is, forty thousand a month."

"Outrageous!" Richard hissed. "We're *not* going to put up with this."

"You're not going to have any choice." Allen Diamond was a big man, broad-shouldered, with black hair and a square jaw. "And if by chance we find that forty thousand a month isn't sufficient, we'll petition for more."

"Does that include your legal fees?" Richard asked nastily.

"No, no." Diamond grinned pleasantly. "That will come from the estate."

"Bullshit! If you think—"

"Gentlemen! Gentlemen!" Cox raised his voice, trying to calm things. "Bickering serves no purpose. The only way this can be resolved is for the will to be found. I suggest we all search for it diligently."

Cox picked up the folder in front of him and tucked it under his arm. "Mr. Diamond, I'll be in contact with you."

Cox left the room, the Warren brothers a step behind. At the door Richard turned and said, "You're not going to see a penny of my father's estate. Not a goddamned penny." He slammed the door so hard the walls shook.

Pamela took out a cigarette and lit it, her hand trembling noticeably. She hated the Warrens, but she was also frightened of them. With their wealth and power, nothing was beyond them. She inhaled deeply and kept the smoke down as long as possible before exhaling. "Do you think they'll find the will?"

"I doubt it," Diamond said, picking up his ostrich-skin briefcase. "I suspect they've already turned the world upside down looking for it."

"What happens if they can't find the will or prenuptial agreement?"

"From an inheritance standpoint, you are the surviving widow."

"What does that mean to me monetarily?"

Diamond shrugged. "It depends. How much was your former husband believed to be worth?"

"About a hundred and fifty million, I guess."

"Then you'll receive about fifty million, maybe a little more. The other two thirds go to his sons."

Pamela stared at the attorney, wide-eyed. Her heart pounded at the thought of so much money. "Are you sure?"

"You're going to be a wealthy woman, Mrs. Warren," Diamond said. "A very wealthy woman."

13

"Sorry I'm late." Joanna walked into the rear of the forensics laboratory carrying a folder of X rays. She nodded to Lori McKay and Jake Sinclair and to another man who was seated in a director's chair, his feet propped up on a countertop. His name was Ed Jacobs and he was considered by most to be the best orthopedic surgeon at Memorial Hospital.

"Have you examined the skeleton?" Joanna asked Jacobs.

"Not yet. I was waiting for you."

"Were you filled in on the victim's history?" Joanna asked, taking out X rays and flipping them up on the viewbox.

Jacobs nodded. "It's not a very long story. A guy gets killed, gets buried, and has a plate in his femur."

"It's the femur we're interested in," Joanna told him. "For openers, can you tell us if the victim had a limp?"

"Maybe." Jacobs got to his feet and stretched. He was tall and well-built with thick, reddish brown hair and an aquiline nose. The front of his scrub suit was spotted with perspiration. "Let's start with the X rays."

Joanna put up the last of the X rays and stepped away from the viewbox as Jacobs approached. Jacobs seemed to move in slow motion when not in the operating room doing surgery. In the OR, he was the exact opposite. He could perform a total knee replacement, skin-to-skin, in under two hours. The house staff had nicknamed him Fast Eddie.

Jacobs carefully examined the X rays, using a magnifying glass to study the flecks of metal near the femur. "Somebody shot him, huh?"

"There are other possibilities," Lori said.

"It's a bullet wound, sweetheart," Jacobs said. "Trust me."

"There are other possibilities," Lori persisted, an edge to her voice. "And I'm not your sweetheart."

"I wish you were." Jacobs grinned, picking up the X ray and holding it up to a bright lamp. "I'd give up my wife for you."

"I'm afraid Lori is right," Joanna said. "It's not a bullet. I had a piece of the metal analyzed and they tell me it came from a grenade."

Jacobs shrugged, unfazed. "Grenades are just oversized bullets."

Lori said, "There are substantial differences between bullets and grenades."

"Not when it comes to wounds," Jacobs said.

"I can give you some references that—"

Jacobs held up a hand and shook his head. "Don't lecture me on bullets and grenades. I spent a year in Vietnam with a MASH unit and I saw more wounds caused by the goddamn things than I care to remember. Bullets are nothing more than flying shrapnel and so are grenades."

Jake nodded to himself. They had guessed right. The victim had fought in Vietnam. Where else would he have gotten wounded by a grenade? "Was the injury bad enough for him to limp?"

Jacobs examined the X rays once more, then went over to the table that held the skeletal remains. He carefully measured the lengths of the femurs and tibias. "There is no shortening of the long bones. I doubt that he had a limp."

Joanna asked, "What about the metal plate?"

"It's a supracondylar plate, held in place by a compression screw," Jacobs said.

"Is there anything unusual about it?" Joanna asked.

"Not by X ray." Jacobs again bent over the skeletal remains and studied the metal plate at length.

"Is there any way to determine when it was made and who it was sold to?"

"Maybe," Jacobs said after some thought. "Have you got a tool kit?"

Joanna pointed to a drawer under the counter. "Right behind you."

Jacobs found the correct type of screwdriver and with great effort he removed the screw that held the metal plate to the femoral bone. The plate had been exposed to the elements and was obviously rusted in places. Jacobs went to a nearby sink and, using a stiff brush and running water, removed the remaining debris from the plate. He reexamined the plate with a magnifying glass. "It was made by Precision Products and it's got a serial number."

Joanna's face lit up. "Great!"

"Don't get your hopes up too high," Jacobs cautioned. "Precision Products was bought out by another company five years ago. It might not be possible to find their old records."

"Christ," Joanna grumbled, making no effort to hide her disappointment. "How can we check it out?"

"With a phone call," Jacobs said. "Where's your phone?"

"Next to the door."

Lori turned back to the X rays and fixed her gaze on the supracondylar plate. The metal plate was so obvious it almost jumped out at her. Yet she had overlooked it at first, not bothering to wonder what might be under the dirt and grime covering it. So stupid! Of course, the plate would have the manufacturer's name stamped on it and in all likelihood it would have a serial number as well. Joanna must have suspected that those things would be there but she needed someone with expertise to give her the particulars. That's why she asked the orthopedic surgeon to have a look.

"Suppose the manufacturer and serial number had worn off or were unreadable. What would you have done?" Lori asked Joanna.

Joanna thought for a moment. "I would have sent it to the FBI lab. They're very good at deciphering nearly impossible markings."

Lori nodded and made a mental note about the FBI lab for future use.

Joanna sat down and wearily rubbed at her eyes. It had already been a long day with autopsies, lectures, conferences and calls. But it was the worry that was getting to her. It had been twenty-four hours since the plasma had been introduced and her sister Kate was no better, still semicomatose, still poorly responsive.

And Joanna was still very afraid that she too might come down with the deadly virus. The nurse from the Virology Research Center was continuing to have fever and chills but no rash had appeared. Thus the diagnosis remained uncertain. If, however, a hemorrhagic rash developed, then the diagnosis would be clear-cut, the evidence overwhelming that the denguelike virus had been transmitted from the sick boy to the nurse. And perhaps to Joanna as well. Mack had made no bones about it. If the nurse got the disease, Joanna would have to be isolated and watched. Joanna kept wondering if she was going to end up in a bed next to her sister. In a grave next to . . .

The door behind her opened and Joanna looked over. David Dellacorte walked into the forensics laboratory with a stack of computer printouts under his arm. He waved to Jacobs, who was leaning against the wall talking on the phone. Then he came over to the group surrounding the table with the skeletal remains.

Dellacorte smiled warmly at Lori. "How have you been?"

"Just fine," Lori said, her voice unusually sweet.

Joanna noticed the change and watched the two exchanging glances. She wondered if they were seeing each other socially. It wouldn't have surprised Joanna. David Dellacorte was handsome, Lori McKay pretty, both bright. But there had to be a fifteen-year difference in their ages. And both were strong-willed; they would probably be at each other's throats half the time. So what? she thought. That wasn't her business as long as it didn't interfere with the investigation.

"Were you able to get the data on the liver transplants?" she asked Dellacorte, pushing herself up from her chair.

Dellacorte placed the stack of computer printouts on the counter-top and flipped through them like a deck of cards. "Here are all the liver transplants we've done at Memorial. Sixty-two cases over eight years. Twenty patients have died and their autopsy reports are included."

"How many patients received their livers from Donors International?"

"Six," Dellacorte said. "All received incredibly good matches. All are still alive, except for William Arthur Warren."

Jake looked up from the skeleton's skull, which he had been intently studying. "What about William Arthur Warren?"

"We're just talking about his transplanted liver," Joanna replied. She quickly introduced the men. They nodded across the table at each other. Joanna refocused her mind on the transplant patients. "So six patients received livers from Donors International and two of the livers developed cysts and adenomas?"

"That's what it looks like so far," Dellacorte said. "We'll know about the other patients once we've done the ultrasound studies."

"Only six cases from Donors International," Joanna said, thinking out loud and wishing the number were higher. She tapped a finger against the stack of computer printouts. "Do these records contain information about the people who donated the livers?"

"Just a brief clinical history and their tissue and blood types," Dellacorte said. "Of course, the donors aren't named."

"Damn," Joanna cursed softly.

"I think you're going to have to talk with the people at Donors International about the donors," Dellacorte said.

"I did," Joanna told him. "They weren't very helpful. They kept saying everything was private and confidential."

"They're probably frightened about being sued. You should go out there and meet with them face-to-face."

"I did meet with them face-to-face," Joanna said, slightly annoyed at Dellacorte's know-it-all attitude. "Getting information from them was like pulling teeth."

"Maybe they're trying to hide something," Jake suggested.

"Maybe." Joanna shrugged, now thinking about Jason Adler and the deal he must be cutting with Rudolph Ettinger to point the finger of blame at Memorial. "But I didn't get the impression they were trying to sweep things under the rug. I think they were just protecting all of their interests. You see, Donors International is really a big medical complex where they do incredible research. Nobel Prize–type research. I just think they don't like outsiders.

That's why they built it in the middle of the Santa Monica Mountains. It couldn't be more isolated."

Jake's ears pricked up. "Where in the Santa Monica Mountains?"

"South of Mulholland Drive," Joanna said. "Perhaps a mile or so west of the San Diego Freeway."

Jake picked up an ulnar bone and twirled it in his fingers like a baton. "That's not far from where we found this skeleton."

Joanna's eyes narrowed. "Are you sure?"

"It sounds like the same general area. Have you got a detailed map of West Los Angeles?"

Joanna nodded. "On the wall in the front lab."

Lori started to follow them out but stopped when David Dellacorte tugged on her sleeve. She smiled at him, studying his face briefly. He was so damn good-looking with his prematurely graying hair. She glanced down at his hand and didn't see a wedding band. "It's interesting stuff, isn't it?"

"Yeah," Dellacorte said and leaned back against the counter. His elbow touched Lori's arm for a moment and he felt her warmth through his white coat. She had the aroma of a freshly opened bar of soap. "I don't see how you learn so much from so little," he said flatteringly.

"It's the training."

"No. It's more than that. A lot more."

"You think so, huh?" Lori smiled at him.

Dellacorte smiled back, resisting the urge to touch her again. "Are you involved with anyone?"

"Not really," Lori said, her voice low.

"Do you go out a lot?"

"I don't have much free time," she said and immediately regretted it. Quickly she added, "I try to keep Saturday night open."

"Want to get together for dinner?"

"Sure."

"Where do I find you?"

"I live—" Lori stopped abruptly as Joanna and Jake walked back into the room. "I'll call your office and leave my number," she said, almost whispering.

Jake came over to Lori. "Have you got the precise location where we found the skeleton?"

Lori closed her eyes and searched back into her memory. For these kinds of details, she had a nearly photographic mind. "It was a mile and a half west of the freeway. The nearest off-ramp was Getty Center Drive."

"So the grave site paralleled Getty Center Drive?" Jake asked.

"Just about," Lori replied. "It was maybe a hundred yards north."

Jake rubbed his forehead, thinking about the new information and fitting it in with what he already knew. He remembered the California Highway Patrol officer at the grave site telling him that there was a women's clinic to the north. He wondered if that was Donors International or something else.

Jake turned to Joanna. "Is there some kind of women's clinic at Donors International?"

Joanna nodded. "An infertility clinic. Why?"

Jake ignored the question and tried to calculate distances. As best he could determine, the grave site and Donors International were separated by at least a mile of rugged terrain. Very rugged terrain. No way anyone was going to lug a body over that ground.

He looked back at Lori. "There weren't any roads heading north from the grave site, were there?"

Lori thought for a moment. "I remember a few hiking trails."

"But they were narrow and steep," Jake recalled.

"Very," Lori agreed. "I don't think anyone could carry a body very far on those paths," she added, seeming to read Jake's mind.

"Do you think there's some connection between the skeleton and Donors International?" Joanna asked, trying to make the association.

"I doubt it," Jake said, then shrugged. "I mean, what the hell would a sniper have to do with a transplant place?"

"A sniper!" Dellacorte said, now keenly interested. He quickly looked down at the skeleton. "How do you know he was a sniper?"

"I'll tell you about it later," Lori said.

Jake looked over at Dellacorte. "What you hear about this case goes no further, understand?"

"Absolutely."

Jake took out a Greek cigarette and lit it, ignoring the disapproving stares of the doctors. He started pacing the floor, concentrating again on the trails and paths between the grave site and Donors International. There were no access roads, as far as he remembered, no way to transport a body over miles of rugged terrain. But Jake decided to look at the area again. This time from the air, using a police helicopter.

Joanna watched Jake pace. She knew that something about the grave site was still bothering him. When it came to investigations Jake was like a bulldog. He was unbelievably tenacious and wouldn't let go until he had all the answers he wanted. Joanna sighed to herself, thinking about her relationship with him. He was so smart in so many ways, yet so stupid when it came to women.

Dellacorte glanced at the wall clock and pushed himself off the counter. "I've got to run or I'll be late for evening rounds."

Joanna's brow wrinkled as she tried to remember a question she'd had for David Dellacorte. Something important, very important, about transplants. Suddenly it came to her. "One more thing, David. I learned that the livers for William Arthur Warren and Rudolph Ettinger came from Hungary and Greece. Even with the use of private jets those livers had to be on ice for at least fifteen hours. Isn't that a long time for organs to sit around before being transplanted?"

Dellacorte shrugged. "Not really. The absolute cutoff time for a liver to be on ice is twenty-four hours. Of course, the sooner it's transplanted the better."

"Is it possible that the long period of time the liver was out of the body could have led to formation of cysts and adenomas?"

Dellacorte considered the idea carefully. "I doubt it. I know of at least three livers that were on ice for twenty-four hours and then transplanted. The patients did fine. But I'll double-check and get ultrasound studies to be sure."

"Got it!" Ed Jacobs yelled as he put the phone down. He walked over to the group, shaking his head. "Christ Almighty! You'd think I was asking them for the keys to the White House."

"What did you find out?" Joanna asked.

"We got lucky," Jacobs said, stretching his neck and shoulders. "Those supracondylar plates are manufactured in lots of a hundred. So each serial number represents a hundred plates. The plate on your skeleton was part of a lot sent to Walter Reed Hospital in 1974."

Joanna squinted an eye. "Are you telling me that this plate with this serial number was put in a hundred patients?"

"That's right," Jacobs said. "So now you know your man is among that hundred."

"Shit," Jake grumbled under his breath. "It's going to take forever to track down a hundred different people."

"And you're going to need a subpoena to get those records from Walter Reed Hospital. That's a guarantee."

Jake waved his hands dejectedly. "That's not a problem. The problem is tracking down a hundred men from over twenty years ago. It's going to take a long, long time. Too goddamned long." Jake started pacing again.

Joanna looked over at Lori and got her attention. Joanna motioned with her eyes for Lori to look down at the skeleton. Lori stared back, puzzled. Joanna discreetly pointed to her own ring finger.

Lori's face lit up. "We can get the answer with a phone call." She shot Joanna a grateful glance.

Jake stopped in his tracks. "How?"

Lori picked up the wedding band. "We know his initials. J.R."

Jake smiled broadly. "We've got our man."

Joanna smiled too, but inwardly she felt no real joy. She looked down at the skeleton and it reminded her of death and she started thinking about her sister Kate again.

14

The pawnbroker was fidgety. He wouldn't look at Jake Sinclair or Lou Farelli while he talked, and he continually twirled a diamond ring around his little finger. "The guy comes in and hocks a Rolex. It happens all the time. I must do ten, fifteen a week in here."

"He seemed like the Rolex type, huh?" Jake asked.

The pawnbroker shrugged. "He was presentable. He wasn't some bum off the street, I'll tell you that."

The door to the shop opened and a well-dressed, matronly woman with silver-blue hair entered. The pawnbroker signaled to an assistant, who stepped forward to help the woman. "And I checked the serial number on the Rolex too. The number wasn't on the alert list the day I took in the watch. You can check your records for the dates."

"I did," Jake said. It had taken the police nearly two weeks to track down the serial number of William Arthur Warren's Rolex. They'd finally got it from a neighborhood jeweler who'd repaired the watch. "Did you serve the guy who hocked the Rolex?"

"My son did," the pawnbroker said. "But I had to okay it."

"So you saw the guy?"

"Oh, yeah."

The pawnbroker was a short, stout man, middle-aged and balding, with rosy cheeks. His name was Maury Glazer. "And I made damn sure he IDed himself too."

"I thought you said he looked presentable," Jake said.

"He did, but I didn't know him," Glazer said. "And if I don't know you I don't trust you. I'm double careful, Lieutenant. I don't have to deal with hot stuff to make a good living."

"So you got his name and address?"

"I got better. I Xeroxed his driver's license."

Jake smiled thinly. "Did he know you Xeroxed his license?"

Glazer shrugged. "Maybe, maybe not. But it wouldn't have mattered. When you're in my store, Lieutenant, you play by my rules."

"I'd like to look at that license."

"It's in the back. I'll get it for you."

Jake stretched his back and looked around the well-appointed pawnshop. There was no merchandise hanging from the walls, no musical instruments or electronic gadgets. Everything was expensive and locked under glass. Even though the store was in Beverly Hills, there were bars on the windows and surveillance cameras and an armed guard off to the side. In the back were small offices where Jake guessed that the rich and famous conducted their business. "It's going to be a phony ID," Jake mused.

"Yeah," Farelli agreed. "No one is that goddamn stupid."

Jake shook his head, puzzled. "Why did he hock the watch in a shop where people would see him and remember him? Why not play it safe and get rid of it on the street?"

"And why leave behind a diamond necklace that's worth three times as much as the Rolex and can't be traced? A real pro would have grabbed that necklace faster than you can blink."

"It just doesn't make sense." Jake reached for his notepad and flipped through the pages, making certain he hadn't overlooked any questions he wanted to ask the pawnbroker. He came to a page on the skeletal remains found in the Santa Monica Mountains. At the bottom were question marks next to the notations "Women's clinic" and "Access roads." He looked over at Farelli. "Did you get that helicopter for me?"

"Tomorrow at four," Farelli said. "They can only give you thirty minutes of air time."

"That's not enough," Jake said. "I need at least an hour to cover that area."

"It was like pulling teeth to get thirty minutes. They've got all their aircraft tied up looking for that freeway sniper."

"That son of a bitch," Jake growled, his face suddenly hard. For the past month someone had been taking shots at drivers on the freeway using a high-powered rifle. Two people had been killed, four badly injured. The sniper liked to work in the early morning hours, but the last shooting had taken place at night. Now the city was up in arms and all police helicopters were going up in the evening as well with spotters and marksmen outfitted with night-vision goggles.

"You know, Jake," Farelli said, thinking aloud, "if you don't see anything from the air you should go over that area on foot again."

"Why?"

"Because that skeleton belonged to a guy who was iced ten years ago," Farelli explained. "If there was a road there and it hasn't been used for years, it'd be overgrown with brush by now, maybe even washed out by the rains. You might not see it from the air, but you could from the ground."

"Good point," Jake said and scribbled a note to himself.

Glazer came back to the front of the shop and handed Jake a photocopy. "Here's the guy who brought in the Rolex."

Jake studied the information on the copy of the driver's license. The man's name was Eric Miller, his address 9000 Sunset Boulevard. He was thirty-eight years old with black hair and blue eyes. His weight was 150, his height 5' 10". Jake studied the photograph on the license. The face was very dark, the contrast poor. But the face resembled the man he'd met in Pamela Warren's hospital room. "What's that guy's name? The sleazy guy we saw in Mrs. Warren's hospital room?"

Farelli quickly flipped through his notepad. "Boyette. Tony Boyette."

Jake showed him the photocopy. "What do you think?"

"It could be him," Farelli said cautiously. "Too bad it ain't a better picture. But, yeah, I'd say it was him."

Jake turned to the pawnbroker and carefully described Tony Boyette, paying particular attention to the man's sharp, chiseled features and long black hair. "And he had beady eyes, too, the kind you don't really trust."

Glazer nodded firmly. "That sounds like the man with the Rolex."

Jake said to Farelli, "Get a good picture of Boyette from one of the guilds or groups he belongs to."

"Right."

Jake turned back to Glazer. "Could you identify this guy in a photograph or in a lineup?"

"In a split second," Glazer said.

"We'll be back tomorrow."

"I'm here until six every day but Sunday."

Jake and Farelli were almost to the door when the pawnbroker called out after them. "Oh, there's one thing I forgot to tell you."

"What?" Jake asked.

"I think I've seen the guy who pawned the Rolex before."

"Where?"

"On television. I think he's some kind of actor." Glazer shrugged and chuckled to himself. "But then again, aren't they all in this town?"

15

"I've got good news and I've got bad news," Mack Brown said. He had his feet propped up on the desk in his office, a Styrofoam cup of coffee in his lap.

"What's the good news?" Joanna asked.

"Your sister's encephalitis is definitely improving. She's far more alert and responsive than when you saw her last."

"Great!" Joanna smiled broadly and clenched her fists, shaking them with joy. She looked over at Mack. He wasn't smiling back. "Has there been brain damage?" Joanna asked quietly, anticipating what the bad news would be.

"No, no," Mack assured her. "There's been no motor loss and her cranial nerves are intact. She's still lethargic, of course, but her cerebral function seems good."

"Then what's the bad news?"

"Kate's liver is not doing well," Mack said gravely. "The inflammation persists and seems to be worsening. She may be developing hepatic necrosis."

A chill swept over Joanna. "Like the necrosis you see in viral hepatitis?"

"Exactly."

Joanna slumped in her chair and shook her head hopelessly. Hepatic necrosis was the worst possible complication. For unknown reasons, some viruses induced massive destruction of liver cells. Within weeks or months liver failure ensued and it was inevitably fatal. There was no known treatment. "What's the evidence that she's going into hepatic necrosis?"

"She has fever and some abdominal pain, and her jaundice is deepening." Mack reached for a laboratory slip on his desk and read it. "Her last serum bilirubin was six milligrams per cent."

Joanna sighed in despair. "Is there anything we can do?"

"I'm afraid not."

"What about giving her more plasma?"

Mack hesitated, tapping his pencil on the desk. "I wouldn't be in favor of that."

"Why not?"

"Because it might make things worse. As a matter of fact, the plasma we gave Kate may have caused even more inflammation of her liver."

Joanna looked at Mack oddly. "How?"

"There're antibodies against the virus in the plasma," Mack explained. "And some people believe that when the antibodies interact with the virus in the liver, the interaction not only destroys the virus, it may also destroy the liver cells. You might think of the liver cells as being kind of innocent bystanders."

"Do you believe that concept?"

Mack shrugged. "Who knows? But Kate's liver function did worsen after the plasma transfusion. We can't ignore that."

"So we just sit around and watch her die?" Joanna said angrily, and immediately regretted saying it. She knew Mack was doing everything possible.

Mack gestured with his hands. "There's always the possibility of a liver transplant."

Joanna stared at Mack for several moments. "Would that work in Kate's case?" she asked. "I mean, with the virus everywhere in her body, wouldn't the virus destroy the new liver too?"

"Not necessarily," Mack said. "Right now Kate is getting better except for her liver. Which means that the virus is dying out except in her liver. If all of her other organ systems remain intact, Kate might do very well with a transplant."

"It sounds so drastic," Joanna said quietly.

"It may be her only chance," Mack said. "But we don't have to make any decisions now. We'll cross the transplant bridge when we get to it. Maybe Kate will surprise us and heal her own liver."

"Right," Joanna said, but she was still thinking about a liver transplant and how she would go about setting it up.

Mack got to his feet. "Let's go visit Kate. I know she wants to see you."

They left the office and walked down a corridor to the area outside the isolation ward. As they put on gowns and gloves, Mack said, "By the way, our nurse with the fever is in the clear. She wasn't infected with the denguelike virus."

"What caused her illness?" Joanna asked.

"A garden-variety adenovirus," Mack said. "We grew it out of her blood this morning."

"Well, at least I don't have *that* to worry about anymore."

Mack pulled up his mask and goggles. "Remember, Kate is better but she may still be contagious. You can touch, but don't kiss."

They entered the isolation unit and went over to Kate's bed. She was propped up on pillows, drinking orange juice through a straw with the aid of a nurse. She didn't seem to see the doctors and stared straight ahead.

Joanna's heart dropped. She had expected Kate to look better, to be more like her old self. But her sister still looked terribly ill. She was so thin, with sunken eyes and deeply jaundiced skin. And the movements of her hands were like an old person's—slow and uncertain.

"Hi," Joanna said finally.

Kate's eyes moved slowly to Joanna. She just stared, her face expressionless.

"Remember me?" Joanna asked, trying to control herself and the tears she felt coming.

Kate continued to stare blankly at her sister. There was no sign of recognition.

Joanna suddenly remembered she was wearing a mask and goggles. She pulled them down for a brief moment.

Kate's mouth opened, her lips trying to smile. "Do I look as shitty as I feel?"

"You look beautiful," Joanna said. The tears came and she

quickly wiped them away with her sleeve. She pulled her goggles and mask back up. "These damn goggles bother my eyes," she lied.

"Particularly when you cry into them," Kate said with effort. Her voice was weak and raspy.

Kate's mind was still good and sharp, Joanna thought, and thanked God for that. "Are you having any pain?"

Kate nodded. "In my stomach. It kind of comes and goes. What's causing it?"

"Your liver is inflamed," Joanna told her.

"Is that why I'm so tired?" Kate asked.

"That's the reason."

Kate took a swallow of orange juice, some of it dripping off her lip and onto her chin. With effort she took a deep breath. "Am I going to get better?"

"Of course," Joanna said firmly. "Dr. Brown will tell you that—"

"He'll lie to me," Kate said and reached for Joanna's hand. "But you won't, will you?"

"No," Joanna said softly.

"Then tell me, am I going to make it?"

Joanna tried to keep her voice even. "We've got a tough fight in front of us."

"How tough?"

"Damn tough."

Kate slowly closed her eyes and seemed to drift off. She was motionless except for her shallow breathing. Her eyelids fluttered for a moment, then opened. "I do my best work in tough places."

"You get some sleep," Joanna said, squeezing her sister's hand. "I'll be back to see you later."

Kate nodded and closed her eyes.

Joanna and Mack quietly left the isolation ward and stripped off their goggles and surgical garb. Joanna peered through the glass window and watched the nurse lower the head of Kate's bed. Even from a distance Kate looked awful. Joanna shook her head sadly, still having difficulty accepting the fact that Kate was so near death. With hepatic necrosis it was a matter of weeks, or months at the most. It was a nightmare, a horrible nightmare.

"Maybe she'll be one of the few lucky ones," Mack said, coming up beside Joanna. "Even with massive necrosis, there are occasional patients who pull through. Last night I read a report in which a patient survived despite substantial hepatic necrosis. I can get a copy of the report for you, if you'd like."

Joanna nodded, but she hardly heard what Mack was saying. She was thinking about liver transplants and how quickly she could set one up.

16

Joanna was in the shower when the doorbell rang. She stepped out and put on a blue-and-gold UCLA warm-up outfit, wondering who it could be. It was almost ten P.M. and outside the weather was cold and blustery, a new storm making its way into Southern California. The doorbell rang again.

Joanna hurried into the living room and looked through the peephole. Jake Sinclair was in the doorway, huddled up against the wind.

Joanna opened the door. "I hope this is business, Jake."

"It is," he said, moving past her and over to the fireplace. He held his hands out at the blaze and warmed them. "Christ, it's cold out there."

"You could have called rather than coming over," she said tonelessly, trying to control her temper. "Believe it or not, I've got a phone."

"Which has been busy for the past two hours."

Joanna grumbled to herself, remembering that she'd taken the phone off the hook to watch the last two acts of *La Boheme* on public television. She went over to the phone and placed it back in its cradle. "Would you like a brandy?"

"Oh, yeah," Jake said gratefully. "Maybe it'll help thaw me out."

He watched her walk over to a small bar. The warm-up suit she was wearing stuck to her wet skin and outlined every curve in her body. Even when she stood still she was sexy. And her bare feet and wet hair seemed to accentuate it. Jake wondered for the hundredth time how he'd ever let her get away.

He pried his eyes away from her and glanced around the spacious living room. It was tastefully decorated and very feminine. The chairs and couch were French antiques and upholstered in deep-blue silk. The walls were covered with oils, lithographs and watercolors. But his favorite part of the room was the old brick fireplace with the bearskin rug in front of it. He smiled to himself, recalling the times he and Joanna—

"Here you are," Joanna said and handed him a snifter of brandy.

They sat on a large couch and sipped their drinks, watching the logs blaze and spit from the heat. Outside the wind gusted and caused the windows to rattle.

"Nice place to be on a stormy night, huh?" Jake said.

"Yeah, I guess." Joanna continued to stare into the flames, but in her peripheral vision she was watching Jake. He had so many good qualities to go along with his good looks, she thought. He could be funny, and there was even a soft spot he kept hidden from everyone except those few who managed to get close to him. But he had a flaw too, a huge flaw. Jake could be incredibly insensitive, and always at the worst time. When it hurt the most.

Joanna shook her head, clearing it. Her relationship with Jake was over and done. Finished. "What is so important that you had to come over on a night like this?"

"I think we got a break in the William Arthur Warren case."

Joanna's brow went up. "Oh? What?"

"Somebody hocked the old man's Rolex."

Joanna turned to face Jake, tucking her legs under her. "The guy can't possibly be that stupid."

"I'll fill you in. Then you tell me what you think," Jake said and lit a cigarette, flicking the match into the fireplace. "Last week the watch was hocked at a Beverly Hills pawnshop. Now, the pawnbroker is a sharp operator and isn't about to get caught with hot goods, so he makes the fellow produce an ID. The guy's name is Eric Miller and he's got a West Hollywood address."

"How do you know it's not a fake ID?" Joanna asked.

"Odds are it is," Jake conceded. "But the address is real—or at least was real. It's on Sunset, and there used to be an apartment complex there. It was torn down a few years ago to put up an office building."

"Has this Eric Miller got a record?"

"Nope. But according to the pawnbroker's description, the guy's got a face that's a pretty good match for a part-time actor named Tony Boyette." Jake dragged deeply on his cigarette and blew a smoke ring at the ceiling. "I met Tony Boyette at Memorial Hospital the day after the murder of William Arthur Warren."

"What was he doing at Memorial?"

"Visiting Pamela Warren."

Joanna smiled. "This is getting kind of interesting." She finished her drink. "You want more brandy?"

"Just a touch."

Joanna hurried over to the wet bar and came back with the bottle. She poured generously. "Tell me about Tony Boyette."

"He's a wanna-be who takes acting lessons a couple of times a week. Pamela Warren is in the same class, and apparently that's where they met."

"Were they sleeping together?"

"Not according to their classmates," Jake said, then shrugged. "But who the hell knows? They could have had a one-nighter."

"So they were just friends, huh?"

"That's how it seemed. They talked a lot. He sometimes walked her to her car. But there was no touching or hand-holding."

"And he supposedly came to the hospital to see how she was doing?"

Jake nodded. "With a bouquet of flowers from her classmates. Farelli checked it out. The class did send flowers."

Joanna ran a hand through her still-damp hair and flicked a water droplet at the fire. It hissed back. "And you figure that Tony got into her purse at acting class, right?"

Jake grinned to himself as he nodded again. Joanna was a forensic pathologist, a doctor, but she thought just like a cop. "He knows she's married to a multimillionaire so he takes a peek at her wallet and gets her address. He makes a copy of her house key and walks right in. That's why there was no forced entry. As long as you use a key to enter, the alarm system doesn't go off."

"Has Tony Boyette got a criminal record?"

"Nope. Nor does anybody else in the class."

Joanna wrinkled her brow, concentrating. "So he slips out during class to one of those shops that makes copies of keys. Or he asks a friend to do it, not saying whose keys they are, of course, so Pamela never becomes suspicious of his absence."

Jake looked at Joanna admiringly. "You should have been a cop."

"In a lot of ways I am," she said, touched by the compliment.

The flames in the fireplace suddenly began to flicker. Joanna reached for a poker and jabbed at the logs, bringing the fire back to life. "I think you've got your man, assuming the pawnbroker is able to positively ID Tony Boyette."

"Oh, I think he will," Jake said. "We're getting a picture of Tony from the actors guild, and I'll bet you dollars to doughnuts the pawnbroker fingers him."

"And if he doesn't?"

"We'll bring Tony down to the station and put him in a lineup," Jake said gruffly. "We'll let him sweat for a while and see if that won't loosen him up."

"Does he seem the type to crack under pressure?"

Jake shrugged. "Who knows? Actors can be pretty good at lying and covering up. Hell, he might even admit to pawning the watch and give us a bullshit story about buying the Rolex from some hustler on the street. It can be a long distance between pawning a watch and convicting a man of murder."

"Unless you've got evidence that puts him at the scene of the crime."

"All we've got are some partial muddy footprints," Jake said. "And they aren't going to help us at all."

He reached for another cigarette but decided against it. He was on his third pack of the day, and his throat was getting raw. "Did anything show up in the cigar?"

Joanna looked at him strangely. "What cigar?"

"Remember the bitten-off cigar at the Warren murder scene?"

Joanna nodded, now recalling the cigar and piece of tobacco

found on the floor in the Warren library. She had sent them to a forensic dentist at Memorial for further study. "I think I've got the report in my office here. Let's take a look."

Jake followed Joanna across the living room and into a large office that had formerly been a spare bedroom. Built-in bookshelves and file cabinets lined the walls. There were two desks, one holding a microscope, the other a computer. A human skeleton wearing a New York Yankees baseball cap hung in the corner. "When did you do all this?"

"A few months ago," Joanna said, switching on the computer.

"Does the apartment manager know?"

"It's not an apartment anymore," she said. "They decided to convert it into condominiums and I bought a unit. The price was irresistible."

"How much?"

"Eighty thousand."

Jake's jaw dropped. "Why so cheap?"

"The real estate group that owned it went bankrupt and the bank foreclosed. They sold the units at auction. There weren't many bidders."

Joanna punched numbers into the computer keyboard and data on the William Arthur Warren murder flashed up on the screen. She punched in more numbers and the results of a study from Memorial's School of Dentistry appeared. Joanna skimmed to the relevant parts, then read aloud. "The cigar was bitten by human teeth. In particular, a human incisor with a small chip on it. The incisor did not belong to William Arthur Warren."

"Maybe it'll match up with Tony Boyette's teeth," Jake said.

"Even if there is a match, it won't hold up in court," Joanna told him. "It's not nearly precise enough for positive identification."

"Like the damn footprints," Jake said sourly.

"There was a small spot of saliva on the bitten-off piece of tobacco," Joanna went on. "They tried to extract it but didn't have too much luck. They're still trying."

"Suppose they could extract it?"

Joanna moved her head back and forth ambiguously. "Sometimes they can get some interesting information from saliva. It contains certain types of enzymes and antibodies."

"That isn't going to help very much."

"Not in a court of law. But it might be useful when you question Tony."

"How so?"

Joanna grinned mischievously. "You might tell him that the murderer bit off the end of a cigar and left some of his saliva on the piece he spat out. And you'd like a sample of Tony's saliva to compare it with. Tell him you want to do some DNA studies and see if there's a match."

"Can you really do that?"

"I doubt it. But you'll sure as hell get his attention."

Jake chuckled softly. "You're a hard woman."

"Tough as nails," Joanna said.

"That would really cause him to sweat blood," Jake said, happily looking forward to the interrogation.

"Particularly if you give him a cigar to chew on. Tell him you want to reenact the murder scene as closely as possible."

Jake nodded, smiling at her. He would never have thought of that.

Joanna switched off the computer and led the way back into the living room. The fire had died down, the temperature in the room dropping. Outside the wind was howling. "It's getting late, Jake, and I've got a long day tomorrow."

He took her arms and held them. She just stood there motionlessly, showing no response. "Thanks for your help," he said warmly.

"Any time."

Joanna reached for the door and opened it. A blast of cold air blew into the living room. In the garden she could see bushes and small trees bending with the strong gusts. "Good night, Jake."

Joanna closed the door behind him and waited a moment before looking out the peephole. Jake was pulling up the collar of his coat, hunching down against the wind and drizzle as he hurried away. For a moment she felt guilty over sending him out into such foul weather. But then she remembered how he wasn't there when she'd needed him the most. Her guilt passed.

She vowed never to become involved with Jake Sinclair again. Never.

17

Pamela Warren was alone with her attorney, Allen Diamond, in the law offices of Cole, Cox and Harrington. She nervously twisted her wedding band and glanced around the room. In the rear wall was a small window behind which—her lawyer had explained—there was equipment to record depositions. Pamela wondered if the machines were on. She had the feeling she was being spied on.

Pamela moved in closer to her lawyer and spoke in a low voice. "Why do you think they called this meeting?"

Diamond shrugged. "I don't know."

"Maybe they found the will."

"Maybe." Diamond shrugged again. "But they didn't need to call a meeting for that. They could have notified us by phone or letter."

"Then why?" Pamela persisted.

Diamond studied his manicured nails briefly. "Perhaps they're going to offer you a settlement."

Pamela's eyes narrowed suspiciously. "What kind of settlement?"

"They give you a fixed amount to relinquish all claims to the estate."

"Forget it!" Pamela said at once. "I want every penny I'm legally entitled to."

"I understand." Diamond nodded agreeably. "But keep in mind, you're taking a risk."

"What's the risk?"

"They could tie you up in court for years."

"And during that time I'd live very comfortably, thank you."

"But they could find the will and prenuptial agreement during that time," Diamond went on, "so you would've been better off taking the settlement."

Pamela thought about the fifty million dollars she'd receive if the will wasn't found and what she'd lose if it was. A world of difference. All that luxurious wealth . . . Pamela felt as if she was at the craps table in Las Vegas with everything she owned riding on the next roll of the dice.

"And remember," Diamond said, breaking into her thoughts, "regardless of the offer, don't accept or refuse it now. Tell them you'll consider it. You can always say no later."

Pamela wondered how much the Warrens were going to offer. Probably a million, two at most. They were such cheap bastards— and ruthless as well. No, she decided, one or two million would never do. Not after what she went through during her marriage to William Arthur Warren.

It was hard for Pamela to believe that she once loved her former husband. Not his money, him. She could still recall the endless list of medical tests and exams he had demanded she undergo to document her excellent health. And then the painful procedures required before she could attempt to become pregnant. It had all felt so damn unnatural. Someone taking your eggs at surgery and fertilizing them in a laboratory with your husband's sperm before placing the eggs back in your uterus. And all for naught. The pregnancies never happened and their marriage became cold and loveless. They slept in separate bedrooms and led separate lives. He treated her like a well-paid servant. The bastard, she fumed to herself, feeling no remorse for her part in his death.

There was a rumble of thunder in the distance, and the large bay window in the conference room vibrated. Pamela glanced out at the bleak weather, gray and drizzly. She decided she might settle for five million.

The door to the conference room opened and Alexander Cox walked in, followed by Richard and T.J. Warren. The men quickly seated themselves. Cox nodded to Pamela and her attorney. The Warren sons didn't bother.

"Thank you for coming on such short notice," Cox said and opened a legal file. He took out a thick manila envelope. "Mr. Richard Warren has an announcement he wishes to make."

"Thank you, Alexander," Richard said formally and cleared his throat. "It is with great pleasure that I announce that my father's will has been found." He smiled smugly as he watched Pamela's expression.

Pamela was stunned speechless. Her face went deadly pale. All that money. Gone!

"I trust that the will has been authenticated," Diamond said evenly.

"Oh, yes," Cox assured him. "The will is twelve years old and was signed and witnessed in this office. The witnesses were secretaries and they still work with our firm. If you wish, I can call them in."

Diamond shook his head. "That won't be necessary."

"Of course, I will make copies of the will for you and your client to examine," Cox added.

"And make copies of the prenuptial agreement," Richard said. "We found that as well. And please underline the part that says his wife receives the full amount agreed on in case of my father's death. We don't think that's valid here. We believe my father meant in case of death from natural causes."

Diamond looked over at Alexander Cox. "Does the agreement say death or does it specify death from natural causes?"

"It simply says death," Cox replied.

Richard moved in closer to the table and fixed his eyes on Pamela. "We think my father's wife insisted on having the clause about his death included in the agreement. And if we can prove she did—well, then, that casts a different light on his murder, doesn't it?"

The accusation hung in the air. Again there was a low rumble of thunder outside.

Pamela stared at Richard Warren and wondered if he was just guessing or if he knew something. Her shock was turning to anger, her hatred for the young man even deeper than usual. She wanted to scream at him and leap across the table and scratch out his eyes.

Under the table she dug her long nails into her palms and tried to keep her composure. "Your father drew up the agreement. I had no say in the matter."

"That's true," Cox said, backing her up. "We only went through one draft of the prenuptial agreement and Mrs. Warren was not present."

Diamond tilted back in his chair and gestured with his hands. "It seems clear that Mrs. Warren is entitled to the full amount agreed upon."

"We'll see," Richard said.

T.J. Warren took out a small cigar and lit it. He blew smoke across the table at Pamela. "And since the matter of the will is now settled, we want this woman out of my father's house within twenty-four hours."

"Whoa!" Diamond said abruptly. "This will has to go through probate and nothing—I repeat, nothing—happens until then. Mrs. Warren will continue to live in the house and the estate will continue to support her."

T.J.'s face reddened. "We want her—"

"I don't care what you want," Diamond said calmly. "It's the law. And besides, this will is twelve years old. Maybe your father drew up another one more recently."

"To my knowledge," Cox said, "there was only one will."

"Well, you never know," Diamond said, bringing his fingers together and forming a steeple. "One day one will miraculously turns up, the next day another will might show up. Stranger things have happened."

Richard Warren glared at Diamond, hating him, and distrusting him as he distrusted all lawyers. "Well, then, we'll just have an appraiser go to the house and list everything and put a value on it. That way this woman won't be able to take things that don't belong to her. And don't tell me I can't, because I know I can."

The sons were like jackals fighting over scraps, Diamond thought. He turned to Cox. "Are these two the major heirs?"

Cox nodded. "Richard and T.J. Warren are the main beneficiaries, along with the now-deceased Jerry Warren."

Pamela's head jerked up. "Who is Jerry Warren?"

"Jerry was the youngest of William Arthur Warren's sons," Cox said sadly. "He died in his twenties a while back." Cox looked down at the table, remembering the day William Arthur Warren had tearfully confided to him that his youngest son had AIDS.

"So that's why he wanted the child named Jerry," Pamela lied softly, her mind racing ahead, now seeing an avenue to get her hands on more of William Arthur Warren's wealth.

Richard's face suddenly lost color. "What child?"

"I'm pregnant with your father's child," Pamela said as all the pieces fell into place. "And of course I'll follow my husband's wishes and name the child Jerry if it's a boy."

"This is preposterous!" Richard Warren was on his feet, his fists tightly clenched. "They didn't even share the same bedroom."

Pamela smiled sweetly. "Oh, every so often we did. Besides, you don't have to make love in the bedroom."

Diamond slowly shook his head—as always, amazed at what money did to people. And the more the money, the stranger and more unpredictable the behavior.

"You probably went out and got yourself knocked up by some guy," Richard blurted out, losing control. "You'll never get away with this. There's no way that child belongs to my father."

"Sure there is and I can prove it," Pamela said and paused to fluff her hair in place. She waited as long as possible, watching the sons squirm and enjoying it. "We'll do tissue typing on the baby. We know your father's tissue type because he underwent a transplant. I'll get myself typed and then we can determine beyond any doubt that William Arthur Warren fathered the child."

Richard and T.J. were dumbstruck. They looked over to their attorney for help. Cox shrugged. He could offer no assistance.

Richard slammed his fist down on the table so hard that it shook. "We're not going to put up with this nonsense. Everyone knows my father was referring to my brother who was alive at the time the will was drawn up. We can easily prove that."

Alexander Cox sighed to himself and wished Richard would sit down, shut up, and stop trying to practice law. If the woman was pregnant with William Arthur Warren's child, everything changed. Will or not.

"And suppose the child is a girl?" Richard snorted. "How are you going to get around that?"

"With the greatest of ease," Pamela said, permitting herself to smile. "You see, Jerry is also a girl's name."

"Wait a minute! Wait a minute!" T.J. suddenly broke in, shifting in his seat as if he had something important to say. "Didn't my father state in his will that he wanted his estate to go to his three *sons*? There was no mention of a daughter."

"It doesn't matter," Diamond said. "If my client's child was fathered by William Arthur Warren, the child will share in the estate."

T.J. jerked his head toward Alexander Cox. "Is that right?"

Cox nodded slowly. "I'm afraid so."

Pamela pushed her chair back and stood. "When the appraisers come to my house to list and evaluate all the contents, please make certain I'm given a copy of the list." She stared at the Warren brothers, making no effort to hide her contempt for them. "I don't want these two taking anything that belongs to William's child."

Pamela spun around and left the conference room. Allen Diamond followed her out and down the corridor to a bank of elevators. An empty car was waiting and they entered.

As the elevator descended, Diamond turned to Pamela. "Are you really pregnant?"

Pamela smiled broadly and winked at him.

"If this is a bluff, Mrs. Warren, it's not going to work," Diamond said seriously. "And if you are pregnant you're going to have to prove that the baby was fathered by William Arthur Warren."

The elevator door opened. Pamela Warren took her attorney's arm as they walked out. "You just do your job, Mr. Diamond, and I'll do mine."

18

"We've done ultrasound studies on twenty-eight transplanted livers from Donors International," Jason Adler said. "None showed any cysts or adenomas. Thus, I think we can safely say that there's nothing in the way we're handling and processing the livers that causes cyst formation."

"I'd like to see the reports as well as the photographs of the ultrasound studies," Joanna said.

"Of course," Adler said evenly, but his jaw tightened at the inference that he might not be telling her the truth. "I should tell you that the studies were reviewed by independent experts who verified the results."

"Who were these experts?"

"Consultants hired by the attorneys for Rudolph Ettinger."

"Great." Joanna groaned under her breath, now realizing that Donors International was working hand in hand with Ettinger's lawyers, feeding them all the information they'd need to nail Memorial Hospital in court. She wondered if that was the payoff Donors International had promised to Ettinger to avoid being sued.

Joanna looked up at the giant video screen in the control room at Donors International, feeling especially irritable. Her neck and back ached from sitting and staring up at the screen for the past hour. Via satellite hookup, she and David Dellacorte had spoken to the doctors in Budapest who had cared for the donor of William Arthur Warren's liver. The Hungarian physicians could offer no insight into why the transplanted liver was filled with cysts.

Now the transplant coordinator was punching numbers into the keyboard at the console, trying to re-establish a connection with doctors in Athens. She puffed away on a cigarette held between her lips, oblivious to the ashes that sprinkled down on the desk.

Joanna waved a hand in front of her face, trying to clear the air, and turned to David Dellacorte. "How many ultrasound studies have you done on patients with transplanted livers at Memorial?"

"Twenty-two," Dellacorte said. "And Ettinger was the only one who showed up with cysts. We also reviewed the autopsy slides from eighteen other liver transplant patients who died and none had cysts."

"So," Joanna concluded, turning back to Adler, "our data clears us from guilt just as much as your data clears Donors International, doesn't it?"

"Perhaps," Adler said. "But Ettinger's lawyers must feel differently. Otherwise, why would they sue Memorial and not Donors International?"

"Maybe they know something we don't," Joanna said and watched Adler's reaction. He shrugged his shoulders and kept his face expressionless. But Joanna still felt he was holding something back. Something important.

There was a loud burst of static as the giant video screen lit up with flashing, zigzagging lines before forming an image. Two heavy men, middle-aged, with thick gray-black mustaches appeared on the screen.

"Good afternoon," Adler said. He was seated at the console next to the coordinator, a microphone in front of him. "Thank you for joining us. We have Dr. Joanna Blalock here with us and she'd like to ask you some questions regarding the young boy who donated his liver for transplantation. Would you please introduce yourselves?"

Joanna watched the Greek physicians closely. The surgeon, Dr. Diodonis, was dressed in a scrub suit; the family doctor, Dr. Pappas, wore a white coat. Both spoke English very well, and Joanna guessed that they had trained in America.

"Dr. Pappas," Joanna began, "thank you for taking time from your busy schedule."

"I only hope I can help." Pappas opened a thick hospital chart and began flipping through pages.

"As you know, the liver that was transplanted has subsequently been found to have hemorrhagic cysts and we're trying to determine why." Joanna paused, giving time for the sound of her voice to carry to Greece. "Was there any history of polycystic disease in the boy or his family?"

"None whatsoever," Pappas said promptly.

"Were his liver or kidneys ever palpable on physical examination?"

"Never."

"Did you ever take X rays of his liver or kidneys?"

Pappas turned to the surgeon and spoke briefly in Greek, then turned back to the microphone. "We did an MRI study following the tragic accident. The liver and kidney appeared normal."

"Is polycystic disease common in Greece?"

Pappas shrugged. "It's uncommon, but not extremely rare."

The images on the screen began to fade, becoming blurred and indistinct. Loud static noise filled the air. The transplant coordinator hurriedly punched numbers into the keyboard, trying to reestablish the video connection with Athens.

Joanna leaned back from the microphone and rubbed the muscles in her neck. The only thing she was getting out of the discussions was a sore cervical spine. She had hoped that at least one of the boys would have had polycystic disease, an unusual disorder in which large cysts formed in the kidneys and sometimes the liver. It was a hereditary disorder, often asymptomatic, that usually didn't become clinically obvious until the teen years or later. But in polycystic disease most of the cysts were in the kidneys, not the liver, and when they were in the liver they usually didn't amount to much. Joanna sighed wearily. She was grabbing at straws and knew it. The images of the Greek doctors reappeared on the screen.

"Dr. Pappas," Joanna started in again, "does the boy who donated the liver have a large family?"

"Are you referring to first-degree relatives?"

"Yes."

"A mother and father and three older brothers."

"I would like ultrasound studies done on the liver and kidneys of all first-degree relatives. We will of course pay for the studies and give each member a fee of a thousand drachmas for the time we take up."

"That will be no problem."

"And I would like copies of the MRI studies that were done to be sent to us for review."

"They'll go out by international courier first thing in the morning."

Joanna quickly glanced down at an index card she was holding. "Did the boy ever have liver disease?"

"No."

"Were liver function tests ever performed on him?"

Pappas squinted an eye, thinking. "A few years ago there was an outbreak of hepatitis at the boy's school. We checked his blood for the virus and did liver function tests. Everything was normal."

"One last question. Did the boy ever take drugs or medications?"

"Not to my knowledge."

"Was he ever exposed to estrogen or testosterone?"

"Never. His sexual development was normal and he had no feminizing features."

"Thanks for your time." A blank wall, Joanna thought. A big nothing. "Dr. David Dellacorte, a transplant surgeon from Memorial Hospital, is here and would like to ask Dr. Diodonis a few questions."

Joanna pushed the microphone over to David Dellacorte. She leaned back and closed her eyes as he introduced himself and began to question the Greek surgeon. They talked about the shape and size and color and texture of the boy's liver. They discussed in detail the area of the liver near the common duct. That was where the largest and most prominent cysts were found.

"The cysts were as large as marbles, you say?" The Greek surgeon's bushy eyebrows arched.

"Some were even larger," Dellacorte said.

"Oh, I wouldn't have missed those," Diodonis assured him. "Not in the area of the common duct. That's the area where we spend the most time when removing the liver."

"They had to have been there," Dellacorte said, thinking aloud.

"Perhaps they were," Diodonis suggested. "But maybe they were so small we missed them."

Dellacorte looked at the screen quizzically. "And then they suddenly grew after transplantation?"

Diodonis shrugged. "Just a thought."

Joanna quickly reached for the microphone. "Have you ever heard of this happening before?"

"Not this rapidly," Diodonis said. "But it certainly happens in polycystic disease. The cysts are initially very small, microscopic in size, and then over years they grow and grow until they squeeze out all the normal tissue."

Joanna's interest was heightened. "And what might cause them to grow like that?"

"Who knows? Maybe immunosuppressive drugs could do it."

"Have you seen this phenomenon occur?"

"Oh, no," Diodonis said easily. "I was just theorizing."

Shit, Joanna cursed to herself and pushed the microphone back to Dellacorte. The last thing she needed was more guessing without any scientific data to back it up.

"However," Diodonis went on, "I did see cysts develop in a transplanted liver once."

Joanna grabbed the microphone again. "When?"

"About two years ago," Diodonis said, then paused, apparently thinking back. "He was a man in his sixties who thought his new liver would rejuvenate everything, including his sex life. Unfortunately, he was impotent and stayed that way after his transplant. So he began taking large amounts of Chinese herbs to enhance his sex drive. It worked well but it also caused cystic degeneration of his liver."

Joanna's mind raced ahead. Testosterone! It had to be testosterone. "What can you tell us about this Chinese herb?"

"It was very popular in Europe because it worked so well. It was not licensed as a drug but was available in health food stores. It was eventually taken off the market because it contained large amounts of testosterone and other substances that no one could identify."

Joanna nodded slowly. "So it's no longer available in Europe?"

"It's no longer available legally, in stores," Diodonis corrected her. "But I'm told the rich and powerful still use it extensively. They send their private jets to China to pick up large quantities of the herb. To an old, impotent man it's like gold, you see."

"Yes, I see," Joanna said slowly, thinking about rich and powerful men, like William Arthur Warren and Rudolph Ettinger, who could send their jets anywhere, anytime. She wondered if they were impotent and had learned of the Chinese herbs in their multinational boardrooms. "Did this herb have a trade name?"

Diodonis smiled thinly. "In most countries it was marketed under the name Superman."

"Is there any chance you could obtain a sample of the herb for us to study?"

"I doubt it, but I'll look around."

"Thanks for your time, Dr. Diodonis."

Joanna leaned back in her chair as the video screen went blank. She wondered if the answer to the cystic transplanted livers was going to be that easy. She'd have to ask Ettinger about it, knowing that he might well lie about using any drug for impotency. Men were funny that way. Of course, she couldn't question William Arthur Warren. But she could talk with his wife. Pamela Warren would know.

"Impotency is common in people with chronic liver disease," Dellacorte mused. "Two of my transplant patients had penile implants done."

"Can testosterone cause this much liver damage?" Adler asked.

"Absolutely," Joanna said. "We've seen livers that were almost destroyed by anabolic steroids."

Adler strummed his fingers on the desk, hoping that Ettinger and Warren had taken some testosterone-laden Chinese herbs. That would be a perfect answer. And Donors International wouldn't have to put up with the incessant demands from Rudolph Ettinger and his lawyers anymore.

Adler turned to the transplant coordinator. "Karen, can you tell us if any of our liver transplant patients were taking Chinese herbs?"

"Sure." The coordinator pressed a button and the video screen turned a deep blue with a white dot in its center. She punched numbers into the keyboard and watched as data flashed across the screen. The word *processing* appeared, blinking off and on. Then the screen went blank and lit up again.

NO HERBAL MEDICINES LISTED.

"Damn." Dellacorte groaned.

"That doesn't mean no one took the herbs," Adler explained. "It simply tells us they weren't listed. Some patients don't consider herbs to be drugs." He looked at Karen again. "Have your assistants check all the raw data compiled on William Arthur Warren and Rudolph Ettinger. See if either patient mentioned Chinese herbs."

"Or impotency," Dellacorte added.

Joanna watched the coordinator walk away from the console. Her gaze went back to the screen and the words *herbal medicines*. So many agents could damage the liver, she thought. Drugs, herbs, toxins, viruses. And sometimes the damage was so intense the liver failed altogether. Like in Kate. Poor Kate! She walks into some damn cave in Guatemala, doing her job, and the next thing she knows she's dying of liver failure. Joanna still had trouble accepting the fact that Kate was dying. But she was, and her only hope was a transplant.

Joanna turned to Jason Adler. "I have to talk with you about a personal matter."

"Of course," Adler said, caught off guard. He glanced at Dellacorte briefly and wondered if Joanna Blalock wanted the surgeon present.

"My younger sister has liver failure and will probably need a liver transplant in the near future," Joanna said quickly.

"I'm sorry to hear that," Adler said sincerely. "Tell me the clinical history."

"My sister is an archaeologist and was on an expedition into a rain forest in Guatemala. The group went into a cave and exposed themselves to a denguelike virus that behaved like ebola. Most of the group have died horrible deaths. Kate survived, but she has terrible liver damage."

"Is there any chance of recovery?"

Joanna shook her head sadly. "Virtually none."

"We'll be glad to help," Adler said and moved his chair in closer. "I take it that Dr. Dellacorte will be the surgeon?"

"Yes."

"An excellent choice," Adler said. "Now, it's up to Donors International to obtain the very best tissue-typed liver for your sister. Let me tell you our procedure. First we tissue-type your sister and put the information in our computer network. As donors become available they're matched up against your sister's tissue type. When a good or excellent match is found, your sister's doctors are notified. If they want the transplant to be done, we arrange to have the liver delivered to Memorial Hospital. Our usual fee is two hundred and fifty thousand dollars, but we do give professional discounts to physicians and their families. Your cost would be two hundred thousand."

"And what if a good match can't be found?" Joanna asked.

Adler gestured with his hands. "Let's hope we don't reach that point."

"But what if we do?" Joanna persisted, her voice rising.

"You might want to consider a lobe transplant from a close family member."

"A what?"

"A lobe transplant," Adler repeated, then added, "It's a new procedure."

"It's risky as hell," Dellacorte interjected. "Both for the donor and the recipient."

Joanna turned to Dellacorte. "Tell me about it."

Dellacorte took a deep breath, wishing that Adler hadn't brought up the subject. "It's an experimental procedure in which one lobe of the liver is taken from a family member and transplanted into the patient. Immunosuppressive drugs are given to the patient to prevent rejection of the lobe. The patient's liver is left in with the hope that it will regenerate itself. If that happens, the immunosuppressive drugs are stopped and the transplanted lobe withers away, which is fine because the patient's own liver is now working. If the patient's own liver never recovers, then the immunosuppressive drugs are continued to prevent rejection of the transplanted lobe."

"The lobe donor has to be a close relative?" Joanna asked.

Adler nodded. "A brother or sister would work best."

Joanna nodded. "If need be, I'll do it. I'll be the donor."

"It's very experimental," Dellacorte reminded her.

"How many times has the procedure been done?" Joanna asked.

"Three that I know of," Dellacorte said.

"And what were the results?"

"Two went badly. One is still alive."

Joanna considered the options. Neither was good, but a complete liver transplant from a well-matched donor seemed best—if a donor could be found.

"I would advise against a lobe transplant," Dellacorte said. "You'd be putting yourself at risk and you'll be giving up a lobe of your liver. That lobe represents the liver tissue you have in reserve if your own liver becomes damaged later on."

Joanna nodded but said nothing.

"If you wish us to proceed," Adler said gently, "we'll require a twenty-five-thousand-dollar deposit. When the appropriate donor is found, the remainder of the bill must be paid in full."

Joanna stared out into space, wondering how she was going to come up with $200,000. She could borrow $50,000 against her pension fund and probably another $25,000 on her condominium, but that still left her $125,000 short. Joanna clenched her jaw tightly, hating what she was doing. She felt like she was in a marketplace, bidding for organs that were being auctioned off. A well-matched liver was going to go to someone who could bid $200,000.

It wasn't right, and Joanna knew it. There were thousands of patients on waiting lists for liver transplants, all waiting patiently for their turn to come up. But if Joanna could swing the financing, she would probably bypass those whose needs were just as urgent. And she had no doubt that some of the money she paid would be secretly funneled to the donor's family, thus ensuring that the liver went to Donors International.

Joanna took a deep breath, disgusted with herself. Any way she looked at it, she was buying a liver for her sister. And that wasn't right. It was wrong, very wrong. But Kate would die without the transplant.

"If you wish to give the matter more thought," Adler said softly, "we'll understand."

"I want to proceed as quickly as possible," Joanna said and pushed her chair back. "You'll have my check in the morning."

19

Joanna stopped outside Rudolph Ettinger's hospital room and took a deep breath, readying herself. As she reached for the door, it suddenly opened and David Dellacorte stormed out. His face was beet-red and the veins in his neck were bulging. He stomped down the corridor, muttering obscenities under his breath.

Joanna hurried after him, catching him by the arm. "What's wrong, David?"

"That son of a bitch," Dellacorte hissed.

"What?"

Dellacorte clenched and unclenched his fists, trying to control his anger. "You offer to help the guy and he bites you. It's like petting a rattlesnake."

Joanna looked at him, puzzled. "I thought the chief of surgery had taken over the case?"

"He has," Dellacorte said, calmer now. "But it seems Mr. Ettinger has developed two very large hepatic cysts that are compressing what little normal liver he has left. The usual surgery to decompress the cysts would be very risky in Mr. Ettinger's case, and the chief is reluctant to operate. So he's asked me to do it, using a laparoscopic technique I've developed. It's far safer and easier on the patient. But it's still risky in someone like Ettinger."

"And Ettinger has agreed to let you do it?"

"Of course," Dellacorte said and waited for a nurse to pass by before continuing. "He's no fool. He's been told that I'm the best there is at this procedure."

"Maybe you'll generate some goodwill when you—"

Dellacorte forced a laugh, interrupting her. "Forget it! He still plans to sue Memorial, and he can hardly wait to begin destroying my reputation in his newspapers and on his television stations. Regardless of how the surgery goes, I lose."

Joanna nodded, now understanding the no-win situation Dellacorte faced. "He'll surely blame you if things go wrong."

"And if things go well, the chief, who will be in the operating room with me, will get all the credit. You know, the usual bullshit—great judgment, the captain guiding the ship through rough seas." Dellacorte sighed deeply. "All I'm trying to do is help and the bastard responds by embarrassing me."

"With so much animosity between you and Ettinger, I'm surprised you haven't dissociated yourself from the case."

"I've given it some thought."

"Then why not do it?"

"Because I'm stupid," Dellacorte said and walked away.

Joanna went back to Ettinger's room, wondering why he was so intent on alienating the people who could help him the most. It was probably because he felt so helpless, Joanna decided. Ettinger was a man of immense wealth and power, accustomed to giving orders, not taking them. But in Memorial Hospital he had no power and was totally dependent on others. He couldn't even pee without doing it in a bottle so the doctors could carefully monitor his intake and output of fluids. Sad, Joanna thought, but it still didn't excuse his rudeness to the staff.

Joanna knocked briskly on the door and entered. Rudolph Ettinger was propped up in bed reading the *Wall Street Journal.* He put down the paper and glared at Joanna over his reading glasses.

"What the hell do you want?" Ettinger grumbled.

"I've got a few questions I'd like to ask you."

"Make it quick."

Joanna moved in closer to the bed. Ettinger seemed thinner than before, and his skin had a peculiar gray pallor that was seen in patients with terminal illnesses. "Mr. Ettinger, have you ever taken vitamins or Chinese herbs?"

"Hell, no!"

"Think hard, Mr. Ettinger," Joanna said, pressing him. "I'm interested in Chinese herbs. Particularly those that are believed to enhance a man's potency."

Ettinger threw the newspaper to the floor and struggled up to a sitting position. "What in the hell are you talking about?"

"I'm talking about drugs or herbs that enhance your sexual powers. Now, did you take them? Yes or no?"

Ettinger's eyes narrowed angrily. "Is this some kind of joke you're playing?"

"It's no joke," Joanna said evenly, staring back at him. "We've learned of another transplant patient who developed liver cysts after he took herbs to make himself more potent."

Ettinger's face softened, just a little. "And he developed cysts like mine?"

"Much the same."

Ettinger shrugged uncomfortably. "I've taken some vitamins and minerals, I guess. And there was some amino acid proteins that help build up your muscles."

"Any Chinese herbs?" Joanna persisted, feeling that Ettinger wasn't divulging everything.

After a long pause Ettinger said, "I don't remember anything like that."

"Is it possible you took herbs?"

"Anything is possible."

If he was taking herbs for impotency, he wasn't going to admit it, Joanna decided. "Mr. Ettinger, would you allow me to go to your home and go through your medicine cabinet?"

"Absolutely not," Ettinger said at once and his face closed. "I don't remember taking any damn herbs and that should be good enough."

"Did you take anything to enhance your sex drive?"

"I've already answered that," Ettinger said brusquely. "Now, I think you'd better leave."

Joanna hesitated, trying to come up with a compromise. Maybe Ettinger was taking herbs but forgot. People with failing livers often had memory lapses. "Would you have one of your associates or family members bring in all the medicines and pills you have at home for me to examine?"

"I think that can be arranged," Ettinger said and lay back on his pillows, now exhausted. "You may not believe this, young lady, but I do want to know why my liver has gone bad, and I do want you to fix it so I can return to decent health."

"Well, to be honest, you're not helping us very much in our investigation."

Ettinger coughed weakly. Phlegm rattled in his throat. He lay perfectly still with his mouth open and looked more dead than alive. "You want to be honest? Good. Let's be honest. My liver is failing and there's nothing you or anybody else can do to reverse it and I'm going to die because of it. So don't expect me to eagerly assist you in some investigation that won't help me one bit." Ettinger coughed again, not bothering to put a hand over his mouth. "This hospital got itself into this mess. Let it get itself out."

"I'm sorry this has happened to you," Joanna said sympathetically. "And if you wish to blame Memorial for your problems, you have every right to do so. But there's absolutely no proof to back up your accusations."

"My lawyers think otherwise."

"Be that as it may, while you're hospitalized here I would ask that you treat the staff with the same courtesy that they've extended to you."

Ettinger smiled thinly. "I see you've been talking with Dr. Pelligrini."

"His name is Dr. Dellacorte, and I would be particularly nice to him if I were you."

"Why?"

"Because he's the one person at Memorial who can give you a bit more time on this earth," Joanna said and walked out.

20

"Christ! I hope I never need bypass surgery," Lou Farelli said.

Jake nodded grimly. "I hear they split your chest open with a saw and then staple you back together."

Farelli winced at the thought. "It's got to hurt, got to hurt."

"But they say it works. It's like getting a new set of coronary arteries."

"I'd just as soon keep the ones I've got."

They were standing outside the Coronary Care Unit at Memorial, waiting for the cardiologist looking after Maury Glazer. The pawnbroker had suffered a severe attack of angina and had been rushed to Memorial in critical condition. Thrombolytic agents had been injected into Glazer's coronary arteries, but he hadn't responded and was now being prepared for bypass surgery.

The doors to the unit opened and both men stepped back as a gurney whizzed by. It carried an old man, an O_2 cannula in his nose, his skin more blue than white. Jake glanced into the unit before the doors closed, looking for Maury Glazer. He saw only doctors and nurses hurrying about.

"I hope the doc lets us talk with Glazer." Jake reached for a large envelope tucked under his arm and extracted a twelve-by-twelve-inch photograph of Tony Boyette. He studied it briefly. "It's a pretty good photo, huh?"

"Damn good," Farelli said, vigorously chewing gum. "The photographer managed to get the sleaze out of Tony's face."

"Did you check out Tony and his actor friends?"

"Everybody's clean. And I also checked for locksmith shops around Tony's acting school. There are none within a mile of the place. The closest one was in North Hollywood."

"Did you show them Tony's picture?"

Farelli nodded. "Nobody knew anything."

The doors to the Coronary Care Unit opened and Dr. Alex Berman walked over. He was a tall, slender man in his forties with gray-brown hair and wire-rimmed glasses. "Lieutenant Sinclair?"

Jake showed his shield. "I appreciate your taking the time to talk with us."

"Not at all," Berman said. He took off his glasses and rubbed at his eyes. "What can I do for you?"

"We need to talk with Maury Glazer."

"I'm sorry," Berman said, "he's unstable enough as it is."

"It's a murder investigation, Doc."

"Lieutenant, I appreciate your problem," Berman said. "But I just don't think my patient can tolerate questioning."

"We've got a killer on the loose," Farelli joined in.

Berman's brow went up. "The freeway killer? The sniper?"

Jake ignored the question. "We need ten seconds of Glazer's time. We show him one photograph. He says yes or no."

"Can you imagine some lunatic shooting at innocent people for no reason?" Berman asked, still thinking about the freeway sniper.

Jake shrugged. Sure, he thought. Just go to East Los Angeles and watch the drive-by shootings that occur every night. "Ten seconds. That's all we need."

Berman hesitated, now deliberating. He nervously scratched at his neck. "Ten seconds. One question. That's it."

"Good," Jake agreed quickly.

"And if he's already asleep from his pre-op medications, tough luck. You're not waking him."

"Okay."

The detectives followed Berman into the unit. It was much larger than Jake had thought it would be. There were no rooms, just beds lined up head first against the walls. All the patients were hooked up to IVs and monitors, some to respirators. The machines made noises, the patients didn't. For some reason Jake found himself walking on his tiptoes.

Maury Glazer was in a bed at the far end of the unit. He was propped up on pillows, his chest clean-shaven and painted with an orange-colored antiseptic. His eyes were closed. A thin, petite woman with silver-gray hair was at the bedside, holding Glazer's hand.

Berman said softly, "Mrs. Glazer, these are detectives who need your husband's help."

"He hasn't done anything wrong, has he?" Annie Glazer asked anxiously.

"No, ma'am," Jake said quietly. "We just need him to identify someone for us."

Annie Glazer looked at Alex Berman, asking silently if it was all right for her husband to be disturbed.

Berman nodded and patted her shoulder reassuringly.

"The man we're after is a killer," Jake explained. "Otherwise we certainly wouldn't bother your husband at a time like this."

Maury Glazer opened his eyes. "You got a picture?"

"Yeah," Jake said, admiring the man's pluck. "How are you feeling?"

"Like shit. Show me the picture."

Jake handed Glazer the glossy black-and-white photograph. "Remember, these photos always make the person look better than he looks in person."

Glazer studied the picture at length. "I need my glasses."

Annie Glazer quickly opened an eyeglass case and placed the horn-rimmed glasses on her husband's face. He smiled warmly at her, then went back to the picture, holding it up to the overhead light.

"Well?" Jake asked.

"I think it's him," Maury said.

"Are you sure?"

Maury Glazer looked at the picture again. Suddenly he grimaced in pain and made a short coughing sound. "Goddamn angina."

"You can take another nitroglycerine pill if you wish," Berman said.

Glazer placed a tablet under his tongue and waited for it to dissolve. Within seconds the pain eased. He looked over at his wife and smiled. "Annie, stop worrying. I'm going to be fine."

Glazer adjusted his glasses and studied the photograph again. "Can I be absolutely sure it's him? No, not a hundred percent. In the photo he looks younger and his skin is smoother. But I'll bet it's him."

Jake asked, "Think you could pick him out of a lineup?"

"Absolutely."

"When you're better we'll put this guy onstage for you."

"It won't be long," Glazer said and turned to his cardiologist. "What do you think, Dr. Berman? Two or three weeks should do it, huh?"

"Maybe a little longer than that," Berman advised.

"Two or three weeks," Glazer insisted. "I'm a real fast healer."

"Your time is up, Lieutenant," Berman said.

As they were leaving the unit, Jake remembered another question he wanted to ask the pawnbroker. Had Boyette signed a receipt or form when he hocked the watch? If so, they'd have a sample of his handwriting and maybe his fingerprints too.

Jake turned and saw a gurney approaching Glazer's bed. Berman was stepping aside; Glazer's wife was crying. Jake took out his notepad and wrote the question down. He'd check with Glazer's son at the pawnshop.

Outside the unit Farelli stopped at the water fountain and took a quick drink. "I'd be scared shitless if I was about to undergo bypass surgery. But Glazer ain't, is he?"

Jake shrugged. "I think he's just like the rest of us. He's plenty worried."

"Are you saying he's putting on a show for us?"

"Not for us. For his wife."

"Yeah," Farelli said quietly, thinking if it was him he'd do the same thing for his Angela. "What do you want me to do about Tony Boyette?"

"Pick his ass up."

* * *

"Where the hell are my goddamn eggs?" Pamela Warren screeched.

"Mrs. Warren," Jason Adler said placatingly, "it's been over ten years since—"

"I don't give a damn how long it's been," Pamela cut him off. "Those are my eggs and I want them. And I want my husband's sperm too."

Adler looked over at Matthew Dunn, director of in vitro fertilization at Donors International. "Perhaps Dr. Dunn can explain the situation better than I."

"Let me tell you what the problem is," Dunn said straightforwardly. "The technique we used ten years ago to freeze eggs was imperfect. We found that after a few years the eggs often disintegrated on thawing. Accordingly, we tended not to keep them for longer periods of time."

Pamela glared at Dunn. "Are you telling me my eggs have been destroyed?"

"I'm saying they might have been," Dunn said. "We'll know more when we check through all of our deep freezers."

"You'd better come up with those eggs," Pamela threatened, "and damn quick."

Dunn stared back at Pamela Warren and her attorney. "And what happens if we don't?"

"You'll find yourself in a courtroom," Pamela snapped.

Dunn's expression hardened. "That doesn't bother me, Mrs. Warren. I'm sure the judge will understand when I tell him that our earlier freezing technique damaged the eggs and we were concerned they could produce abnormal fetuses."

Pamela locked her eyes with Dunn's, wondering if he was bluffing, disliking him as much now as she had ten years before. He was still a gruff, tactless man. And unattractive too, with a forehead that was too broad and lips that were too thin. "You had no right to destroy my eggs."

"I didn't say we did," Dunn said tersely. "I said we may have."

Pamela bristled, realizing that the doctors at Donors International had the upper hand. They could always make up some bullshit story that a judge or jury would believe. "If those eggs aren't found, I'll sue the hell out of you."

Dunn shrugged, unconcerned. "You'll lose."

"So will you," Pamela said angrily. "And you'll lose big time. It'll be the type of lawsuit that the news media love, particularly since it involves William Arthur Warren. When all is said and done, your reputation and the reputation of your program at Donors International will be ruined."

Dunn flicked his wrist disdainfully. "Mrs. Warren, your husband is dead and he's no longer news. And neither are you."

"We'll see about that," Pamela seethed. "We'll see how the media reacts to a young widow trying to conceive a child with her murdered husband. And we'll see if the court won't appoint someone to search through your records and freezers to determine what happened to my eggs. And perhaps the eggs of other women as well."

"Now, now!" Adler interceded quickly. "Let's not be hasty. We just need more time to search through our freezers. I can assure you we are looking for those eggs as diligently as we can."

"Well, I can assure you that if my eggs aren't found in three days, you'll end up in court facing a huge lawsuit." Pamela turned to her attorney. "Mr. Diamond tells me that legally those eggs are my property, not yours. And you can't do anything with them without my permission. Right, Allen?"

"Absolutely," Diamond said. "The eggs and sperm belong to the couple. They have joint custody. Thus, when the husband dies, his wife inherits."

Adler said, "I have no reason to doubt you, but you understand that we must have our lawyers examine the matter. And all of this will have to be disclosed to the Warren estate."

"Examine all you want," Pamela snapped. "Just come up with my eggs." She lit a filtered cigarette and blew smoke into the air. She had a feeling that Adler and Dunn were lying, that they knew where her eggs were. But why would they hold them back? What would they have to gain? And then there was the problem of Adler's discussing the matter with the executor of her husband's estate. The Warren brothers would fight tooth and nail to stop her from obtaining the frozen sperm and eggs. Well, screw them. The sperm and eggs belonged to her and any offspring she produced would be a legal heir.

Pamela puffed on her cigarette and looked out the window of Adler's office. She could see the side of the mountain with trails leading up to the Japanese garden that she and her husband had been shown on their first visit to Donors International. That had been ten years ago. It seemed like a lifetime.

"Mrs. Warren, I don't mean to pry," Adler said delicately, "but could I ask what you wish to do with the eggs? I, of course, know that your husband recently passed away and I was just wondering . . ." He let his words trail off.

"I plan to fertilize the eggs with my husband's sperm and become pregnant," Pamela said without hesitation. She took a deep breath and decided to play it sad. Not too much grief. There was no need to overdo it. She took out a handkerchief and dabbed at her eyes. She lowered her voice appropriately. "It was my husband's wish to have one more child. I promised him we would try again and succeed. My husband may be gone but my promise still holds." Nice touch, she thought. Almost like a deathbed vow.

"I understand," Adler said gently, but he was almost certain the woman was lying.

"Those eggs are very important to me," Pamela said quietly.

"Of course," Adler said, "and we'll do everything possible to find them."

Pamela's face hardened. "You've got seventy-two hours."

"That should suffice," Adler told her. "But again, I must warn you. Even if we find them, eggs frozen by the old method tend to disintegrate on thawing."

"What about the sperm?"

"They last indefinitely," Adler said. He tapped a pencil on his desk slowly, thinking. "Of course, if we found his sperm your best chance to conceive would be for you to undergo the injections that make you superovulate. We could then fertilize the fresh ova and have a much higher success rate."

Pamela shook her head sadly. "I can't take those shots again. I had terrible reactions to the last ones. Remember?"

"Yes, I do," Adler said, now recalling the allergic-type reactions she'd had. "It would be dangerous to try that again. I'm sorry."

"So am I." Pamela pushed back her chair and got to her feet.

21

Kate looked worse, much worse. She was semicomatose again and was now babbling nonsensically. Joanna gently squeezed Kate's hand but got no response.

Joanna glanced over at the nurse. "When did she slip back into a coma?"

"Sometime in the middle of the night," the nurse said. "She was talking coherently before she went to sleep."

"Has she been seen by the neurologist?"

The nurse nodded. "Early this morning." She reached for a thick chart and handed it to Joanna, saying, "I'm going to step out for a moment. If you need anything just press the buzzer."

Joanna flipped through the chart until she came to the neurology consultant's note. He believed Kate had hepatic encephalopathy, a comalike state induced by liver failure. It was thought to be caused by metabolic abnormalities, particularly the accumulation of ammonium in the blood. Sometimes it was reversible, sometimes not. Joanna scanned her sister's most recent laboratory studies. Kate's liver function was deteriorating further, her blood ammonium level elevated. Hepatic coma, Joanna thought sadly, the last stage of liver disease.

She squeezed Kate's hand again and again but got no response. Kate appeared moribund now, with sunken eyes and so much weight loss that she seemed little more than skin and bones. And she wasn't moving, not even a twitch. A gruesome picture suddenly flashed into Joanna's mind. Kate lying in an opened casket. Oh, Lord!

Joanna brought Kate's hand up to her bosom. "Don't die on me, Kate. Please don't leave me," she pleaded softly.

Kate made a low, coughing sound. Joanna quickly leaned over her sister, looking for signs of consciousness. Kate's eyes stayed closed as she continued to cough weakly.

"Kate," Joanna spoke into her sister's ear. "Kate, can you hear me?"

There was no response.

A cough reflex, Joanna thought dejectedly, not a conscious effort.

The door to the isolation unit opened and Mack Brown walked over. The nurse was a step behind him, carrying a plastic bag of plasma.

"Kate went into hepatic coma early this morning," Mack said. He reached across the patient and pried her eyelids open. Kate tried to turn her head away from the light. "But not too deep."

"Is it going to be reversible?"

"Maybe," Mack said, now checking the temperature chart at the foot of the bed. "I heard some rales in her lungs that may signal the onset of pneumonia. Sometimes infections tip patients with liver disease into hepatic coma."

"I take it that Kate's now on antibiotics?"

"Big doses. And I'm going to give her another bag of plasma."

Mack took the plastic bag of plasma from the nurse, double-checked the label and handed it back. "Our friends in Guatemala found another survivor of the epidemic and sent us a unit of his plasma. It contains very high titers of antibodies against the virus. We may as well try it. I don't think it can hurt."

Joanna sighed. "It's desperation time, isn't it?"

"I'm afraid so," Mack said grimly. "Her liver is not going to recover, and unless Kate receives a transplant she'll die. She's been tissue typed and I put her name on the waiting list."

"Do you think the national transplant network can find her a liver?" Joanna asked, checking the clock on the wall. She had an appointment with a banker later in the morning to arrange a loan on her condominium.

"Oh, I think they could if given the time." Mack stepped back as the nurse hooked up the bag of plasma to Kate's IV. "The problem is time and numbers. There are over four thousand people on the waiting list, many of them just as sick as Kate. And unfortunately she's got an unusual tissue type. It's going to be very difficult to find her a good donor."

"I talked with the people at Donors International yesterday," Joanna said. "She's now on their list too."

"They supposedly come up with excellent matches," Mack said, now watching the plasma flow into Kate's arm. "But I hear they charge an arm and a leg."

Joanna shrugged. "You do what you have to do."

"Well, we'll just have to keep your sister going until a good donor comes along, won't we?"

Joanna nodded, thinking about the liver lobe transplant she'd discussed with Dellacorte. A lobe of Joanna's liver could keep Kate alive until a suitable donor was found. She decided to get herself tissue typed and talk with Dellacorte about the sister-to-sister lobe transplant again. Today. "Are we sure the virus has cleared out of Kate's system?"

"Pretty much so. Why?"

"Because I'd hate to see Kate get a new liver only to have it infected again and destroyed again by the same virus."

"I don't think that's a major concern," Mack said easily. But it was a possibility nonetheless. One virus sitting in some corner of Kate's body could infect the liver and multiply and multiply until it destroyed every hepatic cell. It could happen. But Mack wasn't about to discuss that possibility with Joanna Blalock. She had more than enough to worry about already.

"Jesus," was all Jake could manage to say. The skeleton they'd unearthed in the Santa Monica Mountains had been strung together with wire and now hung from a hook in the wall. The man had a face and a body. He wore combat fatigues, boots and a floppy rain cap. Jake moved in for a closer look. "Where are his eyes and hair?"

"We don't have that information," Joanna said.

Jake glanced over at her, puzzled. "You can get the characteristics of his eyes and hair from his military record. I assume that his government photograph wasn't so good, huh?"

"We don't have a name for our man yet," Joanna said. She was sitting on a counter in the forensics laboratory next to the skeleton. "We have four names and we don't know which one is right."

"Let's take it from the beginning," Jake said. "You've got me confused."

"The man here was constructed just on the evidence we found in that grave," Joanna explained. "The skeleton told us his height and shoe size. We approximated his weight from his bones and the size medium garment he was wearing."

"How do you know he was wearing combat fatigues?"

"From bits of clothlike material that had stuck to his bones."

Jake reached up and touched the man's head. It was made of a smooth plasterlike material. "Where'd you get his face from?"

"A computer. We fed in the size and contour and density of each facial bone and the computer came up with a face. No eyes or hair, though."

"I'll be damned," Jake said, impressed. "Now, what's this about four names?"

Joanna was about to answer, but her mind suddenly went to another possible source of money for Kate's transplant. Kate's insurance company. Maybe they'd contribute. They were an HMO, and Joanna knew they would resist like hell paying for any big-ticket procedure. But it was worth a try.

"The names?" Jake prompted.

Joanna motioned over to Lori McKay. "Lori can give you those details."

Jake studied Joanna for a moment and wondered what was bothering her. He'd noticed it when he first walked in. She seemed distracted and not focused, totally unlike the way she usually behaved when hot on the trail of something important. Maybe she wasn't feeling well, he thought, or maybe it was something about him that was bothering her. He knew she was still upset with him for not being there when she needed him. She'd never let him forget that.

"So," Jake said and turned to Lori, "tell me about the four names."

"We contacted Walter Reed Hospital and they were able to come up with four patients with the initials J.R. who had supracondylar plates inserted in 1974." Lori reached into her coat pocket and took out an index card. "There was a James Robert Anderson, a James Robert Butler, a Jerome Robinson, and a Jimmy Rogers. All in their twenties, all Caucasian, all survived their surgeries."

"Shit," Jake growled. "It'll take forever to track them down."

"Why?" Lori asked.

"Because the names are from over twenty years ago," Jake told her. "People move, people get lost, people die. Believe me, it's going to be a bitch finding them."

"Maybe not," Joanna said, sipping coffee from a mug and stealing a quick glance at the wall clock. "I sent our skeleton down for some special X rays. They may narrow it down for us."

"How will the X rays help?" Jake asked.

"You'll see," Joanna said. "The X rays are on their way up now."

She glanced at the wall clock again. One-thirty P.M. In an hour she was going to meet with the people at the credit union to try to arrange a $50,000 loan using her pension fund as collateral. And maybe she could get a little more, but not much. Just count on the $50,000, she told herself. That, together with the $25,000 loan on her condominium, would give her $75,000. She was still $125,000 short, but it would more than cover the down payment. Maybe she could get some long-term financing from Donors International.

"We tried to pick up Tony Boyette," Jake said, breaking into her thoughts.

"Who?" Joanna asked absently.

"Tony Boyette. The guy who hocked William Arthur Warren's watch."

"Somebody hocked the victim's watch?" Lori asked, ears suddenly pricked. "I didn't know that. Nobody told me."

"We just found out," Jake lied.

"Well, tell me about it," Lori said and moved her chair in closer.

Jake groaned to himself, wishing he hadn't brought up the subject of Tony Boyette. He briefly summarized the details for Lori, mentioning his visit to the pawnbroker just prior to bypass surgery. He decided not to tell her about meeting Tony in Pamela Warren's hospital room. She didn't need to know that. "The pawnbroker didn't give us a one-hundred-percent positive ID, but it was close enough."

"You said you tried to pick him up," Lori said. "Did he split on you?"

Jake shook his head. "He's somewhere in the Mojave Desert, shooting a commercial. He's due back tomorrow."

Joanna asked, "Did your pawnbroker come through the surgery all right?"

"Like a trooper." Jake smiled. "He'll have no problem picking Tony out of a lineup. And stupid Tony also signed a receipt at the pawnshop using a phony name. So now we've got a sample of his handwriting. We're going to nail this guy good."

"Cool," Lori said happily.

There was a loud knock on the door. Everyone turned, waiting for it to open. Lori gently fluffed her hair in place and wet her lips.

"Come in," Joanna called out.

The door opened and a hospital messenger entered carrying a stack of X rays. Lori stared at the man, disappointed. She had been hoping it would be David Dellacorte. She had left a message with his office telling him that she'd be in the forensics laboratory between one and three. He wasn't going to show up—just like he hadn't called after their date as he'd promised.

It had been a really good first date, Lori thought. They had talked and kissed and gotten real close. Then his damn beeper went off. He kissed her again and promised to call. But he hadn't. Goddamn him and all men who say they were going to call and then didn't.

Joanna took the X rays from the folder and flicked them up on the viewboxes. "These are copies of X rays taken on the four patients at Walter Reed Hospital after their surgeries. Pay particular attention to the flecks of metal embedded in the femur. It's a shrapnel fingerprint, for want of a better term. Now, let's see which one matches up with the X rays taken on our skeleton."

Joanna reached for the new X rays taken on the skeleton and carefully compared them to the others. She went through all four sets of X rays from Walter Reed Hospital, then came back to one and studied it closely. The metal flecks were in the exact same positions as the flecks in the femur of the skeleton. "A perfect match. Our man's name is James Robert Butler."

"Well, well," Jake said quietly. He turned and spoke to the half skeleton, half man hanging from a hook. "Tell me, James Robert Butler, what were you doing in those mountains and why did they have to kill you for doing it?"

22

Pamela Warren hated the motel room. It was small and sleazy with worn furniture and plaster walls that were cracked and peeling. She could hear a couple arguing loudly in the adjacent unit. A prostitute was yelling at her customer, demanding more money. There were more shouts and threats, then a door slammed.

Pamela lit a cigarette and glanced at the paper-thin drapes covering the window, despising the room and despising herself for being there. This would be the last time, she promised.

The shower in the bathroom came on and Tony Boyette began singing an Italian song he'd learned for a bit part in a movie. Pamela cringed, disliking his voice and manners and everything else about him. She had to get him out of her life. But how? He would hold on to her tighter than a leech, dreaming about the millions and millions of dollars he was promised but would never see. He was really in the way now. She considered the possibility of buying him out, but that wouldn't work either. No matter what she gave Tony, he'd keep coming back for more. Pamela puffed absently on her cigarette, concentrating, trying to come up with a plan. The shower went off and the singing stopped.

"Hi, beautiful!" Tony came into the room, dripping wet. He toweled himself off, spreading his legs slightly as he worked on his groin. Outside there was the noise of traffic rumbling by on Sunset Boulevard in West Hollywood. Tony raised his voice above it.

"Pretty soon we'll be at the real ritzy places, huh? Like the penthouse suite at the Mirage in Las Vegas?"

"You bet," Pamela said, trying to sound enthusiastic. She studied Tony briefly in the bright light. He was starting to age, with obvious crow's-feet and sagging skin on his neck. He wasn't going to age well, she decided, not well at all.

"Look at this damn towel," Tony said and held it up. "It's filthy from that desert sand. I can't get that shit off me." He threw the towel onto the floor by the bed. "But I can't bitch about the money they paid for that stupid commercial. A grand for two days' work in the desert. Not bad, huh?"

"Not bad at all."

"But for us that's going to be like tip money, isn't it?"

She crushed out her cigarette. "If the service is good."

"Ho! Ho!" Tony laughed and jumped into bed next to her. "I'll give you good service, all right."

Pamela automatically put her arms around him, but felt nothing. She closed her eyes and envisioned she was in bed with Tom Cruise. She could get off on that.

Tony sensed her beginning to warm as he gently stroked the skin on her back between her bra and silk panties. Her breathing increased and she pressed up against him. "Oh, baby," he whispered to her, "we're going to have a good life together. And don't worry about the cops. I can handle them."

Pamela quickly pushed him away and sat up. "What cops?"

"They came by to question me," he said calmly. "But I was on the commercial shoot in the desert. They told the apartment manager they'd be back later."

"Something's wrong," Pamela said, instantly on guard.

"So they come back to ask some questions," Tony said, unconcerned. "So what?"

"I'll tell you what," Pamela said sharply. "They saw us together in my hospital room and now they come back to see you but not me. That means they've found out something about you, something that bothers them."

"Hell, I'm clean," Tony assured her. "I've got no record."

Pamela's mind was racing, trying to find any mistakes they might have made. Maybe somebody had seen Tony in the neighborhood the night of the murder. Maybe he'd left a fingerprint somewhere. She looked at him icily. "Did you spend the goddamn money you got from the safe? Did you flash a big roll of bills in front of your friends?"

"No," he said promptly. "I swear it."

"What about the wallet and credit cards?"

"They're at the bottom of the ocean."

"Shit." She growled loudly. They'd made a mistake and everything was going to come undone.

"Oh, come on," Tony said soothingly. "You're making a mountain out of a molehill. The cops are just scratching around to see what they can find. They don't have a damn thing on me."

Oh, yes they do, Pamela thought as she lay back. They've got something that connects you to my husband.

Tony moved in closer and began nibbling on her neck. "Don't worry about it. I can deal with the cops. And remember, there's no way they can hook me up to you except that we both went to the same acting class."

Pamela suddenly smiled to herself. Let the cops pick up Tony and let Tony talk his head off. She would deny everything, except knowing him. There was no evidence to show she had conspired with Tony to kill her husband. And even if they found out she was sleeping with Tony, so what? There was no law against that. She'd deny knowing what he was going to do. She would rage in public at Tony for killing her husband. And if necessary she'd hire a damn good lawyer—maybe the lawyer who'd defended O. J. Simpson. He'd get her off, and Tony would go to jail and maybe the gas chamber. It could work out so well. And she'd be rid of Tony Boyette once and for all.

She felt Tony's hand between her legs and started to think about Tom Cruise again.

There was a sharp knock on the door. "Sorry to bother you, folks. We've got a big water leak in the bathroom beneath yours. I've got to check it out."

"Goddamn it," Tony growled, reaching for the towel on the floor and wrapping it around his waist. He waited for Pamela to pull the sheet up over her, then opened the door.

"D-don't," Tony stammered, backing up, his eyes bulging. He

was looking into the barrel of a large gun. The man holding the weapon was dressed entirely in black, from his hat to his boots.

The man signaled with the revolver for Tony to turn around, then raised a flattened hand and brought it down forcefully on Tony's neck. The karate chop was expertly placed. Tony saw a brief flash of lights. Then everything went dark. He dropped to the floor like dead weight.

Pamela bolted from the bed and reached for the phone. But the man moved quickly and knocked the phone from her hand. He grabbed her by the arm and put the barrel of the gun against her mouth. "Make a sound and you're dead," he said coldly.

"Please don't hurt me," Pamela said, her voice a squeal.

"Just do as I say." The man backed up slowly and kicked the door shut. Then the man kicked hard at Tony's ribs to make certain he was out. Tony didn't move. The man moved toward Pamela. "Lie down on the bed, face down."

"Please—"

"Do it!" the man said hoarsely and jabbed her chest with the gun.

Pamela lay on her stomach, petrified with fear. Desperately she tried to think of a way out. She might be able to make it to the bathroom, but that wouldn't help. It had only a small window high up. She could never get through it. The phone was nearby on the floor. Maybe she could—

"Put your hands behind you," the man ordered.

She followed his instructions and offered no resistance as he quickly taped her hands and feet together. Then he balled up a handkerchief and forced it into her mouth.

"Good," the man said.

Out of the corner of her eye she watched the man open a small briefcase and take out a long piece of cord and several syringes. He moved over to Tony and, picking up the limp body, placed it in a sitting position in a chair near the bathroom door. Then he came back to Pamela.

He turned her over on her back and leaned over her. Gently he bit into the skin of her abdomen, leaving bite marks but not drawing blood. He did it a half dozen times.

"Nice, huh?" the man said, looking up at her. "Want more?"

Pamela was about to nod, thinking he might just be a freak. Maybe she could still get out alive. But then she saw his eyes. Cold, lifeless eyes. She struggled violently against the tape that bound her, twisting and turning.

The man gave her a thin, humorless smile and reached for the syringe.

Lori wondered when David Dellacorte was going to make his move. They had touched and kissed and felt each other passionately, but they still had their clothes on. She wondered if it was something she had done—or not done.

"What's the matter, David?" she asked softly.

He took a deep breath and exhaled loudly. "I'm not sure I want to get involved right now."

"Is there someone else?"

"Was."

"But you're still thinking about her, huh?"

"Sometimes," he admitted.

They were sitting on a couch in the living room of her bungalow in Santa Monica. Before them logs were blazing in a giant brick fireplace that went from ceiling to floor. She nestled her head against his chest. "Were you married to her?"

"We were thinking about it."

"And?"

"And it didn't work out."

"What happened?"

"It just didn't work out," David said, his face now closed.

Men! Lori thought to herself and wondered why they were so frightened to talk about their feelings. It was so stupid to keep feelings bottled up deep inside where they could only gnaw away at you. Getting emotional information from men was next to impossible. Christ! It was like pulling teeth. "Are we going to be able to get around this?"

"I think so."

"How?"

David grinned broadly. "Well, for starters we could get you out of that silk blouse you're wearing."

Lori smiled back at him and climbed on his lap, straddling his thighs. She leaned forward, her nose touching his. "Are you any good at unbuttoning?"

"Totally inexperienced," he said, kissing her lips and chin.

"I'll show you how," she purred and undid the top button on her blouse. As each button came undone, David leaned his head in and kissed the newly exposed area of her chest.

The blouse was half off when the phone rang. "Damn." She groaned unhappily. "I can't believe this."

Lori disengaged herself from his embrace and picked up the phone. She spoke briefly and slowly put the phone down. "I've got to go," she said and began buttoning her blouse. "They've found Pamela Warren dead in a motel room."

"Jesus!" David said, shaking his head. "Was it suicide?"

"They didn't say."

23

The police had left the bodies exactly as they had found them. Pamela Warren was lying on her back, half on and half off the bed, a needle and syringe still stuck in her arm. Tony Boyette was sitting in a chair near the bathroom door, his arms dangling down. A thick cord around his neck was tightly strung over the door and tied to the doorknob on the opposite side. The skin of his face was colored a deep purple. He had clearly hanged himself.

"Looks like fun and games," Lori said, her tone clinical.

"Yeah, I guess." Jake Sinclair was studying a spoon on the floor. It was coated with a sticky black substance. Thai heroin, he told himself, and stirred it with the tip of a pencil. The Thai drug was ten times more powerful than the usual stuff bought on the street. Addicts and shooters with any sense stayed away from it because its potency was so unpredictable.

Jake stood and brushed the lint off his trousers. "You figure Mrs. Warren did the shooting for both of them?"

Lori nodded. "I would think so. She was a nurse, and they're trained to do venipunctures."

Jake scratched at his head, trying to put all the pieces together. "I'll tell you what bothers me, McKay. We've got two people shooting the same poison and for all the world it looks like one died from the shot and the other by hanging."

"I'm not sure I follow you."

"Well, this black heroin is very powerful stuff," Jake explained. "It kills the shooter almost immediately, usually while the needle is still in the arm. Just like in Pamela Warren. Now we're certain Tony got his shot, yet he still had time to hang himself. It doesn't fit."

"Oh, I can think of a dozen explanations for that," Lori said, unconcerned. She held up a hand and counted on her fingers. "First, they may have had different tolerances to the drug. Some people can handle very large doses, others can't. Secondly, maybe she gave her lover a smaller dose and thus he had time to go through all of his shenanigans. Thirdly, maybe she gave him his hit just as he started the autoasphyxiation process. Then the cord would have tightened as he fell forward. Kind of like he hanged himself while he was already dying. And on and on and on. Believe me, all of the explanations I've given you are valid."

"Maybe," Jake said, still unconvinced. He studied the corpse of Tony Boyette and wondered again what the mind-set was in people who shut off their air supply for sexual gratification. Sexual asphyxia. Orgasms were supposedly magnified by briefly depriving the brain of oxygen. But sometimes people went too far too long and ended up like Tony.

Jake shook his head slowly, amazed at what people were willing to do for a little extra pleasure. Crazy. His gaze went to Pamela Warren. Lori was now taking a thermometer from Pamela's rectum and reading it. "How long has she been dead?"

"No more than a few hours. Her body temperature is just at ninety-eight degrees."

Jake carefully stepped around the phone on the floor, its receiver off the hook. He envisioned Pamela Warren suddenly realizing she had overdosed and frantically grabbing for the phone, knowing she was going to die. Too bad, he thought. You play with fire, you get burned.

He glanced into the small bathroom with its stained basins and dripping faucets. The toilet was making a gurgling noise, its seat cracked and off center. Jake wondered what Pamela Warren was doing in a piece-of-shit place like this. Maybe it was the easy availability of drugs on the street. Or maybe she got a kick out of slumming it.

He moved across the room to the door and looked out. Curious guests were lined against the railing on the opposite side of the motel, straining for a better view of the murder scene. They were drinking and laughing and talking loudly. A party atmosphere. A circus.

Lou Farelli hurried up the stairs and came over. He paused for a moment, catching his breath. "The manager knows from nothing. Tony checked in and paid in advance. The manager caught a quick glimpse of Mrs. Warren. He said they'd been here at least a dozen times in the past."

"What about the drugs?"

Farelli shrugged. "He says what people do in their rooms is not his business."

"Suppose we run his ass in?" Jake said brusquely. "Maybe then it would become his business."

"Maybe," Farelli said, "but I don't think the guy's a dealer—if that's what you're getting at."

"How did he happen to find the bodies?"

"The phone in this unit was off the hook," Farelli told him. "The light on the switchboard kept blinking, so the manager came up to see if anything was wrong."

Across the way the crowd by the railing was becoming more unruly. Someone dropped a bottle of beer, and it hit the pavement below with a loud pop. The crowd roared its approval.

"Get all those people back in their rooms," Jake said. "Question them individually. See if anybody saw anything unusual."

Farelli's brow went up. "Did you find something?"

Jake gestured with his hands noncommittally. "Just some things that maybe don't fit right."

Farelli turned to leave, then came back. "There may be something else that doesn't fit right."

"What?"

"I checked with a couple of dealers near here. They swear that black shit from Thailand hasn't been on the streets for months. Nobody will touch it."

Farelli turned to leave again, but he stepped aside to make room for Joanna Blalock. She was dressed in jeans with a leather bomber jacket. A real knockout, Farelli said to himself, thinking that Jake Sinclair was the luckiest man in the world to have had her and the dumbest to have let her go. "Hi, Doc."

"Hello, Sergeant," Joanna said warmly. She moved past Jake with a nod and went over to the bodies.

Lori stared at Joanna, mouth agape. Not again, goddamn it! Not again! She looked over at Jake, seething, furious with him for bringing in Joanna Blalock without bothering to ask.

Jake read Lori's face and moved closer to her. "You think the murder of William Arthur Warren was a high-profile case? Well, it was nothing compared to what this is going to be. A multimillion-aire's widow dies in a cheap motel shooting drugs with a would-be actor who gets his jollies by hanging himself. We're talking big money and kinky sex and probably infidelity. Every newspaper and television station in America will be covering this story day in and day out. Now, the smart move is to bring in all the help we can find. The last thing we want to do is make a mistake here."

"I haven't made any mistakes," Lori snapped.

"Are you sure?"

Lori took a deep breath and tried to calm herself. "You could have at least asked me."

"Yeah, I should have," Jake admitted.

Joanna overheard the conversation as she wriggled her hands into latex gloves. She felt sorry for Lori McKay, knowing the feeling of having someone push you aside because they consider you inexperienced. But Jake was right. There were two deaths in the same prominent family, one murdered, the other a suspected suicide. It would make headlines everywhere, particularly with the sexual angle. Two deaths so close together, probably not related— but who knew? There would be so many possible interconnections, so many nuances that a young medical examiner would miss. Jake was right to bring in someone more experienced, but as usual he hadn't considered the other person's feelings.

Joanna walked around Tony's body, checking the cord on his neck and the deep bruise it had left anteriorly. His face was a pur- plish color, congested with blood. She pulled down the corpse's lower eyelids and saw the small petechial hemorrhages that went along with strangulation by hanging. On his arm were two venipuncture marks, both recently made.

She studied his genitals. No semen, probably no orgasm. No evidence for prolonged or rough sexual intercourse. Next she went to his back. There were no marks, no scratches. Finally, she lifted up his long black hair and exposed the back of his neck. She examined the indentation where the cord had dug into the skin and above that a distinct ecchymotic area at the level of the second cervical vertebra. Carefully she measured the size of the ecchymosis. "Who is he?"

Jake held out his hand and made the introduction formally. "Joanna Blalock, meet Tony Boyette."

Joanna's jaw dropped. "The man who hocked William Arthur Warren's Rolex?"

"The one and the same."

"Son of a bitch," Lori said softly, her voice filled with wonderment. She moved her lips for several seconds before she spoke again. "Pamela Warren's lover killed her husband?"

"Looks that way," Jake said, grinning slightly.

Lori's eyes suddenly widened. "Do you think she was in on it?"

"What do you think?" Jake asked.

"Son of a bitch," Lori muttered again. "She had to be."

Joanna nodded slowly. "And he bashed her head just to throw us off."

"Yeah," Jake said and nodded back, "that was a nice touch."

"And that's how Tony got into the house so easily," Joanna went on. "She probably turned the alarm off for him or left a door open."

"And he didn't take the diamond necklace because it really wasn't a burglary," Jake added. "Taking the old man's watch and the money from the safe was a cover-up. They just wanted to kill him."

Joanna moved over to the body of Pamela Warren. Briefly she studied the needle and syringe still stuck in the dead woman's arm. "Do we know what was in the syringe?"

Jake pointed to the spoon on the floor. "We think it's black heroin."

"Potent stuff," Joanna said, carefully scanning the carpet. She got down on her hands and knees and searched under the bed.

Jake couldn't pry his eyes off Joanna. She had a wonderfully shaped butt, and the tight jeans accentuated it. "What are you looking for?"

Joanna didn't answer. She searched under the spread and beneath the pillows. She even looked into the pillow cases. Nothing. Carefully she rolled Pamela's body on its side and glanced under it. Again nothing.

"Pamela Warren had everything," Lori mused, "and she threw it all away for this. And then she kills herself with some stupid drug."

"I'm not sure she killed herself," Joanna said evenly. "Somebody may have done it for her."

Jake's eyes narrowed. "Why do you say that?"

"Because something is missing," Joanna said.

"What?"

"A tourniquet," Joanna told him. "I can't find the tourniquet."

Jake furrowed his brow, not understanding. "What the hell are you talking about?"

"I'm talking about a tourniquet," Joanna said and searched the bed one last time. "It's usually a length of tubing or rubber that venipuncturists tie around the upper arm to make the veins stand out. It's very difficult to find a vein without using a tourniquet."

Lori thought quickly. "Not always. Some men, for example, have very prominent veins that you can see without using a tourniquet. Or maybe Pamela Warren just used her hand as a tourniquet on the guy. You know, she squeezed tightly on the upper part of his arm."

"That's possible," Joanna conceded. "But only for Tony's injection. What about Pamela Warren? We've been assuming she injected herself, but there's positively no way she could have done that without a tourniquet. And since she died almost immediately upon injection, the tourniquet should be on the bed next to her, and it's not. Which means she didn't inject herself."

Jake rubbed at the back of his neck, thinking. "So you think somebody else did it?"

"Right," Joanna said. "And whoever did it made a mistake. He took the tourniquet with him."

Jake sighed heavily, still not convinced. "We're going to need more evidence than that to prove they were murdered."

"There *is* more," Joanna told him and walked over to Tony's body. She bent his head forward and lifted his long black hair, exposing the back of his neck. "He's got a big ecchymotic area on the cervical spine just below the skull. It was probably made by a karate-type blow."

Jake shrugged. "Maybe it was caused by the hanging."

Joanna shook her head firmly. "In hanging victims, all of the bruising and soft tissue damage is located in the front of the neck. This is very evident in Tony." She tilted his head back and loosened the cord on his neck. "Take a look."

Jake leaned over and examined the deep groove and bruising in the front of Tony's neck. "So you figure the murderer came in, chopped Tony on the neck and shot them up with Thai heroin?"

"It seems that way, doesn't it?"

Lori asked, "Why did the murderer bother with the sexual asphyxia setup? The Thai heroin was enough to kill them, and it still would have looked like they accidentally overdosed."

"The asphyxia business was added window dressing to throw us off," Jake said. "It damn near worked, too."

Lori went over to Pamela Warren's body and examined her arms and hands. "There are no bruises or broken nails. I guess she didn't put up a fight."

Lori removed her hand from Pamela's wrist, but for a moment the latex glove she was wearing seemed to stick to Pamela's skin. Lori quickly took off her glove and felt Pamela's wrist. "There's something sticky on her skin."

Joanna hurried over and felt Pamela's arms from shoulders down to fingers. The stickiness was limited to the wrists. She reached for a magnifying glass and carefully examined the skin over the wrists. Small pieces of white thread adhered firmly to the skin surface.

Quickly Joanna moved to Pamela's legs, again finding stickiness and embedded bits of threads on the skin about her ankles. "Pamela Warren was tied up, hand and foot, with adhesive tape. No doubt about it."

Joanna turned and nodded to Lori. "Good find. I would have missed it."

Lori beamed. Her face began to blush, so she brought up a hand and coughed to cover it.

Joanna checked the floor and bed again, then the wastebaskets in the bedroom and bathroom. "There's no tape. The killer took the used tape with him."

Lori went over to Tony Boyette's body and felt his wrists and ankles. "There's no stickiness," she reported. "He wasn't taped up."

"There was no need," Joanna said. "He was probably out cold from the karate blow."

"So," Jake said, reconstructing the crime in his mind, "the guy comes in, chops Tony, ties up Pamela with tape, shoots them both with heroin, and hangs Tony. Then he unties Pamela, takes the tape and scrams." Jake glanced at the cord around Tony's neck and the needle in Pamela's arm. Somebody went to a lot of trouble to cover up a murder, he thought. "This was done by a real pro. He was no amateur."

Joanna asked, "Who would hire a professional to kill Tony and Pamela?"

Jake smiled thinly. "Who benefits?"

Joanna thought for a moment. "From Tony's death, probably nobody."

"And from Pamela Warren's?"

Joanna thought again, then slowly nodded. "We'd better check her will."

"And the will of William Arthur Warren," Jake added.

Lori looked at Jake, confused. "What does the old man's will have to do with this?"

"Pamela must have inherited a bundle from her dead husband, right?" Jake explained.

"Right," Lori agreed.

"Well, now she doesn't," Jake said. "And maybe that money goes right back into the pot."

Lori nodded, seeing the connection. "And somebody else becomes even richer."

24

"Please open up the safe," Jake said to Richard Warren.

"This safe belonged to my father, not to Pamela," Warren said sharply.

"I don't care whose safe it once was," Jake said, his voice hard. "I've got a search warrant for this entire house, and that includes this safe. Now open it."

"I think you should know that our attorney is at this moment obtaining an injunction to prevent—"

"That's nice," Jake interrupted him. "Meanwhile, open the damn safe."

Warren went over to the wall safe and began turning the dial. He kept glancing over his shoulder at Jake as if to make certain the detective wasn't trying to learn the safe's combination. His first attempt to open the lock was unsuccessful. He cursed under his breath and tried again.

Jake glanced around the library in the Warren home. Nothing had changed since he was last there except that the bloodstains on the wall and floor were gone. He gazed over at the chair where Pamela Warren was supposedly sitting when the burglar entered, then to the place on the floor where she'd dropped her brandy snifter when she jumped up to help her wounded husband. All bullshit. They cold-bloodedly killed the old man for his money. Jake wondered who had pulled the trigger. Probably Tony, stupid

Tony, dreaming of all that money. Well, he wasn't going to be dreaming anymore.

The safe opened and Warren stepped back. "Here you are."

"Please take out the contents and place them on the desk," Jake said. He signaled over to a uniformed policeman to move in closer. With assholes like Warren it was best to have a witness, just in case he decided to claim later that something was missing. The safe contained only insurance policies on the house and its contents. No money. No jewelry. "I need to see a copy of your father's will."

"Why?" Warren asked, now on guard.

"I want to know what your stepmother inherited from your father."

"Nothing," Warren said happily. "She was excluded from the will."

Jake was taken aback. "Are you sure?"

"Absolutely positive," Warren said. "My brother and I are the executors of my father's estate. My father and Pamela had a prenuptial agreement. There was nothing more."

"How much did she get?"

Warren hesitated, wondering how much he had to tell the detective. He wished Alexander Cox would hurry up and get the damn injunction. "Not that much."

"I need a number," Jake said.

"She was to receive two million dollars."

Enough for her to kill for, Jake thought immediately, plenty enough for most people. But there was no way the Warren brothers would have killed Pamela over a couple of mil. That was pocket change to them. "Do you know anyone who would want Pamela dead?"

Warren shrugged. "Nobody I know."

"Would anyone gain from her death?"

Warren rubbed his chin pensively. "Maybe the people she was suing at the reproductive clinic."

"What reproductive clinic?" Jake asked.

"I don't know what its formal name is, but it's associated with Donors International."

Jake reached for his notepad. "Why was she suing them?"

Warren hesitated, hating to go through the nightmare again.

Christ! If the news media got hold of the story they'd have a field day and the Warren name would become a laughingstock. But he knew it was going to come out one way or another. The detective had already gotten the name of Pamela's attorney from Warren. Her sleazy lawyer would happily divulge everything now that his client was dead and thus nonpaying. "When my father married Pamela they decided to have children. They turned out to be infertile, so they went to a reproductive clinic where they tried in vitro fertilization. It never worked."

"So why is she suing them?"

"They froze away some of her eggs and my father's sperm for possible future use." Warren's face suddenly turned hard. "When my father died, Pamela—the bitch—decided that the money she would get wasn't enough. So she went back to the clinic and asked them to impregnate her. That way her offspring would become an heir to the Warren fortune. They couldn't find the eggs and she was going to sue them."

"Jesus." Jake exhaled and shook his head. *Fucking people,* he thought. *What they wouldn't do for money.*

"So," Warren went on, his mood lighter now, "Pamela's death doesn't bother me a damn bit."

Right—Jake smiled to himself—*now you don't have to worry about cutting Pamela and a future child in on the estate.* He studied Warren briefly, wondering if he'd have the balls to have someone knocked off. "When did you learn that Pamela was suing the clinic?"

"Yesterday," Warren said. "I told you earlier that I am an executor of my father's estate. So when the clinic found Pamela's eggs and my father's sperm, their attorneys immediately called my attorneys, who called me. You see, there's a real question as to who owned the eggs and sperm, Pamela or my father's estate."

"Did Pamela know the eggs had been located?"

"I have no way of knowing that."

Jake lit a Greek cigarette, still keeping his eyes on Warren. So if Pamela became pregnant, he was thinking, she'd end up with millions and millions from the Warren estate. And it would probably come right out of the pockets of the Warren brothers. For that kind of money people kill. Or have others kill for them.

"Hey, Jake!" Lou Farelli called out. "Come take a look at this."

Jake crushed out his cigarette and walked over to a small writing desk in the far corner of the library. Farelli was hunched over the opened drawer of a file cabinet. "What have you got?" Jake asked.

"You tell me." Farelli handed Jake a computer disk that was labeled "Medical History—prospective wives (1985)."

Jake studied the label briefly, then looked across the room at Richard Warren. "Mr. Warren, how many times was your father married?"

"Twice," Warren said. "To my mother and to Pamela."

"Is your mother still alive?"

Warren shook his head. "She died in 1976."

Jake handed the disk back to Farelli and pointed to the computer on the desk. "Do you know how to work this thing?"

"Sure." Farelli turned on the computer and removed the disk from its paper folder. He blew dust off the disk and inserted it into the computer. He began punching instructions into the keyboard. Medical data appeared on the screen.

PROSPECTIVE WIFE #1

NAME: PAMELA JORDAN

SEX: FEMALE

AGE: 32

NATIONALITY: USA

RACE: CAUCASIAN

MEDICAL HISTORY: EXCELLENT HEALTH   USUAL CHILDHOOD DIS-
EASES   TONSILLECTOMY—AGE 10

MEDICATIONS: BIRTH CONTROL PILLS

ALLERGIES: NONE

FAMILY HISTORY: PARENTAL GRANDFATHER—DEAD, AUTO ACCI-
DENT, AGE 80   GRANDMOTHER—DEAD, AUTO ACCIDENT, AGE 78
MATERNAL GRANDFATHER—DEAD, HEART FAILURE, AGE 76
GRANDMOTHER—ALIVE AND WELL, AGE 72

LABORATORY: BLOOD TYPE—B POSITIVE   TISSUE TYPE—A1,
A2, A9, A11, A28, B5, B7, B8, B12, B16, DR2, DR4, DR5, DR7

CA: 12-58-47

DOA: 1996

Farelli punched the keyboard again and medical data appeared on another prospective wife. And another and another. William Arthur Warren had extensive health histories on four prospective wives. "This guy really knew how to check out his brides-to-be, huh?"

"Maybe he was a perfectionist," Jake said.

Richard Warren was standing behind Jake, looking over his shoulder. "It wasn't a matter of his being a perfectionist, Lieutenant. My mother died young of colon cancer that ran in her family. I think my father didn't want to go through that again."

"I understand," Jake said, but he wondered why the old man still kept the information in his library when he'd been married to Pamela for ten years. And why would a man collect medical data on *four* prospective wives, every one of them healthy, and then keep the information on a computer disk? A permanent record. Why?

Farelli pointed to the data beneath the tissue type on the screen. "CA: 12-58-47" and "DOA: 1996." "What do you make of these?"

Jake studied the screen briefly. "I don't know what CA stands for, but DOA usually means dead on arrival."

"Yeah," Farelli said, "and the year listed is 1996. Now how did Warren know in 1985 that his wife was going to die in 1996?"

Maybe he planned it, Jake thought. "Give me the disk."

"You got any ideas?" his partner asked.

"Oh, yeah," Jake said. "But none of them make any sense."

He took the disk and left the library.

Joanna slowly put down the phone. The news was good and bad. The good news was that Kate was coming out of her hepatic coma, although she was still very lethargic. The lung infection had apparently precipitated the episode. The bad news was that Kate's liver function hadn't improved despite the infusion of another unit of Guatemalan plasma. One of the hepatic function tests was actually worse. A liver transplant was now inevitable, but a donor had yet to be found either by the national organ procurement network or by Donors International.

Joanna sighed wearily, asking herself again where she was going to get the money if Donors International came up with a good donor. She was still $100,000 short and she'd hocked everything she owned. She wondered again if Donors International had some sort of financing program. Probably not, but she'd ask. It would be humiliating, but she'd ask.

"Got a minute?" Jake called out from the door.

"Sure," Joanna said and pushed herself away from her desk in the forensics laboratory. "What's up?"

"The damndest story you ever heard." Jake told her about Pamela Warren and the frozen eggs and sperm that were lost at Donors International and how she had desperately wanted them found so she could impregnate herself. "And, of course, the child would become William Arthur Warren's heir."

"And Pamela would have control of the child's fortune."

"You got it."

Joanna slowly shook her head. "I thought I had already heard everything under the sun, but this takes the cake."

"And believe me, Richard Warren couldn't have been happier about Pamela's death."

"Of course," Joanna said. "It saved him from a big court battle, which he'd have probably lost. Her death meant millions to him."

"Uh-huh," Jake said, smiling thinly.

Joanna gave him a long look. "You consider Richard Warren a suspect in Pamela's murder?"

"Maybe," Jake said carefully. "Maybe he hired someone to do it."

"I guess anything is possible."

"People do anything and everything for money."

"Yeah," Joanna said absently, thinking about Kate and the $100,000 she needed. She wondered what she'd be willing to do for the money to save her sister's life. Anything, Joanna decided, just about anything. In her mind she went over all of her assets again. There was nothing left to hock.

Jake studied the distracted look on Joanna's face. "The last few times I've been in here I've gotten the feeling that something is really bothering you."

Joanna flicked her hand and muttered, "It's nothing."

"Yes, it is," Jake said. "If it's me or something I've done, tell me.

If you want me to get the hell out, just give me the word and I'm out of here."

Joanna sighed sadly. "Kate is terribly ill and is going to need a liver transplant. It's very, very expensive and I'm a hundred thousand dollars short."

"No problem," Jake said at once. "I'll get it."

"You don't have that kind of money."

"I've got a house I can mortgage."

"Thanks," Joanna said gratefully, "but I can't let you do that."

"It's done," Jake said firmly. "When do you need the money?"

Joanna stared at Jake, caring about him more than she'd ever let him know.

"When?" Jake persisted.

"Soon," she said softly.

"I'll get the paperwork going the first thing in the morning. Okay?"

"I'll pay you back," she promised, "with interest."

"When the bank sends me a monthly bill, I'll just send it on to you. How does that sound?"

"Perfect."

"Good." Jake reached in his pocket and took out a computer disk. "I need—"

Joanna jumped up and grabbed Jake, kissing him hard on the mouth.

"That was pretty good." Jake grinned. "But at a hundred thousand a kiss I don't think I can last very long."

"If only you weren't such an insensitive pain in the ass," Joanna said.

"I know," Jake said and pecked her on the lips. "Now I need your help on something."

"As strange as Pamela Warren and her eggs?"

"Damn near." Jake handed her the computer disk. "This came from a file cabinet in William Arthur Warren's library."

Joanna read the label on the disc. "Medical History—prospective wives (1985)." "What is this?"

"It's detailed medical data on four women, and Pamela is one of them."

Joanna inserted the disk into her computer and began

punching numbers on the keyboard. She moved in closer to the screen and carefully studied the medical information. "Pretty complete, isn't it?" Joanna went back to the data on Pamela Warren. "Do you have any idea why he did this?"

"His son says it's because Warren's first wife died of colon cancer and he wanted to avoid that happening again."

"That's possible. Some forms of colon cancer run in families."

"But don't you think it's strange to keep all this medical data on prospective wives? Shouldn't this type of information be in a doctor's office?"

Joanna shrugged. "Maybe it was. Maybe William Arthur Warren just wanted a copy of the data for himself."

Joanna moved down the computer screen to Pamela's tissue type. She enlarged the area so the numbers of the type were easily readable.

Jake studied the data on the screen. "Why would he want his future wife's tissue type?"

"Some tissue types are known to be associated with certain diseases," Joanna explained. "For example, type B27 occurs with great frequency in ankylosing spondylitis. People who are B27 positive are fifty times more likely to get the disease than those who are B27 negative."

Jake pointed to the data listed as "CA: 12-58-47" and "DOA: 1996." "What does this mean?"

Joanna concentrated on the abbreviations, then slowly shook her head. "I'm not sure. CA usually refers to cancer or carcinoma, but the numbers after it don't make sense. DOA is the common abbreviation for dead on arrival, but I don't think it means that here."

"Why not?"

"Because it's listed under laboratory data. There's the blood type and tissue type, then CA and DOA."

"Could it be some sort of special laboratory test?"

"That's a possibility. There are so many new tests today that it's—" Joanna stopped in mid-sentence and quickly pushed a button on the keyboard. Now all of the medical data on Pamela Warren could be visualized on the computer screen. "I've seen this format for medical information before. Same form, same listings."

"Where did you see it?"

"At Donors International."

"And they do blood and tissue typing tests out there?"

"Oh, yeah."

Jake rubbed at his chin. "That place keeps coming up again and again, doesn't it?"

25

Rudolph Ettinger jerked out of his sleep. One moment he was in a nightmare, the next moment half awake, but never really out of his sleep. In the darkness he saw dots of light glaring at him. Eyes of animals! Animals waiting to attack, ready to pounce on him. Panic gripped Ettinger, and he grabbed at the bedsheets and tried to yell for help. Then the sharp pain in the side of his abdomen jabbed at him and he suddenly realized where he was. In a hospital room at Memorial. His heart was pounding, sweat pouring off him.

Ettinger took a deep breath, trying to calm himself, and looked around the darkened room. The small dots of light he'd thought were animal eyes were on some type of monitoring machine next to his bed.

As his vision accommodated to the darkness, Ettinger saw the door partly ajar, a thin streak of light coming in from the corridor. Now he remembered being moved from the surgical ICU, where he had been observed after the surgery to decompress his liver cysts.

Christ! He hated the ICU, with its dying patients lined up in a row, every one of them hooked up to tubes and monitors and IVs. And when one of the patients died, the staff would quickly pull the curtains around the bed, as if that would somehow contain death and stop it from spreading to the other patients. When the man next to him died, Ettinger demanded to be moved out of the ICU and into a regular room.

Ettinger tried to prop himself up in bed, but the pain stabbed at him again, much sharper this time. He considered calling the nurse for another pain shot, then decided against it. The last shot had probably caused the nightmare and befuddled his mind. He wanted to think clearly. He could push the pain aside. It wasn't that bad.

Let's see, he thought. Where was I? Oh, yes, the ICU and patients lined up like sheep, waiting to die. But that's not going to happen to me. Hell, no! They found one liver for me, they can find another to transplant into me. And if they can't, my people will.

Ettinger peered into the darkness and thought about the instructions he'd given to his second-in-command. *Comb the world, using all of our power and influence and money, and find me another liver. Make sure it's a good or excellent match and offer the donor's family as much money as it takes.*

Ettinger's roots were middle European, his father Hungarian, his mother Czech, and that's where a matching liver was most likely to be found. Agents working for Ettinger were now making inquiries at every major hospital and clinic in Hungary and the Czech Republic as well as in America, England and Canada, where immigrants from Central Europe had once flocked. They'll find one, Ettinger thought confidently. He was offering a million dollars to the donor and a million to the person who found the donor—if the match was excellent.

The door opened halfway and light flooded into the room, hurting Ettinger's eyes. He looked away, blinded for a moment. "What do you want?" he growled.

"Just checking on you, Mr. Ettinger," a nurse said. "Do you need anything for pain?"

"No."

The nurse came over to the IV stand and turned on a small light. She checked the monitor through which the IV line ran and made certain the flow rate was correct. "Everything is fine."

"Then stop bothering me so I can get some sleep."

"We'll do our best." The nurse turned off the light and walked away.

The door closed and Ettinger returned to his thoughts. They'd come up with a new liver, he repeated like a mantra. People would do anything for that kind of money. And once the new liver was found it would be put into the Donors International network, thus assuring that the organ would come to Ettinger and to no one else. And under no circumstances would the surgery be done at Memorial. They had screwed him up once. They wouldn't get a second chance. All they were going to get was a huge lawsuit.

A new liver, he thought, and pictured himself healthy and robust again. It would come.

Ettinger closed his eyes and drifted off, snoring lightly. He slept for only a few minutes before a loud clap of thunder awakened him. He glanced over at the rain-splattered window and the blackness beyond. He snuggled under the sheets, careful not to stretch out and aggravate the pain in his side.

The door opened again and quickly closed. A crack of light still came into the room, and Ettinger could see a figure in the shadows.

"Who's there?" Ettinger asked, eyes straining in the dark.

"Just here to check your IV."

"Not again!" Ettinger said, exasperated. He watched as the figure in a scrub suit approached. "I'm trying to get some rest and you people keep bothering me every five seconds."

"I'll make sure you're not bothered again."

Ettinger looked up and tried to see the nurse's face. All he saw was a face mask. "Are you an intern?"

"No."

The figure bent over and inspected the rubber tubing at the end of the IV line, holding something that reflected light in the dimness. It was made of glass or plastic. Ettinger strained again, trying to identify the object. His eyes suddenly widened. It was a syringe. "What are you doing?"

"Just flushing the line."

Ettinger felt uneasy. Something was wrong, something was out of place. But what? What? He searched his mind desperately trying to come up with an answer. Then it came to him. How did the nurse know the IV line needed to be flushed? The line couldn't be seen in the darkness. And besides, the IV tubing went through a monitor that sounded an alarm if the flow stopped or suddenly decreased.

Frantically, Ettinger kicked the sheets off and tried to get out of the bed, but he found himself being sat on, held in place, as the contents of the syringe were injected into the IV line.

Ettinger fought with all of his might, but in his weakened state he was no match for his assailant. He tried to yell, but his voice was little more than a squeak.

It's a nightmare, he told himself, *just another nightmare. I'll wake up in a second.*

Ettinger felt a terrible burning in his arm, and then his heart began to flutter wildly. The room started spinning, and he heard himself gasping for air.

Wake up! Wake up! his brain screamed. *Please! Please . . .*

26

"There's a beautiful Japanese garden behind those trees," Joanna said.

Jake tried to see through the forested area. "In there?"

"Yes," she said and took his arm. "Come on. I'll show you."

They left the main road leading to Donors International and walked down a pebbled path that was lined with thick shrubbery. Above them the sunlight was blocked out by the intertwining tops of the trees. Nearby a bird screeched loudly, then flapped its wings and flew away.

Jake picked up the pace. He hated closed-in places, particularly when the light was poor. The path sloped upward and around a huge boulder. They walked out into an open area and came to the lovely garden.

"It's striking, isn't it?" Joanna asked, watching a big goldfish swim in a clear pond.

"When you charge people a quarter of a million dollars for an organ, you can afford nice things," Jake said.

"But they deliver, Jake. And they deliver the best."

"Everything's got a price," Jake said and looked beyond the garden to what looked like a dormitory. "What's that structure behind the chain-link fence?"

"A school for children with learning disabilities," Joanna told him. "They set it up as a model program to see how well it would work."

"You mean they wanted to see how profitable it would be."

"I guess."

Jake studied the empty schoolyard and wondered where the swings and jungle gyms and other playthings were. He moved in closer to the fence. In one of the windows of the building he saw a face. A child's face was staring at him. Then it was gone. Jake heard a whining sound overhead and looked up at a surveillance camera on a light pole. "They keep a careful eye on the kids, huh?"

"The children come from wealthy families," Joanna explained. "They would make perfect targets to kidnap and ransom."

Or to kidnap and molest, Jake thought. The world was now so fucked up that defenseless kids needed high fences and surveillance cameras for protection.

"We'd better head back to the road," Joanna said.

"Where's the main building located?"

Joanna pointed to a patch of trees just to their north. "That way. But I think we have to go back to the road to reach it."

"Let's try a shortcut."

They walked out of the garden and down a dirt path, muddy in places from the heavy rain of the night before. Overhead the sky was gray and threatening again. They went through a stand of pine trees and came to a hilly area where the trail sloped abruptly downward. Carefully they inched their way down the soggy path. At the bottom were wooden planks and beyond them were steps leading up to the main buildings of Donors International.

"Jesus," Jake said, impressed. "I had no idea it was this big. Are all of these buildings part of Donors International?"

"Yup." Joanna nodded and pointed with an index finger. "The first building is the reproductive clinic. The second is for organ procurement, and the third one is used for transplant research."

"What's the fourth building?"

Joanna looked over Jake's shoulder at a fourth structure, located behind the research building. She hadn't seen it the first time she visited, and Jason Adler hadn't shown it to her. It was small, less than half the size of the research building, with slit-like windows high up. On the roof was an air-conditioning or ventilation system. As they moved in closer, Joanna could see that the small building was actually attached to the research center by an enclosed walkway.

"Hello!" Jason Adler called out from the patio next to the research building. He came over to meet them. "It's nice to see you again, Dr. Blalock, but I wish it weren't under such tragic circumstances."

Joanna introduced him to Jake, then Adler guided them to a wooden table with park benches. "I hope you don't mind if we talk out here. The rain last night leaked into my office and caused a real mess."

"This'll do fine." Jake touched the bench, making sure it wasn't wet, and sat next to Joanna, facing Adler. "We're investigating the death of Pamela Warren and need your help on some matters."

"Of course," Adler said.

"First, let me tell you this is a murder investigation."

Adler's eyes widened. "But the newspapers reported—"

"Forget the newspapers," Jake said, watching Adler's surprised expression. "She was murdered, and so was the man she was with."

Adler slowly shook his head. "Why would anyone do that?"

"That's what we're trying to find out." Jake took out his notepad and flipped through pages. "When was the last time you saw or heard from Pamela Warren?"

Adler thought for a moment. "A few days ago. She was here with her lawyer."

"And she wanted her frozen eggs and her husband's sperm, right?"

"Correct."

"And you couldn't produce them?"

"We had trouble finding them," Adler said, nodding. "You see, Lieutenant, we have thousands and thousands of ova and sperm frozen away here. The Warren specimens were from ten years ago."

"And she threatened to sue you?"

"Unless we came up with them," Adler said evenly. "She gave us three days."

"So you must have been very relieved when you located them."

"To say the least," Adler said and exhaled heavily. "The last thing we wanted was a multimillion-dollar lawsuit."

Jake flipped a page in his notepad. "Did you notify Mrs. Warren immediately?"

"I notified our lawyers first," Adler said. "From a legal standpoint there was some question as to who owned the frozen ova and sperm—Mrs. Warren or the Warren estate. My attorney advised me to notify Mrs. Warren as well as Mr. Warren's sons, but not to give anyone the specimens under any circumstances."

"What time did you notify Mrs. Warren?"

"In the early afternoon. I left a message on her machine."

"So you can't be certain she got your message?"

Adler gestured with his hands. "I left the message. She didn't call back."

Joanna asked, "How many eggs did Mrs. Warren have frozen away?"

"Four," Adler said.

"So this was her last chance?"

Adler nodded. "And to be frank, her chances weren't very good. The technique we used a decade ago wasn't very sophisticated. Those eggs would have probably disintegrated with thawing."

"What happens to the frozen eggs and sperm now?" Joanna asked.

"We'll keep them until we receive instructions from our attorneys," Adler said. "But I would guess they'll belong to the Warren estate."

Jake tapped his pen lightly against the table, wondering if Pamela Warren really meant to use the eggs. "Was Mrs. Warren aware of the low probability of a successful pregnancy?"

"Absolutely," Adler assured him. "I stressed that point. But she was still insistent. She wanted those eggs."

Sure, Jake was now thinking, she'd want the eggs, even though they might not work. She could always ransom them off to the Warren brothers, who would pay nicely just to get her out of their hair. Everything in this murder revolved around money. Everything.

A loud engine roared to life on the hillside. A tractorlike earthmover began digging a wide channel through the rocky terrain.

Workmen quickly cleared the dirt away and rolled large drainage pipes into the trough.

"The heavy rains have soaked the mountain and caused some landslides," Adler said above the noise. "We're hoping the new drainage system takes care of the problem for us."

Jake studied a segment of the huge pipe. Its diameter was at least three feet. He wondered why such a large pipe was needed just to drain water from a mountainside.

As he turned back to Adler, Jake's notepad slipped from his hands and fell to the ground. He reached down for it and noticed a man sitting behind them at a nearby table. The man was dressed in a scrub suit and was reading a newspaper with his back to them, but his head was rotated so he could overhear the close-by conversation.

Abruptly the man leaned forward and intently studied his newspaper. Jake nodded to himself. The bastard was listening in and knew he'd been spotted and was now trying to cover it up. Jake wondered how long the man had been there.

"Who's the doctor right behind us?" Jake asked.

Adler looked past Jake. "That's Matthew Dunn, director of the women's clinic. Why?"

Because he's been listening in on us, Jake wanted to say, but he held his tongue. "Would he know about Pamela Warren's eggs?"

"Oh, yes."

"I'd like to talk with him."

"Surely," Adler said, then called out to Dunn. "Matthew, could you join us for a moment?"

Dunn glanced up and threw his newspaper aside, obviously annoyed by the interruption. He came over and sat next to Adler. "I've only got a few minutes before my next case."

Adler said, "I think you remember Dr. Blalock. And this is Lieutenant Sinclair. They're investigating Pamela Warren's death."

Dunn barely nodded. "What can I do for you?"

"Tell us about Pamela Warren's eggs," Jake said.

"There's not much to tell. We had the eggs frozen away and had trouble finding them. She threatened to sue if we didn't find them, but luckily we did. End of story."

"Where'd you find her eggs?" Jake asked.

"In our freezer," Dunn said at once.

"You just opened the freezer up and there they were?"

Dunn's face hardened. "We spent hours and hours looking for those damn eggs."

"And you're certain they are her eggs?"

"Positive."

"Did the Warren estate ask that those eggs be tested to make sure they came from Pamela Warren?"

Dunn's eyes narrowed noticeably before he nodded. "Just as a formality."

Jake smiled thinly. "To make certain the eggs weren't switched?"

Dunn stared at Jake, the veins in his neck bulging. "Are you accusing me—"

"I'm not accusing anybody," Jake said, not trusting the man, not even a little.

The noise from the earthmover started again, louder this time. Jake looked over at the hill, wondering if the frozen eggs really belonged to Pamela Warren. If they did, Donors International would be off the hook and Pamela Warren would have had her eggs—either to get pregnant with or to ransom off. Probably the latter. Pamela Warren was a careful woman. Why risk the eggs' disintegrating when they were thawed? The only losers would be the Warren brothers. But would they kill over this? Oh, yeah, Jake decided, for this kind of money they'd kill.

But what if the eggs didn't belong to Pamela? Then the Warren boys would win and Pamela Warren would lose. No! No, she wouldn't, Jake thought again. Pamela would still have won. She would have sued the hell out of the doctors and would have gotten millions and millions. Donors International would have been the big loser.

Jake needed to know if those eggs were Pamela's. It wouldn't tell him who had killed her, but it would tell him who benefited the most from her death.

As the noise from the earthmover faded, Jake turned to Joanna. "What's the best way to determine if those eggs belonged to Pamela Warren?"

Joanna thought for a moment. "Check the DNA in the eggs

against Mrs. Warren's DNA. It should be a perfect match if the eggs are hers."

Jake looked at Dunn. "We'll need a sample from those eggs."

"Nobody touches them," Dunn snapped. "Not without a court order."

"That shouldn't be a problem," Jake said easily.

An outdoor public address system went on. There were brief musical chimes, then the message. "Dr. Dunn, OR four, please."

Dunn got to his feet. "If you have any more questions, they'll have to wait."

"Oh, I'll have more questions," Jake said. "A lot more."

Adler glanced up at Dunn. "Matthew, I'm certain the lieutenant has a very busy schedule and—"

"So do I," Dunn said and stormed away.

Adler watched Dunn leave, then turned back to Jake. "This has been a legal nightmare for us. We're all under a great deal of strain."

"Right," Jake said and scribbled down a note, then looked over to Joanna. "See if Dr. Adler can give us a hand with those computer disks."

"Dr. Adler," Joanna said, picking up the questioning, "there's one more matter you might be able to help us with."

"I'll try."

"We found a computer disk in the library of the Warren home. It belonged to Mr. Warren." Joanna took the disk from her purse and handed it to Adler.

Adler reached for his reading glasses and read the label. "Medical histories on prospective wives? What is this?"

"Apparently Mr. Warren kept medical files on a number of prospective wives. They included extensive personal and family histories as well as blood and tissue types."

Adler handed the disk back. "That's a bit unusual, isn't it?"

"It seems that Mr. Warren's first wife died young of a hereditary form of colon cancer, and he didn't want anything like that to happen to him again."

Adler rubbed his hands together, thinking, then nodded. "I can understand that. Did he do DNA studies to see if there were any abnormal genes present?"

"Not that I know of," Joanna said. "But all of the medical information was listed on a form that appeared to be identical to the one you use on your prospective donors."

Adler was suddenly on guard, his expression much more serious. "We certainly weren't involved in that. I should tell you that most of the information on our donors comes from outside physicians. We just tabulate the data."

"Pamela Warren was one of the prospective wives," Joanna said evenly, watching Adler's reaction.

Adler breathed a sigh of relief. "That explains it. On all of the couples who participate in our in vitro fertilization program, extensive medical histories and tissue typing are performed. We do that to protect ourselves and the parents. It's important to know, for example, whether there are any hereditary diseases on either the father's or mother's side of the family. Or if there's a history of congenital abnormalities. Clearly Mr. Warren modeled his data form on the one we use for our donors."

"Why do tissue types?" Joanna asked, already knowing the answer.

"Certain tissue types are known to be associated with some very unpleasant diseases."

"And why the blood types?"

"To avoid Rh incompatibility between the mother and the newborn."

Joanna leaned back. Adler had all the right answers. "Do you have any idea why he kept medical data on four prospective wives?"

Adler shrugged. "Not at all."

Joanna reached in the pocket of her blazer and handed Adler a slip of paper with CA 12-58-47 and DOA 1996 written on it. "Do you know what these abbreviations represent?"

Adler studied the paper at length, then shook his head. "I have no idea what they are."

"Could they be some specialized laboratory test?"

Adler studied the slip again, muttering the numbers under his breath. For a moment his eyes seemed to light up, but then he shook his head. "No, that's not it."

"What?"

"I thought the CA might stand for carcinoembryonic antigen.

You know, the antigen in the blood that is sometimes seen in colon cancer."

Joanna squinted an eye. "But the usual abbreviation for carcinoembryonic antigen is CEA."

"Exactly," Adler agreed. "And the numbers after it don't make sense."

Joanna's beeper sounded loudly. She quickly pressed a button, silencing it. A chill went through her as a picture of Kate flashed into her mind. "Where's a phone?"

"Here." Adler reached into the pocket of his white laboratory coat and handed her a cellular phone.

Joanna punched the numbers for her office and spoke briefly. Slowly she put the phone down, a stunned expression on her face.

"What's wrong?" Jake asked.

"They found Rudolph Ettinger dead in his bed at Memorial."

27

"Ettinger damn well better have died from natural causes," Simon Murdock growled. "He goddamn well better have."

Murdock was circling the dissecting table that held the body of Rudolph Ettinger. The autopsy room was deserted, doors locked. All of the other tables had been cleared of bodies. The only people present were Murdock, Joanna Blalock, David Dellacorte and Harry Crowe.

Murdock spun around and pointed a finger at Dellacorte. "And if he bled to death from your newfangled surgery, your days here will be numbered."

Dellacorte glared back at Murdock, hating him and the power he held over everyone at Memorial. "Mr. Ettinger was doing very well postoperatively when—"

"He was doing so goddamned well he died," Murdock snapped and started circling the body again.

Joanna slipped on a pair of latex gloves and watched Murdock pace. She had never seen him so agitated, so out of control. But she understood why. Ettinger had been an extremely powerful and well-known figure, and if his death had been caused by physician error, Memorial's reputation would suffer immeasurably. The news media would never let go of it, particularly after they learned he was already in the process of suing Memorial because his transplanted liver had become cystic.

"Why the hell didn't he die at home?" Murdock grumbled.

Joanna waited for Murdock's anger to quiet down. She didn't want him ranting and raving and breaking her concentration during the autopsy. She felt like telling him to sit and be still and stop wasting time. But she had to admit that Murdock's fury had served a purpose. When he heard of Ettinger's death, Murdock ran to the hospital room and screamed and yelled at everyone in sight, making certain no one touched or changed anything on the body. Even the IV tubing and monitor had been left in place. Ettinger had been rolled down to the morgue in his hospital bed.

Joanna studied the nude body of Rudolph Ettinger. He was a small man to begin with, but death made him seem even smaller. Death always did that, and for some reason it was more obvious in men. Joanna glanced at Ettinger's genitals. They were so shriveled they looked like wrinkled folds of loose skin.

Murdock stopped pacing, but he was still cursing under his breath.

"All right, let's begin." Joanna moved in closer to the dissecting table and adjusted the overhead, voice-activated microphone. Ettinger's chest and abdomen had already been cut open, the crown of his skull sawed through. "The patient is a sixty-eight-year-old Caucasian male with a protuberant abdomen and obvious wasting of his extremities. There are small ecchymotic areas on his legs and recent venipuncture marks on his arms. An intravenous line is in place and runs through a monitor."

Joanna reached over to the IV tubing and examined the plastic switch that regulated the rate of flow. "Who turned the IV off?"

Dellacorte thought for a moment and shrugged. "One of the nurses, I guess. The IVs are usually discontinued when a patient is found dead."

Joanna looked over at Murdock. "Who was in the room when you got there?"

"The nurse who discovered the body and Dr. Channing, the chief of surgery," Murdock said.

"No one else had been in the room?" Joanna asked.

"Not to my knowledge," Murdock replied.

"Who was the last person to see Mr. Ettinger alive?"

"The same nurse. She checked on him just before midnight. He was fine."

Joanna nodded to herself. "Would you call Dr. Channing and ask if he or the nurse shut the IV off?"

Murdock tried to think of the significance of the closed-off IV, but couldn't. "Why is that important?"

"Just being thorough," Joanna said evenly. "Please make the call."

Murdock went to a wall phone and made a quick call. When he returned Joanna was peering into Ettinger's thorax, examining the lungs. "What's that?" he asked, pointing to a thick, fibrous area.

"A scarred pleura," Joanna told him. "It doesn't mean much. What did Channing say?"

"He didn't turn the IV off," Murdock said. "He's checking with the nurse now."

Joanna carefully studied the lungs, looking for bleeding or clots in or around the great blood vessels. "The lungs seem fine. There's no evidence for pulmonary emboli."

"Shit," Murdock muttered sullenly. He had hoped to see a big embolism in one of the pulmonary arteries. That would have tied everything up nice and neat.

"Simon," Joanna said, trying to hold her patience, "would you mind not barking into the microphone? It's voice-activated and the typist isn't going to know what to transcribe."

"She can figure it out," Murdock snapped. "Are you sure there are no emboli?"

"Positive." Joanna reached up and pushed the microphone away. She decided to speed up the autopsy and look for obvious possible causes of death. For Murdock's benefit. Once he was gone she'd do a more complex postmortem examination and dictate the report.

Joanna dissected out the heart and lungs en bloc and removed them from the thoracic cavity. She studied the exterior of the heart, then sliced into the walls of the ventricles and measured their thickness. "The heart is normal-sized and I don't see any thrombi."

"What about the coronary arteries?" Murdock asked.

Joanna looked for areas of infarction and didn't find any. She carefully cut into the small arteries that fed the heart. "His coronary arteries are clean."

"Christ," Murdock said disgustedly. "He must have died from something."

Oh, he died of something, Harry Crowe thought. But a horse's ass like Murdock wouldn't know that in a third of all sudden death cases no cause could be found. They just died. Harry believed that God controlled death and that when He wanted to kill somebody He just did it. And if some stupid pathologist couldn't find out why—well, that was too bad. God didn't give a damn about that. Harry glanced over at the body of Rudolph Ettinger, split open and gutted like a fish. He wished Joanna Blalock would hurry up. There were a dozen autopsies waiting to be done.

Now Joanna was inside Ettinger's abdominal cavity. Everything looked normal except for the liver. "His liver is a mass of hemorrhagic cysts." She pointed to an incision in the lower lobe of the liver. "You can see where the laparoscopic surgery was done."

Murdock leaned over, his nose almost touching the cystic liver. "Do you see any hemorrhage?"

"None."

Murdock glanced over his shoulder at David Dellacorte. "You're lucky. If we had found a big hemorrhage you would have had a one-way ticket out of here."

Dellacorte gritted his teeth and tried to hold his temper. The veins in his temple bulged. "Laparoscopic surgeries don't cause bleeds. That's why we do them."

"And they never cause infections either, huh?" Murdock shot back, thinking about a middle-aged woman who'd had laparoscopic surgery on her gallbladder and had been terribly infected with an antibiotic-resistant staphylococcus. She had died and the family was now suing Memorial. "What about septic shock?" Murdock quickly turned to Joanna. "Could Ettinger have gotten an infection from the surgery and died of sepsis?"

"That's always possible," Joanna said. "But we have no evidence for that."

"And besides, Mr. Ettinger was receiving high doses of antibiotics," Dellacorte added.

"He still could have been infected," Murdock persisted.

"You show me a positive blood culture," Dellacorte said, an edge to his voice. "Then we can talk about sepsis."

"We'll see if we just can't come up with that." Murdock turned to Harry Crowe. "Did you take blood cultures for bacteria?"

"And urine cultures too," Harry said.

"Good," Murdock said approvingly. He hoped they could find something that would point the blame at Dellacorte. Wrecking an individual doctor was a lot better than destroying the whole damn hospital.

"Let's do the brain," Joanna said, not wanting to get between Murdock and Dellacorte. She inserted her fingers beneath the crown of the skull—where it had been sawed through—and tried to pry it off. It didn't budge. She tried again, straining. "Harry, I need some help here."

Harry Crowe hurried over. He grabbed the edge of the skull and worked his fingers in, then gave it a forceful pull. The crown of the skull popped off. A small clot of blood flew out and across the table.

"What was that?" Murdock asked, startled for a moment.

"A small clot that was located just outside the dura," Joanna explained as she peered into the cranial cavity and examined the convoluted folds of brain tissue.

Murdock's face lighted up. "A subdural hematoma?"

"An extradural hematoma," Joanna corrected him, "but it was very small. It didn't cause any problems."

She carefully lifted the brain out of the cranial vault. On gross inspection there was no evidence of hemorrhage or thrombosis of any major artery. "Nothing here."

Murdock sighed dejectedly. Things were going from bad to worse. Without a cause of death, he could see another lawsuit on the way.

The wall phone rang and Murdock hurried over to it. He spoke for only a moment and returned to the dissecting table. "Neither Channing nor the nurse turned the IV off."

"Somebody did," Joanna said, concentrating her mind.

Dellacorte asked, "But you don't think Ettinger died because somebody turned off his IV, do you?"

Murdock had to agree. "Stopping his IV fluids certainly wouldn't kill him."

"That's not the point," Joanna said.

"Then what is?" Murdock asked impatiently. "What the hell is so important about the IV being turned off?"

Joanna looked into space and tried to fit all the pieces together. "We know the IV was still running when Ettinger was last seen alive, right?"

"Right," Murdock said.

"Then somebody turned it off while he was alive."

"So what's the big deal?"

"Whoever turned it off didn't want anyone to know the IV was turned off."

Murdock looked at Joanna, puzzled. "How can you be so sure?"

"Because the alarm on the IV monitor never sounded," Joanna explained. "Whoever shut off the IV knew enough to turn off the alarm."

Murdock nodded slowly, still not aware of what Joanna was driving at. "So you're saying it had to be somebody who was familiar with IVs? A doctor or a nurse?"

"Yes."

"But why?"

Joanna pulled the IV from Ettinger's arm and quickly plugged the end of the needle, making certain no fluid escaped. "You tell me. Why would anyone turn off an IV that is running in a patient's arm? Under what circumstances?"

Murdock thought at length. "One reason would be that you were going to pull the IV needle out. You'd shut off the IV first to prevent fluid from spilling out onto everything."

"The IV was still in his arm," Joanna reminded him.

Murdock wrinkled his brow in thought. "You'd stop the flow if you wanted to inject something into the IV tubing near the vein. That way it goes directly into the patient, undiluted. You know, like a drug or—" Murdock quickly reached for the patient's chart and flipped pages until he came to the medication sheet. He read it carefully. "Rudolph Ettinger didn't receive any drugs intravenously last night."

"You mean he didn't receive any IV drugs that were ordered," Joanna said softly.

"But why would somebody want to inject—" Murdock's jaw suddenly dropped. "Oh, Christ!"

28

Joanna came into the forensics laboratory just as a giant ultracentrifuge automatically switched off. The noise from the motor whined down, then the room was quiet. Off to the side the lights on the wall phone blinked, all lines on hold, all incoming calls now routed to the hospital operator. Joanna leaned against the door, exhausted, her feet and back aching from standing at the autopsy table for so long. And despite the time spent, she still didn't know how Rudolph Ettinger had died.

With effort Joanna pushed herself away from the door and walked over to the freezer. She carefully placed the specimens of bodily fluids and tissues from Rudolph Ettinger into the deep freeze, then went to a large blackboard, where she made a long list of the tests she wanted done on the samples. Tissue from Ettinger's liver would be studied extensively for viruses, toxins, drugs, and any other agent that might conceivably cause cystic degeneration.

Joanna stepped back from the blackboard and made certain she had written down all the tests she wanted. Then she remembered the Chinese herb medicine for impotency that induced the formation of hepatic cysts. One of Ettinger's aides was supposed to drop off all of Ettinger's medications for Joanna to examine.

She went into her office and switched on her computer. The screen indicated she had some E-mail. That could wait. She brought up the file on Rudolph Ettinger and studied it. The medi-'

cations he kept at home had never arrived. And now they'd have a difficult time getting anything out of the Ettinger family, particularly with the suspicious circumstances surrounding his death.

Joanna tilted back in her chair, thinking about Ettinger's death and wondering if he too had been murdered. Everything pointed to it, but they would have to find the drug or toxin to prove it.

Joanna punched in a code on the keyboard and the first E-mail message appeared on the screen.

> We need to talk. I'll be in my office until 7 p.m.,
> then over at the Alamo.
>
> Mack

A streak of fear shot through Joanna as she wondered if Kate had taken a turn for the worse. Joanna had been so tied up with work that she hadn't checked on Kate since early morning. She glanced up at the wall clock. It was almost eight. She grabbed her coat and umbrella and hurried out of her office.

Outside the weather was miserable. The rain was coming down hard, pounding against the cement, and a brisk wind pulled at Joanna's umbrella. She wondered if she should go back and get her car, but she decided not to. *To hell with it,* she thought, and pushed on.

A car sped by and sent up a wave of water that splashed on the sidewalk, dousing Joanna's legs. She cursed at the driver but trudged on, remembering a similar incident in San Francisco when a car splashed water over her and Kate, soaking them. They had laughed and laughed at each other. But nothing was funny now. Everything smelled of gloom. Joanna had to fight the depression she felt coming on.

The Alamo was crowded and noisy. All of the tables were taken and customers were standing two-deep at the bar. Joanna took off her coat and searched the room for Mack.

"Hi," Chrissy the waitress said. "Kind of wet out there, huh?"

"Yeah," Joanna said sourly and looked at her damp skirt and soaked shoes. "Is Mack here?"

Chrissy motioned with her head to the small stage at the rear of the room. Mack was sitting next to Patsy Willis, the blonde singer. They were tuning their guitars.

"Is he any good?" Joanna asked, surprised.

"Not bad."

Chrissy led the way to Mack's table and pulled out a chair for Joanna. "He's two ahead of you. You want to double up?"

"No, no," Joanna said quickly. "One at a time is fine."

"Better double up," Chrissy advised. "What with the wet weather and all."

Joanna watched Chrissy walk away, recalling that the waitress had a partially deaf little boy who was studying to learn how to speak. Everybody had their heartaches, Joanna thought sadly, everybody.

The microphone gave out a loud squeal and Joanna looked up at the stage. Mack and Patsy were laughing, still tuning their guitars. Joanna wondered how many sides there were to Mack Brown. He was a damn good doctor and an easygoing cowboy, and he could move from one to the other with hardly any effort. But there was a lot more to Mack Brown than that, Joanna decided. He was a man who knew how to get your attention and hold it.

Mack and Patsy began singing. His voice was good and blended in nicely with hers. Joanna leaned back and closed her eyes, listening to the sweet ballad. "If tomorrow never comes, will she know how much I loved her?" they wailed in harmony. The song was about a cowboy who is lying next to his sleeping lover and wondering if she'd know how much he'd loved her if he didn't awake in the morning. Joanna wished she had a relationship like that. And for the hundredth time she wondered why she didn't.

"Here you go," Chrissy said, placing two shot glasses of tequila and a beer in front of Joanna.

"The salt comes first, right?" Joanna asked.

"Always."

Joanna licked at a pinch of salt, then swallowed the tequila and chased it with beer. "Nice," she pronounced. "It didn't burn at all."

"The good stuff never does," Chrissy said. "Are you and Mack close?"

Joanna hesitated a moment, caught off guard. "Not really."

Chrissy watched Joanna blush and grinned at her. "But you want to be?"

"I didn't say that."

Chrissy smiled broadly and winked.

"What's so funny?"

"People," Chrissy said and walked away.

The song ended. Mack kissed Patsy on the cheek and thanked her for letting him sit in. He bowed to the scattered applause, then came over to the table.

"You've got a good voice," Joanna said.

"Oh, you say that to all the boys." Mack grinned and signaled Chrissy for another round.

Joanna grinned back at him, feeling better already. Then she remembered the E-mail she'd gotten from him and her smile faded. "I got your message. Is Kate worse?"

"She's the same," Mack said. "But I thought I should tell you about a new antiviral drug they're studying at the NIH. A colleague mentioned it to me on the phone this afternoon."

Joanna leaned forward, ears pricked. "Tell me about it."

"First, don't get your hopes up too high. It's not a wonder drug."

"Give me the details," Joanna said impatiently.

"It's got a name that's about a mile long, and in some cases of overwhelming viral infection it seems to help. But it has dangerous side effects."

"How many patients has it been used on?"

"Six. Two got better."

"And the other four?"

"Dead. Two from cardiac irregularities that might have been caused by the drug."

"Christ," Joanna said dejectedly. "The drug killed as many as it helped."

"It's risky, real risky," Mack agreed.

Joanna thought at length, then said, "Would you advise we use it?"

Mack shook his head. "Too risky. A transplant would be safer. But I thought it only right that you know all the options."

"We'll go with the transplant," Joanna said firmly.

Chrissy brought the fresh round of drinks over and announced, "These are Jose Cuervo Eighteen Hundreds. The best tequila under the sun."

"What's the occasion?" Mack asked.

"The bartender likes your singing," Chrissy said.

Outside there was a loud boom of thunder and the entire bar shook. Everybody roared their approval, a few letting out earsplitting cowboy yells. Joanna and Mack swallowed shots of tequila in unison and chased them down with cold beer.

"I think I'm getting smashed," Joanna said.

"Want some coffee?" Mack asked.

Joanna shook her head and smiled. "I'll just keep the feeling going with a little Bud Light, thank you."

As Patsy launched into another bittersweet ballad, Joanna thought about Jake and all the wonderful times they'd had. But that was over, she told herself, and pushed him from her mind.

Joanna leaned her head on Mack's shoulder and listened to the beautiful tune, sipping her beer, then more tequila. She began to float pleasantly, her eyes closing.

"I think I'd better get you home," Mack said.

"You might have to carry me," Joanna said drowsily.

"How much do you weigh?"

"About a hundred and twenty."

"I can handle that."

As soon as they stepped outside a blast of rain hit them. Joanna held her umbrella up, but it didn't help much. The rain was coming down in sheets, at times pushed horizontally by a strong wind. There wasn't a taxicab in sight.

They huddled together and walked quickly down the sidewalk. At the corner the drains were clogged and the intersection was flooded with at least a foot of water.

"Shit," Mack grumbled, "now we've got to go the long way back to Memorial."

"How far is it?"

"Six or seven blocks."

The downpour drenched them as they turned and trudged their way against the wind and rain. The first block was tough going, the second block even tougher because it was uphill. And to make matters worse, Joanna was wearing high-heeled pumps that kept slipping off her feet.

Joanna leaned against a light pole and rested. "I'm not going any farther. Not an inch more."

"If you stay out here you'll probably drown." Mack grinned at her. She was soaking wet and strikingly attractive in the half darkness.

"Too bad then," Joanna said, looking up at the rain and letting it splash on her face. "Too fucking bad."

Mack put his arm around her and they started out again, but she kept leaning on him more and more and her shoes slipped off every other step. He finally lifted her up and began to stagger, now feeling the effects of too many tequilas himself.

Mack laughed out loud, enjoying the wind and rain that reminded him of his boyhood in Texas. With effort he steadied himself and continued down the street. Then he saw a Holiday Inn.

"We're saved," Mack announced.

"Excellent," Joanna said, believing they were back at Memorial. "Take me to my car."

"We're going to spend the night at the Holiday Inn."

Joanna looked up at him, giggling. "Did you make reservations?"

They walked into the hotel lobby, soaking wet, staggering slightly, and laughing. As Mack checked in, the desk clerk stared down at Joanna's bare feet. "Do you have any luggage?" the clerk asked.

"It'll be here later," Mack said promptly.

The clerk nodded knowingly and handed Mack a key.

Their room was large, with a king-size bed and sliding glass doors that overlooked a pool. There were no robes in the closet. Mack handed Joanna a large towel and gently steered her toward the bathroom. "You'd better get out of those clothes."

Joanna studied herself in the bathroom mirror. Her hair was wet and stringy, her light makeup gone. She looked like hell. Her head was still swimming pleasantly, so she had to hold on to the basin while she wriggled out of her wet clothes and wrapped the large towel around herself.

She came out of the bathroom and saw Mack standing by the sliding glass doors, staring out at the pool. He also had a large towel wrapped around himself.

Joanna went to his side and leaned against him. "What are you thinking about?"

"I don't know if I can keep my hands off you," Mack said.

"Is that a song?"

"No. It's a fact."

"Good," Joanna said and let the towel drop from her body.

29

"It's an open-and-shut case," Jake said. "Tony Boyette murdered William Arthur Warren."

"Yeah," Lou Farelli agreed. "There's enough stuff here to convict him twenty times over."

They were standing in a small room at the rear of the police station. In front of them was a table that held all the evidence against Tony Boyette. A muddied pair of sneakers, ten thousand dollars in crisp new bills, and a plastic envelope containing a bitten-off cigar.

"Tony was so stupid." Jake picked up a sneaker with his ballpoint pen and studied the mud and blood smeared on its sole. "He keeps a pair of rotten old sneakers in his closet. Don't ask me why, but he does. And of course the sneakers match the footprints found in the Warren house and the mud on the shoes is identical to the mud on the carpet. And for good measure he steps in some of William Arthur Warren's blood on his way out. Then he pawns the poor bastard's watch instead of dumping it."

"And he hides the money," Farelli said scornfully. "He puts it in the pocket of a coat hanging in his closet. It was the first place I looked."

Jake placed the sneaker down and looked over at the bitten-off cigar. The bite mark on the cigar had matched up perfectly with Tony's teeth. "Tony was too much of an idiot to plan the murder of William Arthur Warren. Pamela had to be the brains behind it."

"All for money," Farelli said, thinking aloud. "She must have wanted that money real bad."

"And her plan might have worked if she hadn't picked a dumb schmuck like Tony for her partner."

Farelli scratched at his head. "You've got to wonder why she chose a piece of sleaze like that for a partner, don't you?"

"Probably because he was willing and able."

Jake lit a cigarette and spat a piece of tobacco from his lip. "I figure it this way. She meets Tony at the acting class and devises a plan to kill her husband. She rubs up against Tony in the class and breathes in his ear. They end up in a motel room screwing their brains out. Tony falls in love, and when he finds out she's really wealthy he falls even deeper in love. She convinces him to help her bump off the old man, and Tony thinks about nothing but being laid and getting his hands on millions and millions of dollars."

"Could be she fell in love with Tony," Farelli suggested. "Some women like sleaze."

"Could be," Jake said, "but I don't think so. My guess is she was just using Tony. Tony had no future with Pamela Warren."

Farelli nodded slowly. "If she was cold-blooded enough to ice her husband, she would have had no trouble doing the same thing to Tony."

"Well, now all of them are dead."

Jake began to pace around the room, a trail of cigarette smoke just behind him. "And their murders are all connected."

Farelli squinted an eye. "How do you figure that?"

"You show me two murders in the same family within a month and I'll show you two murders that are connected."

Farelli caught a puff of Jake's cigarette smoke in his face and breathed it in, loving it. It had been six years since his last cigarette, and not a day passed that he didn't think about lighting up. Farelli brought his mind back to the problem at hand. He remembered what Jake had told him about Pamela's frozen eggs and her idea to get pregnant in order to cash in on more of the Warren fortune. "I can't see the Warren brothers knocking off Pamela because of those eggs. Hell, even the doctors said those frozen eggs weren't going to work. It was a long shot at best for Pamela."

"Yeah, but just suppose that Pamela did get pregnant," Jake

countered. "That child would have been entitled to a third of the Warren estate. You're talking about fifty million dollars. And that is very serious money."

"I guess," Farelli reconsidered. "But why knock off Tony?"

"That's a problem," Jake admitted, "because Tony was a big zero who nobody cared about. Nobody was going to pay a pro big money to ice Tony."

"Maybe Tony just happened to be in the wrong place at the wrong time."

"Uh-uh," Jake said, shaking his head. "That ain't going to work. The killer came prepared to kill two people. He had rope, tape, syringes, heroin. It was well planned. He knew there were two people in that motel room."

"But why knock off Tony?" Farelli asked again.

"I think Tony was just part of the camouflage to make it look like kinky sex and an overdose," Jake said, then smiled thinly. "Tony was just playing a role, another bit part."

"But we're still left with the same question: Why was Pamela Warren killed and who did it?"

Jake mashed out his cigarette. "Maybe the hooker down the hall can help us with the who did it."

They walked out of the office and down a long corridor past rain-streaked windows. Outside the day was dark and cold as the stubborn storm refused to move off Southern California. They stepped around a small puddle on the floor. The ceiling just above them was leaking.

"What's the hooker like?" Jake asked.

"Like most of them. Young and pretty and tough. And she's scared shitless, although she's trying to hide it."

"Has she got a sheet?"

"Nope."

They entered a brightly lit interrogation room. A young woman was sitting at a long table, facing them. Behind her was a uniformed policewoman.

Jake took a seat across from the hooker and offered her a cigarette.

"I don't smoke," she said.

"Do you mind if I do?" Jake asked politely.

The prostitute shrugged, not caring. "I want a lawyer."

"Why? Have you done something wrong?"

The young woman said nothing. She just stared at Jake. If there was any fear in her eyes, he didn't see it.

"Answer my questions and you'll walk out of here," Jake said evenly. "Lie to me and I'll see to it that every time you step out on the sidewalk a patrol car pulls out from the curb and follows you."

The young woman swallowed silently. "What do you want to know?"

"What's your name?"

"Cherrie."

"You do most of your business at the Paradise Motel?"

Cherrie nodded, now examining her nails.

"How many times a week?"

"Like, uh, every day."

"How many times a day do you use a room there?"

"Maybe two or three."

Jake studied the woman's face. She was pretty with catlike features, but her eyes seemed very sad. "And you were there the night they found the dead couple, right?"

"Right."

"Tell me what you saw."

"Well," Cherrie began, "I was tiptoeing out of my—"

"Why were you tiptoeing?" Jake interrupted her.

"The guy I was with had paid for an all-nighter," she explained. "But he fell asleep. Hell, I wasn't going to lie there and watch him snore."

"So you were tiptoeing out," Jake said. "Go on."

"Well, I see this guy dressed in black, everything black, standing at the door down the way," Cherrie continued. "He's knocking on the door, saying he's there to check a leak in the bathroom. Now I know the manager, and the guy in black ain't him."

"So what did you do?"

"I got the hell out of there," Cherrie said indignantly, as if only an idiot would do otherwise. "When I saw the gun I figured the guy was a jealous husband or something."

Jake moved his chair in closer. "The guy had a gun?"

"Yeah. I saw it when the person inside opened the door."

"Well, now," Jake said amiably, "if you were close enough to see the gun, you were close enough to see his face."

Cherrie hesitated, lips moving, but she didn't say anything. She took a deep breath. "It was really dark and he was dressed in black. He even had on a black hat."

"What kind of hat?"

"You know, a pointed one. Like Humphrey Bogart used to wear."

"Was the guy young or old?"

"Kind of old," Cherrie said without hesitation. "You know, like in his forties."

Jake groaned to himself, suddenly feeling ancient. His forty-sixth birthday was coming up. "Was he short or tall?"

"My height. Maybe five-eight with a stocky build."

"What about his face?"

"I told you it was dark."

"Are you sure?" Jake pressed her. "You'd better not be lying."

"Goddamn it! It was dark," Cherrie said, irritated. "I didn't see his face, and I sure as hell didn't see it when he turned the light out."

Jake jerked his head up. "What light?"

"The light by the door. The guy reached up and unscrewed the bulb."

Jake thought back to the motel room and the light next to the door. It was in a plastic fixture. A person would have to reach up and over the fixture to unscrew the bulb.

Jake turned to Farelli. "The guy's fingerprints ought to be all over that lightbulb."

"Maybe he was wearing gloves."

Cherrie shook her head. "I don't think so. He kind of touched the light and took his hand away. You know, like it was hot."

Farelli nodded, smiling. "No gloves."

Jake reached for the phone.

30

"This is what we started with." Jake inserted a slide into the projector and an image of a grave site appeared on the screen. It showed a human skull and scattered bones in a pool of mud.

"And here is the skeleton laid out on the table in the laboratory with the metal plate in place," Jake said and went on to the next slide. "And this is the computer-generated picture of the victim's face."

The image on the screen showed a triangular-shaped face with a squared-off jaw. There were slits where the eyes, nose and mouth should have been. "And here's our guy in the flesh." Jake pressed a button on the projector and the final slide flashed up. "Here is James Robert Butler."

Joanna carefully studied Butler's features. They were remarkably similar to those generated by the computer. His face was triangular and his jaw very square. Even the computer image's eyes and mouth were close. Butler was thin-lipped and his eyes seemed little more than slits.

Joanna wondered if he had squinted at the moment his picture was taken. She moved in closer to the screen and pointed to Butler's eyebrows. "Are those scars I see?"

"Yeah," Jake said. "They show up a lot better under the magnifier."

"So our guy was a brawler, huh?"

Jake nodded. "With a real short temper."

Lori McKay stared at the screen and tried to see the scars Joanna was talking about. Gradually they came into view. Two, maybe three of them. Jagged scars partially hidden by the eyebrows. "Somebody did a shitty suturing job."

"I doubt if there was any suturing done," Joanna said. "Macho types don't go to emergency rooms. They just put a Band-Aid over the cut and let it heal."

Lori smiled. "Big, tough guys afraid of needles, huh?"

"It's not that," Jake explained. "They like battle scars that show. It makes them look tough."

Joanna studied James Robert Butler's face again. It did have a mean quality to it. A coldness. "What do we know about this fellow?"

"Plenty." Jake switched off the projector and turned on the lights in the forensics laboratory. He waited for Joanna to take down the screen, then reached for his notepad. "James Robert Butler was born in 1951 in San Diego. He was raised in a middle-class family but always seemed to be in trouble. As a teenager he was arrested three times for being drunk and disorderly and twice for assault and battery. The last time he beat the hell out of some kid for no reason. He fractured the boy's skull."

"Did he spend any time in jail?" Joanna asked.

"Are you kidding?" Jake said, scorning the legal system. "They put him on probation and sent him for counseling—whatever the hell that means." Jake turned a page in his notepad. "Butler finally graduated from high school and went to some vocational institute where he was thrown out for fighting. His grades were pretty good, so he wasn't stupid. Then he worked as a bouncer for a year before he decided to join the army and become a Ranger."

Lori asked, "What's a Ranger?"

"One of the army's elite combat groups," Jake told her. "Kind of like the Special Forces."

"Did he have a specialty?" Joanna asked.

"He was a sniper, an incredible marksman. According to his records, he had pinpoint accuracy up to a thousand meters."

"Whew!" Joanna uttered. "That's over half a mile."

"He was damn good," Jake went on. "The military discipline was apparently what he needed. His record was clear, and he rose to the rank of sergeant before he was wounded in Vietnam. His leg was shattered by a grenade fragment and he was sent to Walter Reed Hospital for major surgery. That's when he got the metal plate. Following his discharge, he drifted for a while, then settled in San Diego in 1982. He got married and worked as an auto mechanic. He lived a normal life."

"No more fights?" Joanna asked.

"None." Jake flipped another page. "He had a sister he was very close to. She decided to be a surrogate mother for some infertile couple. Apparently they paid her ten grand to do it. Anyhow, she got pregnant and moved in with Butler and his wife. Things went fine until she got close to delivery. That's when she decided she wanted to keep the baby."

Joanna groaned softly. What a nightmare! To carry a child inside you for nine months and then have to give it away. "Was the child conceived using eggs from Butler's sister or from the wife of the infertile couple?"

Jake shrugged. "I'm not sure. Does it matter?"

To Butler's sister it might have, Joanna thought. It might have mattered a hell of a lot. Joanna shrugged back at Jake. "Just curious."

"I'll check it out," Jake said, then continued. "The sister wanted to keep the baby, but she was threatened with a lawsuit. So she gave up the child. Then she sank into a deep depression—real deep—and committed suicide."

Lori's face suddenly paled. "Are you sure it was suicide?"

"For sure," Jake said. "She left her brother a note, then climbed into a tub of hot water and slit her wrists."

Lori shook her head sadly, thinking back to her residency in Baltimore. She was two months pregnant and trying to decide whether to have the child or have an abortion. The problem was solved when she had a miscarriage. Yet she was depressed after it happened, so depressed that thoughts of suicide had gone through her mind. She'd had to take Prozac to get herself back on an even keel. But she still grieved for that child, and not a day went by that she didn't think about it.

Jake stared at Lori for a moment. "Are you all right?"

"I'm fine," Lori said evenly. "Please go on."

"Well, like I said, Butler and his sister were very close and her death hit him pretty hard. He stopped going to work and just sat around the house all day. He didn't watch television or read or do anything like that. He just sat and stared into space. The guy would go days without speaking to anybody. His wife thought he'd eventually get over it, but he didn't.

"Then one day she walked into their bedroom and saw the damndest thing she'd ever seen in her life." Jake reached for a cigarette and lit it, inhaling deeply. "There in the bedroom, standing in front of the mirror, was her husband dressed in full combat gear. He had on camouflage fatigues, floppy hat and boots, and he was holding a rifle with a big telescopic sight attached to it. And get this—his face was painted black, like some warrior from hell. It scared the bejesus out of his wife. Butler walked out without saying a word and never came back. That was in 1986."

"What did the wife do?" Joanna asked.

"She waited and waited and eventually got married again. She figured he'd gone off somewhere and killed himself."

Lori nodded, thinking that's what she would have concluded too. "Did the wife have any idea why he went into those mountains where we found him?"

"Not a clue."

There was a soft knock on the door. A young technician entered and hurried over to Joanna. "Sorry to interrupt, Dr. Blalock, but I thought you'd want to see the results on Rudolph Ettinger right away."

Joanna reached for the sheet of laboratory data and studied it at length. "Are you sure of these numbers?"

"Positive," the technician assured her. "We ran the specimens in triplicate and got the same values every time."

Joanna waited for the technician to leave, then turned to Jake and Lori. "Rudolph Ettinger didn't die of natural causes."

Jake squinted an eye. "What causes did he die from?"

"Potassium," Joanna said simply. "A massive overdose of potassium." She tilted her chair back and rocked, reconstructing the crime in her mind. Thinking aloud, she said, "That's why the flow of IV fluids was stopped just above the monitor."

Jake looked at Joanna, puzzled. "You've lost me. What's this monitor?"

Joanna went to the blackboard and quickly drew a diagram. First she illustrated a plastic bag and, coming from it, a long, narrow tube. The tube went through a square that she labeled MONITOR and then the tube continued into a human arm. Joanna pointed to the plastic bag. "The IV fluid runs from this plastic bag into a narrow tube. The tube goes through a monitor which calibrates the flow, and then the tube goes into a vein in the patient's arm. Got it?"

"Got it," Jake said.

"In Rudolph Ettinger, somebody stopped the IV flow just above the monitor. At least that's the way we found it. So we tested the IV fluid in the plastic bag and the fluid in the tubing near Ettinger's arm. The potassium content in the tubing near the arm was a thousand times greater than the potassium content in the plastic bag."

Joanna put the chalk down and pointed to her forearm. "Somebody injected concentrated potassium chloride right into Rudolph Ettinger's vein."

"And what does that do?" Jake asked.

"It causes cardiac standstill."

Jake wetted his lips. "Are you talking murder?"

"Beyond any doubt."

31

Kate Blalock heard someone calling her. It was a distant, female voice.

"Kate! Kate!"

She tried to open her eyes, but they were too heavy. A chill ran through her body, and she reached for the sheets, pulling them up. The air felt very cool, just as it always did when the sun went down in the jungles of Guatemala. The days there were insufferably hot, the nights surprisingly pleasant. So it must be night, she thought.

Maybe they were still in the cave with its dampness and quiet. Yes, that must be it! No! That couldn't be right! Everybody got sick in the cave. Tommy and Dan and Marcia and Kim. All sick as hell with fever and chills and unable to keep anything down, not even water. It was malaria. That's what the guide said. But they all took pills to prevent malaria. So why—

"Kate! Can you hear me?"

Kate opened her eyelids halfway and saw a figure wearing a surgical mask and cap. She closed her eyes tightly and opened them again, confused. What was a nurse doing out in the jungle?

"Do you know where you are?" a male voice asked.

"In Guatemala," Kate whispered.

"No, you're in Los Angeles."

"No, I'm in Guatemala. Ask Tommy or Marcia or Kim. They'll tell you."

"What part of Guatemala are you in?"

"In the jungles to the north."

"Are you sure?"

"Positive. Ask Kim."

"Do you know what month it is?"

Kate thought the voice had asked, *Do you know what a moth is?* "It's a winged insect," she said.

Joanna reached down and gently squeezed Kate's hand. "It's Joanna, Kate."

"It's July? Already?" Kate took a deep breath and, closing her eyes, she drifted off.

Joanna shook her head sadly and looked over at Mack Brown. "How long has she been this way?"

"Since this morning," Mack said. "She was very lethargic at breakfast, but she was oriented. Then it just got worse and worse."

"Was there any precipitating cause?"

"She may have a urinary tract infection that induced another bout of hepatic encephalopathy. We're checking it out now."

Kate started babbling nonsensically. Some of her words were in English, some in Spanish. "Over here! Oh, not yet! *Qué pasa, hombre? Qué?* That's a good one, really good." Kate swallowed loudly several times. Then she was quiet again.

"Kate," Joanna whispered urgently, but her sister didn't respond.

"Kate," Joanna tried again, but still there was no response.

"Come on," Mack said, taking Joanna's arm and guiding her out of the unit. They stripped off their masks and looked through the window. Kate started thrashing about in her bed. A nurse hurried over to restrain her.

Joanna sighed wearily. "She's getting a lot worse, isn't she?"

"I'm afraid so," Mack said. "Her encephalopathic episodes are occurring more and more frequently."

Joanna nodded, facing up to the inevitable. "And you're sure we've tried everything short of the transplant?"

Mack hesitated, picking his words carefully. He didn't want to give her any false hopes. "There's one more type of therapy we could try. But," he quickly cautioned, "it's never been used against this form of virus."

"Tell me about it," Joanna said, hope against hope.

"It's called hyperimmune gamma globulin therapy," Mack told her. "The idea is to give the patient concentrated gamma globulin which contains antibodies against the virus."

"Wait a minute," Joanna said, puzzled. "We've already given Kate plasma from the Guatemalans who survived the infection. That plasma contained antibodies against the virus and it didn't work."

"But that wasn't *concentrated* antibodies," Mack explained. "What I'm suggesting is that we obtain four or five units of plasma from the survivors and extract the gamma globulin fraction from the plasma. That way we'll end up with a concentrated purified preparation of the antibodies against the virus. And that can be given to Kate intravenously."

"Who would make the preparation?"

"Our immunology department. They're very good at it."

Joanna nervously ran a hand through her hair. "Does this gamma globulin therapy have any risks?"

"Some, but they're minimal."

"How soon can we get more plasma from Guatemala?"

"It's being flown up at this moment."

Joanna smiled appreciatively. "The health officials in Guatemala have been very good to us, haven't they?"

"They sure have," Mack agreed. "But they also have an ulterior motive. They're scared shitless that another outbreak of the virus is going to occur, and they want us to come up with some form of therapy."

"How long will all this take?"

"Four or five days."

"Are you sure Kate can hold on that long?"

Mack shrugged. "There are no guarantees."

He glanced back into the unit. Kate was becoming more agitated, grabbing and shaking the side rails of her bed. "I should tell you that I got a phone call from Donors International this morning. They think they may have a liver for Kate. It's not an excellent match, but it may be a good match. They're double-checking the tissue type of the donor now."

"Could we try the gamma globulin therapy first?"

"We could, but if we pass up this liver it will go to somebody else. You'd be taking a gamble."

Joanna thought quickly, trying to weigh all the options. "If necessary, we could always use a lobe transplant from me to tide Kate over."

"You'd still be taking a big gamble," Mack warned her. "Remember, neither the lobe transplant nor the gamma globulin therapy has any track record."

Joanna tapped a finger against her cheek, concentrating, trying to reach a decision. "If you were in my position, which would you choose? The gamma globulin or the transplant?"

"The transplant," Mack said without hesitation. "We know that works."

"I guess you're right." Joanna sighed wearily and turned to leave.

Mack touched her arm. "About the other night, Joanna. I feel like hell."

"Why?"

"Because I'm married and we were drunk and . . ." He trailed off helplessly.

"Don't worry about it."

"I feel guilty as hell," Mack went on, keeping his voice down. "You were really vulnerable because of Kate's illness and I kept ordering tequilas and the next thing you know we're in bed together."

"So?"

"So, damn it, I took advantage of you."

"No, Mack. We took advantage of each other."

Jake could see at once that something was wrong. Joanna was sitting in the shadows of her laboratory, staring into space and absently puffing on a cigarette. She didn't turn as he approached.

"Are you all right?" Jake asked.

"Kate's not doing well," Joanna said.

"I thought she was holding her own."

Joanna slowly shook her head. "She's worse, Jake. I think she's dying."

"Oh, Jesus!" Jake pulled up a chair and sat facing Joanna. "Can't they do anything?"

"They're trying their best." Joanna held her cigarette absently and a large ash fell onto her shirt. She ignored it.

"What about the transplant?"

"They're searching for a donor now."

"They'll find one," Jake said, nodding to himself. "And I'll bet Kate does great with a new liver."

Joanna hardly heard him. She was still weighing the therapeutic options for Kate. The gamma globulin therapy was untried and the lobe transplant was still experimental and the results were spotty at best. And the whole liver transplant wasn't a sure bet either. The liver found by Donors International wasn't an excellent match and it might not even turn out to be a good or acceptable match. *And while you're sitting here debating,* Joanna thought, *your sister is dying.*

Reaching into his coat pocket, Jake took out a check and placed it on the desk. It was made out to Joanna for $100,000. "Now you can get Kate a damn good liver."

"Thank you, Jake," Joanna said softly. "I'll pay back every penny. That's a promise."

"I want something else for the check," Jake said.

"What?"

"I want you to listen to why I didn't call or come around when you had that breast cancer scare."

"You don't have to apologize," Joanna said sincerely. "We were already apart by then. I had no right to expect you to—"

"I ran," Jake admitted. "I ran away because I was terrified."

"Of what?"

"Losing you."

Jake stood and began to pace around the room. He kept his head down, staring at the floor. "My father died when I was a young boy. He was a cop who got shot trying to stop a holdup. It was just me and my mother left. There was no other family. And we had it hard as hell. The police pension was next to nothing. She had to work her fingers to the bone just for us to get by."

"Jake, you don't have—"

"She was the sweetest lady you ever met," Jake went on, his voice even lower. "She always made sure I came first. She would do without so I could have just a few of the things that kids normally had. During my last year in high school she found a lump in her breast. She ignored it. Doctors cost money, and she was trying to save up enough to send me to the city college. She convinced herself that the lump was nothing. It would go away. It didn't, and the cancer spread all over her body. She died the day after I graduated from high school."

Jake stopped and reached for a cigarette, then decided against it. He started pacing again. "When you told me about your lump, all I could think of was losing another person I loved. I just couldn't handle that. I couldn't stand that kind of pain again. I wasn't brave enough. So I ran."

"Oh, Jake!" Joanna said softly.

Jake came over and touched the end of her nose with his finger. "I know I blew it, but I'll never run again. You can bet on that."

Joanna waited for him to leave and close the door. Then she put her head down on the desk and cried.

32

"Is this really necessary?" Simon Murdock asked.

"Yeah, it's really necessary," Jake said.

"Please keep in mind that this is a hospital."

Jake looked at Murdock sharply. "And you keep in mind that somebody was murdered up here."

Murdock winced at the word *murder*. There was a press conference scheduled in less than an hour, and he still didn't know what he was going to tell them. "What I meant is that we have very sick patients on this ward and the last thing we want to do is to upset them."

"Then close all the doors and keep them closed while we're here. And tell the staff to keep their mouths shut around patients."

Jake glanced down the corridor to the nurses' station, where yellow police tape had been put up to seal off the area. "All right, let's go."

Jake started down the corridor with Joanna at his side. Just behind them were Murdock, David Dellacorte and the head nurse, Nancy Fine. The hallway was filled with the distinct scent of an air deodorizer. It had a sickly sweet aroma and Jake wondered what had made the smell that they were trying to cover up. Overhead the ventilator system switched on, but the air barely moved.

They came to a fire escape door and Jake slowed. "Is that door ever locked at night?"

"Never," Dellacorte said. "But it only opens from the inside out."

"So nobody can get in from the fire escape?"

"Right."

Wrong, Jake thought. All a pro needed to do was place a piece of tape over the inner lock and he could enter from the fire escape whenever he wanted to. "How many people were working on this ward the night Mr. Ettinger died?"

Dellacorte rubbed at his chin, thinking back. "A lot. Fifteen or twenty. Maybe more."

"Let's narrow it down to midnight."

"Still at least fifteen."

Jake groaned to himself. "Why so many?"

"The surgical ICU was a madhouse," Dellacorte explained. "We had a small plane crash in Santa Monica and the passengers were really mangled. Only one ended up surviving."

"And then there was the pileup on the Golden State Freeway," Nancy Fine added.

Dellacorte nodded. "That's when all hell broke loose. We had to move people out of the ICU to make room for the more critically injured ones."

"So you were on the floor all night?" Jake asked.

"Off and on," Dellacorte said. "Between midnight and two in the morning I was in the emergency room, then back up here briefly, then in the OR most of the night, then back up here."

"So there were a lot of people coming and going?" Jake asked.

"A lot."

"Did you see anybody you didn't recognize?"

Dellacorte thought for a moment, then shrugged. "I knew all the doctors and nurses. But some of the orderlies and X-ray technicians . . ." He shrugged again. "I can't be sure."

Jake looked over at the head nurse. "How about you?"

Nancy Fine shook her head. "Everybody I saw, I knew."

The group entered the room Rudolph Ettinger had died in. It was vacated and Joanna had arranged for everything to be positioned exactly as it was the evening Ettinger's body was discovered. An IV pole was by the bed. Hanging from it was a plastic bag filled with 5 percent glucose in normal saline. A narrow tube went from the plastic bag, through a monitor, and down to the bed. The needle was stuck in a rolled-up towel that represented Ettinger's arm.

"So," Jake said, carefully eyeing the IV setup, "our killer comes in some time after midnight, walks over to the bed and injects concentrated potassium chloride into Ettinger's IV. Right?"

"Right," Joanna said.

"How long you figure it took him?"

"Or her," Joanna corrected him automatically. "No more than a minute or two."

"That's assuming our killer knew his or her way around IVs and monitors."

Joanna nodded. "I think that's a correct assumption. The killer knew how to switch off the monitor alarm. And he knew he had to stop the IV flow before he injected the potassium or the potassium might have gone up the tubing rather than into Ettinger's arm. Yeah, he knew what he was doing."

"So," Jake said, "our killer has got to be someone familiar with IVs. Like a doctor or nurse or technician."

"I don't agree with that," Murdock argued. "I could teach a high school student how to switch off a monitor and inject something into IV tubing. That doesn't require a rocket scientist."

Jake shook his head. "Our guy knew his way around IVs and hospitals. He was no amateur."

"You can't be sure of that," Murdock said.

"Sure I can," Jake said easily, disliking Murdock and his arrogance a little more than usual. He obviously was afraid of the scandal of finding a murderer on his hospital's staff. "This hit had to be planned and committed by someone who knew hospitals. Let's start with Rudolph Ettinger being in a regular hospital room."

"What's so unusual about that?"

"Murdock had been in the surgical ICU," Jake said. "They moved him to a regular room in the early evening, maybe six hours before he was killed. Now, who would know he had been moved out of the ICU?"

"Perhaps the killer posed as a visitor and—"

Jake cut him off, dismissing his theory. "Read the doctors' orders in Ettinger's chart. He was not to have any visitors, and according to the nurses' notes he didn't. Now, with that in mind, who would have known Ettinger had been moved out of the ICU?"

"Someone on staff," Murdock had to admit.

"And who would have known that he had an IV in his arm and that the IV was attached to a monitor?"

Murdock nodded weakly. "I see your point."

"And the killer picked the right time, too," Joanna said thoughtfully. "He waited until the ward was like a madhouse, when everyone would be preoccupied and dashing around. That way the killer could move about without drawing attention to himself."

"And if everybody was busy as hell with accident victims," Jake went on, "chances are the staff wouldn't have time to check on Rudolph Ettinger through the night. The killer figured they wouldn't find Ettinger until morning and the killer was right. He had plenty of time to be long gone and cover his tracks."

Murdock shook his head slowly. "I still can't believe that someone from this hospital could commit such a terrible act."

"Well, somebody from your hospital did."

Jake looked around the room, now spotlessly clean. The Crime Scene Unit had gone over the room for hours and found nothing, not even a hint of a clue. But Jake had expected this. Joanna had told him that when a patient dies in the hospital, the room is carefully and thoroughly scrubbed down with soap and water and bleach. Any clue the killer might have left behind had been washed away.

Jake glanced over at the bed where Rudolph Ettinger had died. "Did Ettinger know he was dying?"

"Maybe," Joanna said. "Concentrated potassium chloride burns like hell when it's injected intravenously. Why do you ask?"

"Well, if he was awake and knew something was wrong, why didn't he reach for the buzzer?"

"Maybe he tried," Joanna suggested. "But maybe the killer knew about the nurses' buzzer too."

"Yeah," Jake said sourly. "This guy had all the bases covered, didn't he?"

As Jake led the way out, he noticed that the door of the room directly across the corridor was cracked open. It closed quickly. "Who's in that room?"

Dellacorte reached for his index cards and flipped through them. "Mrs. Ethel Ryan."

"I'd like to talk with her if I could."

"Now wait a minute, Lieutenant," Murdock objected. "We can't disturb our sick patients like this. I will not allow you to upset them."

Jake gave Murdock a long stare, then turned to Dellacorte. "How sick is this woman?"

"She has a tumor of the biliary tract," Dellacorte said. "But she's up and walking about."

"Can she talk with us briefly?"

"I don't see why not."

Dellacorte knocked on the door and waited a moment before opening it slightly. "Mrs. Ryan, may we come in?"

"Sure," Ethel Ryan called out.

As the group entered, she carefully studied each of the visitors. "Lord! What is this, some sort of committee?"

Dellacorte smiled and moved over to the bedside. He patted the woman's shoulder gently. "The police are investigating a matter for the hospital," he said delicately, "and they'd like to ask you a few questions, if you don't mind."

"Somebody stole something from that dead man's room, didn't they?" Ethel Ryan asked the question as if she already knew the answer.

Jake stepped forward, ignoring the question. "I'm Detective Lieutenant Sinclair. Could I ask you a few questions about the room across from yours?"

"So I was right," Ethel said, nodding to herself. "Somebody did steal something."

"Did you know the man in the room across from you?"

"Personally? No." Ethel smiled at the detective, liking him instantly. He had a rugged, handsome face, and he looked like he didn't take any crap from anybody. Unconsciously she began to primp, wetting her lips and fluffing up her red-orange dyed hair. "But I remember when he died."

"You mean the morning of his death?"

Ethel nodded. "And the night before. The staff kept checking on him. You know, a lot more than they usually do."

"How do you know they kept checking on him?" Jake asked, taken aback.

"Because I keep my door open most of the time," Ethel Ryan said promptly. "Hell, if something goes wrong with me I'm going to scream. They'll ignore a buzzer, but they'll run like hell when they hear you scream."

Murdock cleared his throat. "Have you been left unattended when you needed assistance?"

"Nope. And I'm not going to be either," Ethel said, smiling. She turned in bed, adjusting the sheets. She was wearing a silk nightgown and robe.

"Let's go back to the night before the man's death," Jake picked up the questioning. "Can you remember things that happened around midnight? Were you still up?"

"Oh, sure," Ethel said positively. "I watch the *Tonight Show* every night. I don't go to sleep until one or two in the morning."

"And what did—"

Ethel Ryan suddenly grimaced with pain. She grabbed at her side and pressed on it. Gradually the pain left her face. "When are you going to take this goddamn tumor out?" she asked Dellacorte.

"As soon as your prothrombin time returns to normal," Dellacorte said, patting her shoulder again. "If your blood doesn't clot correctly you could bleed massively at surgery. And we don't want that, do we?"

"No," Ethel Ryan said agreeably. "But we do want this goddamn tumor out, don't we?"

"Soon," Dellacorte promised.

"Sorry, Lieutenant," Ethel said. "You were asking?"

"Do you remember anybody going into the room across the corridor around midnight?"

Ethel thought back, concentrating. "Let's see now. It was just in the middle of the *Tonight Show* and . . . and— Yeah, I remember a nurse knocking on his door and going in."

"How long was she in the room?"

"Like a minute or so. Real quick."

"Did you see her face?"

Ethel pointed to Nancy Fine. "It was her."

Jake nodded to himself. That checked with the nurses' notes in

Ettinger's chart. They stated that Nancy Fine visited Ettinger's room at 12:02 A.M. "Were there any visitors after the nurse?"

"One more," Ethel said.

"When?"

"Maybe five or ten minutes later," Ethel recalled easily. "A guy wearing a scrub suit went in."

"Was it a doctor?"

Ethel shrugged. "Maybe. But he could have been an intern or a medical student. Hell, they all look alike to me."

Jake moved in closer to Ethel Ryan's bed. "Did you see his face?"

"No. But I heard his voice."

"What did he say?"

"Something like, 'I'm going to flush your IV.' "

Jake turned to the nurse. "Why would somebody go in to flush Ettinger's IV?"

"They wouldn't," Nancy Fine said. "His IV was running perfectly."

Jake turned to Ethel Ryan. "You're sure you didn't see the guy's face?"

"Positive."

"Did you recognize his voice?"

"No. I really wasn't paying attention," Ethel said. "I was on my way into the john."

"Was he still in the room when you came out of the john?"

"I didn't notice. I got back in bed and switched to an old Fred Astaire movie." Ethel closed her eyes and sighed. "Fred Astaire and Ginger Rogers. They were so great."

"Yeah," Jake said. "Really great. Thanks for your help."

They filed out of her room and started back down the corridor. A large group of doctors and nurses were gathered at the nurses' station, watching, all knowing about the murder of Rudolph Ettinger. The news had spread through the hospital like wildfire.

"This doesn't prove that it was one of our staff who did it," Murdock said.

"I think it does," Jake told him. "Somebody had to plan all this, and somebody had to know all the routines that go on in this hospital."

"That's still not proof," Murdock said firmly.

"But everything points to it, Simon," Joanna said, nodding to herself. "The killer knew his way around. And he just waited for the right time. Then he walked into Ettinger's room with a syringe loaded with potassium chloride and—" Joanna stopped in mid-sentence and quickly turned to the nurse. "Where do you store your potassium chloride?"

"In the medicine room," Nancy Fine said.

"So you keep an inventory?"

"Sure. That way we know when we're about to run short."

"Please check your inventory list right now. See if it matches up with the number of potassium chloride vials you still have on hand."

"It'll just take a minute," Nancy Fine said and hurried away.

Jake looked at Joanna admiringly. He knew exactly what she was driving at. And Jake would have missed it because Joanna knew something he didn't. That potassium chloride came in vials. So damn simple and such an important clue.

Jake stretched his back, then glanced over at Murdock and Dellacorte. On the surface, they would be the ones who would gain the most from Rudolph Ettinger's death. The old man was going to destroy the hospital and the reputations of both men. But why would they kill him now? The lawsuit charging the doctors and hospital with malpractice had already been filed. Even with Ettinger dead, the lawsuit would still proceed, and so would the ruinous publicity it would generate. And Ettinger's death might even strengthen his case in court. No, Jake decided, they wouldn't have killed him. Neither they nor the hospital would benefit from his death.

Nancy Fine ran up to the group and paused to catch her breath. "We're missing four vials of potassium chloride."

"So our guy knew his way around the nurses' station," Joanna concluded.

"And he could move in and out of there without anyone becoming suspicious," Jake said, then turned to Murdock. "You've got a murderer walking the halls of Memorial Hospital."

33

"I think we have a liver for your sister," Jason Adler said. "We're double-checking the tissue type now."

"Who's the donor?" Joanna asked.

"A teenager in Scotland. He was shot in the head accidentally while hunting with friends."

Adler led the way into the control room at Donors International. The room was dimly lit, with most of the light coming from the blank video screens on the wall. Karen Kessler, the transplant coordinator, was sitting at the console, rapidly punching numbers into a computer keyboard while she talked into a telephone headset.

"How long will it take for the liver to reach here?" Joanna asked.

Adler squinted and counted in his head. "About twelve hours if the planes are on time."

"Too bad the Concordes don't fly into Los Angeles."

"Maybe one of these days," Adler said and turned to the transplant coordinator. "Karen, show Dr. Blalock the clinical data on the prospective donor."

Karen entered a code and the central video screen lit up. The clinical information on the Scottish donor appeared.

PROSPECTIVE DONOR

NAME: ROY MCGREGOR
SEX: MALE

AGE: 16 YEARS

NATIONALITY: BRITISH

RACE: CAUCASIAN

CLINICAL HISTORY: ACCIDENTAL GUNSHOT WOUND TO THE HEAD.
   CLINICALLY DEAD. TWO EEGs AT EDINBURGH INFIRMARY SHOW
   NO ACTIVITY

PAST MEDICAL HISTORY: EXCELLENT HEALTH USUAL CHILDHOOD
   DISEASES

MEDICATIONS: NONE

ALLERGIES: NONE

FAMILY HISTORY: PARENTS HEALTHY; NO SIBLINGS
   GRANDFATHER WITH GOUT GRANDMOTHER WITH
   PULMONARY FIBROSIS

LABORATORY EVALUATION:

BILIRUBIN	.8
SGOT	24
SGPT	40
ALKALINE PHOSPHATASE	100
GGTP	52
ALBUMIN	4.4
BLOOD TYPE	B POSITIVE

Joanna studied the video screen, concentrating on the donor's age. He was only sixteen. So young! And an only child. The boy's family had to be devastated. She'd never really thought much about the personal side to organ donation.

"And we may have a match for the boy's kidneys and heart," Adler said, breaking into her thoughts.

"He's so young," Joanna said, thinking aloud.

"Much too young," Adler agreed. "But his death means others will live."

One family grieving, Joanna thought, three other families rejoiced and were filled with hope. She felt almost ghoulish, as if she was preying on the corpse of an almost dead person. But the boy's death could save Kate's life, and that was something that Joanna was willing to move heaven and earth for.

Joanna's eyes went back to the video screen. "Where's the boy's tissue type?"

Karen Kessler brought up a second video screen.

	CRITICAL ANTIGENS		
DONOR		KATE BLALOCK	
A	2, 10	A-	2, 10
B-	8, 16	B-	8, 16
DR-	??	DR-	4, 6

"The boy's A and B tissue antigens are clear-cut," Adler explained. "We tested him for two antigens from group A and two from group B. These antigens match your sister's perfectly. It's the boy's DR group that's causing our problems. For some reason we're having trouble determining the DR type. We've sent the specimen to a very excellent laboratory in London and they are retesting for the DR antigen now."

"So," Joanna said, "if the boy's two DR antigens match Kate's DR antigens, he's a perfect match."

"An excellent match, not a perfect match," Adler corrected her. "Even if all six antigens from groups A, B and DR match, there is still a twenty percent chance that the recipient will reject the liver."

"And if there's one mismatch?"

"The rejection rate goes up to forty percent."

"And two mismatches?"

"With two mismatched antigens we don't even attempt to do the transplant," Adler told her. "The rejection rate is a hundred percent. So the six antigens we test for are not the only antigens, but they certainly appear to be the critical ones."

Joanna's eyes narrowed. "Is that what they're commonly called? The critical antigens?"

"By most. Why?"

Joanna looked up at the video screen and studied the heading "CRITICAL ANTIGENS." She searched her mind, thinking back to the recent past. "I've seen the term 'critical antigens' before, but not in this context."

Adler shrugged. "Well, there are a lot of critical antigens in human biology. The blood group antigens A, B and Rh, for example."

"No, no," Joanna persisted, the answer almost on the tip of her tongue. "It had to do with something on a computer, I think."

Adler was about to say something, then shrugged again. "You'll have to be more specific than—"

A soft buzzing sound came from the console and a red light on the wall began to blink. There was a sudden tension in the room. Karen reached over and pushed a button, then spoke slowly into her headset. Joanna couldn't hear the conversation, but Karen's face was dead serious.

"That's a private line," Adler said, his expression equally serious. "Only urgent calls are put through."

Karen quickly scribbled down notes as she spoke. The room was very still, and now Joanna could hear parts of the phone conversation. "Is she being admitted?" and "We'll call in our own specialist." Then, "Right, right. Thank you."

Adler remained motionless and kept his eyes glued to the transplant coordinator's face. The moment she finished the phone conversation, Adler said, "Bad news?"

Karen Kessler sighed wearily. "One of our surrogate mothers was in an accident on the Ventura Freeway."

"Who?"

"Joyce B."

"Was she hurt badly?"

"Nothing was broken." Karen reached for a cigarette and nervously lit it. "But she started to spot a little blood in the ER at Memorial."

"Damn!" Adler grumbled. "She's not even six months into her pregnancy. Do they think she's going to have a miscarriage?"

"They can't be sure, but they're worried. She's being admitted to the obstetrical service."

"Make sure our obstetrical specialist sees her tonight."

"Maybe she'll be lucky and not abort," Karen said and punched in the phone number of Robert Goodall, M.D.

Adler picked up a pencil and tapped it rapidly against the desk.

He grumbled a profanity under his breath, then began to pace around the console. "What in the hell was she doing driving on the freeway on a night like this? It's raining so hard you can barely see in front of you."

He turned quickly to the transplant coordinator. "Tell Goodall I want a report as soon as he sees the patient."

Karen held up a finger and nodded. She was still trying to reach the doctor through his answering service.

Joanna asked, "Do you use many surrogate mothers at Donors International?"

"We employed quite a few early on, when we first started," Adler replied. "But most of them were young women and they presented a lot of problems."

"Such as?"

"Mainly immaturity and greed. Most of the surrogates did it for money, of course. We paid ten thousand dollars for their services, and that amount seemed fine to them at first. But you'd be amazed at the number of women who demanded more money at the end of the pregnancy. And then there were those who decided they wanted to keep the babies despite the contracts they'd signed. On a few occasions we had to actually threaten them with legal action."

"So ten years ago you were employing a fair number of surrogates?"

Adler thought for a moment. "I'd say one in five of our pregnancies was carried by a surrogate mother."

"Did you ever use the surrogate mother's ova and the husband's sperm?"

"Never," Adler said at once. "The ova and sperm always came from the infertile couple."

Joanna thought back to the sister of the man whose skeleton was found in a grave a mile from Donors International. "Do you do any follow-ups on the surrogate mothers after they're delivered?"

"No. Once they deliver they're paid and that is the end of our contractual agreement." Adler gave Joanna a long look. "Why the interest?"

"One of the cases we're studying over at Memorial involves a surrogate mother."

"At Donors International?" Adler asked, suddenly alert.

"I'm not sure," Joanna said evenly. "She was a surrogate mother some years ago. Her name was Diane Butler. Is that name familiar to you?" She watched his face, waiting for a reaction. There wasn't any.

Adler shrugged. "Not offhand. But I can have someone check into it for you if you'd like."

"Please."

"Let me make a quick call to our records department."

Adler walked over to a wall phone on the far side of the control room. He spoke briefly, his back to the others, then returned. "I forgot it was after eight. We have only a skeleton crew on now, so I'm afraid we'll have to delay a records search until tomorrow morning. I'll call you as soon as we get the information."

"That'll be fine," Joanna said.

Karen Kessler removed her headset and slowly stretched the muscles in her neck and back. "Dr. Goodall is finishing a C-section at Santa Monica Hospital. He'll see our patient within the hour."

"And he knows to call us?" Adler asked.

"He knows."

A green light on the computer-phone linkup behind the console began to flash. Karen leaned over and studied the message being typed out on the printer. She pushed a button that transferred the information to the video screen. "The tissue typing from London is coming in."

Everyone's total attention went to the video screen.

TISSUE TYPE
(LONDON)

KATE BLALOCK		DONOR	
A-	2, 10	A-	2, 10
B-	8, 16	B-	8, 16
DR-	4, 6	DR-	PROCESSING

Joanna's heart pounded in her chest. *Just let one of the DR antigens match,* she prayed. *Just one!* That would be matches on five out of six, good enough for a transplant. *Come on,* Joanna pleaded silently, *just one DR antigen match!*

The video screen went blank for a moment, then printed the data again, including the DR types.

TISSUE TYPE
(LONDON)

KATE BLALOCK		DONOR	
A-	2, 10	A-	2, 10
B-	8, 16	B-	8, 16
DR-	4, 6	DR-	3, 7

"I'm sorry," Adler said. "The DR antigens are a mismatch. The boy is not a suitable donor."

Joanna sighed and made no effort to hide her disappointment. So close, she thought. Only two antigens apart. Close, but not close enough. "You'll keep trying to find a donor?"

"Of course," Adler said sympathetically. "We'll eventually find a liver for your sister. She'll just have to hold on until we do."

"I'm not sure how much longer she can last," Joanna said softly. "They're starting her on an experimental type of treatment with hyperimmune gamma globulin, but no one is very confident."

"Perhaps it will buy us a little more time."

Joanna took a deep breath and exhaled slowly. "A lobe transplant from me to Kate may be my sister's only chance. We match up pretty well, don't we?"

Adler nodded and signaled to Karen Kessler, who rapidly punched numbers into the keyboard. Joanna had sent her blood to Memorial Hospital and Donors International because she wanted it tested in the same laboratories that had determined Kate's tissue type. It was done to verify and double-check the results. Kate and Joanna Blalock's tissue types appeared on the screen.

KATE BLALOCK		JOANNA BLALOCK	
A-	2, 10	A-	2, 10
B-	8, 16	B-	8, 16
DR-	4, 6	DR-	4, 7

"Only one mismatch," Adler said. "You'd be a suitable donor for your sister."

"I'll begin making plans for the surgery," Joanna said, her voice hushed.

"Perhaps we'll find a donor before we need to take that step," Adler said hopefully. "We also have two more accident victims now being tissue typed as prospective donors. Maybe one of them will match up with your sister."

"Maybe," Joanna said, but deep down she believed a lobe transplant was inevitable. She glanced up at the video screen and studied the data comparing her tissue type with Kate's. At the top of the screen was the heading:

CRITICAL ANTIGENS

Joanna's eyes suddenly widened as she focused in on the capitalized letters *C* and *A*. CA! Her mind flashed back to the computer files found in the library of William Arthur Warren. The file of each prospective wife had had the same cryptic notation—CA, followed by six numbers. Six antigens! The six critical antigens! Oh, my God! Joanna spun around in her chair and stared up at Adler.

"Is something wrong?" Adler asked.

"I need William Arthur Warren's tissue type," Joanna said. "I need to know his six critical antigens."

Adler looked at her oddly. "May I ask why?"

"Just bring it up on your computer, please."

Adler nodded to Karen, and within seconds William Arthur Warren's tissue type was being typed out on the printer.

"Here you are," Adler said, handing the printout sheet to her.

Joanna snatched it from his hand and hurried out of the room.

34

Joanna couldn't believe how fast the cars were going on the San Diego Freeway. Rain was coming down so hard that the windshield wipers could barely keep up, yet drivers were whizzing by at sixty miles an hour or more. Joanna stayed in the slow lane and tried to keep her speed down, but the car behind her was right on her tail and she had to go faster and faster.

"Goddamn it! Why don't you back off?" Joanna seethed, taking a quick glance in the rearview mirror. The automobile behind her was either a truck or a sport utility vehicle. Its headlights were high and shone directly into Joanna's mirror. She speeded up and put a little more distance between them. Three more exits and she was off the damn freeway, she thought, then ten minutes to Memorial Hospital and she'd have her answer.

Her mind went back to the files of all of William Arthur Warren's prospective wives. The cryptic data had to be their critical histocompatibility antigens, their tissue types. It had to be. There was no other explanation. And it was easy to prove. All she had to do was compare Warren's critical antigens with those of his prospective wives. If all were perfect or excellent matches, then the puzzle was solved. William Arthur Warren had selected his wife based on her tissue type. He wanted the woman's organs.

But don't jump to conclusions, Joanna warned herself. Wait

until you do the comparisons. Wait. But she knew she was right. The old bastard knew . . .

A big oil tanker sped by and sent up a gigantic spray of water. It thudded against Joanna's windshield and for a moment she was blinded. She leaned forward, trying to find the road. She felt her tires running over the markers that separated the lanes on the freeway. On her left a horn blasted loudly. Instinctively she jerked the steering wheel to the right as another truck zoomed by.

"Jesus!" Joanna muttered to herself, shaken. She gripped the steering wheel tightly, eyes glued to the road. Behind her the big vehicle with the bright lights was still there. And it was tailgating again. So damn close! Maybe the driver was some nut. A crazy with nothing better to do. Joanna speeded up again.

The rain began to slacken. Up ahead Joanna saw a sea of red lights. Drivers were slowing as they went through the Sepulveda Pass, a stretch of freeway that inclined uphill before it reached the Brentwood area. Two more exits and Joanna would reach the well-lighted Sunset off-ramp. The car behind her slowed and backed off.

The rain was down to a drizzle, so Joanna opened the window halfway and let the cool air blow against her forehead. Fifteen minutes more and she'd be at Memorial Hospital. Then at least one of the riddles would be solved. But a lot of unanswered questions would still remain. Most important, why were the transplanted livers filled with cysts? Why? She still had no explanation for that, not even a clue.

The car behind her suddenly pulled out into the next lane and came alongside. Joanna looked over at the sport utility vehicle, its window rolled all the way down. The driver looked back at her. Their eyes met and locked for a brief moment. Joanna glanced back at the road, then back at the obnoxious driver. The light was poor and he was dressed in black. She couldn't make out his face.

She stepped down on the accelerator and her car lunged forward. But the vehicle beside her speeded up as well and stayed alongside. She cursed under her breath, now thinking he was some idiot playing games on the freeway.

Again Joanna glanced over to glare at the man. She saw his outstretched arm holding a gleaming metallic object. It took a moment for her to realize it was a gun. There was a flash as her window exploded and shards of glass flew into her face and neck. Her hands came off the steering wheel as her car spun out of control.

Joanna heard tires screeching and metal slamming into metal, then a final shot just before everything went silent and black.

35

"Why are the Feds being so hush-hush about this guy?" Farelli asked.

Jake shrugged. "They didn't say. But for some reason the FBI doesn't want to talk about him on the phone."

"They did get a good set of prints off that lightbulb though, didn't they?"

"A perfect set."

Jake lit a Greek cigarette and inhaled absently, his mind drifting back to the lightbulb outside the motel room where Pamela Warren and Tony Boyette were murdered. The killer had reached up and unscrewed the lightbulb to darken the area. And in the process he left behind a clear set of fingerprints. The pro probably had gloves on, Jake thought. At least initially he did. But the fixture that held the bulb was small and wouldn't admit a gloved hand. Jake had gone back to the motel and tried it. It was a tight squeeze for even a bare hand. So the pro took off his glove without thinking and unscrewed the bulb. He had fucked up—big time.

Outside there was a loud crack of lightning, then thunder. The lights in the conference room at FBI headquarters in West Los Angeles dimmed momentarily, then came back.

Jake glanced over at the rain-streaked window and the blackness beyond. "Think this rain is ever going to stop?"

"One of these years," Farelli said sourly. "But at least it keeps the freeway sniper quiet. I guess the bastard doesn't like to get wet."

"Or maybe he doesn't like water dripping on the lens of his telescopic sight."

"You figure he uses a sight, huh?"

Jake nodded. "He's hit too many people. This guy isn't taking random potshots."

The door to the conference room opened and Agent Robert Henry walked in. He sat at the long table facing the detectives. In his hands were two thin folders. "The man you're looking for is Luis Vega. He's one mean son of a bitch." Henry pushed a folder across to Jake and waited for him to open it. "Luis Vega was born and raised in Havana, Cuba. He came to the United States in the late seventies during the Muriel Boatlift."

Farelli asked, "What was the Muriel Boatlift?"

"A nightmare, that's what it was," Henry said, his face hardening. "During the Carter administration, we bitched and moaned about Fidel Castro denying his people the right to emigrate out of Cuba. So Fidel decided to accommodate us. He opened up his prisons and sent us all of Cuba's most violent criminals. Murderers, rapists, deviates. The worst of the worst. They came to Florida in flotillas of vessels of all shapes and sizes. It became known as the Muriel Boatlift because one of Cuba's meanest prisons was named Muriel."

"Jesus Christ!" Farelli said disgustedly. "We let those bastards in?"

"Of course," Henry said, tilting back in his chair. "You remember the movie *Scarface* starring Al Pacino? Well, those psychopathic killers depicted in the show were from the Muriel Boatlift. That movie was as close to being fact as you can get."

Jake studied Vega's file. It consisted of two pages. "He's got a strange record. During his first five years in America he was as clean as a choirboy. Then all hell broke loose."

"That's what his *official* record says," Henry said carefully.

"And what does his unofficial record say?" Jake asked.

Henry hesitated while he chose his next words. He was middle-aged and well built with a crew cut. "What I'm about to tell you was obtained via back channels with another intelligence unit. This information no longer exists. It's gone, disappeared, buried so deep it'll never see the light of day."

Jake nodded. "You're saying his record has been scrubbed?"

"Exactly," Henry said. "And our friends who did the scrubbing expect it to stay that way. Understood?"

"Understood."

"I think I'll have one of your cigarettes," Henry said and reached across the table for the pack. He lit the cigarette and inhaled deeply with obvious pleasure. "I limit myself to three a day, and I enjoy the hell out of each of them."

Farelli was tempted to reach for the pack, but he resisted. One cigarette and he knew he'd soon be smoking a pack a day.

"Well, back to our friend Luis Vega," Henry said. "As soon as he got off the boat, our boy went into the drug business and did very, very well. His group ended up controlling half the drug traffic in Miami. But then things turned sour. Other gangs moved in on his turf and drug wars broke out. People started dying, and Vega's suppliers got antsy. Finally, one of his lieutenants was caught knee-deep in heroin and cut a deal with the DEA. He gives them a ton of evidence against his boss. Luis Vega is convicted and sentenced to a thousand years in jail. And he never serves a day."

"He squealed too, huh?" Farelli guessed.

Henry shook his head. "No. Vega was too smart for that. Squealers in protection plans have a funny way of ending up dead."

Henry took another drag on his cigarette and felt guilty. This wasn't his third smoke of the day, but his sixth. And he had another one in his car, and he knew he'd smoke that on the way home. Shit! He'd thought he had such control of it. "Luis Vega is a very bright man with a college degree, if you can believe that. He's fluent in Spanish, English and Italian. And he can pass for any of those nationalities too."

Henry slid a second folder across the table. Jake opened it and studied the twelve-by-twelve-inch, glossy black-and-white photograph. Vega had swarthy good looks with prominent cheekbones and thin lips. His black hair showed no gray. Jake guessed he was in his early forties. "How old is this photo?"

"It was taken four years ago," Henry replied. "Anyhow, the DEA

boys thought that Vega, being so sharp, would be perfect to infil-
trate the Latin American drug cartel. They offered him a deal to
spy on the cartel and have his record scrubbed clean. He grabbed
it and ended up doing wet work for a Columbian organization."

Jake and Farelli looked at each other and exchanged nods. Wet
work was the Agency's code for assassination.

"Things went fine," Henry continued, "until the mid-eighties.
Then Vega decided to do contract work on the side. In America,
for chrissakes! Well, the Agency can't put up with that. Killing in
Bogota is one thing, killing in New York City is another. The
Agency disassociated itself from Vega and told him he was on his
own. They destroyed every scintilla of information that might con-
nect Vega to the Agency and cut him loose."

"And that's when his record suddenly lights up with criminal
activity," Jake said, now glancing at Vega's sheet. "Assault and battery, possession of a deadly weapon, extortion, attempted murder.
Twelve arrests and no convictions?" Jake's brow went up.

"Not even close to a conviction on any count," Henry said miserably. "Like I told you, he's a very smart son of a bitch."

"And now he's a hit man."

"That's what we hear." Henry reached across for the folders and
closed them. "He specializes in *accidental* deaths."

"That fits." Jake told Henry about the murders of Pamela
Warren and Tony Boyette in the motel. "And Luis Vega would
have no trouble getting Thai heroin."

"He could get a ton of it with one phone call," Henry agreed.
He closed his eyes and in his mind reconstructed the crime scene
Jake had described earlier. "He left the needle and syringe in her
arm, huh? That's a nice touch."

"He's a very clever guy," Jake said. "But this time he screwed up
and left some clues behind."

"The same thing happened in New York," Henry said, nodding
to himself. "There was this judge who was paid to do a favor for
one of the families in New York. The judge took the money but
forgot to do the favor. Vega was brought in to ice the old man.
They found the judge in his bathroom, floor wet, tub filled with
water. He apparently had slipped and bashed his head on the edge
of the tub. It turns out that the judge couldn't take baths or even

showers because of a skin condition. He could only sponge himself, and even then he had to use special oils and emollients to
keep from getting terrible rashes. Vega had set the bathroom
scene up, then bashed the judge's head against the tub.

"Did a witness put Vega at the scene of the crime?" Jake asked.

"Oh, yeah," Henry said at once. "An eyewitness saw him leaving
the judge's condominium. There's a warrant out for Vega's arrest.
But of course, proving that Vega did the deed is going to be
another matter."

Jake scratched at his ear, thinking. "You said that Vega worked
for one of the families in New York."

Henry nodded. "A very well-connected family. As we understand it, he works for them exclusively. He does no side work."

Jake looked at Henry strangely. "Are you saying that Pamela
Warren and Tony Boyette were somehow involved with the mob?"

Henry stood and carefully stacked the folders against the
tabletop. "What I'm saying is that if Luis Vega did the killings, then
it was the mob who wanted them dead."

36

Jake Sinclair burst into the hospital room. A doctor in a long white coat was leaning over Joanna, examining her eyes with an ophthalmoscope. Jake moved in closer, now seeing Joanna's arm and the IV in it, and the flashing monitors behind the bed.

The doctor turned and stared at Jake. "Who are you?"

"Family," Jake said tersely. "How is she?"

"Not bad, considering what she's been through." The name tag on the doctor's coat stated that he was Robert Wills, M.D., from the Department of Neurology. He turned to Joanna. "You seem to be pretty much intact, although I think your head is going to ache for a while."

"My vision is a little blurry," Joanna said, "and I'm having trouble concentrating."

"That's because you've had a concussion," Wills told her. "Things might get worse before they get better. If you notice any change—like weakness or numbness, even if it's transient—let us know immediately."

"I will."

As the neurologist moved away from the bed, Jake saw Joanna's face and his heart twisted. She had an egg-size purplish lump on her forehead, and her cheek and neck were covered with cuts and scabs. "My God, Joanna. You look like you've been through a war."

Joanna winced as the door closed with a thud. The noise caused her head to ache even more.

Jake pulled a chair in close to the bed. He touched her nose with a finger. "Are you in a lot of pain?"

"Every part of me hurts," Joanna said quietly. "I feel as if somebody beat the hell out of me with a board."

"From the Highway Patrol's description of your car, you're lucky to be alive."

Joanna nodded slowly, her mind flashing back to the accident. She remembered the sounds of tires screeching and metal crunching into metal. Then everything had turned upside down.

"What happened out on that freeway?" Jake asked.

"Someone took a shot at me."

"What!" Jake brought his chair in even closer. "Are you sure?"

"Positive," Joanna said slowly. "I saw his arm and I saw the gun he was holding." A pain stabbed at her temples and she clenched her teeth together, grimacing. Gradually it eased.

"You feel up to talking about it?"

"As long as my headache doesn't get any worse."

"Start from the beginning," Jake said and took out his notepad. "Where were you coming from on the freeway?"

Joanna reached for some ice chips in a shallow tray on the night table and wet her lips. Her mind was still fuzzy and recent events seemed jumbled together. "I—I remember being at Donors International," she said hesitantly, trying to gather her thoughts. "They believed they had a donor for my sister, but they retested the boy's tissue type and it didn't match up." Joanna closed her eyes and a voice within her brain kept repeating: *Close! So close! Only one mismatch.* There was something else she'd learned at D.I., but her mind was too fuzzy to bring it into focus.

"What happened next?" Jake prodded her gently.

Joanna reached for more ice chips. "I was on the freeway and a car was tailing me, then pulled up alongside. I saw a man with a gun, then a flash and the window exploded in my face."

Jake's jaw tightened. "A goddamn freeway shooter! Maybe the same nut who's been taking potshots at drivers from the hills is now staying in his car, warm and dry."

"I don't think so," Joanna said, recalling the bright lights in her rearview mirror. "This guy followed me for at least a mile. I'd speed up, he'd speed up. Then he suddenly pulled into the next lane, and that's when I saw the gun."

"Probably just some nutty bastard with a gun," Jake said and scribbled down a note to check with Highway Patrol to see if there had been any other freeway shootings last night. "Did you see the guy's face?"

Joanna shook her head slightly, and even that motion caused her temple to throb. "It was too dark. But he was dressed in dark clothing. I'm sure of that."

Jake's eyes narrowed. "Was he wearing a black hat?"

Joanna thought for a moment. "I can't be sure. It was so dark."

"Think," Jake urged her. "A black hat—like one that Humphrey Bogart used to wear."

Joanna tried to concentrate, to see the man's face. All she saw was the gleaming gun. "I just can't say. Why is that so important?"

"Because the pro who killed Pamela Warren and Tony Boyette was dressed in black. And he was wearing a black hat."

Joanna stared at Jake, fear flooding through her. "Why—why would he want to kill me?"

"I don't think it was the same guy."

"But it could be."

Jake shook his head firmly. "It ain't the same guy. A freeway shooting wouldn't be this pro's MO. He's too slick for that."

"Do you know who the pro is?" Joanna asked.

Jake nodded and told Joanna about Luis Vega and the fingerprints he'd left behind on the lightbulb outside the motel room. And about the killer's expertise at making murder look accidental. "He now works as a hit man for the mob."

Joanna propped herself up on an elbow. "Mob? Do you think Tony Boyette was hooked into the mob?"

Jake shrugged. "We're looking into it."

"So it was a mob hit?"

"That's what we think. But we don't have a clue as to why."

Joanna eased herself back down. "There are so many bits and pieces of information here that don't fit together. Everything is unconnected, a riddle, or a puzzle within a puzzle."

Joanna closed her eyes. Jake's presence seemed to steady her and memories from the evening before began to come back. She was at Donors International, watching the video screen with Adler and Karen Kessler, waiting for the tissue typing results to come in from London. Then a phone conversation. What was that conversation about? What? An accident of some kind. Somebody was hurt. A patient? No, no. It was a—a pregnant woman. A surrogate mother. Joanna opened her eyes. "Did you know that Donors International uses surrogate mothers for some of their infertile couples?"

"How did you find that out?" Jake asked.

"Jason Adler told me," Joanna said, her memory on that point crystal-clear.

"Did you ask him about Diane Butler? You know, the sister of our skeleton-man?"

Joanna nodded. "He didn't recognize the name and he showed no reaction when I mentioned her."

"We're getting nowhere with this Diane Butler," Jake said frustratedly and flipped pages in his notepad. "We talked again with the skeleton's ex-wife and she wasn't any help except to tell us the name of the hospital where Diane Butler delivered her baby."

"Did you get her hospital records?"

"They're sealed by court order."

"Then get them unsealed by court order," Joanna said briskly.

Jake smiled. The trauma to Joanna's head hadn't affected her sharpness. "We're in the process."

"And there's one more thing," Joanna said, events coming back slowly. "Remember the computer disk you found in William Arthur Warren's library? The one with the files that had the abbreviation CA followed by six numbers?"

"Yeah. What about it?"

"I think the letters CA stand for critical antigens," Joanna said. In layman's terms, she briefly explained what the six critical antigens were and their importance in determining whether an organ from one person could be transplanted into another person without rejection. "In other words, Warren was testing prospective wives' tissue types for suitable organ donors."

Jake looked at Joanna, puzzled. Then his jaw dropped. "Jesus!

Are you saying he picked his wives based on their ability to donate an organ to *him?*"

"Exactly," Joanna said. "He wanted someone who matched his tissue type."

Jake pushed his chair back and started pacing the floor. "Jesus Christ!" he kept saying over and over again. He reached for a cigarette to help him think better, but then remembered he was in a hospital room. "Can you prove it?"

"Oh, yeah," Joanna assured him. "All we have to do is match William Arthur Warren's six critical antigens against those of his prospective wives. If there's a perfect match we have our answer. He considered marrying them for their tissue types."

"So they could be his organ donors," Jake concluded, still pacing the room. He thought he'd heard or seen just about every imaginable crime on the face of the earth, but marrying a woman so you could kill her if the need arose and take— He stopped in his tracks and turned quickly to Joanna. "Wait a minute! William Arthur Warren had his transplant last year, and the liver sure as hell didn't come from Pamela Warren."

Joanna smiled without humor. "She was his ace-in-the-hole, his backup donor."

"You're depraved." Jake grinned at her and started pacing again. "So the old man gets his liver the usual way via Donors International?"

"I didn't say that," Joanna broke in.

"Then how did he get his liver?"

"Maybe from one of the prospective wives he didn't marry."

"This gets more insane by the second," Jake said, shaking his head. "There must be a way to find out where William Arthur Warren's liver came from. Donors International would have to give us that information if we asked for it."

"They've already given it to me," Joanna told him. "According to their records, the liver came from a young boy in Hungary."

Jake gestured with his hands and shrugged. "Well, there's your answer."

"Not really," Joanna said. "Maybe Warren arranged for one of his prospective wives to go to Hungary on an all-expenses-paid trip. She has an accident in Hungary—one that's set up, of course—and

Leonard Goldberg

sustains a serious head injury. She's declared brain-dead. And it's her liver, not some little boy's, that is sent back to America."

Jake looked at her oddly. "You just can't substitute organs that way."

Joanna shook her head, and her headache came back with a vengeance. She quickly pressed on her temples with her fingers and the pain eased. "Jake, you don't have to switch organs. Remember, all transplant matching is done with blood samples. The donors never see the recipients and the recipients never see the donors. Even the doctors don't know one another. It's all accomplished with blood samples. So, imagine we have the ex-prospective wife in an ICU in Budapest and her blood shows a tissue type that matches William Arthur Warren's. Her liver is removed and sent to America. The doctor who removed the organ is paid hush money to say that the liver came from a young boy. That false information is sent electronically to this country and becomes part of the medical records at Donors International. That way there's no possible connection between Mr. Warren and his donor. Now who's to know the difference?"

Jake nodded slowly. "Do you think Donors International is involved?"

"Maybe, maybe not. They could have just been used as a conduit by William Arthur Warren and never have known it. By using Donors International, Warren assured himself he and nobody else would get the liver."

Jake scribbled down a note. "We'll have to check and see if those prospective wives of his are still alive."

"The first thing to check is Warren's tissue type to see if it matches with the types of his prospective wives."

"How do I get his tissue type?"

"It's in my purse," Joanna said. "I got a printout of his tissue type before I left Donors International last night." She reached for the night table, then remembered that all of her valuables would be held by the hospital for safekeeping. "Check with the nurse at the front desk. She'll give you my purse. And remember, we don't need a perfect match. Five out of six matched antigens is good enough for a transplant."

"Five out of six," Jake said, writing down the information.

Joanna's face suddenly lost color as a wave of nausea swept through her. She tried to swallow it away. "Those dizzy spells are coming back."

"Want me to get a nurse?"

"Please."

At the door Jake turned and looked back at Joanna. She was sucking on ice chips, her eyes closed. He reconsidered her theory about how William Arthur Warren had gotten his liver. It would take a whole lot of arranging to set that up, Jake thought. Then he reminded himself that people with power and money were very good at arranging things.

Joanna leaned over the side of the bed and began retching.

Jake ran for the nurse.

37

The head nurse stepped out from behind the nurses' station. "Hi, Dr. Blalock. What brings you up to the obstetrical floor?"

"My doctors want me to walk around a bit," Joanna said. "They think it'll speed up my recovery."

"I heard about your accident," the nurse said, trying not to stare at the bruises and scabs on Joanna's face. "Did you know that one of our patients was also in a freeway accident the same night you were?"

Joanna nodded. "That's what someone told me. Is she doing all right?"

"Oh, she's fine. She had a little spotting, but that's stopped, and there's no evidence of fetal distress." The nurse lowered her voice. "Did you know that she's one of those surrogate mothers?"

The look on the nurse's face told Joanna that the nurse didn't approve of surrogates. "Oh, yes, I'm aware of that," Joanna said. "As a matter of fact, we may have a mutual acquaintance."

The nurse smiled awkwardly, her face coloring. "Well, Sara certainly seems like a nice person. Very nice."

"Would it be possible for me to visit her?"

"Sure. She's in room 810."

Joanna walked down the corridor and stayed close to the wall, just in case she started to lose her balance. She was still a little woozy, and at times her head seemed to swim. A step behind her was a nurse's aide who was sent along to accompany Joanna and keep an eye on her.

As they approached room 810, Joanna turned to the aide. "You can take a break now, if you wish."

The aide hesitated. "They told me to stick by you."

"Why don't you grab a cup of coffee in the nurses' lounge?" Joanna told her. "If I need you, I'll ring the nurses' buzzer."

"Great," the aide said and practically skipped down the hall.

Joanna knocked gently on the door of room 810 and entered. Sara was propped up in bed, a bunch of pillows tucked behind her. She was young—in her early twenties, Joanna guessed—with a pretty, freckled face and long auburn hair.

"Hi," Sara greeted her uncertainly.

"Hi," Joanna greeted her back. "I'm Joanna Blalock."

"And I'm Sara Smith."

"Can I visit for a while?"

"I'd like that." Sara watched the attractive visitor with the livid bruises and scratches on her face. She wanted to ask her about them, but politeness restrained her.

"I was in a car accident last night, too," Joanna explained, striking an instant chord of sympathy with Sara. "The nurse mentioned that you were a surrogate mom," Joanna added quietly.

"That's right," Sara said, thinking that her visitor might be considering using a surrogate mother to carry a child for her. "Are you interested?"

"In a way," Joanna said evasively. "Can you tell me how you get to be a surrogate mother?"

"Most of us hear about it by word of mouth," Sara said easily. "Although there is some advertising done, I'm told."

"How did you learn about the program you're in?"

"You mean Donors International?"

"Yes," Joanna said, keeping her voice and expression even.

"Well, I heard about it from a girlfriend in Santa Barbara who was in the program. So I gave them a call and they had me fill out an application and come in."

"They have a Donors International in Santa Barbara?"

"No, no. I called them from Santa Barbara, where I live. After they got my application, they sent a car and drove me to their clinic in West Los Angeles."

"The one in the mountains?"

"Right," Sara said, nodding. "It's in such a beautiful setting, isn't it? It doesn't even look like a clinic."

"What happened next?"

"Well, they interview you and put you through a hundred different tests before they even let you see the gynecologist. Then you see him and if everything is fine they accept you into the program."

"You went through a lot of testing, huh?"

"Lord! More tests than you can count," Sara told her. "They do everything, and if anything is wrong with you they disqualify you. The girl who is chosen to have your baby will be in perfect health, you can bet on that."

"I'm glad to hear that," Joanna said, now realizing that Sara Smith thought that Joanna was interested in finding a surrogate mother to carry her fertilized egg. Good. That would make the questioning easier. "After they implant the embryo into you, do you keep coming back to Donors International?"

"You see them every three months," Sara said. "But you visit an obstetrician in your hometown every month and he sends a report to Donors International."

"So there are girls from all over California in the program?"

"Oh, yeah." Sara reached for a Kleenex and quickly blew her nose. "From San Diego to San Francisco."

Joanna was about to ask Sara if she'd known Diane Butler, the sister of the skeleton found in the hills. Then she remembered that Diane Butler had committed suicide over ten years before. "So you knew others in the surrogate program?"

"Some of them. We'd be at the clinic at the same time for our checkups and we'd talk."

"Do you ever get to see the baby after delivery?" Joanna asked gently.

"Never, I'm told," Sara said at once. "They say they don't want any bonding between the surrogate mother and the baby—which, of course, is a bunch of bull. You don't carry a baby inside you for nine months without some kind of bonding. It would be impossible not to feel close to the child, don't you think?"

"Absolutely," Joanna agreed, feeling for the young woman.

"I'm told they won't even let you see the baby in the delivery room," Sara said angrily. "Jesus! You'd think they'd let you do that. You know, see the baby once."

"Yes, I would."

"But that's part of the agreement. You and your services are bought and paid for, like it or not." Sara shook her head slowly. "You never see your baby."

"Perhaps if you could find out who the biological parents were?"

"You'd better not try," Sara said ominously.

"Do you know somebody who did?"

Sara nodded and lowered her voice. "A friend of mine from Santa Paula. She wanted to see that baby so bad, but she didn't have the money to hire a lawyer."

"So what'd she do?"

"Hired a private investigator to find the biological parents of the baby."

"And what happened?"

"The private investigator started snooping around and thought he was close to getting some answers. Then he suddenly disappeared. He went out in a fishing boat on Lake Piru and never returned. They found his boat, but they never found him."

"Did your friend continue her search for the biological parents?"

"Are you kidding?" Sara said and looked at her strangely. "Would you?"

There was a soft knock on the door. It opened and the nurse's aide peeked in. "We'd better be getting back, Dr. Blalock."

Joanna stood and her head started to swim. She quickly reached for the back of her chair and steadied herself.

The aide rushed over. "Are you okay?"

"I'm fine," Joanna said, the vertigo subsiding.

"Just the same," the aide said, "I'd better hold on to you."

Joanna smiled at Sara. "I enjoyed our chat. May I come back tomorrow?"

"I'd like that a lot," Sara said.

They took the elevator back to the surgery ward and walked slowly back to Joanna's room. Joanna leaned against the aide, her legs tired and becoming weaker with each step. She wondered how long it would be before her strength returned and the dizzy spells stopped. Hopefully not the weeks and weeks the neurologist had predicted. Joanna tried to concentrate on the information Sara Smith had given her.

So the private investigator supposedly died by accident on a fishing trip, his body never found. And just when he was getting close to some answers too. How convenient! Of course, that didn't mean his death was related to the surrogate program at Donors International. Private investigators have a lot of clients and are always sticking their noses in places where they're not welcome. But still . . . Joanna planned to visit Sara Smith again and get some names. Jake could look into it.

Up ahead Joanna saw David Dellacorte and Lori McKay standing by the door to her room. They waved and quickly came over.

"How are you feeling?" Lori asked.

"Better and better," Joanna lied, her legs now rubbery. She leaned heavily against the aide. "Just a little tired from my walk."

"I'd better get you into bed," the aide said, holding tightly on to Joanna's arm.

David saw the color draining from Joanna's face and grabbed her other arm. "You've got to take it easy. It takes a while for things to come back."

David and the aide helped Joanna into bed. She lay back, her head beginning to swim again.

Lori said, "Lieutenant Sinclair stopped by a few minutes ago and said to say hello."

Joanna smiled, straining to keep her eyes open.

"And he left a message," David said. "He said to tell you that the contents of your purse were strewn all over the freeway. All the hospital had was your wallet and some keys. The data on William Arthur Warren was missing."

"Do me a favor, David," Joanna said, her eyelids half closed.

"Sure. What?"

"Get me William Arthur Warren's tissue type."

"No problem," David said. "Why do you want his tissue type?"

"Because I think it'll tell me where his liver came from," Joanna said drowsily. She closed her eyes and drifted off into a deep sleep.

38

Joanna twisted and turned in her nightmarish sleep. She was back on the freeway and her car was spinning out of control, its tires skidding on the wet pavement. Joanna screamed as her car flipped over and over and landed on its roof. She was upside down, strapped in by her safety belt. A horn was blaring. A *loud* horn. A huge oil tanker was bearing down on her. Frantically, she tried to get out. The car door was jammed shut. She pushed at it, screaming at the top of her lungs. The trucker slammed on his brakes. Too late! The tanker crashed into Joanna's car, dragging it along the freeway. Sparks flew. A fire started. Joanna pushed desperately at the door, the flames now engulfing—

Joanna awakened in the darkness with a start, unsure of where she was. Then lightning flashed outside and blue light filled the hospital room. A nightmare, Joanna told herself. The same nightmare she'd had the night before, but this one had been worse, more real. Her heart was pounding and perspiration soaked her thin gown. And her head was aching and spinning again. Lord, when would it stop? When? She became aware of her parched throat and reached over for some ice chips, but the chips had melted and the tray was filled only with lukewarm water. Joanna licked at the moisture on her fingers, wondering what time it was. It was so dark. It had to be the wee hours of the night.

Joanna suddenly tensed, her senses heightened. She thought she heard something move inside her room. Quickly she looked into the darkness in the direction of the sound. Everything was still. The only noise was the sound of her own breathing.

Joanna remained motionless, concentrating, certain she'd heard something. Lightning flashed outside again and the room lit up briefly. There were shadows and forms silhouetted against the wall. One of the shadows looked like a man with his arms upraised. Joanna was about to yell when the lightning flashed again. The shadow came from a television set suspended from the ceiling by two metal rods.

Joanna lay back and closed her eyes, sensing a wave of nausea coming on. *Not again,* she thought miserably, and tried to swallow it away. Earlier that evening she had awakened with nausea and vomiting so severe that they'd had to give her Compazine and start an IV infusion to prevent dehydration. She had done too much on her first day out of bed, and the end result was that she'd made her condition worse. *Stupid! So damn stupid!* She sighed wearily, resigning herself to a long, slow recovery.

Outside thunder roared and the rain pelted down so hard it caused the window to rattle. Joanna snuggled up under the sheets and drifted off to sleep, listening to the weather. She had slept for only a minute before she jerked up in bed once more. She had heard the sound again. Louder this time. It was a thudlike noise and it came from the direction of the door.

"Who—who's there?" Joanna asked nervously.

The door opened wide and light came in from the corridor. A man dressed in white entered. "Just here to check your IV."

A male nurse, Joanna thought and rested her head back on the pillow. "I think it's fine."

"Let's make sure."

Joanna glanced over at her arm where the IV needle was securely taped in place. All of her jerking and twisting around in bed hadn't displaced it, she thought thankfully. Joanna had small veins, and it usually took the venipuncturist two or three tries to get a needle properly inserted.

The male nurse was checking the amount of saline remaining in the plastic bag that hung from the IV pole.

"Is everything all right?" Joanna asked.

"Couldn't be better," the man said. He turned his back to Joanna as he reached into his pocket.

"Is there enough saline to get me through the night?"

"Plenty."

Joanna felt another twinge of nausea. "Could you bring me more ice chips when you have a chance?"

"Sure."

"Thanks," Joanna said, watching him step away from the bed and tear off a long strip of two-inch tape. He was wearing white pants and a short-sleeved white shirt with black loafers. Joanna looked away, then suddenly looked back and studied the man's outfit, realizing that something was wrong. The nurses on the surgery floor all wore scrub suits. All of them. All the time. Joanna pushed herself up, still staring at the man, and reached for the nurses' buzzer. "Who the hell are you?"

"What?"

"You're not a nur—"

The man slapped the buzzer away and clamped a hand over Joanna's mouth. Joanna fought and clawed at the man, trying to get out of bed. But he was on top of her, his weight pinning her to the mattress. She bit down fiercely on his hand and broke the skin.

The man jerked his hand away, and Joanna opened her mouth to scream. But as she shrieked, thunder roared and drowned out her yell for help. Before she could scream again he struck her face hard with an open palm. Scabs opened and her facial wounds began to bleed.

"Bitch!" the man seethed, and he applied a broad strip of tape across her mouth.

Joanna saw stars as a terrible pain shot through her head. He was still on top of her, and she now saw him take out a needle and syringe and reach for the IV tubing. *Oh, God! Oh, God!* Joanna's mind screamed. *He's going to kill me!*

She tried to push him off, but her strength was ebbing rapidly. Twisting and turning, she clawed at him, but he barely budged.

Joanna watched helplessly as the man injected the contents of the syringe into the IV tubing. She felt a burning sensation in her arm. Then the light dimmed and the room began to spin. Her last conscious thought was of her sister Kate. Who was going to look after her now?

39

"What the hell do you mean she just walked out?" Jake glared at the others in the hospital room, giving each a hard stare. First Simon Murdock, then David Dellacorte, then the head nurse. "Sick people don't walk out of the hospital in the middle of the night, do they?"

"Sometimes patients with head injuries do peculiar things," Dellacorte explained lamely.

"You mean they act funny? Go off their rockers?" Jake snapped.

"Sometimes it happens."

"Let me get this straight," Jake said, trying to hold his temper. "Two days after a woman is in a car accident she's up and walking around. She's acting normally, she's thinking normally. But she's still quite weak as hell. Then suddenly she decides to walk out into a storm in the middle of the night. Is that what you're saying?"

"Maybe she fell out of bed," Dellacorte suggested. "Maybe she struck her head and worsened an already serious concussion. She could have forgotten who she was and where she was."

"That's probably what happened," Murdock said, agreeing. "And that would explain why there's blood on the sheet and pillowcases."

"I see," Jake said, not seeing at all. "Joanna hits her head, crawls back into bed and bleeds, loses her memory, gets out of bed, puts on her robe and slippers, then walks out of Memorial without any-body noticing. That's how you figure it?"

"It's quite possible," Dellacorte said. "Late at night there's only a skeleton crew on duty. She could have walked right off the floor. And she would know how to avoid people. Remember, Dr. Blalock knows every nook and cranny of this hospital."

Jake looked at Dellacorte incredulously. "Are you telling me that Joanna couldn't recall who she was or where she was, but she could still remember every nook and cranny at Memorial?"

Dellacorte gestured with his hands. "Just trying to come up with an answer."

"Well, that ain't it." Jake began to pace the room, studying the closet with Joanna's clothes, the sheets and pillowcases with her blood on them. Too many things were out of place, he thought, too many things were wrong. Particularly the blood that was on the sheets and pillowcases but not on the floor. If she cracked her head open on the floor, there should be plenty of blood there.

Jake walked over to the night table and looked down at the plastic dish used to catch vomit. "Dr. Blalock wasn't feeling well last night, I take it?"

The nurse nodded. "The nausea and vomiting returned. We had to restart her IV."

"Did she throw up in bed or in the bathroom?"

"In bed," the nurse said. "She felt so nauseous and dizzy. I don't think she could have made it to the bathroom."

"So we've got a woman lying in bed sick as hell," Jake said, then turned to Dellacorte. "And you're telling me she walked out of here and kept walking to God knows where?"

Dellacorte shrugged. "I can't come up with any other explanation."

I can, Jake said to himself, and walked over to the IV pole. He gazed up at the plastic bag half filled with saline, then at the IV tubing that went from the bag through the monitor. The end of the tubing with its needle still attached dangled in the air. There was no fluid coming from it. Jake checked the needle on the IV line, then looked down. "How come there's no saline coming through the tubing?"

Dellacorte walked over and examined the tubing. "There's no saline coming out because the line has been closed off."

"And who closed it?" Jake asked pointedly.

Dellacorte shrugged and looked over at the head nurse.

"It was closed off when we came in this morning," the nurse said nervously.

"Who closed it off?" Jake asked again, staring at the others. He waited for an answer but got none. He shook his head, exasperated now. "You're not going to tell me that Joanna got up after hitting her head, pulled the IV from her arm and remembered to close off the line so fluid wouldn't leak on the floor—you're not going to tell me that, are you?"

There was an awkward silence in the room. All eyes went to the IV setup, then to the bloodstained sheets.

Murdock broke the silence. "Well, if Joanna didn't close it off, who did?"

Jake studied the IV tubing again, his mind going back to the murder of Rudolph Ettinger. He remembered Joanna telling him that the tubing had to be closed off before anything else could be injected into it. Otherwise the new material would flow up the tubing rather than into the person's vein. "Maybe it was done by the same guy who did Rudolph Ettinger."

Murdock's face suddenly lost color. "You—you think someone tried to kill Dr. Blalock?"

"Maybe he succeeded," Jake said hoarsely.

Dellacorte waved a hand disdainfully. "You don't have any proof for that, Lieutenant. There's no real evidence of foul play here."

"Sure there is," Jake said, reconstructing in his mind what had happened to Joanna. He again glanced up at the half-filled bag of saline, then looked over to the nurse. "What time was Joanna's IV last checked?"

The nurse flipped quickly through the chart. "At eleven-thirty P.M."

"And do you know how much saline was in the plastic bag at eleven-thirty P.M.?"

"Of course."

"And you know the flow rate of the IV fluids?"

"Yes."

"Good," Jake said, nodding. "Now look at the plastic bag and see how much fluid remains. That'll tell you how much saline went into Joanna between eleven-thirty P.M. and the time the IV line was closed off. Right?"

"Right."

"And if you know the amount of saline infused and the flow rate, you should be able to tell me what time the IV was stopped."

It took the nurse a minute to do the calculations. "The IV stopped at approximately twelve forty-five A.M."

Jake began pacing the floor again, glancing back and forth between the door and the bed. "At around twelve forty-five A.M., someone entered this room. Joanna's in bed sick, feeling like hell, maybe asleep. The guy starts to fiddle with the IV and Joanna wakes up. She knows something is wrong and maybe tries to scream or get out of her bed. The guy slugs her and her facial cuts open and bleed. Maybe she's got a split lip. She bleeds all over the bed, still fighting, but she's weak and sick. It's no problem for the guy to hold her down and inject something into the IV tubing."

Dellacorte nodded slowly. "And he had to close off the IV tubing to make certain that whatever he injected went directly into Joanna's vein."

"Yeah," Jake said sourly. "I'll bet it's the same bastard who did Ettinger."

"Probably some nut," Dellacorte guessed. "Some damn maniac."

Jake shrugged, thinking of the gunshots fired at Joanna on the freeway. The two attacks on Joanna's life weren't random. They weren't coincidence. Somebody wanted her dead.

"This hospital is turning into a madhouse," Murdock said disgustedly, "a madhouse with a maniac on the loose. And when the press gets wind of this, they're going to crucify us. I can see the headlines now: MURDER AT MEMORIAL . . . AGAIN!"

Dellacorte rubbed his chin pensively. "But if Joanna Blalock is dead, where's her body?"

Jake felt an icy chill, having no answer for that question, his mind resisting even contemplating it. But if he wanted to find Joanna, he had to force himself to think it through. Why take the body? What purpose would that serve? None, as far as he could see.

And moving a dead body was no easy matter. You couldn't just sling it over your shoulder and walk out the door. Of course, there was a slim possibility that she was still alive. Real slim. Could be, though, he thought, hoping against hope. Chances were she was dead, and he knew it. "Maybe the Crime Scene Unit will be able to help us with that," he said curtly, herding the others to the door. "Everybody out. And nobody—I mean nobody—comes in this room until I say so."

As he stepped into the corridor, Jake saw Lou Farelli coming toward him. Jake moved away from the group and took Farelli aside. "What have you got?"

"Nothing, *nada*," Farelli said. "Nobody in this whole fucking wing saw anything."

"Check again," Jake said in a low voice. "Get a list of everybody who was on the floor between twelve-thirty a.m. and one a.m. last night. That's when Joanna disappeared."

Farelli jotted down the times, then looked into Jake's eyes. "You okay?"

"No," Jake said honestly.

"I'm sorry about the doc, Jake. Really sorry," Farelli said and hurried back down the corridor.

Jake walked over to the group and asked the nurse, "How many people would have been working up here last night after twelve-thirty a.m?

"Maybe six, seven at the most," the nurse said, counting in her head. "That's the graveyard shift."

"And all the patients would have been sleeping?"

"Almost certainly."

Jake sighed wearily and started down the hallway, the group just behind him. He slowed as he approached the room where Rudolph Ettinger had been murdered. Two murders two doors apart. Same technique. It had to be the same guy.

Jake moved on. Across the corridor he saw a door cracked open slightly. It closed quickly. "Is Ethel Ryan still in that room?" Jake asked, gesturing with his head.

"Yes," Dellacorte answered. "She developed an infection and we had to postpone her surgery again."

"How is she doing now?"

"She's better," Dellacorte said. "She's on the schedule for tomorrow."

Jake knocked on Ethel Ryan's door and waited for her reply, then entered.

Ethel Ryan sat up in bed and fluffed her carefully coifed red hair. There was an IV running into her arm. "Hi, Lieutenant. I see you're still investigating, huh?"

"Trying," Jake said warmly, liking the woman. "Do you feel well enough to answer a few questions?"

"Sure. Why not?"

"Were you awake last night between twelve-thirty A.M. and one?"

"Absolutely."

"No doubt about it?"

"I'm positive," Ethel said, nodding firmly. "I watched the *Tonight Show* until twelve-thirty, then I watched an old Loretta Young movie. Don't you just love her?"

Jake smiled, thinking that you could tell someone's age by the movie stars they liked. "Did you stay in bed all the time?"

"Naw," Ethel said, waving a hand. "With this damn IV you've got to pee every five minutes."

"So you got up a lot?"

"A bunch."

"Was your door opened?" Jake asked.

"Always."

"So, did you see anything unusual?"

Ethel thought for a moment. "No, nothing unusual."

"Hear any unusual noises?"

"Nope. But of course half the time the thunder outside was so loud you couldn't even hear the TV."

"Well," Jake said, trying not to show his disappointment, "thanks for your time."

"You bet."

Jake was almost to the door when he turned. "Did you happen to see any of the staff last night after twelve-thirty? You know, interns or residents?"

"Nope. Just a guy with a laundry cart."

"I see," Jake said and turned for the door. Suddenly he stopped and spun around. "What kind of laundry cart?"

"You know, one of those big ones," Ethel said, spreading her hands wide apart. "It had to be four feet across, maybe more."

Jake looked over at the nurse. "Is there any reason for a big laundry cart to be up here at twelve-thirty at night?"

The nurse shook her head. "None whatsoever. There's never a need to pick up laundry at that hour."

"Son of a bitch!" Murdock hissed under his breath.

Ethel Ryan studied the expressions on their faces. "What? What? Was it something important I said?"

Jake ignored the question and quickly left the room, the others a step behind. He closed the door before he spoke. "That's how the guy did it. That's how he made her disappear. He put her body in that laundry cart and covered it with dirty linen. And he wheeled that cart right the hell out of Memorial Hospital."

"Maybe we should check the laundry," Murdock suggested.

"We will," Jake said. "But don't get your hopes up. Chances are she's long gone."

"But why take the body?" Murdock asked. "It doesn't make sense."

Yes, it does, Jake thought to himself. It makes a lot of sense to whoever did the killing. Otherwise he wouldn't have gone to all the trouble of moving the body out of Memorial. But why? Jesus H. Christ! *Why?*

Jake looked down the corridor to the nurses' station. Farelli was talking on the phone, signaling excitedly for Jake to come over.

Jake broke into a half run until he reached his partner. "What?"

"We've got all of Diane Butler's records unsealed by a friendly judge. They're being flown up to us," Farelli said as he put the phone down. "We've got us a lot of records."

"You mean medical records, right?"

Farelli nodded. "Those and a bunch of court records."

"What court records?"

"It seems that shortly after Diane Butler gave birth, she hired a lawyer to petition the court to let her know the name and where-abouts of her baby."

"And?"

"And two parties immediately went to court to prevent Diane Butler from learning the whereabouts of her baby."

Jake thought for a moment. "Donors International was one of the parties."

"Right."

"Who was the other?"

"The baby's biological father."

"You got a name for the father?"

"You ain't going to believe it."

"Try me."

Farelli smiled thinly and slowly articulated the name. "William . . . Arthur . . . Warren."

40

Joanna awoke disoriented, all of her senses out of kilter. She thought she could see, but everything was black. She could hear, but the only sound she heard was her own breathing. Her head was aching and spinning, and when she tried to sit up something stopped her. She tried again, harder. But again there was a restraint of some sort. She took a deep breath, gathering herself, and wondered where she was. Slowly her memory returned. She remembered the accident on the freeway and the concussion she'd suffered and her hospitalization. Hospital! Yes, the hospital. And then she recalled the man in her room whom she'd fought with. What did he want?

For a moment Joanna thought she was still in her hospital bed. But then she touched the surface she was lying on. It was very firm and smooth, like plastic or leather. And there were no sheets and her head wasn't resting on a pillow. And why couldn't she sit up? Why? It was very quiet. The darkness seemed to press down on her. Suddenly she felt terror, thinking she was entombed. Buried alive! Oh, Jesus! Oh, Jesus!

Joanna fought to control herself. She tried to push her panic aside, but the idea of being buried paralyzed her with fear. Desperately she searched around, looking for a speck of light. Everything was black. And there were no sounds. None. The thought that she was in a coffin underground caused her to shake uncontrollably.

With effort she calmed herself a little. *Think! Think!* she commanded herself. *You may not be in a coffin. Don't jump to conclusions. Think!* She tried to swallow, but her throat was dry and she coughed and coughed again. The sound seemed to travel. Abruptly, Joanna's brain shifted into a scientific mode. The sound carried, so there must be plenty of space around her. She quickly sucked at her cheeks and mouth, gathering up saliva, then turned her head and forcefully spat. She waited, counting off the seconds. One . . . two . . . The saliva hit the floor with a soft thud.

Joanna breathed a sigh of relief, knowing she was on a bed or table in a room. But where? Again she tried to sit up but couldn't. Then she sensed the restraint across her chest. Her hands were free, and she reached up and touched the Velcro strap. She began wriggling down the bed so her fingers could grasp the strap.

Suddenly she stopped. She heard muffled voices. Two men, she thought, maybe more. The voices grew louder. A lock turned and the door opened, letting in a streak of light. Joanna looked up and saw the kettledrum-shaped lights above her. An operating room! She was in an OR.

"Is she still out?" a male voice asked.

"I checked her twenty minutes ago, Dr. Adler," another man said, "and she was out like a light."

Adler! Jason Adler? What was he doing at Memorial? Then Joanna remembered hearing a lock turn as the door opened. The ORs at Memorial had swinging doors. There were no locks. *I must be at Donors International!* But why? The memories rushed back to her. The man in her hospital room, sitting atop her, injecting something into the IV tubing. *Jesus! I've been kid—*

"Let's check her again," Adler said.

Abruptly the room was flooded with light, the intensity so great it hurt Joanna's eyes. She heard footsteps approaching and closed her eyelids, pretending to be unconscious.

"See? Like I told you. She hasn't moved an inch."

"We don't want her too deep," Adler said. "She's got to be up and around for everything to go as planned."

"Maybe we should give her something to wake her up, then."

"That shouldn't be necessary," Adler said and moved in closer.

"Assuming you gave her the correct dose of Valium, she should be coming around shortly."

"Maybe the drug worked too good on her."

"There's one way to find out."

Joanna readied herself for what she knew was coming. A painful stimulus of some sort. People in deep anesthesia didn't respond to pain at all, and those on lighter levels withdrew from the pain and groaned. She felt Adler grasp the skin on her arm and pinch. The pain was sharp and piercing and it took all her willpower to keep her face expressionless and her body still. The pain became almost unbearable as Adler's fingernails cut into skin. Joanna groaned weakly and moved her arm away from the source of the pain.

"She's still pretty deep," Adler said. "But she'll start coming around soon."

"When should I check her again?"

"In twenty minutes."

Joanna heard the men walking away. The lights went out and the door closed. She was back in total darkness.

Patiently she waited to make certain the men weren't coming back. She counted slowly to fifty, listening and looking in the direction of the door. With effort she wriggled down the table until her fingers reached the Velcro restraint. She undid the strap and pushed herself up to a sitting position. Her head began swimming and aching, but not as much as before.

She sat on the edge of the table and took deep breaths, trying to regain her balance. Again she attempted to sort things out. Why had they kidnapped her? Why had they brought her here to Donors International? What did she know that was so important to them?

Her mind went back to the night of the accident and the meeting she'd had with Adler at Donors International. She remembered learning about the six critical antigens and how they were listed in the files of William Arthur Warren's prospective wives. And she'd asked Adler for the list of Warren's six critical antigens so she could see if they matched up with those of the four women.

So that was it! They did match up. William Arthur Warren's prospective wives were in reality his prospective organ donors.

That's why he'd put them through so many tests. To make certain they and their organs were in perfect health. The bastard probably had one of the women killed in a foreign country and her liver shipped—

No! He didn't have to kill anyone outside the country. He had them killed here at Donors International and they used this OR to remove the liver. Holy Christ! It was a perfect setup. If anyone saw the OR, they believed it was used to do experimental transplants in animals. Maybe it *was* used for that, but it was also used for humans. And Adler and Donors International were part of it all. They had to be. And now that Joanna knew everything they'd have to kill her. She was as good as dead unless she could find a way out.

Quickly she stepped down to the floor. The tiles felt very cool, and Joanna realized she didn't have her slippers on. That could be a real problem if she managed to get outside. The terrain around Donors International was rugged and rocky. It would cut her feet to shreds. *The hell with it! Get outside, then worry about your feet.*

She walked carefully in the darkness, waving a hand in front of her. Jesus! It was so dark. The last thing she wanted to do was to run into something and knock it over, causing a racket. Slowly she went forward, shuffling her feet in short steps.

She came to a wall, smooth and cold, and tapped softly on it. Glass. A window, she thought, her hopes soaring. Then she felt a metal handle and pulled on it. The built-in cabinet opened. Shit! Joanna moved on, her legs weak and heavy. And the dizziness was starting to return. She put her back against the wall and slowly slid down to a sitting position on the floor.

You've got to push on, she told herself, *otherwise you're dead. You know too much, and they can't let you stay alive.*

Joanna reached up and found a very hard edge to hold on to. She pulled herself up and felt around the curved edge until she got to the faucet. A basin! She searched for the faucet handles but couldn't find them. Then she remembered that water flow from OR basins is controlled by pedals on the floor. She stepped on a pedal and water blasted out noisily. Quickly she removed her foot, hoping no one had heard the loud noise. She gently pushed down on the pedal and water came out of the faucet with a minimum of noise. Joanna cupped her hands and gulped down mouthfuls of water. Then she splashed cold water on her face and neck.

Joanna stared into the blackness. She felt better now, but she needed light. Without it there was no chance of escape. She worked her way along the wall until she reached the door. Quietly she turned the doorknob. Locked. Pressing her ear against the door, she listened intently and heard nothing. Then she reached up and tried to find the light switch. She could feel only the tiled wall. *Damn it! It has to be here.* Unless the switch was outside the door. Again she tried to find it and again she felt only a tiled wall.

Her legs were weakening and she had to resist the urge to sit. She began to flex and extend her knees and did a few squats, trying to make the muscles work and increase the blood flow to them. She did a deep knee-bend, thinking that her only chance was to find a window and use a metal stool to punch a hole in it big enough to crawl through.

She moved her arms, stretching them back and forth. Yes, they'd kill her and bury her somewhere out in those mountains, and no one would ever find her body. Unless the rains came and washed away the mud, exposing her bones, like they did for James Robert Butler. Christ! They probably killed him too. But why? Why not just chase him away?

Don't worry about him, Joanna thought. *Worry about yourself and what they're going to do to you. I've got to get out of here before they kill me.* Joanna wondered why they hadn't killed her already. They could have killed her at the hospital with an injection of potassium chloride, just as they had murdered Rudolph Ettinger. Or they could have easily killed her here. One bullet and she'd be dead and buried where no one would find her. Why were they keeping her alive? They must have some purpose in mind for her.

Her legs felt a little stronger now, and she walked on, one hand touching the wall, the other waving in front of her. *I need a window. Lord, I need a window!*

She heard the muffled sound of voices, then footsteps coming. A lot of footsteps. Quickly she tried to work her way back to the operating table. First find the door, she told herself. Then the basin, then turn right and walk straight to— Was the OR table straight ahead or off at an angle? Off at an angle, Joanna decided frantically.

She reached the door and heard voices just outside. She moved along the wall to the basin, then veered off. The doorknob turned. Desperately Joanna floundered in the darkness, her hands groping for the operating table.

The door opened and the OR abruptly lit up.

Joanna spun around, blinded for a moment by the bright lights. "I thought you said she was still out?"

"She was," Adler said. "I swear she was."

Joanna squeezed her eyes shut and opened them again, not believing what she was seeing. She stared at David Dellacorte, her mouth agape. "What are you doing here?"

Dellacorte gestured with his head to Luis Vega. "Get her back on the table."

"What's this all about, David?" Joanna asked as Vega pushed her down and strapped her on the table.

"It's about you sticking your nose in business that doesn't concern you," Dellacorte said.

Joanna's head began to spin and she had trouble concentrating. "What are you talking about? The cystic livers were—"

"I'm talking about William Arthur Warren's tissue type," Dellacorte cut her off. "You discovered where he got his liver from, didn't you?"

"From his prospective wives," Joanna said. "That's why he had them tissue typed before he would consider marrying them."

"You aren't so bright after all, are you?" Dellacorte asked derisively. "But eventually you would have figured it out."

"Figured what out?"

"That William Arthur Warren had all those women tissue typed to find a few whose tissue type matched his. And when he found one whose type was almost identical to his, he married her."

"To get her liver," Joanna said, still not believing the nightmare.

"To get her ova," Dellacorte corrected. "And we incubated her ova with his sperm in vitro and ended up with a fertilized egg. That egg was implanted into a surrogate mother who gave birth to a child whose tissue type was nearly identical to that of William Arthur Warren. It was the child who was his organ donor."

"Oh, my God," Joanna uttered, horrified, thinking about the young children in the nearby day-care center. "The children in the day-care center are being kept like animals, to be sacrificed when needed?"

"And if an organ was needed before the child reached the necessary size, we could always use the wife as the donor. Of course, the wife wouldn't work out as well. Although her critical antigens matched up well with Mr. Warren's, there was a fair number of mismatches among the other antigens. The child, on the other hand, matched up beautifully, with only an occasional mismatch here and there. The child was for all intents and purposes a perfect donor."

Joanna glared at him. "This sounds like something the goddamn Nazis would do."

"Not really," Dellacorte said, unperturbed. "It's the future."

"What? Murder?"

Dellacorte shrugged. "We do it every day in medical centers across America and think nothing of it. We rip out fetuses—which are surely alive—and kill them in abortions. We then take some of that fetal brain tissue and implant it into the brains of patients with Parkinson's disease and the patients improve. We're killing those fetuses and taking their tissues for transplantation."

"But an abortion is different from murder."

"Oh?" Dellacorte scoffed. "Tell me about it! Tell me about the anencephalic babies who can live for weeks, but who are killed as soon as we find a baby who needs those organs. Killed! We pull the plug on those babies so they'll die and we can get their organs. Hell, we do that all the time in ICUs. Some of those patients are alive only as long as they're kept on life-support systems. And as soon as we need their organs, we do an EEG and get the family to sign a consent form and we pull the plug. You can call it murder if you like. I call it making the best of an awful situation."

"And what do you call it when you kill those children you've raised here?"

Dellacorte thought for a moment, then shrugged. "We are just helping others."

"For a quarter of a million dollars a patient."

"It's a moneymaker," Dellacorte agreed. "And we put a lot of that money back into research. We do good things here. Maybe not according to your rules, but we do good things."

Dellacorte checked his watch and turned to Luis Vega. "I want her at the back of Memorial Hospital at six A.M. sharp. Make certain she can walk. That's important. We want her up and about when the accident happens."

Joanna's eyes bulged with fear. "What accident?"

"You're going to be hit by a car and crushed. You'll be rushed into the ER at Memorial and placed on life-support systems. I'll happen to be in the ER at the time. You'll be near death and I'll remember that your sister needs a liver transplant and that your tissue type is a good match for her. We'll take your liver and give it to your sister before you die."

"Beautiful!" Vega said admiringly. "The newspapers and TV shows love this kind of shit."

"And, of course, your death will be considered accidental," Dellacorte went on. "You know, you'll be a patient with a bad concussion who wandered out the back door of Memorial and got hit by a car. It all works out very well."

"Beautiful," Vega said again.

Dellacorte turned to move away, then turned back to Joanna. "Oh, there's one more thing. The cysts in the livers of William Arthur Warren and Rudolph Ettinger were caused by hormones we gave the children. We wanted to speed up their growth and maturation, so we gave them human growth hormones as well as sex hormones. I think it was the testosterone that induced the hepatic cysts, don't you?"

Joanna stared at him, wondering if this was all some terrible nightmare.

"Yes, I think so," Dellacorte answered himself. "Well, that won't be a problem again. We don't use sex hormones anymore. They don't help that much with organ maturation."

"You bastard!" Joanna seethed and tried to get off the operating table. Vega pushed her back down.

"Keep her quiet for the next four or five hours," Dellacorte told Vega.

"How much Valium should she get?"

"A half cc," Dellacorte said, reaching for the door. "And I want her checked every fifteen minutes. Got it?"

"Every fifteen minutes." Vega reached for a syringe and filled it to the half cc mark with injectable Valium. He roughly grabbed Joanna and turned her on her side. She twisted with all of her might and tried to get out of his grip. "Hold still, bitch!" Vega said and jabbed the needle through the robe into Joanna's buttock. She twisted and jerked again as the needle penetrated her muscle.

Vega pushed down on the plunger of the syringe and met with resistance. He pushed harder, and some of the fluid squirted out from the area where the needle was attached to the syringe. Vega wondered if he should stick her again with more sedative. Maybe a little more. Screw it! Vega decided. Enough of the Valium had gotten in. That would hold her.

41

Jake Sinclair and Lou Farelli exited the elevator and walked quickly toward the grand ballroom at the Beverly Hilton Hotel. Up ahead the hotel manager and two security guards stood beside the closed doors.

The manager stepped forward to meet them, glancing pointedly at Jake's sport coat. "May I help you, gentlemen?"

Jake flashed his badge and introduced himself. "You have the seating arrangement for this affair?"

"Yes, we do."

"I need to speak with Richard Warren and Alexander Cox. We'd appreciate your getting them for us."

"They're going to be starting the presentations shortly," the manager said. "Can't this wait?"

"No, it can't," Jake said.

The manager looked Jake in the eyes. "You might be interested in knowing that the mayor of Los Angeles is here."

"That's nice," Jake said. "But we don't want to talk with him. It's Cox and Warren we want. Now, either you get them or I use the PA system. You make the choice."

The manager nodded slightly. "Please wait here."

The security guards opened the doors for the hotel manager. Jake moved in, making sure the doors stayed open. The ballroom was huge, with enough space to seat a thousand people comfortably at circular tables. At the front was an elevated dais for the distinguished guests. There were sparkling chandeliers overhead. A band that Jake couldn't see played soft dinner music.

"So this is the grand gala for the new music center, huh?" Farelli asked.

"Yeah."

"Wonder what a seat costs."

"A grand or more, depending on where you sit."

Farelli whistled under his breath. "What the hell are they serving that's worth a thousand bucks a plate?"

"Influence," Jake said and reached for a cigarette. He lit it and coughed, his throat raw from the two packs he had already smoked that day. *Got to quit,* he reminded himself, thinking of the promise he'd made to Joanna over a year before to stop smoking. Jake sighed audibly. He wasn't good at making promises and even worse at keeping them.

His mind drifted back to Joanna and her disappearance. Maybe she was still alive. Just maybe. They had checked with the laundry at Memorial and verified that no one had been authorized to pick up laundry on the surgical ward at 12:30 A.M. And a laundry cart was found on the loading dock at the rear of Memorial and shouldn't have been there. At the bottom of the cart were bloodstains. And the blood from the cart matched the blood found on Joanna's bed. Joanna had been in that cart and she was still bleeding, which meant she was probably still alive. But why kidnap her? What purpose would that serve?

"We don't allow smoking here, Lieutenant," the hotel manager said and extended his hand. "May I have your cigarette?"

Jake took a final drag on the cigarette before handing it over, still wondering why someone would want to kidnap Joanna. It was damn difficult to grab someone from a hospital and get the person out the door without being seen. The chances of getting caught were very real, even with careful planning. Someone must have wanted Joanna, or her body, really badly. But why?

Richard Warren came through the ballroom doors, tight-lipped. "You'd better have a damn good reason for this intrusion."

"Let's try murder," Jake said evenly.

"What!" Warren said, taken aback. "What murder?"

"Something that happened a long time ago," Jake said. "We've just got a few questions for you. First, were you aware that your father fathered a child ten years ago?"

Warren's jaw dropped. "You've got to be kidding!"

"I couldn't be more serious, Mr. Warren. We have plenty of proof to back it up."

"This is crazy," Warren said nervously. "My brother T.J. and I are my father's only living children. And I don't give a goddamn what kind of papers you have."

"So you never knew or met this other son?" Jake asked, unfazed by the man's anger.

"Absolutely not! I've never—" Warren stopped in mid-sentence as Alexander Cox came through the doors. He hurried over to the lawyer. "Alexander, you're not going to believe what I'm hearing from these detectives. They claim my father had another son. You know that's all a bunch of crap. You know damn well—"

Alexander Cox held up his hands, palms out. "Let's start from the beginning. What's this about another son and why are the police so interested in the matter?"

"We're investigating a possible murder," Jake explained. "In the course of our investigation we learned that William Arthur Warren fathered a boy ten years ago. It seems that nobody ever heard of the child and, other than the birth record, there's no mention of the child in any document or government file. It seems that the child just disappeared."

Cox asked, "And there's no question that the child belonged to William Arthur Warren?"

"None at all," Jake said. "The boy was born to a surrogate mother. Mr. Warren actually went to court shortly after the birth of the child to prevent the birth-mother from learning the whereabouts of the child."

Cox's eyebrows went up. "Did you say surrogate mother?"

"That's right," Jake replied. "Mr. Warren was named as the biological father."

"This is insane," Richard Warren blurted out. "This is—"

Cox held up his hand again and Warren fell silent. "So William Arthur Warren and Pamela had a child using a surrogate mother. Is that what you're saying?"

"Exactly," Jake said.

"I was never informed of this."

"Are you sure?"

Cox hesitated briefly. "To the best of my knowledge."

"That's odd," Jake said, smiling coldly. "Very odd. Because the court records on the child list you as William Arthur Warren's lawyer."

Cox didn't blink. "You must be mistaken. I would have remembered that."

"Well, you're named as the attorney in the court proceedings."

Cox thought for a moment. "And the court was petitioned here in Los Angeles?"

"No. In San Diego."

"That explains it," Cox said, nodding. "We opened a branch of our firm in San Diego some years ago. My son, Alexander, ran the San Diego office."

"How can we reach him?"

"I'm afraid that's not possible," Cox said sadly. "My son died of leukemia five years ago. We closed the office shortly after that."

"I'm sorry," Jake said and made a mental note to check and see if the old man was telling the truth about his son. "So, William Arthur Warren never mentioned this to you, is that right?"

"Never," Cox said. "But that wouldn't be unusual for him. He was a very secretive man and liked to keep things close to his vest. That was his style."

Richard Warren waved his hands disgustedly. "I still don't believe it. My father would never have a child that way."

"Well, he did," Jake said firmly. "He and Pamela Warren are listed as the biological parents."

"That bitch," Warren hissed. "She put him up to this. She would have done anything to get her hands on the Warren money."

Jake turned to Alexander Cox. "Mr. Cox, I need to see your son's file on William Arthur Warren. It might tell us something about the child's disappearance."

"May I ask why you are so interested in something that happened ten years ago?"

"Because it might help us solve a murder-kidnap case we're working on now," Jake said at once, his intuition telling him that everything here was interconnected. The murders of Pamela Warren and Rudolph Ettinger, the disappearance of the child, the kidnapping or worse of Joanna, the buried skeleton of James Butler. All interconnected. But how? "That file could be very helpful."

"I see," Cox said, giving the matter serious consideration. "And William Arthur Warren may somehow be involved in this case?"

"Indirectly," Jake hedged.

Cox sighed heavily, still weighing the matter. "You must understand that even though Mr. Warren is dead, I'm still bound by the attorney-client relationship. I still have to protect his interests and name."

"Damn right," Richard Warren said. "If my father did anything wrong, we're not going to help you prove it."

Jake was wasting valuable time and knew it. And he didn't want to go through all the paperwork to get a court order to open the file. That would take up even more time. "Let's strike a deal," he said to Cox. "You screen your son's files on William Arthur Warren. If you find anything that incriminates him, you don't show the file to me. If there's nothing incriminating, I get to read it."

Cox considered the offer carefully, then nodded. "Agreed. I'll review the file tomorrow and give—"

"You'll review it *tonight*," Jake said, cutting him off.

"That's quite impossible," Cox said promptly. "Some of those San Diego files are on microfilm. Some are still in boxes in our storage room. It would take us hours and hours just to find the Warren files."

"Who is in charge of the files in your office?"

"Our office manager."

"Give him a call and have him meet us at your office immediately. Tell him he may have to spend the whole night looking for a file."

Cox hesitated. "Why the urgency, Lieutenant?"

"Because somebody's life may be at stake."

"Let me see if I can reach our office manager," Cox said.

"I'm coming along," Richard Warren said, still thinking about losing a third of the Warren fortune to a stranger. "As executor of my father's estate, I'm entitled to know the contents of that file."

"Do you have a problem with that, Lieutenant?" Cox asked.

"None," Jake said.

"There's a bank of phones by the men's room," Richard Warren said, taking the attorney's arm.

Jake watched the men walk away and turned quickly to Farelli. "Get a couple of patrol officers over to Cox's office pronto. Tell them to stand at the door and not let anybody in until we get there."

Farelli took out his cellular phone. "You think they'd try to hide something?"

"I think they would if they had a chance to."

Farelli shrugged. "It seemed to me that they were surprised, like they really didn't know anything."

"Nobody knows anything," Jake said, shaking his head in disgust. "People are being murdered, people are disappearing, and nobody knows a goddamned thing."

"Well, at least we know the doc is still alive," Farelli said, punching numbers into his cellular phone. "You know, the blood at the bottom of the laundry cart and all."

Jake nodded, but he wasn't at all sure that Joanna was alive. The blood stains at the bottom of the cart could have come from a dead body as well as a live one.

Farelli spoke briefly into the cellular phone, giving instructions, then pushed the off button. "There'll be a black-and-white there in ten minutes."

"When we get out of here, make another call to get the paperwork started for a court order to open up the files on William Arthur Warren."

"But Cox has already agreed to let us take a look."

"And suppose he finds something incriminating and decides not to let us see the file?"

Farelli scratched his ear absently. "You really think that file is going to tell us something important, don't you?"

"It sure as hell better," Jake said. "Otherwise we got nothing, absolutely nothing."

42

Joanna awakened to the sound of a door opening and closing and opening again. Then bright lights came on. She closed her eyes and remained motionless.

"I keep forgetting that the damn light switch is outside the door," Jason Adler said from a distance.

"See? She's still asleep."

"She hasn't moved any?"

"Not an inch."

"Good. When you check her next, sit her up and get her moving."

The door closed and the lights went out. Joanna waited, making sure they'd gone, then opened her eyes. She expected to see blackness, but instead saw a hazy, deep gray. Gradually things began to come into focus. Above her were the kettledrum-shaped lights, off to the sides the gleaming tiled walls of the OR.

She tried to sit up, but the Velcro belt across her chest restrained her. Wriggling down the table, she reached up and unstrapped herself. With effort she pushed herself into a sitting position. Her head began to swim and a wave of nausea swept up from her stomach, but it lasted for only a moment. She took long, deep breaths and collected herself, remembering what had happened before they injected her the last time. She could still see the smug expression on David Dellacorte's face as he gloated over what he was doing. It was unbelievable! Conceiving babies and raising them to serve as organ donors. They were killing people for their vital organs. And Joanna was next.

Another wave of nausea came and she retched briefly. She brought up nothing. The nausea passed.

Her mind went back to Dellacorte and his plans for her. They would take her to the road behind Memorial Hospital in the early morning, where she would have a fatal accident and be rushed to the ER. Early morning! Joanna wondered what time it was and how much time she had left.

Slowly she eased herself off the operating table, then began to move in the half darkness. The tiled walls and basins were becoming more distinct now, the glass cabinets reflecting light. Light! Where was it coming from? Joanna glanced up at the far wall near the ceiling and saw the windows. They were more like slits and appeared to be made of frosted glass.

She found a small table with thick legs and quietly pushed it across the room. She climbed onto the table and reached up to examine the window. It was rectangular, made of thick frosted glass, and about two feet in height. *Maybe I could squirm through it. Maybe. But first I've got to break it.*

There was a loud, rumbling sound outside and the window began to vibrate. Then Joanna saw giant raindrops pelting against the glass. She climbed down from the table and looked around for something she could use to break the window. A hammer would be perfect, she thought, or some other heavy, blunt instrument. A wrench or pliers would do. But a hammer was best. And if she timed the blows of the hammer to coincide with the thunder outside, no one would hear her.

Thunder roared again, and Joanna looked up at the window. The light coming through was more intense. Dawn was breaking. Panic flooded through her as she realized that time was short, very short. How often were they checking on her? Every fifteen minutes, Dellacorte had ordered. And on the next check they were supposed to get her up and moving. Joanna wondered how much time she'd used up since the last check. Five minutes at least. Probably more. Again she felt the panic and tried to push it aside.

Stay cool, she commanded herself. Find the goddamn hammer and break the window. Now, where would a hammer be? Or a wrench? Maybe by the anesthetic equipment. It had all sorts of knobs and screws to turn and sometimes they got stuck.

Quickly she went back to the operating table and squatted down next to the tanks of oxygen and anesthetic agents. The light in the OR dimmed, and for a moment Joanna could hardly see anything. Then the light came back. Probably a cloud blocking out the early morning sun, she guessed. She found a metal drawer and opened it. There were screwdrivers, pliers, a wrench. All small. Too small to break through thick glass. Disheartened, she closed the drawer and looked over at the wall. Then she saw it. A small fire extinguisher, fully loaded. She lifted it and felt its weight. It was plenty heavy enough. She'd use it like a battering ram.

Joanna placed the fire extinguisher on the table under the window and climbed up. Carefully she brought the extinguisher to her shoulder and held it there, ready to strike, waiting for the next roar of thunder. *Come on! Come on, damn it!* She waited and waited. A minute passed, maybe more. Another minute, she told herself, and the window had to go, thunder or not. Then she heard the sounds of approaching footsteps and muffled voices.

Quickly, Joanna put the extinguisher down and jumped off the table. *I'm dead! I'm as good as dead!* She moved rapidly to the operating table and was about to lie down when she saw the standing tray with surgical instruments on it. She grabbed a scalpel and a roll of tape next to it. Hurriedly she taped the scalpel to the inner surface of her forearm and covered it with the sleeve of her hospital robe.

The lights went on and the door began to open.

Joanna lay back and fastened the Velcro strap across her abdomen.

"All right, let's get her up," Adler said.

Joanna tried to relax and keep her muscles limp. She felt herself being lifted up, strong hands holding her in a sitting position. Groaning softly, she moved her head in a bobbing motion.

"Christ! We've got to get her walking and she's not even awake," another man said.

Joanna let her legs dangle off the table, then made the sound of someone about to vomit.

"And now she's going to throw up. Shit! You must have over-dosed her."

"No, I didn't," Luis Vega protested. "Half the stuff didn't even go in." But no one was paying any attention to him.

"Let's get her outside. Maybe she'll do better in the fresh air," Adler said.

Joanna kept her body flaccid as Luis Vega picked her up and threw her over his shoulder. Her head and arms hung down loosely. She had her eyes open now, staring at the back of his black coat. They were moving through a door and down a corridor. A long corridor. Joanna smelled the odor of caged animals and immediately knew where they were. She remembered the area from her tour of Donors International with Jason Adler. They would be outside shortly. Luis Vega slowed.

"Let me get the door," Adler said and hurried ahead.

Joanna untaped the scalpel from her forearm and held it tightly, the blade pointed at Vega's back. They stepped outside. The air was misty and cool, the rain still falling.

"I'll get someone to help you," Adler said, walking away.

"Yeah, do that," Vega said and shifted Joanna up higher on his shoulder. He put his free hand under Joanna's robe and felt her buttocks and anus and pubis. His hand moved slowly back and forth. Suddenly he grabbed a handful of pubic hair and pulled.

"Ohh!" Joanna yelled, caught by surprise.

"So you're not so much asleep, huh?" Vega laughed. A cold, humorless laugh. "Let's try it again."

Joanna waited until his hand was feeling her buttock again. Then she raised the scalpel and plunged it into his back.

Vega dropped to his knees, screaming. Frantically he reached back, trying to find the source of the terrible pain. By the time he pulled out the scalpel, Joanna was sprinting up a nearby hill. He struggled to his feet, the pain still awful. "Get her! Get her!"

Joanna scrambled and fought her way up the hill, the gravel and rocks cutting into her bare feet. Behind her she heard angry voices, yelling and screaming obscenities. She turned to see where they were and she tripped and fell, her face mashing into the soft dirt and leaves. Quickly she was back up, but now she was disoriented. She looked around, panic-stricken, trying to get her bearings. At the top of the hill was a path, she remembered. It led to the road out.

She tripped once more, almost falling, but kept going. *Get to the top,* she told herself. *It's the way out.* Again she heard the voices behind her, closer now, and she pushed herself on. The mist was lifting and she could see the top of the hill. A man was standing there, waiting for her. A security guard! She was trapped, with no avenue of escape. The security guard moved toward her, planting each foot carefully in the mud. Suddenly the ground gave way and the guard tumbled down the hill, his leg twisted awkwardly underneath him. His body hit a large rock near Joanna and the man shrieked with pain. Joanna saw the guard's ripped pants, his leg bent, a bone sticking through the fabric.

Another guard was almost upon her and grabbed at Joanna's ankle. She kicked him hard in the groin and wriggled free, stumbling and groping her way up the hill.

Behind her a voice yelled, "Get her! But don't shoot! Don't shoot!"

She was on top of the hill now and ran for the stand of tall pine trees. The brush was thick and tangled, each step an effort. Her energy was almost gone and she needed to rest badly, if only for a little while. She crawled in behind a dead log, gasping for air. The treetops blocked out most of the light, and the mist was thickening. *Maybe they won't find me,* she thought. But she knew they would when the daylight grew and the mist lifted.

Joanna quickly examined herself. She ached everywhere, but nothing was broken. Her robe was in tatters, her arms ripped and bloody. But no broken bones, thank God! She took long, deep breaths, filling her lungs with cool air as she tried to devise a plan of escape. The only way out was the main road, and that would be heavily guarded. And she couldn't go over the mountains, not in her condition.

Then she remembered the dormitory where the children were

housed. They would have a phone there. One call was all she needed. It was her only chance.

The rain started to come down heavily again, the visibility even less now. With effort Joanna got to her feet and began to move through the brush. She heard footsteps nearby and slowly backed up against a tree. At least two men, Joanna thought. The footsteps came closer and closer.

Joanna froze. She was still exposed but she thought: *Don't move!*

"We'll never find her in this brush," a voice said. It couldn't have been more than ten feet away. "Let's get the bloodhound."

Joanna waited as the footsteps moved away. When she could no longer hear them, she dashed through the trees and down a pebbled path that led to the Japanese garden. She glanced around the open area and saw no guards. Taking a deep breath, she ran across the manicured lawn and over a small bridge and then to the fence surrounding the dormitory. The gate was open and she entered. There were no people, no sounds.

She hurried up the steps to the dormitory and looked over her shoulder before going inside.

A dozen children sitting at small tables looked up at her. Their faces were expressionless, their eyes almost lifeless. They showed no fear or interest in Joanna.

"Is there a phone here?" Joanna asked hurriedly.

The children stared and didn't respond.

"A phone!" Joanna raised her voice. "I need a phone."

The children just stared.

A door at the rear of the room opened and a matron entered. She was pushing a cart filled with platters of eggs and pancakes and bacon. At first she didn't see Joanna, but then she did and her jaw dropped. "Who are you?"

"I need help," Joanna said desperately. "I have been kidnapped."

The children rose with their plates in their hands and moved toward the breakfast cart. "Food! Food!" they said in unison, their voices a dull monotone. "Food! Food!"

"Help me! Please!" Joanna pleaded.

The matron reached for the police whistle around her neck and blew it loudly. The children scurried about, bumping into one another, not knowing what to do.

Joanna ran out the front door—but she saw guards coming across the wooden bridge. There were two of them, one with a bloodhound on a leash. Joanna hurried back into the dormitory, slamming the door and locking it.

She dashed for the back door, zigzagging among the children. The matron tried to block Joanna's way with the food cart. Joanna grabbed the front handle of the cart and shoved it into the matron, knocking her backward. The cart toppled over, eggs and bacon and pancakes spilling onto the floor. The children quickly went to their knees and, like animals, shoveled food into their mouths with their hands.

The front door crashed open and the guards charged in. They rushed at Joanna, but their shoes slipped on the floor, made slick by eggs and bacon pieces, and they fell hard. The bloodhound stopped to eat the food on the floor and paid no attention to Joanna.

Joanna ran out the back door, then through a kitchen area, then through another door, and then she was outside. The rain was falling so hard it stung. She wiped the water from her face and looked to the tall mountain on her left. Too high. Too steep. She'd never get up that. To her right was a stand of tall pine trees and beyond that was the medical complex. If she went that way she'd be running right back into the hands of her captors. Behind her she heard the guards coming, the bloodhound baying loudly.

Joanna made a dash for the pine trees. She could hear men yelling all around her, even in front. Christ! They were everywhere. She was almost through the pines now, thinking that if she could get to the rear of the medical facility she might find a path or trail. The hills weren't as high there, she remembered.

She came to a clearing and looked down at the medical complex. On a patio below, Jason and the man she'd stabbed were looking up at her. The hound was very close, howling at the top of its lungs. And more guards were climbing up the hill to capture her. *Work your way down the mountain at an angle,* Joanna thought frantically, *away from them.*

Carefully she started down at an angle, but the guards below veered off too and stayed in line with her. They weren't hurrying now. There was no need to rush. They had their prey trapped.

The earth suddenly moved. Everyone froze in their tracks. The dog went silent. Then the earth moved again. Joanna's heart stopped for a moment. An earthquake, she thought. But the ground began to slip from beneath her feet and someone yelled out, "Landslide!"

Joanna scrambled, falling, groping her way up and away from the sliding mud. Men were yelling and screaming as they were swallowed up by the avalanche of mud and debris. Joanna fell and tried to get back up, but water came gushing down the mountain, taking her with it. Joanna tumbled head over heels downhill, and for a second she blacked out. When she opened her eyes she was choking, half buried in the mud and rubble.

Then she heard a terrible groaning sound. The front of the mountain was collapsing, taking the Japanese garden and dormitory down with it. Tons of soggy earth slid and gained momentum, then crashed down on the back section of Donors International, half burying it with mud.

Joanna got to her feet and tried to outrun the moving earth. Rocks and trees flew by her as she headed downhill. She fell again, tumbling, blinded by mud and rain. She landed in a trench of some sort. Frantically she wiped at her eyes and cleared her vision. A ditch. She saw a large drainage pipe just as the earth shuddered violently. Joanna dove into the pipe a second before the avalanche of mud hit.

Mud and water thudded against the pipe again and again. The noise was deafening. Then abruptly it stopped. In the blackness Joanna could hear only the sound of her own breathing. She felt the wall of the pipe above her. It was made of some type of cement. On her hands and knees she crawled down the tube, scraping her knees and elbows. It came to an end. Something made of metal was blocking the way.

She crawled backward to the opening of the drainage pipe. It too was blocked by debris and wood and something cold and soft. It had five tentacles and—Joanna jerked her hand away. She was feeling a human hand. Probably one of the guards who had been caught in the avalanche, his body now plugging the opening of the pipe.

Joanna dug around the guard's hand, pushing his arm aside. Suddenly mud and water flowed in. Then the guard's body came back into place at the mouth of the pipe and the inflow stopped. Terror gripped Joanna as she realized that she was buried alive. She pounded on the walls and screamed at the top of her lungs, crying out for help, but the only sounds she heard were her own screams and the echoes they made.

Luis Vega slowly pulled himself out of the rubble and dirt and got to his feet. The pain in his back was sharp and piercing, even worse than before, and he reached behind to see if he was still bleeding. He felt a warm ooze and quickly placed his handkerchief over it and waited for the cloth to stick in place. Floating dirt and debris were settling out of the air now, and he could see the devastation caused by the landslide. Half of the mountain was gone, and it had taken the dormitory and Japanese garden with it. Everything below was buried under mud, including the rear portion of Donors International.

Vega climbed up onto the patio and looked around for survivors. There was an eerie stillness. Nothing seemed to move. In the distance he heard the bloodhound baying. Then it stopped. Vega walked across the patio, its cement cracked and buckled by the pressure of the sliding mud. Up ahead he saw Jason Adler sitting on a step, a dazed expression on his face.

"Are you all right?" Vega asked.

"I guess so," Adler said. He had a deep scratch on his cheek and blood was trickling from it. "Are any of the others alive?"

"No way." Vega examined his gun and checked the barrel to see if it was clear of mud. "Everybody is buried under a ton of mountain."

"Maybe someone . . ."

"Forget it," Vega said, holstering his gun. "They're all dead and buried."

The hound howled again, a low, mournful cry.

Adler struggled to his feet with Vega's help. "What about Joanna Blalock?"

"I saw the whole mountain come down on her. She was either crushed or suffocated to death."

Adler walked around in small circles, checking himself to see if any bones were broken. He looked over at the wall of mud that had rammed into the rear building and flattened it. "We're lucky to be alive."

"Yeah," Vega said tonelessly. "Now what do you want to do with this mess?"

"Well, I—" Adler began hesitantly, "I think we should call for help and see if anyone managed to survive under all this rubble."

Vega looked at Adler strangely, wondering if the doctor was as stupid as he sounded. "You want strangers digging through here with shovels, uncovering dead bodies? Suppose they find Joanna Blalock and those children? What are you going to tell them?"

"You're right," Adler said and nervously rubbed his hands together. "We can't take that chance."

Vega knew what had to be done—and quickly. He was an expert at covering up tracks. "Is anyone working in these buildings now?"

"No. Our personnel don't arrive until eight A.M."

"So no one is here but us?"

"That's correct."

"Good," Vega said, again surveying the mountain and the damage caused by the mudslide. "Let me tell you what we have to do."

"Perhaps we should call Dellacorte first."

"Later," Vega said, taking command. "First, close Donors International to everyone because of the mudslide damage. Give the staff two weeks off with pay. Nobody will bitch."

"Then what?"

"Then we call in some friendly construction people who owe the family favors. They'll bring in earthmovers and take down what remains of that mountain. If they see anything, they'll keep their mouths shut."

Adler nodded approvingly. "Just flatten it, huh?"

"And pave over it. Then construct a new building on top of it."

"How long will all this take?"

"Does it matter?"

Adler shrugged. "I guess not."

"Stay put while I check around."

Vega walked to the end of the patio and carefully climbed down into the mud, sinking in it up to his ankles. With effort he plowed through the sticky slime and debris. Only a few things in the rubble were recognizable. There were some shingles from the roof of the dormitory, and farther up the hill a section of the wooden bridge from the Japanese garden.

Vega stepped over a toppled pine and sank deeper, half up to his knees. Off to his left he saw a child's hand sticking out of the mud. He reached down and touched it. Ice cold. He forced it back down and covered it with dirt and debris.

Vega started back to the patio, the going even tougher now. *The mud and goo will swallow up everything,* he thought. It's like a swamp. The bodies and debris will sink deeper and deeper, never to be found. Good. Just bring in a couple of earthmovers and push the rest of the mountain into this sinkhole. Everything and everybody will be buried for eternity.

Vega spotted a light-blue piece of clothing and picked it out of the slime. Its sleeves were tattered and covered with bloodstains. It was a robe. And inside was stenciled "Memorial Hospital."

Vega climbed up onto the patio and walked over to Jason Adler. "Look what I found."

Adler examined the robe and the marking inside. "It's hers?"

"Got to be."

"Did you see her body? Did you actually see her dead body?"

"Hell, no!" Vega blurted out, losing his patience. "That mud is like slimy goo. You sink in up to your knees just standing still. Nobody is going to find anything or anybody in that shit."

"I just want to be double sure."

"We'll be double sure when the whole damn area is paved over," Vega said, now thinking about the child's hand that had popped up and wondering if anything else was going to surface. "I've got to get rid of this robe."

Adler watched the hit man walk away, unsure if he should follow Vega's advice. After all, Vega was nothing more than a hired gun, rough and deadly, and thinking only of himself. No, Adler thought, better not trust Vega's judgment. Better to contact Della-corte and come up with a plan.

Adler looked back at the collapsed mountain and the rain

324   *Leonard Goldberg*

falling on it, just a drizzle now. But the sky was darkening and filled with clouds, and he knew more rain was coming. And more rain could wash away the mud and expose bodies.

Adler's mind flashed back to James Butler, the crazy man who had been distraught over the suicide of his sister and had sent threatening letters to Donors International. They had investigated the man's past and learned he was once a Ranger and an expert marksman. They'd had to kill him before he killed them. And they had buried the body deep, very deep, but the rain had still uncovered it a year later. Maybe Vega was right. Best to pave over everything.

Adler heard a car coming and quickly turned to the road below the patio. It was a Chevrolet, unmarked, with two men in it. Adler strained his eyes, trying to identify it. God damn it! Who were they and what did they want? And why hadn't the guard at the gate stopped them? Adler hurried over to the steps that led down to the road. The car doors opened and two men got out.

Adler quickly straightened his mud-splattered white coat and waved. "Hello, Lieutenant!" he called out, wondering what the police wanted and why they were here so early in the morning. His heart was pounding in his chest, but he kept his expression even.

Jake came up the steps, Lou Farelli just behind him. At the top he stopped, taken aback by the destruction he saw. "Jesus! What happened here?"

"I'm afraid we had a landslide," Adler said, surprised at the calmness of his voice.

"Was anybody hurt?"

"We don't think so. Only the rear building was destroyed, and fortunately no one was in it at the time of the slide."

"Lucky. Damn lucky," Jake said, now looking up at what remained of the mountain. "You'd better get some experts out here to determine how stable that mountain is."

"We plan to do that as soon as we finish our head count," Adler said, wiping at his forehead with his sleeve. "We have to make certain everyone is accounted for. That's our first priority."

"As it should be," Jake said, taking out his notepad and opening it. "I just need a little information from you."

"Regarding what?"

"Some missing children."

Adler's heart stopped, then started again. "What missing children?"

"It seems that William Arthur Warren and Rudolph Ettinger were the biological fathers of children born to surrogate mothers. And now these children have disappeared." Jake paused and watched Adler's face for a reaction. There wasn't any. "Since everything was arranged through Donors International, we thought you might be able to help us with this investigation."

Adler stared at Jake Sinclair, wondering how much he knew and how much to tell him. The dog started howling again, and Adler looked in the direction of the sound, thinking, trying to come up with answers.

Farelli was achingly fatigued, exhausted from staying up all night searching for William Arthur Warren's legal file. They had finally found it. In the lawyer's notes it was mentioned that Rudolph Ettinger had also fathered a son at Donors International and had won a court battle preventing the surrogate mother from ever seeing the child. Warren's lawyers had used the Ettinger case as a precedent. Farelli watched Adler. The doctor seemed at ease, but his right hand was clenched into a fist.

"Can you help us with this?" Jake asked again, wondering if Adler had heard the request.

Adler shrugged. "We usually don't do any follow-up on the children once they've gone to their biological parents. I doubt if we have any information on them."

"We'd appreciate it if you could check your files. Particularly the files that relate to the lawsuits that were brought against Donors International by the surrogate mothers of the children." Jake thought he saw Adler's face tighten but he couldn't be sure. "Those files could prove very beneficial."

Adler shrugged once more. "Again, Lieutenant, we usually don't keep records on the children. Those children don't belong to us, they belong to their parents."

"No, they don't," Jake snapped. "Those children belong to the state of California. And their parents, like all parents, are just guardians. If the parent in any way abuses, hurts or endangers these children, the state steps in and takes the children away." Jake gave Adler a hard look. "And if the parents or anyone else has harmed those kids, it's a crime. A felony."

"And rightly so," Adler said, his brain racing to come up with a way to delay.

"Now, we want to look at those files."

"All of our computer files are in there," Adler said and pointed to the middle building. "The ground has shifted and the walls of the structure have wide cracks in them. I'm not going into that building until someone tells me it's safe. And I don't think you should either."

Jake could see the cracks running all the way up to the roof. "Get some structural engineers to check it out. We'll be back tomorrow with our own computer expert. And a court order."

That will give us plenty of time to alter the files, Adler thought. "We'll be glad to open our files to you or any other authorized person."

Jake started down the steps, wondering if he should post a guard to make certain no one went into that building. Behind him he heard a voice call out, "Hey, Adler, the power is off and the damn shredder won't work."

Jake turned and saw a man coming across the patio. The man was dressed in black and was holding a piece of clothing in his hand. Jake studied the man's face for a moment before recognizing it. Luis Vega!

Luis Vega spotted the detectives and had his gun out in an instant, assuming the firing position.

"No! No!" Adler yelled out, running at Vega. "They can't prove—"

Vega squeezed the trigger on his semiautomatic Beretta. The first two shots went into Adler's head and chest. Adler dropped like a dead weight, giving Vega a clear field of vision.

Jake dove for the steps as bullets whizzed by him. There were more shots, and he heard Farelli scream with pain. Quickly Jake eased himself down the steps, gun out, head up, eyes fixed on the top of the wooden steps. He heard a loud groan. It sounded like Farelli, but Jake couldn't be sure. Then he heard another groan before everything became silent.

Jake waited, staying absolutely still, his hearing concentrated to any sound that would give away Vega's position. A streak of sunshine broke through the clouds, and Jake saw a human shadow looming above him, moving toward him, growing larger and larger. *Vega! He's coming!* Jake aimed his weapon at the top of the steps and waited. Suddenly the shadow disappeared. Vega had dropped to the prone position, Jake thought, and he was crawling to the edge of the patio. He had to find out if Jake was dead or not.

Jake saw the barrel of Vega's gun come over the edge of the patio. Jake waited, his eyes fixed on the barrel. *Soon it will move,* he told himself. He steadied his weapon against the wooden step. Seconds passed and then more—maybe thirty altogether, but the barrel stayed stationary. More time passed. Nothing. Then Jake heard a noise in the nearby muddy slush.

Son of a bitch!

Jake rolled off the steps just as Vega came around from the side. Vega turned abruptly to follow the moving target, and for a brief instant he lost his balance in the mud. Jake fired off two rounds. The first went wide. The second went into Vega's left eye.

Jake slowly got up and cautiously approached the body, his gun still drawn. Vega was on his back, staring up at the sky with his remaining eye wide open. Jake kicked hard at Vega's ribs. Vega didn't flinch. With his foot Jake turned Vega over and saw brain and bone dangling from the back of the head.

Jake holstered his weapon and quickly went up the steps to the patio. Farelli was on his feet, holding his bloodied shoulder.

"You all right?" Jake asked.

"Yeah," Farelli said. "He just winged me."

Jake took off his tie and wrapped it around Farelli's upper arm, stemming the flow of blood. "That'll hold you until we can get to the hospital." Jake leaned over for the gun that Vega had used as a decoy and placed it in Farelli's holster.

"You get the bastard?" Farelli asked.

Jake nodded. "He's got half a head left."

"Will you please tell me what a mob hit man is doing here?"

Jake shrugged. "It gets crazier and crazier, doesn't it?"

Farelli grimaced and grabbed at his shoulder. "I'd better lie down for a minute."

Jake helped Farelli down to the cement and saw the piece of

clothing Vega had been carrying. He picked it up to use as a pillow for Farelli, then noticed that it was a robe. A robe from Memorial Hospital. "Jesus! Look at this!"

"Wha—?"

Suddenly the earth groaned as the mountain began to slide again. Jake helped Farelli up and they ran for their lives.

43

David Dellacorte hurried into the preop area and glanced up at the schedule board. His patient, Ethel Ryan, would have her exploratory laparotomy done in OR two at eight A.M. Dellacorte's eyes went to the clock above the board. It said 7:30. And he still hadn't gotten a call from the ER regarding Joanna Blalock. Something must have gone wrong, he thought, wondering what and why.

"Your patient is over there," a nurse said and pointed to the far wall. "We'll get Mrs. Ryan set up as soon as the anesthesiologist arrives."

"Why is he late?" Dellacorte asked.

"A flat tire."

Dellacorte grumbled under his breath, but he was pleased with the delay. It would give him time to find out why Joanna Blalock wasn't in the ER on life-support systems. The accident should have occurred an hour ago. "Do you have any idea when he'll get here?"

The nurse shrugged. "Soon, I hope."

"Page me when he arrives."

Dellacorte walked over to the gurney by the far wall and patted Ethel Ryan's shoulder. "How are you doing?"

"Not bad, considering," Ethel said and smiled nervously.

"Are you drowsy?"

"Not enough." She shifted around on the uncomfortable gurney, her eyes never leaving Dellacorte's face. "Make damn sure you get all the tumor out."

"I'll do my best."

"The hell with your best! Get it all out."

"Every drop I see," Dellacorte said, knowing already that the cancer was unlikely to be resectable and that he'd probably end up doing bypasses to prevent further obstruction in the biliary tract. This would give the patient more quality time in the life she had remaining. "There's always chemotherapy if any tumor cells are left behind."

"The hell with that," Ethel said tersely. "Get it all while you're in there."

Dellacorte patted her shoulder reassuringly and left the preop area. He went into the doctors' lounge and looked around to see if anyone else was there. A toilet flushed loudly. Dellacorte hurriedly picked up a magazine from the coffee table and pretended to scan through it.

What could have gone wrong? he asked himself again. There was no way Joanna Blalock could have escaped, not with Luis Vega watching her. Vega was so dependable, so good at what he did. But then again, maybe she had escaped, or maybe she'd died out there. No, he decided at once. Had that occurred Adler would have notified him. What had happened, then? Maybe they'd done as they were told, but Joanna wasn't—

The door to the bathroom opened and a resident stepped out, tightening the drawstring of his scrub suit. The resident passed by Dellacorte, nodding, and walked out.

Dellacorte grabbed the phone and rapidly dialed the number of Donors International. It rang twelve times. No answer. He dialed again. Twelve rings. Again no answer. Something *had* gone wrong. Dellacorte was certain of it now. But what? Maybe they were having trouble causing the accident behind Memorial. Or maybe the accident had been carried out. Maybe she was in the ER and they just hadn't called him yet. Yes! That was probably it. She would have come in near death and it would take time to get her on life-support systems and to get scans to assess the extent of the injuries to her head and brain.

Dellacorte picked up the phone and started to call the ER, then decided against it. No. Better to let them call him. He was chief of the transplant service. He did the harvesting of the organs. Only him. They would call.

But Dellacorte reached for the phone again, wanting to know for certain if Joanna was in the ER. He picked it up, hesitated, then placed the phone down. Better to wait. *And besides, what the hell would I ask the people in the ER? Has Joanna Blalock arrived with her head bashed in?* And what if she hadn't?

Dellacorte glanced up at the wall clock: 7:45. He started to pace the floor, worried, his mind racing. *Check and see if she's in the ER,* Dellacorte told himself. *Casually walk into the ER and tell them you've come for a cup of coffee while waiting for your next case.* And if she wasn't there, then what? Perhaps he should drive out to Donors International and find out what had happened. But he wouldn't have time to do that. The drive out there took twenty minutes one way, on a good day without all this fucking rain.

Dellacorte considered delaying the surgery on Ethel Ryan. If the anesthesiologist didn't show up soon, Dellacorte would let another case be done in OR two. He could reschedule Ethel Ryan for later in the day. That would give him time to get to Donors International and back.

The door to the lounge opened and the surgical resident looked in. "Dr. Dellacorte, the ER called. They just brought in Joanna Blalock."

"Is she all right?" Dellacorte asked, hiding his relief and appearing very concerned.

The resident slowly shook his head. "It's bad. Real bad."

Dellacorte quickly got to his feet. "Are you assisting me on Mrs. Ryan?"

"Yes, sir."

"If the anesthesiologist arrives before I return, get Mrs. Ryan under and get her prepped."

"Right."

Dellacorte hurried from the room and down the corridor, breaking into a half run. *Perfect,* he thought, *absolutely perfect.* The resident had said Joanna was real bad. Which meant she was still alive—but not by much. With life-support systems, they could keep her vital organs perfused while her tissue type was placed in the donor network. Her heart, lungs and kidneys would go elsewhere. Joanna's liver would be reserved for her sister.

He got to the elevator and impatiently pushed the down button. He glanced at the floor indicator. All the cars were going up. Quickly he moved across the corridor and went through the fire escape doors. He took the stairs down two at a time, making a list in his mind of things he had to do. First, call Mack Brown and tell him of the tragedy that would give Kate Blalock the liver she needed. The transplant could be done later that day, or even the next day. The next day would be better, Dellacorte decided. No need to rush if they could continue to keep Joanna going on life-support systems.

Second, he wanted to make an anonymous call to a local TV station, telling them the story of Joanna's disappearance and reappearance and how the terrible accident that killed Joanna would give her sister life. The news media loved stories like that. They'd play it up big, emphasizing the sister-to-sister transplant and giving the story a semihappy, bittersweet ending. That would take some of the heat off Memorial Hospital and its staff.

Dellacorte exited the fire escape and raced down the corridor into the ER. He stepped aside as an aide carrying two units of blood hurried by. Up ahead the nurses' station was in a state of organized chaos. Phones were ringing unanswered, residents and nurses scurrying back and forth yelling messages and orders above the din. Dellacorte almost bumped into a nurse coming out of one of the examining rooms. She was wearing gloves and mask and a scrub suit splattered with blood.

"Where's Dr. Blalock?" Dellacorte shouted above the noise.

"Trauma room one," the nurse shouted back.

Dellacorte cut across the nurses' station to another noisy corridor. Down the way was trauma room one, a red light flashing above its door. As he approached the room, Dellacorte saw a gurney outside the door. The sheet atop it was badly soiled with mud. There were also some spots of blood mixed in.

Dellacorte pushed open the doors and entered the trauma room.

He stopped in his tracks, not believing what he was seeing. Joanna Blalock sat quietly on the edge of the examining table while a nurse gently cleaned her face of mud and blood with a washcloth and soap and water.

Dellacorte spun around—but his way was now blocked by Jake Sinclair. And behind Sinclair were two uniformed policemen, and behind them two more.

Dellacorte felt himself being turned around, and he felt hand-cuffs being applied to his wrists. Then he was pushed toward the door.

Behind him he heard Joanna's voice, hoarse and weak from screaming. It took him a moment to understand the word.

"Bastard."

EPILOGUE

Kate Blalock was sitting up in bed, sipping a chocolate milk shake through a straw. "So you were going to give me a part of your liver, huh?"

"I was thinking about it," Joanna said.

"That's not what Dr. Brown told me," Kate said, sipping more milk shake and making a loud, slurping sound. "He said you were all set up to go."

"Well, it was just a little piece of my liver," Joanna said jovially. "I didn't have much use for it anyhow."

"Liar!"

Joanna leaned over the bed and gave Kate a hug and a kiss. "Oh, Lord! I'm glad you're better."

"It was a close call, wasn't it?"

"Closer than you'll ever know," Joanna said, studying her sister's face. The jaundice was almost gone, and pinkness was returning to her cheeks. "I think that hyperimmune gamma globulin saved your life."

"Dr. Brown thinks so too, but he's not sure," Kate said and lay back on her pillow, her energy nearly gone. "That's why he flew down to Guatemala yesterday. He's going to set up a big study using that gamma globulin."

Joanna's eyes widened. "Has there been another outbreak of the virus?"

"Not according to Dr. Brown. He's just going down there to get things set up in case it does come back."

Joanna thought for a moment, then said, "I'll bet there's been another outbreak."

"I'll bet against it."

"Why?"

"Because Dr. Brown told me he was taking his wife with him," Kate said. "He also mentioned they were going to some beach in Costa Rica afterward."

Joanna nodded and smiled, happy that Mack was back with his wife again. She hoped it would work out for them this time. For a moment she thought about Mack and how he had been there for her when she really needed someone, but they both had realized that was hardly the basis for a lasting relationship. "Well," Joanna said, getting to her feet, "I've got to run. I have a date with a guy who tries to pass himself off as a homicide detective."

"How is Jake?"

"He's still a pain in the ass."

"But he's a good-looking pain in the ass." Kate giggled. "I'd love to see him again."

"I'll bring him in next time," Joanna said and kissed Kate's cheek. "Now, you get some rest and keep drinking those milk shakes. You're still skin and bones."

Joanna left the room and strode down the corridor to the elevator. She got into the car just behind a group of interns. They were talking about the transplant scandal at Donors International and David Dellacorte's involvement in it. The story had been at the top of the news for weeks and showed no signs of letting up.

"So they were killing people for their organs?" one intern said.

"That's what I heard," a female intern replied. "And Dellacorte was making sure the organs went to special people who were willing to pay big bucks."

"Who were the people who got killed?"

"They're trying to figure that out now."

Oh, they've figured it out, Joanna wanted to tell them, right down to the last detail. And with time there would be leaks to the news media and the whole gruesome story would come out. As of yet the media hadn't learned that babies had been conceived only to serve as organ donors later in life. Somehow the authorities had managed to keep a lid on that aspect of the story. But it was just a matter of time before the whole world would know. And maybe some good would come from it. Maybe, finally, the infertility clinics and the organs for transplant facilities would come under strict federal control. Maybe.

The elevator came to a stop.

An intern next to Joanna adjusted his knapsack on his shoulders and turned to his colleagues. "Who would pay a zillion dollars for an organ and not know where that organ came from?"

"Someone who needed it to live," Joanna said, and left the elevator.

She walked across the corridor and into the forensics laboratory. The workbenches were deserted, the technicians gone for lunch. Against the wall centrifuges were spinning at full speed, humming nicely, their automatic timers on and finally working as they should.

On the message board was a note from her secretary. It read: "Dr. McKay called. Can you meet for dinner tomorrow?" Joanna pocketed the message, now thinking about Lori. Poor Lori! She had been crushed when she learned of David Dellacorte's involvement in the transplant scandal. The young coroner felt so hurt and betrayed, her heart broken into a hundred pieces. But with time she'd get over it. Lori McKay was plenty strong.

The door to the rear laboratory was open and Joanna peeked in. Jake was standing near the skeleton of James Robert Butler, examining the femur with the supracondylar plate still attached.

"Do you see anything interesting?" Joanna asked and strolled over.

Jake shook his head. "I was just thinking. This is where it all started. The rain came and uncovered a skeleton and we had to find out who he was."

"A man hell-bent on avenging his sister's suicide. That's who he was," Joanna said. "And he got himself killed trying to do it."

Jake nodded, still looking at the femur. "What do you plan to do with the skeleton?"

Joanna shrugged. "Give it back to the coroner's office, I guess."

"They'll just bury him in some unmarked grave, and he deserves better than that," Jake said respectfully. "He was a veteran; he served his country in war."

"So what should we do?"

"I'm going to contact the Veterans Administration and see if he can't be buried in a VA cemetery."

Joanna nodded and smiled, touched by Jake's thoughtfulness. "That's a good idea, Jake. I like it."

"You ready for lunch?"

"I'm famished."

Joanna took off her white laboratory coat and Jake helped her into a navy-blue blazer. She noticed that his hands were still covered with cuts and bruises and small areas where the skin had been gouged out. He had gotten the injuries while frantically digging through the mud and debris to find her. "How are your hands doing?"

"Better."

"Thank God you've got a brain in your head," Joanna said, shivering to herself. "Otherwise I'd still be buried in that mud."

"No big deal," Jake said as they walked out into the corridor and headed for the main doors of the hospital.

"Oh, yes it was," Joanna said, taking his arm. "You knew that robe from Memorial Hospital belonged to me. And you heard that bloodhound howling. So you got the dog and let him sniff the robe, and he ran to the exact spot where I was buried."

"That dog had a great sense of smell," Jake said, now holding open the door to the stairway. "Farelli tells me that hounds have a sense of smell a thousand times greater than humans. He picked up your scent pronto."

"I owe that dog big time," Joanna said appreciatively. "Where is he now?"

"The pound, I guess."

"The *pound?*" Joanna gave Jake a long, hard stare. "Nobody will claim that wonderful dog, and they'll put him to sleep. They'll kill him."

"Well, maybe it was some other animal shelter the police department took him to."

"You'd better find out where," Joanna said sternly. "You find out where that dog is. You understand?"

"Right."

"And he'd better be alive."

Joanna shook her head, still angry. One moment Jake could be so sensitive and thoughtful, the next so cold and detached. She despised that quality in him, really despised it. But she knew he would never change.

"Well, the important thing is that you're out of that grave you were in," Jake said, switching subjects. "It must have been absolute hell."

Joanna shuddered. "It was so terrifying down there."

"I can imagine."

"No, you can't," Joanna said. "It's horror beyond belief. You're trapped in a cement pipe, a tomb, buried under five feet of mud. You know you're going to die. You're going to suffocate to death. You scream and yell and the only thing you hear is the echo of your own voice."

"Well, it's over now," Jake said and squeezed her shoulder.

"No, it's not," Joanna said softly. "I still have those damn nightmares. Not as often as before, but I'm still having them." She clenched her jaw tightly. "That's what I'd like to do to David Dellacorte. Let him know what it's like to be buried alive."

Jake opened the door on the first floor and they walked across the main lobby of the hospital. "He *is* going to be buried alive—in a prison—for a long, long time. Of course, Davey Boy is screaming his ass off that he's innocent, but we've got enough evidence to convict him five times over."

"What about the others at Donors International?"

"We questioned Dunn and Rhinemann and Karen Kessler. They claim they didn't know what was going on, but I don't buy that. Nor does the district attorney." Jake nodded to himself. "They were in on it. They had to be."

Jake and Joanna walked out the front door and into brilliant sunshine. Jake lit a Greek cigarette and said, "Dellacorte and Adler were the masterminds. As best we can determine, Adler was the brains and Dellacorte provided the money and connections."

"Where did the money come from?"

"We traced the ownership of Donors International to a New York holding company that's controlled by the mob. I guess they figured there were big bucks in the organ transplant business. Organized crime just moves in to supply what's in demand, whether that's liquor in the thirties, or prostitutes, or drugs. Now there's a shortage of organ donors, so there's plenty of money to be made illegally."

"How did Dellacorte become involved with the mob?"

"Easy," Jake said, and waited for a group of nurses to pass. "The family that owned Donors International was once controlled by David Dellacorte's grandfather. And some of Dellacorte's relatives are still in positions of power. When Dellacorte told them about the big money to be made in human organs, those guys must have jumped at the chance."

Joanna squinted an eye. "I don't think David was smart enough to come up with the idea of Donors International."

"I think he and Adler did it together. According to Simon Murdock, Dellacorte was thrown out of his surgical residency fifteen years ago for smoking pot while on call. Then they let him back in after he did a year of immunology research back East. Want to guess whose research laboratory he worked in?"

"Jason Adler's," Joanna said at once.

Jake nodded. "And they did it all for money. The goddamn money."

"And maybe for the fame and glory, too," Joanna added, envisioning the disgrace and embarrassment Dellacorte must have felt when he was dismissed from his residency. He would have been so driven to prove himself, to show the world how great a transplant surgeon he really was.

They strolled across a large patio lined with benches and manicured shrubbery. People were sitting on the lawn, enjoying the warm, clear day. The sun was so bright that Joanna had to put on her sunglasses.

"Where are you parked?" Joanna asked.

"In the no-parking area," Jake said.

"That figures."

They got to the edge of the patio and started down the steps.

A bloodhound began howling loudly.

Joanna quickly looked over at Jake's car. Standing next to it was

Lou Farelli. He was holding a leash. Beside him was a large bloodhound.

"Damn you!" Joanna said and playfully hit Jake's chest.

"Farelli's kid wanted a dog," Jake told her. "We decided to call him Sniff."

Farelli let the dog loose and it ran full speed right to Joanna. She went to her knees and petted the dog, scratching its ears. "Farelli told me that all the rescuers thought I was dead," she said, looking up at Jake. "But not you. You kept digging and digging, not letting anyone stop for even a moment. And when your shovel broke you dug with your hands. Is that true?"

"I had something spurring me on."

"What?"

"The thought that I was about to lose the most important thing in my life."

"Oh, Jake," Joanna said softly. She stood up and embraced him, nestling her head against his chest. "Let's you and I get it right this time, huh?"

AUTHOR'S NOTE

There is a desperate need for transplantable organs in America. According to the United Network for Organ Sharing, nearly 45,000 patients are currently on a waiting list for organ transplants. With the passage of time, this number is certain to grow. As the general population expands, so will the number of patients with vital organ failure who can benefit from transplants.

Unfortunately, the organ donor systems now in place are inadequate to meet current needs, and this inadequacy is becoming more and more obvious. The need for organs is so desperate that people are resorting to measures once considered unthinkable. For example, animal organs are being transplanted into patients with greater and greater frequency. Baboon hearts and livers and bone marrows have been transplanted into humans without success thus far. Genetically engineered pigs are being developed so their livers and perhaps their hearts can be used in humans.

And most striking of all, children are now being conceived and raised for the purpose of being organ donors. In a well-publicized case, a California couple conceived a child so that the infant could serve as a bone marrow donor for a sibling who was stricken with chronic myelogenous leukemia. Admittedly, bone marrow donors are not sacrificed and suffer no harm as a result of being donors, and their bone marrow rapidly regenerates. Nevertheless, it is a straightforward fact that babies are now being conceived solely for the purpose of serving as organ donors.

—Leonard Goldberg, M.D.

• A NOTE ON THE TYPE •

The typeface used in this book is a version of Baskerville, origi-
nally designed by John Baskerville (1706–1775) and considered to be one of the first "transitional" typefaces between the
"old style" of the continental humanist printers and the
"modern" style of the nineteenth century. With a determina-
tion bordering on the eccentric to produce the finest possible
printing, Baskerville set out at age forty-five and with no previous experience to become a typefounder and printer (his
first fourteen letters took him two years). Besides the letter
forms, his innovations included an improved printing press,
smoother paper, and better inks, all of which made Baskerville
decidedly uncompetitive as a businessman. Franklin, Beau-
marchais, and Bodoni were among his admirers, but his typeface had to wait for the twentieth century to achieve its due.

GOLDBER Goldberg, Leonard S

Deadly harvest

DUE DATE

AUG 2 9			
OCT 2 0			